Lynne Graham was born
has been a keen romance r
She is very happily marrie
husband who has learned t
started to write! Her five children keep her on her toes. She has a very large dog, which knocks everything over, a very small terrier, which barks a lot, and two cats. When time allows, Lynne is a keen gardener.

Cathy Williams can remember reading Mills & Boon books as a teenager, and now that she's writing them she remains an avid fan. For her, there is nothing like creating romantic stories and engaging plots, and each and every book is a new adventure. Cathy lives in London. Her three daughters—Charlotte, Olivia and Emma—have always been, and continue to be, the greatest inspirations in her life.

Also by Lynne Graham

The Italian's Bride Worth Billions
The Baby the Desert King Must Claim

Cinderella Sisters for Billionaires miniseries

The Maid Married to the Billionaire
The Maid's Pregnancy Bombshell

Also by Cathy Williams

Bound by a Nine-Month Confession
A Week with the Forbidden Greek
The Housekeeper's Invitation to Italy
Unveiled as the Italian's Bride
Bound by Her Baby Revelation

Discover more at millsandboon.co.uk.

TWO SECRETS TO SHOCK THE ITALIAN

LYNNE GRAHAM

A WEDDING NEGOTIATION WITH HER BOSS

CATHY WILLIAMS

MILLS & BOON

First published in Great Britain 2024
by Mills & Boon, an imprint of HarperCollins*Publishers* Ltd,
1 London Bridge Street, London, SE1 9GF

www.harpercollins.co.uk

HarperCollins*Publishers*, Macken House, 39/40 Mayor Street Upper,
Dublin 1, D01 C9W8, Ireland

ISBN: 978-0-263-32002-2

04/24

This book contains FSC™ certified paper
and other controlled sources to ensure responsible forest management.

For more information visit www.harpercollins.co.uk/green.

Printed and Bound in the UK using 100% Renewable Electricity
at CPI Group (UK) Ltd, Croydon, CR0 4YY

TWO SECRETS TO SHOCK THE ITALIAN

LYNNE GRAHAM

MILLS & BOON

CHAPTER ONE

ARISTIDE ANGELICO, BILLIONAIRE FOUNDER of Angelico Technologies and a once legendary playboy, rested back in his limousine as he was ferried to Luke Walker's memorial service. Six feet four inches, he was built like an athlete, lean and muscular in every long line with unruly black curls, bright green eyes and a startlingly handsome face.

He questioned what he was doing.

'Why are you going to this?' his PA had asked him casually that morning. 'You hardly knew the man.'

The answer?

Aristide was attending out of pure, unvarnished curiosity. The death of an innocent cyclist in busy traffic on his very first day of permanent work had ironically made the news. Aristide had been stunned when he recognised the photo.

He had not, however, been keen to see his ex, weeping over the coffin of her late husband. It would all have been a fake show, a demonstration of the reality that she had about as much emotional depth as a puddle. So, he had ducked the funeral, choosing to attend the memorial service instead.

Aristide had Scarlett Pearson, the dewy-eyed primary schoolteacher, in his bed for almost a year and he had believed he knew her inside out. But, surprise, surprise, he reflected cynically, he had proved to be just as foolishly trusting as many men when it came to a tiny, beautiful redhead. Certainly, Aristide had been stunned when, within weeks of becoming inexplicably unavailable, Scarlett had announced—by cowardly text—that she was getting married to Luke Walker. Luke, her *best* friend from childhood, and a relationship that she had repeatedly assured Aristide was pure and platonic.

More fool him for trusting her! In spite of all the precautions Aristide had taken to keep himself invulnerable, he had ended up almost being a fool for a woman, just as his grandfather and father had been, just as his late twin brother, Daniele, had been. The Angelico men had a poor track record with the opposite sex. As a teenager, Aristide had sworn to remain a playboy and for years that resolve had held fast. The golden years of youth, ignorance and irresponsibility, he labelled that period now. He was only twenty-nine, but he had been a stud at eighteen, determined never to tie his future to either a cold-hearted shrew like his mother or to a cheating gold-digger as his unfortunate younger brother had.

And now the world was threatening to turn full circle, he acknowledged grimly. His mother was putting pressure on him to marry years before he was ready to embrace the institution. Why was he even listening to her? Unfortunately, Daniele's last heartbreaking request of his brother had been that Aristide strive to be kinder and more understanding of their mother's unpleasant nature. It was a tall order, but Aristide was still attempting to be tolerant out of respect for his late twin's memory and to make allowances for his mother's tragic past.

'For the sake of the family,' Daniele had urged, because family had meant everything to his twin...sadly, a great deal less to Aristide.

Suitable marital prospects were served up to Aristide at every family event he attended, and it had become seriously annoying. After all, his plan had always been to stay single until he was middle-aged. Only then would he marry to provide the next generation. He had no perfect candidate in mind, but then he didn't believe a perfect woman existed. He had, however, already considered the desirable attributes his wife should possess. She would have to be beautiful, wealthy in her own right and of a maternal nature. That last trait was non-negotiable. Nobody knew better than Aristide what it had been like to grow up with a cold, cruel mother.

'You're exhausted,' Edith, Scarlett's mother-in-law, sighed in a sympathetic undertone in the church foyer, scanning the younger woman's shadowed eyes.

'You are as well,' Scarlett pointed out ruefully as she acknowledged that the sudden unexpected death of her husband a year earlier had ripped the heart out of the whole family circle.

Luke had essentially died in a cycling accident on the way to work, only the shell of him had lingered in a hospital bed for two long months afterwards. There had, however, been no real hope that he would emerge from his coma during those dreadful weeks and eventually she and her in-laws had agreed for the machines keeping him alive to be switched off. He had been twenty-four years old, newly qualified as an accountant and a much-loved only child with everything to live for still ahead of him. And in the blink of an eye he was now gone and nothing could change that reality.

Scarlett dragged in a ragged breath.

She was empty of tears now. The weeks during which Luke had lain unresponsive in his hospital bed had drained her of the first sobbing desperation of grief. In addition, she was no stranger to family loss. Her adoptive parents had died soon after her marriage, one from a long-standing illness, the other from a massive stroke, brought on, she suspected, by the shock of bereavement. Becoming an adult orphan had made Scarlett even more grateful to have Luke and his parents in her corner. He had helped her build their family with *two* parents. Now, without Luke around to steady her, she felt as though the foundation of her world had collapsed and she knew that she had to get over feeling that way because she still had two young children to raise.

Just about the very last thing Scarlett was prepared to handle was the shocking vision of her ex, Aristide, striding up the path to the church door where she and Luke's parents were greeting their friends. Impossibly elegant in a dark suit, so beautifully tailored it could only have hailed from an Italian designer, Aristide Angelico looked utterly untouched by the passage of time.

Not that that surprised her, because she had learned the hard way that nothing much touched Aristide deep and it *had* only been two years since she had last seen him. That two years for her, however, had been packed tight with her pregnancy, her marriage, the birth of her twins and a new life darkened by the loss of Luke, but an utterly different life from what she had once had while she was with Aristide.

Gleaming black curls that caught the sunlight and were a little too long for tidiness tumbled above a lean, stunningly handsome face. Aristide was a male whom few women failed to notice. Scarlett could feel her knees weakening as though some insidious spell had entered her bloodstream the instant she saw him. It brought back bad memories of how lost she had once got in Aristide, of how vulnerable she had become in the grip of her fear of losing him. And that disturbing surge of recollection hit her at the exact right moment and put her back in control as he grasped Edith's hand, bowed his gorgeous dark head in polite acknowledgment of the sad occasion and murmured conventional words of regret. And then it was Scarlett's turn…

She collided reluctantly with glittering emerald-green eyes as cutting as diamond blades and she didn't hear what he said, didn't even register his hand gripping hers briefly because she *felt* the burning animosity and scorn powering his gaze down into her very bones. Her pale heart-shaped face flamed as though a blowtorch had been turned on her. Involuntarily, she took a tiny step back from him as he turned to address Luke's father, Tom.

Still in shock at being exposed to the passionate aura of charisma that Aristide emanated like a forcefield, Scarlett had to be prompted by Edith's hand on her arm to swivel back and greet the next person approaching. Her brain, her very consciousness and control, still, however, seemed lost to her.

She was remembering what she didn't want to remember: Aristide, smiling, concerned and effortlessly captivating the very first time she had met him when she had turned an ankle out jogging. She had not believed that love at first sight existed until that day. The attraction had been *that* instant and overpowering. By the time she truly understood *who* he was, *what* that wealth and status meant in the world and *how* it would colour his every expectation of *her*, she had already been in too deep to pull back. Loving Aristide had made her too forgiving in that she had kept on making excuses for him when he'd disappointed her. No, *no*, she told herself angrily, not going there now, not today, which was her best friend Luke's day…

Aristide sank fluidly down in a pew, his attention locked on the grieving widow's profile. That porcelain-clear skin of hers showed everything. Even though months had passed since her husband's death, she still looked pale, dark shadows bruising her remarkably blue eyes, her skin wildly outclassed in brilliance by the dark auburn fall of hair like molten copper, which she had restrained in an ugly bun. Surprisingly, he wasn't as pleased to see Scarlett still looking wretched as he had assumed he would be. Did that mean that he was a kinder person than he had ever believed he was? He didn't think so.

Once again, he thought how fortunate it was that he had made himself let Scarlett go in every way. He hadn't spied on her from a distance, keeping tabs on her life. Oh, yes, he had been tempted, because curiosity could be a killer, but he had known that ultimately it was better for him simply to turn his back and move on without wondering how her new life with another man might be developing.

Even so, questions were still bubbling up like burning lava in the back of his mind, the sort of questions he had suppressed two years earlier, questions that he considered *beneath* him. Had she always loved Luke Walker? Had she set up Aristide as a rival to inspire jealousy and finally win her best friend's sexual interest? Or had she been cheating on Aristide all along? In one of those twisted can't-commit-can't-let-you-go relationships?

But she *had* been a virgin, not that Aristide had ever chosen to openly acknowledge that fact lest he encourage his lover to have expectations. And he never ever made that mistake with women. He was always very clear about what he was and what he *wasn't* offering. She had accepted the status quo just as all the women he had ever met did. Even so, Scarlett had continually strained against the boundaries of that acceptance. She had refused expensive gifts and holidays, refused to acknowledge that his needs as the CEO of an international business empire should naturally take precedence over her own humbler calling. Indeed, Scarlett had sometimes been so blasted difficult that he had wondered why he was still with her.

Even so, Aristide was no fool. Scarlett Pearson/ Walker still intrigued him because she had ditched *him* and she was the only female who had *ever* walked away from him. Of course, that fact still rankled with a guy whom Scarlett had once accused of having an ego as big as the planet. It was natural for him to wonder why she had picked another man, nothing more complex than that.

He attended the community-hall sandwiches-and-tea gathering that followed the memorial service. He had rarely felt so out of his depth anywhere, listening to impromptu speeches being made about Luke Walker, who had apparently been a noted youth and outreach volunteer in the local church and various organisations. A Mr Perfect, Aristide decided, wondering what murky secrets Scarlett's husband had been hiding below that squeaky-clean surface because Aristide was that much of an innate cynic.

He couldn't imagine Scarlett with a man like that, but he could imagine her *admiring* a man like that, which set his teeth on edge. When he had first met her, Scarlett's every free hour had seemed to be devoted to similar philanthropic interests, he recalled belatedly, only she had slowly fallen away from all that do-gooding once he pointed out that she was never available when he wanted to see her. Without warning though, Aristide was inexplicably feeling as though he had never really known Scarlett at all and it annoyed him that in many ways he had refused to acknowledge the kind of world she had grown up in. A settled, conventional and conservative realm, which he could barely comprehend because it was the very opposite of the hyper-sophistication, the cold silences and the bitter secrets and dramas that had soiled his own far more dysfunctional background.

Aristide didn't know what family warmth and support was. From what he had witnessed over the years, his parents had *always* detested each other. His father, who had proved to be a most reluctant father and husband in reality, was indifferent to him. His mother, however, idolised him, her sole surviving child, while Aristide quietly despised and avoided her. Regardless of those unpleasant facts, maintaining the Angelico family line entailed presenting an appearance of unity, dignity and doing one's duty. Aristide, however, had only ever truly cared about one other person and that person had been his beloved twin, who had taken his own life six years earlier. A world shorn of Daniele's bright optimistic spirit still seemed like a very bleak place, but it had somehow felt a little less bleak while Scarlett was by his side.

As Aristide approached her through the gathered cliques of guests, Scarlett froze because, prior to that moment, seated with Luke's parents, she had been covertly watching Aristide's every move. In a crowd he was easily spotted by his sheer height and he was even more strikingly noticeable in his immaculate business attire with an expensive gold watch and cuff-links on display.

Everyone around him was ordinary and Aristide Angelico had never been ordinary even at birth, born as he had been into a fabulously wealthy Italian business dynasty. A monogram AA would be stamped on all his handmade apparel like the shirt she still had somewhere in her belongings. And he was gorgeous, unbelievably, impossibly gorgeous. That was a stray thought she suppressed as soon as it came into her mind as she concentrated on wondering instead why he had attended the service when he hadn't, as far as she knew, attended the funeral.

After all, Aristide must've met Luke in passing a dozen times without ever showing the smallest real interest in her best friend. No doubt he would have exerted himself to be a little more charming had her best friend been a woman. Although he had never voiced a word of criticism or sought to interfere, she had eventually worked out that Aristide didn't like her having a close friend the same sex as himself. By then, she had become adept at recognising what annoyed Aristide, bringing a cool light to his shrewd gaze or a faint curl to his lip or even a very subtle edged intonation. In fact, so good had she become at reading Aristide, she could have written a book about him long before she broke up with him.

'May I have a brief word?' Aristide enquired, smooth as glass.

Scarlett rose from her seat, her legs slightly wobbly. 'Of course.' Stepping away from her in-laws, she murmured tightly, 'Why are you here?'

'I was curious.'

* * *

Aristide gazed down at her, scanning the slice of porcelain skin exposed only at the throat by the plain dress, wanting to see more, suddenly exasperated that there was no prospect of such a development. Black lashes pitched low over his spectacular eyes, he studied the ripe curve of her soft lips while involuntarily remembering the taste of her.

For a split second he was knocked sideways by the raw arousal shooting a lightning pulse into his groin. It was inappropriate, wrong, tasteless, everything he was *not* and it outraged his powerful pride. He didn't *still* want her, of course he didn't! It was some crazy throwback to the past combined with unwelcome memories, he reasoned fiercely. But possibly a shot of unvarnished lust was painfully overdue, he conceded, considering that he had not been with a woman in a very long time.

'Why would you be curious?' Scarlett asked in seemingly genuine surprise. 'What would you be curious about?'

A current of pure rage rippled through Aristide, who prided himself on never ever losing his temper. She was playing games with him, of course she was, but what other option did he have other than to play?

'Why you walked away,' he pronounced with gritty reluctance.

Scarlett stared back at him in apparent wonderment, sapphire-blue eyes widening. 'Surely that was obvious?' she responded flatly, turning away as someone else addressed her.

Obvious? Not to Aristide. He wanted an explanation, closure, that was *all*, he assured himself. Clearly, he should have moved on by now, leaving the detritus of that period behind him, but Scarlett had stayed with him like a thorn in tender flesh, nagging at the back of his mind, regardless of how often he threw thoughts of her back out again. He shouldn't have attended the service, he conceded grimly. It was the wrong place, the wrong time.

Feeling drained and yet strung out with nerves, Scarlett finally reclaimed her seat. Edith leant closer and rested a reassuring hand on Scarlett's trembling knees. 'Is that *him*?' she asked very softly. 'He's the living image of our grandkids.'

Scarlett lost colour at that instant recognition while also conceding how very wise and far-seeing Luke had been when he had insisted that there should be no secrets kept from his parents. At the same time, he had admitted that he was gay. 'Yes,' she confirmed flatly because, with their olive skin, black curls and bright green eyes, Rome and Alice were like miniature doppelgängers of their father.

'I'll bring the kids back in an hour,' Edith told Scarlett on the phone. 'They're having fun on the slide. I'll give them lunch and then they can come home and go for a nap, which will give you a break.'

'I don't need another break,' Scarlett pointed out gently. 'I'm not working today.'

'I'm sure you've got stuff round the house to catch up on.'

Indeed, she had, Scarlett conceded as she unloaded the washing machine and carted the washing out to hang it on the line in the back garden. She was tired but then she had been consistently tired since Luke's passing and she reckoned that that weight of exhaustion could well be part of the grieving process. Her life was harder and lonelier without Luke, but she was very lucky to have a pair of adoring grandparents living in the apartment above theirs.

For the past few weeks, she had been back at work at the primary school where she had been employed since graduation. At present though, she was still only working part-time and once she had got through the summer she would have a better idea as to whether or not she wished to return to full-time hours. Luckily for her, Luke had been well insured when he died and she could have afforded to stay home with the children for a while anyway. At present, however, Scarlett knew she needed the stimulation of work and mixing with other adults to stay on a more even keel.

The Walkers had remodelled their spacious detached home into two apartments and had invited their son and his wife to move into the ground-floor one, believing that the children needed outdoor space more than they did. In reality the two couples and the twins had intermingled to such an extent that the garden was freely shared between them and Edith's husband, Tom, was still tending the garden, finding it a relaxing pastime when he wasn't at his accountancy office.

When the doorbell shrilled, Scarlett frowned because she wasn't expecting anyone and her closest friend, Brie, was at work. Leaving the kitchen, she walked through the narrow hall and pulled open the front door with a smile, assuming that it was a delivery.

Her smile fell away and she froze and took a harried step backwards when she saw who stood on her doorstep. It was Aristide, his green eyes veiled and shrewd as he absorbed her dismay at his sudden appearance. 'I would've phoned to warn you that I was planning a visit but I don't have your current number.'

'Aristide…' she breathed hoarsely, dry-mouthed, throat closing over when she needed to breathe in deep and long to inflate her struggling lungs because the sight of Aristide Angelico at her front door filled her with nothing short of panic.

Her first thought was to thank heaven that the children were out with her mother-in-law and her second was to wonder if she had cleared away the toys in the living room. Of course, there were photos of the children in there as well. Much better to keep him outside, she decided, rigid with discomfiture as she moved out into the fresh air to join him. 'What are you doing here?' she asked stiffly, unable to think of a single reason why he would visit her.

'I'm not prepared to discuss that with you standing out in the garden,' Aristide assured her drily.

Coins of pink sprang up over her cheekbones. With very poor grace she backed into the apartment again and opened the living-room door, inwardly praying that she had tidied up, stuffing the innumerable clutter that went with raising young children into the plastic toy boxes hidden behind the sofa. To her relief, a clear wooden floor greeted her anxious gaze and she glanced up at Aristide.

He was so much taller than she was that he towered over her. She was four feet eleven inches in her bare feet and she *was* in her bare feet, got up in worn jeans and a T-shirt. She had no make-up on, so her face was bare, and her hair had last been brushed at dawn. Every morning, Rome climbed out of his cot and nagged her out of bed but not before he gave her a big cuddle. He was extremely cuddly for a little boy sired by a non-cuddling father.

'I asked you a question when we last met. It wasn't the right place or time, for which I apologise, but I would still like to hear an answer,' Aristide outlined.

Scarlett could hardly believe her ears. 'It's been two years, Aristide. Why would you come and ask me now?'

'Is there harm to you in me asking that question?' An ebony brow lifted.

'You've got to admit that it's more than a little strange when you didn't care enough at the time to seek me out,' Scarlett countered tightly, fingers snapping into fists by her side. 'But it's no big secret. It was Cosetta Ricci and that big formal ball you took her to in London. You didn't mention it to me, you didn't explain it. She was the last straw. I could hardly compete with a model and an heiress, and I wasn't prepared to *try* and compete either.'

'I never said that we were exclusive—'

'And the minute I realised that we definitely *weren't* exclusive, I wanted out,' Scarlett completed without embarrassment.

'You didn't want out. You wanted to marry your best friend,' Aristide quipped without expression, emerald-green eyes lethal as knives hitting a target.

'I've given you the explanation that you said that you wanted,' Scarlett retorted flatly. 'Now you can leave—'

'Cosetta Ricci,' Aristide repeated in disbelief. 'She meant nothing to me—'

'Neither did I,' Scarlett slotted in before she could think better of making that point. Goodness knew, she had not had a problem working out that hard fact when she'd never heard from him again after that text. He hadn't fought for her, hadn't confronted her, hadn't argued with her, he had simply let her go.

'She was a friend, nothing more. It was a fund-raiser sponsored by the Angelico charitable trust and my mother invited Cosetta to attend as my partner—'

A fine brow elevated in unforgiving doubt. 'Like you couldn't have said no! Please leave now,' Scarlett urged thinly, walking back out to the hall to yank the front door open in invitation.

Aristide took the hint but came to a sudden halt on the doorstep to proclaim in seething disbelief, 'You're seriously trying to tell me that Cinderella didn't get asked to the ball and that that's why you walked away and married another man?'

Her face hot as fire, Scarlett slammed the door in his face and stalked back to the kitchen to pace in angry circles of frustration. There was so much she could have said to him, so many good reasons that she had made the choices she had, that he would still have been standing there at midnight had she actually started to talk. But she didn't owe Aristide any humiliating truths or insights into her behaviour, she didn't owe him anything!

In fact, she had done him a *huge* favour. She hadn't saddled him with children he didn't want and a society scandal when word of their out-of-wedlock birth inevitably escaped. The Angelico family and Aristide, in particular, were never out of the newspapers in Europe and their every move attracted publicity.

Scarlett, however, had never been good enough for Aristide or his posh family. He had kept her well away from them until his mother had sought her out at a party and had cruelly mocked her for her working-class background and supposedly unknown parentage as an adopted child. Elisabetta Angelico had made it painfully clear that Scarlett was the lowest of the low in her eyes and no more than a passing fling in her son's life.

In actuality, Scarlett had long known who her birth parents were. Schoolkids, they had moved on with their lives quite happily after surrendering her at birth. Her birth mother, whom she had met at eighteen, enjoyed a high-powered career in fashion and had had little interest in pursuing an ongoing relationship with the daughter she had given up. Her birth father had died in a motorbike crash in his twenties. Her exploration of her true beginnings had been a dead end when it came to establishing the new family connection she had secretly craved. And that had been the direct result of the fact that she had had nothing whatsoever in common with the adoptive parents whom she had, nevertheless, deeply loved.

* * *

The following week, Aristide returned to Scarlett's home a second time. He was annoyed that he had not been able to resist the temptation to see her again, impatient to satisfy the curiosity she inspired but equally keen to walk away again, miraculously cured of what was beginning to feel like an obsession. He hit the doorknocker and heard footsteps approaching. The door opened on Scarlett's slender blonde mother-in-law. Unexpectedly, the older woman smiled in welcome. 'Mr Angelico. I'm afraid Scarlett's at work but she finishes for the day in fifteen minutes.'

A very young child lurched up and hugged her leg and then another one appeared to hug her other leg, two upturned little faces staring up at Aristide with huge curious eyes. There was something about the duo, something about their faces, that was weirdly familiar.

Frowning, Aristide asked where Scarlett worked and if he could have her phone number to warn her that he was coming to pick her up. Both his queries were answered pleasantly. There appeared to be no awareness that he had ever been anything other than a casual friend of Scarlett's and for some reason that annoyed him. But then, for several months, Aristide had recognised that he was out of sorts, awash with impulsive responses that were as much out of character as the restlessness afflicting him. For a disciplined, unemotional male, that lack of control was maddening.

He wondered vaguely who the children belonged to as he swung back into the limo and directed his driver to the school. He texted Scarlett, anticipating her alarm with sudden wicked amusement. He was surprised that she was still working at the same place and equally surprised that she was still apparently living with her in-laws. But then, she had rejected his lifestyle, even his gifts, leaving behind everything he had ever given her when she left him. Clearly, Luke Walker and his family, however, had been exactly what she wanted in her life. As usual, the thought rankled.

He had picked her up at the school before and she had been ridiculously embarrassed because people had stared at the limousine, but when he had turned up in a Ferrari some weeks later, she had been no more pleased. Now he sat watching her stalk down the pavement towards him, a beige raincoat floating back from her narrow shoulders, an even more boring brown skirt and top worn beneath. Her hair was descending in little copper strands from her updo and she was flushed. But dress Scarlett up in designer fashion and, tiny though she was, she was a total showstopper. Involuntarily, he thought what a shame it was that she wouldn't be available to be his partner at his unwelcome thirtieth family birthday party, which he was due to attend in two weeks.

He hadn't asked his parents for the party and he didn't want it. He had considered simply not turning up, a response that would have humiliated his very socially sensitive mother in front of friends and relatives. That no-show option would have been utterly cruel, in his late twin's parlance, and Aristide had gritted his teeth and decided to attend on that basis. On the balance side, however, the sight of Scarlett back in her son's life would wondrously enrage his lady mother and enliven the evening for Aristide, and Scarlett's presence would certainly keep the marriage groupies at bay. And then he thought, well, why shouldn't he ask her? It was not as though he would be asking her to get into a bed with him again.

Scarlett slid into the back of the limo at speed, wanting the opulent car to move off again fast, wanting people to stop staring. She was furious with Aristide, furious that he had contrived to surprise her. It had always been a mistake to second-guess Aristide, to underestimate what he was capable of when he was challenged. But she hadn't challenged him, hadn't done anything to reanimate his interest or his wretched curiosity!

'What on earth are you doing here?' she demanded as she turned to look at him.

And the impact of Aristide that close engulfed her like an avalanche. Bright green eyes clear as water against smooth bronzed skin, cheekbones sharp enough to cut glass, a wide sensual mouth set in a sculpted jawline dark with stubble. Drop-dead gorgeous at any time of day but even more stunning when seen without warning and after the passage of time.

Only two years, she reminded herself afresh, but it seemed more like a lifetime since her fingers had last tingled with an overwhelming desire to touch him. *Touch* the silky black curls that tangled round her fingers, *smooth* away the frown etched between his level dark brows, *trace* the sultry, sexy shape of his lips.

Being that near Aristide after so long shook her inside out with guilty longing.

'I have something you left behind—'

'Stick it in the post,' Scarlett urged tightly.

'As it was something precious to you, I didn't like to risk it,' Aristide drawled.

His dark deep voice vibrated down her spine and travelled into more intimate territory. She shivered and froze rigid, Aristide still in her mind's eye even though she was no longer allowing herself to look at him. Aristide in a smooth dove-grey suit, elegantly cut to enhance every line of his lean, powerful body, a white shirt at his bronzed throat, a blue silk tie. He was like catnip and she was the cat, she thought crazily. She couldn't even think about the conversation. Her mind was a blank and her whole body was braced in a defensive position as if she were awaiting an attack.

Aristide studied her, almost wincing as she crossed her slender legs in the pencil skirt and he caught a glimpse of a smooth silken inner thigh. A glimmer of arousal pulsed a warning at his groin and he tensed in immediate denial. He wondered why she was in such a nervous state, why she wouldn't look at him, why she hadn't even asked *what* it was that she had left behind in his apartment. And then he asked himself why he was questioning such random issues and even why he would care what was wrong with her.

The limousine drew up outside his townhouse and the passenger door was opened by his driver. Scarlett's head swivelled. 'Where are we?' she mumbled in confusion.

'At my place. We'll have lunch and talk before I take you home and return to the office,' Aristide murmured in a tone of unnatural calm as if such an idea were perfectly normal.

'We have nothing to talk about!' she gasped.

'You may yet be surprised,' Aristide quipped.

But Scarlett didn't like surprises and her heart sank like a stone because it was entirely possible that Aristide had somehow found out about the children or, at the very least, become suspicious. On wobbly legs, she scrambled out of the limo, her tummy rolling like a ship in high seas, every nerve on overdrive.

CHAPTER TWO

ARISTIDE HAD LIVED in a penthouse apartment when Scarlett had known him. Now she was standing outside a tall Georgian townhouse in one of London's most famous garden squares.

'You've moved?' she breathed, accompanying him up the steps to the front door already standing open on a gracious hallway.

'It was originally my grandfather's property. I inherited it last year after he passed away,' Aristide confided smoothly as an elderly man in the smart dark jacket of a very superior manservant greeted them with great formality at the door.

'James…my guest, Miss Scarlett Pearson—'

'Walker,' Scarlett inserted.

'Mrs Walker,' Aristide conceded very drily. 'I thought you weren't a fan of a woman taking a man's name.'

Scarlett flushed. He was correct. That had been her opinion only until she became pregnant and her adoptive mother had flinched every time she was addressed as 'Miss'. But then that sort of label had been hugely important to her adoptive parents, who would have been heartbroken and mortified had she become pregnant without a respectable husband on the horizon. And Luke, bless him, had stepped up when she needed him to fill that space.

'Why would I have lunch with you?' Scarlett whispered, intimidated by the grandeur of the hall.

Aristide shrugged. 'Why wouldn't you? We didn't part as enemies.'

It was true. There had been no final confrontation, no bitter exchanges. She had expected one, had expected to have to tell lies to support her story. She had dreaded the possibility, imagining Aristide's shrewd and far too clever green eyes digging into her as she voiced those same lies. But Aristide had made no attempt to see her again. He had let her walk away, proving that she meant nothing to him, proving that she had merely been another body in his bed. His indifference had devastated her even while it had best suited her needs at the time.

She was shown into an elegant dining room. Aristide slid her coat off her taut shoulders and passed it to the older man. Drinks were offered. She accepted a moisture-beaded glass of white wine, while striving to recall when she had last enjoyed an alcoholic drink. She watched Aristide like a hawk, trying to work out what he wanted from her. Certainly, he wouldn't be in the market for a list of complaints relating to her departure from his life. He had to have some other motivation to seek her out and she tensed because she had never been able to out-think Aristide.

As she sipped her wine, he dropped a small, worn box down into her lap. She blinked in surprise and then recognition raced through her at speed and she set her drink down hurriedly to open the box. As she had hoped, it was the tiny pearl stud earrings her parents had bought her for her twenty-first birthday.

'*Real* pearls,' her mother had stressed with immense pride.

'I thought I'd lost them!' she exclaimed.

'No, you left them behind. I meant to send them on to you but I forgot about them until I moved in here,' Aristide volunteered, reckoning that she wouldn't thank him for the rest of the stuff she had left behind.

Possibly she didn't want to remember the cobweb-fine lingerie he had bought and she had finally worn for his benefit. She hadn't understood how much he *loved* seeing her in items like that. She had deemed that risqué, like sex in daylight and sex other than in a bed. Once upon a time Scarlett had had a lot of inhibitions and Aristide had had the enjoyable challenge of moulding her into *his* perfect woman. And she had been perfect for months, she had been perfect as long as he sidestepped the awkward questions about where their relationship was heading and any fatal meeting with her parents, which would only have destined her to disappointment. She had wanted more from him, but Aristide had never been with a woman who *didn't* want more from him. It had not occurred to him until it was far too late that Scarlett would leave him sooner than settle for less.

And now she sat there in a little patch of sunlight that suffused her in gold tones. Titian highlights glimmered from her hair, gilding her cheekbones as she smiled at him, delighted to receive her insignificant earrings back. Of course, she had left behind a pair a good deal larger and more valuable, which he had given her. His strong jawline tightened at the memory. No, whatever else he could say about her, Scarlett was not a gold-digger. Not that that had been much of a consolation when she'd suddenly vanished from his life, he conceded grudgingly.

'Thanks,' she said with the first genuine warmth she had shown him as she bent down to tuck that cherished little box into her bag.

'Come and sit down,' he invited, spinning out a chair for her at the table, and he was drowning in memories. Scarlett greeting him with three-course meals when he came home, Scarlett enveloping him in the affection no other woman had ever shown him, Scarlett smiling up at him in bed, so happy, always seemingly so happy that he had been shattered when without warning she told him that she was marrying another man.

Scarlett rose and settled down at the table. 'Was there a reason you wanted to see me?' she dared, stiff as a plank in her seat.

James reappeared and set a tiny ornamental quiche adorned with baby lettuce leaves down in front of her. It was so exquisite a creation that she was almost afraid to touch it. Mouth-watering pastry melted in her mouth and she looked at Aristide enquiringly.

'I have a favour to ask,' Aristide confessed.

Scarlett had braced herself for some reference to her

children and her shoulders dropped in relief even as a frown line indented her brow, because Aristide Angelico didn't ask for favours. Other people asked *him* for favours, but Aristide wanted very little and what he did want he *bought*.

'A favour…from me?' she questioned in surprise.

'My parents are holding a thirtieth-birthday bash for me in two weeks and I need a partner. I'd be very grateful if you would agree to accompany me to the party.'

Blue eyes widening, Scarlett gazed back at him, almost stunned into silence. 'Are you serious?'

'Deadly serious.'

'But why me?'

'Because you wouldn't read anything deeper into the invitation,' Aristide returned smoothly. 'It would be strictly platonic. Essentially, you would shield me from all the wannabes my mother will serve up for my appreciation. She's desperate for me to get married… and I'm not in any hurry—'

'At our one meeting it was clear that your mother despised me, so I should be the last person you would ask,' Scarlett pointed out, although she wondered why she was even bothering to make the point since there was no prospect of her accepting his invite.

'No, it makes you the best option,' Aristide countered with a grim smile. 'I don't mind annoying my mother and your reappearance in my life will shock her and persuade her to back off…at least for a while.'

Scarlett shrugged awkwardly and pushed away her empty plate. 'I couldn't do it—'

'The school term is due to finish. You will be on

holiday,' Aristide reminded her evenly. 'It will only be for a weekend.'

Scarlett went pink, thinking how very deeply ironic it was that Aristide should finally be inviting her to a family event now that they were no longer in a relationship. Italy was essentially his home, but he had only once taken her to Rome for a weekend. Of course, he would never have asked her to socialise with his parents while they were still together lest she begin dreaming of wedding rings. The sole reason she had met Elisabetta Angelico was that the older woman had sought her out to satisfy *her* curiosity and shoot her down in flames.

'I'm sorry I couldn't do it,' she told Aristide flatly, thinking of Rome and Alice because she was no longer free to come and go as she pleased. In addition, could she spend more time with Aristide without making an accidental slip about the fact that she was now the mother of two toddlers?

'Think it over. Thirty-six hours in the Italian sunshine and naturally I would cover any and all expenses.'

The main course arrived. Scarlett concentrated on her food because she had nothing more to say. She was grateful for the return of her earrings, but she could not see any reason why she would want to spend time with Aristide again. He had hurt her too much. He was a mistake she needed to keep firmly in her past. Although, how could she think of her children as a mistake when they had brought her so much happiness? And without Aristide, she wouldn't even have Rome and Alice, she reminded herself.

Aristide studied her down-bent head while she ate only a single mouthful of the chocolate mousse dessert that was an old favourite of hers. He couldn't even get a conversation out of her and just at that moment he was reluctant to rake up their incendiary past to provide useful fodder. Her quietness called to mind how silent she had become during the last weeks of their affair. Quiet, *secretive*, he had later decided in disgust, although whatever she was hiding from him had not kept her out of his bed or made her any less keen to be with him. No, her unexpected unavailability had only begun during that final month and a flood of lame excuses had come his way: illness, family occasions, work events, relatives and friends visiting.

'I should be going,' Scarlett remarked stiffly. 'I'm supposed to be going shopping with my mother-in-law this afternoon.'

Aristide gritted his teeth, discovering that her reluctance merely sharpened his desire to spend more time with her. That kneejerk reaction incensed him.

'A break would do you good,' he murmured softly, waving away the coffee tray James held in the doorway.

Unexpected tears stung the backs of Scarlett's eyes because Aristide could sound so considerate, but it was a superficial level of caring. Once he had comforted her when she'd wept over the return of her father's cancer following several operations, but Aristide would neither go to the hospital with her nor visit her parents' home. He had always carefully avoided doing anything that might suggest that their relationship had any real staying power. He had kept her at a distance, shut her out, refusing to even explain why he had little time for his own family.

Determined not to respond, Scarlett rose from her chair and gathered up her bag. 'Don't you need to get back to work?' she muttered in desperation.

'I decide my own schedule.' Aristide vaulted upright, interrupted in the rousing recollection of the hot, tight embrace of her body and thoroughly irritated by his own susceptibility when his quarry wasn't even making a tiny effort to attract him.

'You should go to Italy with him,' Edith Walker recommended, sharply disconcerting Scarlett the evening of the same day. 'Use it as the perfect opportunity to tell him about Rome and Alice.'

Scarlett was stunned by that advice. 'I can't believe you're even suggesting that.'

'Some day you will *have* to tell your children the truth of their parentage and their father has a right to that same information. You can't ignore the facts for ever.' The older woman sighed ruefully. 'Luke's not here to be hurt now and, sadly, Rome and Alice no longer have a father. Even if Mr Angelico was only marginally interested in the twins, he would surely be better than no father at all.'

Scarlett had paled. She was shaken by that frank opinion.

Edith rested a reassuring hand down on hers. 'We wouldn't be having this conversation if my son were still alive. Luke adored being a father. I would have waited a few years before saying these things to you both, but everything has changed and now your ex has brought himself back into the picture, I think it's time for him to be told the truth.'

'Aristide won't *want* to know.'

'If that's true, then your honesty will still have been for the best. You will know where you stand and will be able to advise the children accordingly in the future. If you do this favour for Mr Angelico, he should be better disposed towards you. Try to keep the relationship civil.' Edith sighed. 'But be prepared for him to be very angry that he is only now being told about the twins. A young man as blessed by advantage as he has been in life will be unfamiliar with the sensation of being blindsided.'

Scarlett went to bed that night with a lot on her mind. As the older woman had reminded her, Luke's death had changed everything. For the first time she was being made to recognise that her children had rights too, rights that it would be wrong to ignore. They deserved to know exactly who they were even if it was only out of a desire to receive an accurate medical background.

In the future would Rome and Alice want to know Aristide and his relatives? In staying silent, she reflected, she had overlooked half of their DNA inheritance and the whole family that were part of that. For an instant she felt quite sick at the prospect of confessing what she had concealed from Aristide two years earlier.

But how much would her secret really matter to him? Aristide had never appeared even mildly interested in children and had been reluctant to discuss his opinion of them. At the time she had suspected that he felt that she had no right to ask such personal questions and instead she had read between the lines, as no doubt intended. He had quipped that he didn't want offspring until he was at least fifty and had casually referred to having had to contest two separate paternity claims in the years prior to their meeting, both ultimately proving to be false.

Furthermore, he had never taken the smallest risk with contraception. Even though she had been taking the pill, he had still utilised his own precautions. Aristide gave no woman his full trust. Scarlett still had not the slightest idea how the twins had been conceived. She hadn't missed any pills and hadn't suffered any illness or taken any medication that could have interfered with her birth control. But even so, one morning she had woken up early feeling as sick as a dog and the writing had been on the wall. She had been terrified, not only at the threat of an unplanned pregnancy but also at what such a development would do to her relationship with Aristide.

Wallowing in the past, however, wasn't doing her any favours, she castigated herself, and she sat up in bed to switch on the light and reach for her phone before she could lose her nerve. If she had to tell Aristide that he was a father, it would, she was convinced, be easier to do it when their children were fully out of sight and hearing. She would tell him in Italy. Edith had made it clear that she and Tom would be happy to keep the twins that weekend.

She texted him.

I will go to Italy.

Aristide, working late, reached for his phone and a wide smile lit up his lean dark features. It was two o'clock in the morning and he bet she hadn't noticed the time. Scarlett could be a very anxious little creature. She would've lain awake in bed fretting about his invitation, weighing up pros and cons but, ultimately, choosing the kindest option. Only that once with that unforgettable text had she not been kind or caring with him, he recalled bleakly. He knew her well enough to picture her lying nibbling at her lower lip, brow indented, troubled eyes flickering. She had done a lot of late-night stressing in silence before they parted, he conceded more reflectively. Exactly what had she been worrying about?

You won't regret it.

And she wouldn't, he swore to himself. All of a sudden instead of dwelling on the past and his disillusionment with her, Aristide was recklessly awash with good intentions. He would be a complete gentleman, he decided. Just like one of those stupid, perfect knights in the fairy tales she liked to read to children. Unluckily for him, a steady diet of that kind of conditioning and refinement had not prepared Scarlett for a normal contemporary guy with flaws. Not only would he ensure that he kept his mother well away from her, but if Cosetta Ricci was on the guest list he would keep his distance from her as well rather than offend Scarlett.

Energised by such good ideas, Aristide was on a high. He would *protect* Scarlett from any adverse influence. What could possibly go wrong?

Receiving a text from Aristide early the following morning, Scarlett phoned to ask him, 'What do you mean, there are dresses arriving?'

Aristide groaned, old memories stirring. 'Scarlett, this is an exclusive social event and you won't have anything in your wardrobe that will be suitable. Just imagine being underdressed in my mother's vicinity,' he suggested.

Scarlett shuddered at her end of the phone.

'You're doing this for my benefit, so I will provide the fancy trappings…okay?'

Scarlett heaved a sigh. 'Okay.'

'The seamstress will take your measurements and adjust whatever you choose to a perfect fit and the stylist will provide the clothing.'

'My goodness, you are taking this very seriously.'

'If you feel that you're looking beautiful you will relax and enjoy yourself.'

As she came off the phone, memories wafted Scarlett back in time. Her final year at college she had lived with Brie and two other friends in a smart apartment in Hampstead. The apartment had belonged to Brie's parents, who had been travelling abroad, and Brie had always hated living alone. Scarlett had seen Aristide out jogging several times before she actually met him. She couldn't possibly have kept up the pace he maintained but she had definitely noticed him. Unfortunately, he hadn't seemed like the sort of male who would ever deign to notice her until her foot slid off the kerb one morning and she twisted her ankle and fell. Aristide had come to her rescue. He had picked her up off the pavement…literally picked her up as if she were a doll and carried her into a café to check her ankle.

Someone had arrived with a first-aid kit. She had assumed his security team were his friends. Aristide had even attended to her bleeding knee. He had knelt at her feet and when she'd looked straight into those stunning black-lashed green eyes of his she had been mesmerised, stumbling over her words and giggling when he'd flirted with her. Later she had cringed at that recollection of acting like an airhead. Although she had been sweaty and tousled, it hadn't seemed to matter to him. He had asked her out to dinner that night and just as fast, before she'd even got his name, she had agreed.

'He must live somewhere nearby,' Brie had mused, checking out the name online and then gasping and going into whoops. 'For goodness' sake, Scarlett. If I'd known Aristide Angelico was out there running on the street, I'd have lain in wait for him and tripped him up for myself! Is that him?' she had demanded, angling her phone screen at Scarlett to show Aristide, black curls cropped short, clad in a very sharp suit. 'Honestly? How can you be so lucky?'

And Scarlett had felt like the luckiest girl in the world for those first few dates. Aristide had immense charm and he'd taken her places she could never have afforded to visit alone. She had always been sensible and she had tried to keep her feet on the ground and not allow Aristide's wealth to affect either the way she saw him or the way she behaved with him. She'd also seen his imperfections. He was arrogant and he had the incredibly high expectations of a young man who had never had to settle for less than the best. He was also very reserved and reluctant to talk about his family.

She'd been in the middle of her final exams when he'd asked her to fly out to the Caribbean with him. He had struggled to accept that she had to study and that he had to wait. But in the end, he *had* waited until she was free and she had flown out to Dominica with him for a week and finally shared a bed with him. Secretly she had thought that that intimacy was happening too soon, but she had also known that for the first time ever *she* wanted a man as much as he wanted her and she had gone with her gut instincts and stopped holding back.

'Have a good time with Aristide,' Brie had encouraged. 'But accept up front that it's not going to last. The world's his oyster and he'll move on eventually. Just try not to get hurt.'

With hindsight she wished she had listened more to her friend because Brie had had the experience to recognise that Aristide was not at an age where he wanted to commit to any woman and he ruthlessly guarded his freedom. Scarlett, in contrast, had begun with infatuation and quickly launched into love. Before very long, she had been virtually living in Aristide's apartment when he was in London and she had been moulding her life around him, dropping out of volunteering projects because she'd no longer had the time, telling white lies to her parents to excuse her absences, rather than admit that she was seeing a guy, who winced if she so much as mentioned him meeting her family.

There had been inevitable conflicts between them. Aristide had been continually buying her expensive jewellery and she had given way but only to the extent of wearing the pieces when she was out with him, always knowing that she would leave them behind when they broke up. But when he had asked her to drop everything and fly off somewhere exotic for an occasional week, she had had to say a flat no because she'd valued her job and once the school holidays were over, they were over. Once or twice, he had gone ahead alone, and worrying about what he could be doing without her had killed her pride and much of her resistance.

He'd given her conflicting messages. The night he'd suddenly informed her that they weren't exclusive, she had said, knowing that, if that was true, she had to break up with him, 'So, you're content for me to see other men?'

'No!' he had fired back at her in astonishment, for once losing his cool.

'Well, if it's only you who retains that option then it won't work for me,' she had warned him. 'I'm not the sort of woman who will be content to sleep with you and with other men at the same time. If you want to be with other women, then you don't want to be with *me* and that's fine. The choice is yours.'

And she had returned to Brie's apartment that night in floods of tears knowing that she had had to draw that line in the sand for her own sanity, but heartbroken that he didn't really appreciate what they had together. After all, aside from those occasional fights, Scarlett had been deliriously happy from the moment Aristide had walked into her life and the idea of life without him again had cut her in two.

'You're in too deep with him. Maybe it's better to step away now,' Brie had consoled her.

'If he's already hurting you like this, you're better off without him,' Luke had told her apologetically that same evening.

What had felt like the worst week of Scarlett's life had followed. She had wondered if she had got too caught up in labels and unnerved Aristide. To be fair to him, while she had been with him she had never had the smallest suspicion that there were any other women in his life, but he refused to make an actual promise or a commitment of any kind that might restrict him.

At the end of the week, Aristide had shown up at the door. 'I miss you,' he had admitted stiffly. 'Right now, I don't want anyone else. That is the truth.'

And the silence had hung there while she'd considered that and it had been the uncertain, anxious light in his eyes that had won her over. He hadn't said much, just enough to warm the cold place in her heart. *Right now*, though… Those two words had engulfed her like the crack of doom, reminding her that he didn't see her as figuring in his long-term future. But he had tugged her into his arms and kissed her with a flattering amount of desperation and she had shelved her concerns and insecurities, telling herself that there was always the possibility that she would get bored with him first.

Only in the end it had been the trauma of discovering that she was pregnant that had forced them apart.

CHAPTER THREE

SCARLETT CERTAINLY WASN'T prepared for the arrival of several rails of clothing to be wheeled in for her inspection and the tailor or the bubbly stylist and her assistant who accompanied them. Sadly for her, she was no longer the same size she had been two years earlier, the size Aristide had naively assumed she still was. Pregnancy had changed her shape. She was fuller at breast and hip and no longer rejoiced in quite the same tiny waist.

The tailor, who took her measurements, clicked her teeth in dismay. The twins were mercifully down for a nap and she had Brie with her for a second opinion.

'With your colouring, I would suggest *this* for the big event.' The stylist extended a dream of a dress. The rich emerald shade reminded her of Aristide's eyes. It swept to the floor in beaded, shimmering luxury.

Scarlett swallowed hard and took it across the hall to try it on in privacy. It was rather too tight and she returned to the now cluttered lounge feeling pretty self-conscious.

'That's gorgeous…if you have it in a larger size,' Brie commented.

'It will be specially made to Mrs Walker's exact

measurements to ensure a perfect fit,' the tailor assured her.

Accessories were produced and then the shopping experience took on another dimension when outfits were produced for Scarlett to travel in. Thinking that that was excessive, Scarlett excused herself to phone Aristide from the hall.

'How many outfits are you planning to buy me? *Travelling* clothes?' she complained critically.

'The paps are everywhere. I want you to look the part the entire time you're with me. It's no big deal, *bella mia*. It's like a stage role. The clothes are only props.'

Silenced, Scarlett came off the phone again, recalling Edith's advice, which had virtually been to keep Aristide sweet in advance of the shocking news she had to share with him while she was away. Arguing with him would only annoy him and since she was doing this favour for him, she might as well do it to the best of her ability. What it cost him to put on a show with her in a starring role was no concern of hers.

'You look amazing,' Aristide proclaimed with satisfaction when he picked her up at the apartment.

Scarlett was still sucking her tummy in as she picked her careful way into the limousine in very high heels. She wore a light jacket teamed with a silk camisole and flowing trousers. Her carefully straightened hair fell in a coppery tumble of smooth strands round her shoulders and her face was equally well made up. She had even had her nails done at a local beauty salon. Barely an inch of her was as nature had brought her into the world, she conceded ruefully.

Aristide feasted his attention on her. She glowed with her coppery hair swirling round her heart-shaped face, her cupid's bow mouth glistening, her eyes lit up like stars. As she settled, the jacket fell back on the camisole exposing the bountiful swell of her breasts and his attention lingered there, only slowly dropping to take in the rest of her. She looked ridiculously sexy without exposing any flesh. She had looked equally good the very first time he'd seen her with her curvy little body and shapely legs revealed by her close-fitting exercise gear.

Aristide was sheathed in faded designer jeans that fitted him like a glove and a shirt rolled up to his elbows, effortlessly elegant and far more casual than her in appearance, but then he didn't want her to look casual and potentially sloppy, she reminded herself wryly. He wanted the perfect, polished version of her that he had so rarely seen two years earlier because she had been too relaxed about being with him to spend hours agonising about her appearance and working on it.

She scrutinised him in a series of crafty little sidewise glances, not quite trusting herself to properly withstand the full spectacular effect of Aristide head-on. She looked and she expected to feel nothing because it had been so long since she had experienced any type of physical attraction. But little warm glimmers of awakening pulsed as she took in his bronzed profile, shifted down to a broad shoulder encased in cotton and to a sleek midriff rippling with muscle before lingering on a powerful masculine thigh and the potent swell at his crotch.

Reddening, she hastily glanced away again, registering in dismay that she was far too susceptible to even *look* at Aristide. It had been too long since she had been touched, held, driven mad with desire. Two years, not that long in the scheme of things, but two years in a sexless marriage had left its mark. She had shut down that part of herself that only Aristide had known, had just got on with her life, telling herself that she was more than happy with what she had established with Luke.

The atmosphere in the back of the limousine was tense and she slowly sucked in a breath, finally acknowledging how fiercely apprehensive she was of what lay ahead of her. When exactly was she planning to unveil her shocking truth to Aristide? Not at the party tomorrow, probably not before it either as she would have to take time getting dolled up for the event. Tonight? Where were they staying? Would there be other people there? She didn't want an audience if he lost his temper. After the party? What time would that be? Again, would they be alone? And they were flying home the next morning…

'You're very on edge,' Aristide scolded, closing a big hand over hers where she had braced it on the seat between them. 'I promise not to leave you alone with my mother.'

'I'm not scared of her!' Scarlett declared, fingers flexing in the light warm hold of his before pulling free as her head turned and inevitably her gaze met his. In all her life she had never been so conscious of another person's proximity.

Eyes as green as her party dress, startlingly bright against his bronzed skin, met her troubled scrutiny. Sudden heat curled up at the heart of her, little atoms of pure sexual awareness fizzing like live sparks through her bloodstream. Every tiny muscle in her body clenched tight and gooseflesh pebbled her arms below her jacket. Her mouth ran dry and her breath rattled in her lungs.

'Don't look at me like that…unless you want the consequences,' Aristide breathed with a ragged edge to his dark deep drawl.

Scarlett blinked rapidly and turned her head away, her whole body bubbling with nervous energy. 'I don't know—'

'I *do* know and so do you,' Aristide contradicted. 'But that's not why we're here together. I said platonic and I *meant* platonic but that also denotes that *both* of us have to respect the rules.'

Scarlett felt as if she were burning up inside her clothes and she stared straight ahead of her.

Aristide was rigid with self-control and hard as a steel girder. She had looked at him with longing and desire had leapt up in him so fast he was still gritting his teeth in a vain effort to control his libido. That *he* should have to remind *her* of the rules! He hadn't expected that little twist, hadn't been prepared for her to give him a look of that nature. Hungry, needy. And she couldn't hide it, was actually refusing to look back at him again while her cheeks were flushed as red as a traffic light.

'I suppose this was to be expected. Familiarity knocks us back into old behaviour patterns,' Aristide quipped much more lightly than he felt about the problem.

'Yes,' Scarlett squeezed out her agreement in a small tight voice. 'That's all it is.'

'So, let's move one step ahead and get our curiosity out of the way now,' Aristide suggested. 'One kiss and then we leave it there.'

Scarlett was so taken aback by that offer that she turned back to look at him in disbelief, sapphire-blue eyes wide and anxious.

'I bet we won't feel anything,' Aristide forecast with confidence.

Scarlett neglected to say that she had never been a woman who bet on what struck her as a surefire loss but she understood what he meant and intended. If she felt nothing, she knew that it would be a huge relief.

'One kiss?' She checked the boundaries tautly.

'One should be enough to prevent us from ripping each other's clothes off before our flight,' Aristide mocked. 'And we need to work on your attitude to me before we float our pretence in front of an audience. You can't continue to pull away from me as though you're scared of me.'

'Of course I'm not scared of you!' Scarlett told him vehemently, even though she knew she was terrified of what he could make her *feel*.

'Good to know.' Aristide studied her with frowning force. 'I don't want to grab you but you're sitting a long way away.'

Scarlett swallowed with difficulty as he extended a lean hand to urge her closer. She grasped it and shifted along the back seat like a mouse told by a cat that she was not on the dinner menu but not really trusting the assurance.

Aristide curved long brown fingers to her cheekbone and tipped up her face. She collided with bright green eyes and it was as if an electrical charge shot through her veins. Quickly she closed her eyes and he lowered his head.

'Stop playing dead with me. It makes me feel like a lion hunting prey.' Taking his time, Aristide brought his mouth down on hers and slowly, smoothly tasted the parted promise of her lips.

She shivered, muscles snapping taut, every sense heightened as he drew her very slowly into his arms like a male determined not to spook her. She had almost forgotten what it felt like to be in his arms, but intense response raced up through her and, involuntarily, she pushed closer.

The scent of him washed over her, warm, male and achingly familiar even after all the time that had passed. Her body was frighteningly hungry for sensation and her lips parted in helpless invitation. He plucked at her full lower lip and ravished the moist interior of her mouth with his tongue. Her heartbeat hit earthquake mode, pounding inside her chest at such a speed that she was breathless. A tiny sound was wrenched from her.

The pressure of his lips grew more urgent and an explosion of fireworks flared and burst inside her, showering her with sparks and enveloping her in response. The feverish pulse between her thighs kicked up a heated notch. She wanted *more*, that fast she wanted *more* and it panicked her and drove her into instantaneous retreat as she broke away from him to surge back into her corner of the back seat.

'That was an enlightening experiment,' Aristide pronounced with finality. 'But we won't be repeating it any time soon.'

Inflamed by the aching pulse at his groin and angrily ignoring it, Aristide gritted his teeth in the humming silence and lifted the jewellery box beside him. 'I thought you might appreciate the return of this stuff for the occasion. Make use of it. Diamonds are acceptable at any time of day,' he informed her.

Grateful to have something to do with her hands, Scarlett clutched the box and flipped it open. Inside, in a careless tangle, lay every piece Aristide had ever given her. With a trembling hand she tugged the slender gold watch free and replaced her own. She couldn't believe that he had kept it all heaped in a box, almost as if he had gathered it up in one angry swoop and hidden it hastily away without making use of the jewellery boxes she had left in a drawer. Slowly, she teased the diamond and sapphire pendant out of the tangle. It had hurt to leave that glittering gem behind. He had given it to her the morning after their first night together in Dominica and she had loved it.

Aristide twitched it gently free of her grasp. 'Turn round,' he told her.

The coolness of the gold settled against her skin as he clasped it at her nape. Goosebumps broke out on her skin again and she shivered.

'Earrings,' he prompted.

She searched out and found the matching sapphire earrings and slowly attached them to her ears. 'The bracelet would be overkill,' she told him shakily.

'Up to you, but I would like to see you wearing most of it tomorrow evening,' he warned her.

With an absent fingertip she traced the exquisite diamond necklace still in the box. He had given it to her their one and only Christmas together and he had been annoyed when she'd taken it off to go home and enjoy Christmas lunch with her family instead of him, but he hadn't given her any warning that he would be spending the day with her. She couldn't possibly have worn a small fortune in diamonds and explained it to her parents' satisfaction.

She thought about that single wildly exciting kiss and burned with the guilt tugging painfully at her. She had fallen into that kiss and melted like ice cream on a hot grill. And he had known it too. Yet she *had* been happy with Luke, she reminded herself remorsefully. She had had so much in common with her best friend because they had shared the same outlook and similar interests. Luke had desperately wanted to be a father and he had been an amazing father for the brief months he had had with the twins.

Sadly, Rome and Alice wouldn't remember him

helping with all those late-night feeds, soothing them when they cried by rocking them in his arms, tirelessly searching out toys that might catch their attention. Luke had adored Rome and Alice, and as a family they had flourished, would still have been flourishing had Luke's life been spared. She swallowed the lump in her throat and blinked back tears. Unfortunately, though, there had been a hollow at the heart of their relationship and both of them had had needs and dreams that the other could not fulfil.

In a daze of recollection, Scarlett boarded Aristide's private jet and sudden panic assailed her as she thought of the explanation that still lay ahead of her. She just wanted to get it over with, she acknowledged unhappily. She didn't want to try and pick some imagined perfect moment because truthfully there *was* no perfect moment in which to make such a revelation. But here they were trapped on a plane in privacy for a couple of hours. Didn't it make sense to come clean during the flight rather than risk being around other people when she told him?

'Have you become a nervous flyer?' Aristide enquired, watching her do up her belt on the other side of the opulent cabin with trembling hands, wondering why she had chosen not to sit beside him.

'Er...no,' Scarlett muttered unevenly. 'I just have something rather challenging to tell you and it's eating me alive with nerves.'

Aristide quirked an ebony brow. 'I can't imagine what that would be.'

He looked amused, emerald-green eyes alight with the hope that he was about to be entertained.

'It's not something you're likely to laugh about,' she warned him, more than ever intimidated by what she had to tell him because he was in no way prepared.

The jet roared down the runway and she breathed in slow and deep as it lifted up into the sky. In the silence that followed, Aristide summoned the stewardess with the buzz of a call button. 'You need a stiff drink,' he told her with a teasing grin.

As the stewardess retreated again, Scarlett released her seat belt and tried to relax with a glass of wine gripped in one hand. 'I have two children…' she began.

Aristide frowned, released his belt and plunged upright wearing an expression of shock at her announcement that she was a mother. She had become a parent with Walker? She had had a child with *him*? That cut something deep in him that he didn't understand, and it hurt like the devil. He couldn't interpret that distorted feeling of loss and betrayal and he took refuge in outrage at the news.

'Two?' he questioned as that latter fact sank in. 'You were barely married a year before his accident! How on earth could you have had two children in that space of time?'

'They're twins,' Scarlett almost whispered, knowing that he had once had a twin brother, who had passed away, but knowing little more detail beyond that. 'They're eighteen months old, a little boy and a little girl. They're *yours*.'

Aristide had frozen beside the built-in bar at the front

of the cabin, his big powerful body rigid with savage tension. Unfortunately, it was as if a red mist of incomprehension had suddenly come down over him and captured him and he couldn't think straight because he had no idea what she could feasibly be talking about. How could her children possibly be his?

'You were married to Luke Walker. If you had children, they can only be his. Why would you tell me that they're mine? Do you need money for some reason?' he prompted in a very detached voice.

'I'll just pretend I didn't hear you say that,' Scarlett said, flinching from that suspicion. 'I'm not in need of money, I assure you.'

'Why else would you suddenly tell me that you have kids and that they're mine?' Aristide demanded. 'This kind of discussion should be taking place in my lawyer's office, not directly with me. I don't deal with this kind of nonsense, not personally I don't,' he added.

'Whatever you choose will be fine with me,' Scarlett responded quietly. 'But I don't want any money and I'm not even asking you to have anything to do with the twins if you would prefer not to. I only spoke up because now that I've seen you again and so much has changed, it seemed time to tell you the truth.'

Aristide compressed his wide sensual mouth and dropped back into his seat, reaching automatically for his laptop. He still couldn't think straight but he was seething with a host of uneasy feelings that were deeply unfamiliar to him. The very thought of Scarlett having had children with Luke Walker made him feel vaguely nauseous. And she was acting out of character, which bewildered him. Scarlett had always been sensible. She was the last woman alive he would ever have thought would approach him with such an unlikely story. But it was crazy what people would do for money. He had learned that young. He had learned that being very wealthy merely made him a target just as it had made Daniele a cash cow for a greedy woman.

'I couldn't possibly have got you pregnant. I'm far too careful in that line,' Aristide informed her with startling abruptness.

'I was very careful too,' Scarlett countered defensively. 'It still happened. I don't know how. But it *did* happen and they *are* your children.'

'Who's listed on their birth certificate?' Aristide shot at her.

'I had to leave it blank.'

'There you are, then,' Aristide quipped very drily.

Silence filled the cabin as Aristide flipped through columns of numbers, barely able to focus on the screen while his brain worked busily in the background on the problem she had set before him. Denial roared through every inch of his lean, taut body. All he could think was that she had succumbed to temporary insanity or that she had financial problems and was hoping to make him step up now that she was on her own again.

But how could she try to con him when she knew that he would demand a DNA test as proof? Scarlett was intelligent and sensible, by no means a fool. Why would she do that? And even as he pondered that conundrum, another idea was burgeoning at the back of his brain.

Aristide stood up again. 'Are you telling me that there was a mistake?'

'A mistake?' she echoed tentatively.

'Because that makes sense. If you slept with both of us around the same time,' Aristide contended grittily, his lean, dark face hard as iron. 'Perhaps you conceived then and you assumed that *he* was responsible. That's why you left me and married *him*, isn't it?'

'No, it isn't!' Scarlett snapped back, shaken by the grubby picture he had fashioned of their past and the depth of his distrust.

'And then presumably when the children were born or some time afterwards, you and Luke realised that I had fathered them and *not* him,' Aristide suggested grimly. 'I have heard of such mistakes but I can't credit your claim in the first place because I always used contraception with you—'

'Oh, for goodness' sake, Aristide,' Scarlett groaned, appalled at the direction his inventive mind was now taking him in. 'Nobody but you could be the twins' father. Luke and I didn't have sex. He was gay. He married me because he was very keen to be a father and he thought he never would be. He married me when I was three months pregnant with your children!'

CHAPTER FOUR

ARISTIDE SHOT HER a look of scorching condemnation for all the false assumptions she had left him to make, both two years ago and in the present.

He was slowly absorbing what she had told him. On the outside he was now monitoring his every visible response but on the inside he was aware of a sensation that could only be described as intense relief... Luke Walker had been gay. Scarlett had *not* slept with him. Scarlett had *not* lied when she told him that her love for Luke was platonic. Together, those two facts were very important to Aristide. And last of all, if Luke couldn't be the father of her children, the chance that Aristide *was* the father now seemed rather more likely, even if he still couldn't grasp how Scarlett could have conceived on his watch. He was stunned into silence as the shock waves of all that information gradually trickled through him.

'You're shocked,' Scarlett conceded anxiously, rising out of her seat to approach the bar and seek out the white wine again for herself. 'I think I need another drink.'

Aristide watched her hold the bottle with a hand that still shook and he steadied it for her. He had never seen her drink even two glasses of wine in quick succession. She was shaken up, scared. Good, she should be, after what she had done and the indescribable mess she had created. And all without good reason, he reflected in stunned, angry disbelief. Why the hell hadn't she told him she was pregnant?

'Aristide...say something.'

'If your claim is correct, you and your husband literally *stole* my children from me!' he framed accusingly.

Scarlett looked up at him in stark dismay and hastily quaffed more wine in a nervous movement. 'It wasn't like that—'

'Do you have a photo of them?'

All of a sudden, Aristide was recalling the young children clinging to the older woman's legs when he had called at Scarlett's home.

Scarlett blinked in surprise and went back to her seat to grab up her capacious travel bag, rifling through the clutter to extract the small personal photo album she had brought with her, although she hadn't expected Aristide to ask to see a photo of the twins so quickly. Especially not directly after he had accused her and Luke of stealing his children from him. That accusation had cut like a knife when she had done everything within her power to protect him and her own family from the fallout of her accidental pregnancy.

Aristide took the album and began to flip through it. Image after image assailed his shrewd gaze and it grew a little glazed because he was viewing children overflowing with clear Angelico traits. Like him they had inherited the same wretched curls and naturally the little boy hadn't had a haircut yet because Scarlett had always hated it when Aristide got his curls cropped short. The little girl, on the other hand, was like a little curly-haired doll, much smaller than her brother. They were incredibly cute but he refused to say so.

'What are their names?' he asked instead.

'Rome and Alice.'

'Why Rome?'

Scarlett coloured and took another gulp of her wine. 'I worked out that that's where it must have happened… once the doctor told me the delivery date. It can only have been that weekend we spent there.'

'A vivid memory. I suppose I'm lucky you didn't call him Rhett or Ashley to follow family tradition.'

Her adoptive mother had been an enormous fan of the movie *Gone with the Wind* and christening her daughter Scarlett had probably been the most adventurous and colourful choice she had ever made in her life. But Nancy Pearson had waited until she was middle-aged to finally acquire a daughter and when that daughter finally came along, even her husband was unable to change her mind about what she chose to call her.

'Tell me why you did this,' Aristide murmured intently, suppressing his anger with every fibre of his being. 'I need to understand *why* you did such a wicked thing.'

Scarlett dealt him an anxious glance. 'It *wasn't* wicked.'

'But it was,' Aristide contradicted firmly. 'You didn't tell me. You didn't give me a choice.'

'But you didn't want children with me.'

Aristide gritted his even white teeth. 'What I wanted shouldn't have entered into the equation once you realised that you had conceived. We were a couple. Normal couples deal with such situations together.'

'We weren't a normal couple. You were away a lot of the time and there were other women in your life.'

Aristide stiffened. 'There *were* no other women.'

Scarlett dealt him a pained appraisal. 'Cosetta Ricci?'

'Cosetta is an old friend,' Aristide explained. 'She's a family friend, more than anything else.'

'But I didn't know that at the time!' she flared back at him in frustration. 'You were determined not to fully commit to our relationship and you were always reminding me that you planned to move on from me eventually—'

'That should have had no bearing on the discussion we should have had the minute you discovered that you were pregnant,' Aristide sliced in with ruthless bite. 'But we didn't have that discussion because you decided to keep your condition a secret from me.'

Scarlett lifted her chin in a defensive movement. 'I thought it was for the best all round. My father was dying of cancer and my mother was already distraught. I couldn't go home and tell them that I was about to become an unmarried mother. They would've fallen apart at the seams. They didn't deserve all that drama at that trying stage of their lives and they deserved better from me.'

Aristide had heard enough. Everyone but him had received due consideration. Luke had offered her a wedding ring and Scarlett had leapt at it to paper over the cracks and please her narrow-minded parents. Nobody had worried too much about how Aristide would feel or what he might want. Yet according to her that little boy and girl were *his* children, *his* blood, *his* responsibility. Rage settled like a heavy stone deep down inside him where he rigorously contained it.

As the silence smouldered, Scarlett began to speak again. 'I didn't want a termination or to part with my child to adoption. I knew you wouldn't want me to have them—'

Green eyes pierced her like steel knives. 'You knew *nothing*!'

'You said you didn't want children until you were middle-aged,' she reminded him doggedly.

Aristide's mouth took on a sardonic tilt. 'And like every other human being on this planet, I adapt to changing circumstances when I have to.'

'I didn't want you to feel that you *had* to do anything for me!' she shot back truthfully.

'No, you were too busy being a coward to do the right thing and *talk* to me. There is no excuse for your lies of omission, no excuse for a woman who walked away from the father of her children and denied him his every legal right to marry another man,' Aristide completed tautly, and he sank back down into his seat, struggling to contain the fierce emotions washing through him in wave after sickening wave.

'Aristide…' Scarlett began uncertainly a few minutes later.

'I don't want to hear any more. To be frank, I've

heard quite enough for the moment,' Aristide admitted flatly, seriously dissatisfied with the explanations he had received. 'But could you please transfer your wedding ring to another finger for the duration of the weekend? It will incite less comment. You can change it back once we leave.'

Scarlett looked down in dismay at her hand and swallowed hard. Even aware of a panicky need to placate Aristide in any way she could, she rebelled against the concept but, an hour later, she slid the ring off her finger and threaded it covertly onto her other hand. He was furious with her. He didn't understand what she had done or why she had done it. How could he?

Her parents had been elderly compared to his, raised in a generation with rigid moral and religious values. Aristide had never felt that he owed a debt to his parents as she had. Her home had been so loving and caring that she had always tried to be the best daughter she could be and the threat of breaking their hearts at an already challenging time in their lives had been more than she could bear.

Had she taken the easy way out? Had she been immature and foolish? But whatever Aristide might say now, he had *not* wanted children two years ago, he would have been highly suspicious of her falling pregnant and her conception would still have destroyed their relationship.

Photographers tried to ambush them at the airport in Florence but Aristide's security team headed them off. Shaken by the flash of the cameras and the level of interest in Aristide, Scarlett was belatedly very grateful to be dressed as the most polished version of herself as she climbed into the limousine that picked them up.

'Where are we going?' she asked stiffly.

'The family home where the party is being held. It's belonged to me since my grandfather died. He didn't like my parents much and he skipped their generation in his will,' Aristide told her wryly. 'That caused a lot of grief in the family circle, but then my home has always been a battlefield, so it was nothing new.'

Scarlett winced at that information. 'You must have been close to him.'

'Much closer than my parents were,' he conceded. 'But I could have done without the bad feeling incited by that will. My grandfather went through two nasty divorces that cost him most of his fortune, but the family properties like the one here and the one in London were held in trust and kept safe. After the second divorce, he spent his time travelling, so I didn't see much of him the last few years of his life.'

'That's sad.'

Aristide shrugged. 'It wasn't. He was happy. In the Angelico clan, happiness is not a given.'

'Why is it like that?' she asked, genuinely curious.

'Too many damaging events, too many bitter people. We have a complex history, but you and I have shared enough negative stuff for one day, so I won't get stuck into it right now, if you don't mind,' Aristide murmured, his strong profile clenching hard, green eyes cool as ice.

So, her children were a negative, Scarlett acknowledged with a sinking heart. But perhaps she wasn't being fair. He was right. She had not given him any choice. She had not spoken up when she should have done. She had not respected his rights as a father. Instead, she had grasped at the nice tidy solution she had seen in marrying her best friend.

'The twins are *not* a negative. I was referring to all the other stuff that goes with them…your silence, your marriage, the choices you made without consulting me,' Aristide specified curtly. 'That is all a very bitter pill to swallow.'

The car turned up a long steep driveway that carried them through deep woodland that slowly petered out into lawn. It was hauntingly beautiful.

'Is this the house?'

As the vast velvety stretch of lawns gave way to a gravel frontage, Scarlett stared wide-eyed at the building ahead, a vast stone property of ancient splendour such as she had never seen except in a history book. 'My word,' she whispered in consternation. 'It's a palace!'

'Palazzo Angelico. We're lucky the repairs have been completed in a timely manner. That's the main reason I suspect it was left to me. My parents let it go to rack and ruin—'

'But this *is* where you grew up,' Scarlett broke in, her wonder at such a childhood background patent and her curiosity on a high. 'Isn't it?'

'Daniele and I…yes. *Madonna santa!*' Aristide erupted without warning. 'It looks as though we're receiving a reception committee. What the hell are my parents doing here?'

'Perhaps something to do with the party?' Scarlett suggested weakly as she walked round the car to join him.

'They have their own home miles away,' Aristide said grittily, disconcerting her by closing a big hand over hers. 'Don't mention the twins, your marriage, anything. Anything you do and say can and will be held against you in their kind of company.'

'I wouldn't dream of it. Your mother paralyses my tongue,' she confided, but she was touched by his unexpected protectiveness.

'Cosetta is here as well. That's her car. Why is *she* here?' Aristide demanded wrathfully.

'Calm down. It's not important,' Scarlett murmured quietly as he urged her up a wide, shallow flight of steps into a huge echoing hall decorated with colourful frescoes.

Four people awaited them. One was clearly staff, standing a fair distance away. Another was an older man with grey hair, who bore a strong resemblance to Aristide. By his side stood an emaciated older but still very attractive brunette sporting giant pearls round her throat, a very smart dress and a bolero jacket. The third was a tall, leggy blonde, whom Scarlett also recognised from the magazine she had first seen her in, Cosetta Ricci.

Elisabetta's welcoming smile for her son fell off her face as though she had been slapped when she saw Scarlett. 'Aristide,' she purred in English, immediately turning to him as though Scarlett were invisible. 'We've moved in for the weekend and, of course, Cosetta, the darling that she is, has been helping me with the party planning. I must say the house is looking ravishing right now.'

'It must have cost you a king's ransom,' his father remarked with a faint air of disapproval.

'It's a shame you left it in such poor condition,' Aristide said drily.

'You look wonderful, Aristide...' Cosetta stepped forward to treat him to a continental kiss on both cheeks, which he tolerated but did not reciprocate. 'And *this* is...?'

It was the first time the little group had acknowledged her presence and Scarlett summoned up as warm a smile as she could manage. 'Scarlett Pearson—'

'Aristide's ex from years ago. How kind of her to step up for the occasion,' Elisabetta Angelico informed her husband, Riccardo.

'Scarlett is *not* my ex,' Aristide contradicted levelly. 'She's my special guest this weekend.'

In all, that welcome was a ghastly, awkward experience. Cosetta smiled continually but Scarlett was a woman too and she guessed that the blonde beauty had expected Aristide to walk through the door alone and be delighted by her presence. Spots of colour highlighted Cosetta's perfect cheekbones at his cool reaction. She did have better manners than Aristide's parents, however, because she made small talk until Aristide intervened to introduce Scarlett to the hovering male member of staff, who was called Andrea and managed the palazzo. Without further ado and with very few words more spoken to his silent parents, he guided Scarlett towards the grand marble staircase.

'My first mistake was agreeing to the party,' Aristide lamented in an undertone. 'Now I've got a home invasion to handle—'

'It's a *huge* house,' Scarlett pointed out gently, resting her hand on the carved balustrade of the stairs. 'Surely you need hardly see them? Your mother looked annoyed when you walked away so quickly.'

'It won't do her any harm,' Aristide bit out and then added, 'No, I don't mean that. Daniele begged me to be more forgiving in his last letter to me and I'm *trying*, but it's a challenge when my strongest memory of her is of her taking a belt to my little brother and calling him stupid because he was dyslexic.'

Scarlett was appalled. Unhappily she could picture Elisabetta being cruel because she had the superior assurance of someone who demanded high standards and punished those who failed her expectations. 'Maybe she's learnt better since then and regrets her treatment of him?' she suggested uncertainly.

Andrea spread open double doors on a big bedroom. Behind them, their luggage was brought up. As Aristide spoke to the man in Italian, Scarlett turned and noticed that all their luggage had been brought to the same room.

'Refreshments will be served out on the balcony,' Aristide breathed, striding across the room to throw open a door and disappear from view.

Scarlett followed him at a slower pace. He stood looking out over the gardens, his strong shoulders and back rigid with raw tension. The *home invasion*? He really didn't like his parents, and that image he had given her of his brother being beaten hadn't warmed her opinion either. As for his father almost sneering at him for repairing a property he and his wife had apparently failed to maintain while they lived there, Scarlett was no more impressed.

What she had to say now sounded terribly trivial in comparison to what she had witnessed. 'You didn't warn me that you were expecting me to share a room with you.'

Aristide swung round and raked impatient fingers through his curls. 'I wasn't expecting you to share with me but their presence in the house doesn't give me another option. We would look fake if we didn't share a room.'

Scarlett nodded agreement. 'I'll sleep on one of the sofas—'

'No, I will,' Aristide assured her apologetically.

Scarlett said nothing. He was far too tall to spend a night on one of those dainty sofas while she, being very much shorter, would manage fine and they did at least look well upholstered and comfortable.

The stone balcony with its shaded roof and ornamental facades was set up for comfort with padded seats and a table. She doffed her jacket and kicked off her shoes, determined to make the most of the sunshine and relax.

'I'm sorry about all the heavy-duty angst,' Aristide framed, his lean, darkly handsome face taut. 'This wasn't how I planned to introduce you to my Italian home.'

'Let's face it, I put you in a bad mood before we even

got off the plane.' Scarlett sighed. 'The reception committee was just the cherry on the cake.'

'I was planning to take you to my favourite restaurant in Florence for dinner this evening, but I suppose it would be rude to abandon my uninvited guests. Shall we be rude?' Aristide dealt her a hopeful look.

'No. You can take me there for lunch tomorrow instead. How would that be?'

Aristide frowned. 'Won't you be spending the afternoon getting ready for the party?'

Scarlett went pink and shook her head. 'I don't have an extensive beauty routine and I prefer to do my own hair.'

'You take everything in your stride like a trooper. Is that the teacher training coming out?' Aristide quipped as a maid in a tunic joined them with a laden tray.

Scarlett wrinkled her nose. 'It could be that I'm just lazy!'

He laughed, green eyes glittering in the sunshine. He had calmed down and she was relieved but still on edge. After all, he hadn't yet had the time to consider her unexpected announcement that he was a father and once that news settled in, how would he react? She dropped down into a comfy seat and poured the coffee. She wanted to ask more about Cosetta Ricci, who was clearly a great favourite with his mother, but she held her tongue because Aristide had had a trying enough day.

CHAPTER FIVE

SCARLETT DONNED A print cotton maxi and her sapphire pendant for dinner and emerged from the opulent marble-lined bathroom to see Aristide sheathed in a fashionable dark blue suit that looked amazing on him.

'You wore that dress in Dominica,' he recalled, studying her fixedly, picturing her shedding it on the sand and walking into the sea like a curvy little goddess who made his heart race and his blood run hot as lava.

'Yes, it's not designer,' she acknowledged ruefully. 'But I didn't come prepared for the number of social occasions that have suddenly cropped up ahead of us.' In fact, she was embarrassed that she had been so careful with what she had accepted in the weekend wardrobe. Aside from travelling outfits and the party dress, she had accepted only one other dress and it was short and unworthy of a dinner with his parents in a palazzo.

A slanting smile tilted Aristide's expressive mouth. 'It's still remarkably pretty.'

But Scarlett could tell by the rampant glow of his emerald gaze that he wasn't really talking about the dress, more likely he was remembering her casting it off at his instigation and abandoning her inhibitions to swim naked on his villa's private beach. And no doubt he remembered even better what they had done once they had emerged from the water again. Her face burned but the clenching sensation in her lower body made her shift her feet uneasily, a tight hunger she was painfully aware of surging through her whenever he looked at her in that certain way.

Dinner was a grand event in the splendid dining room with a table large enough to seat two dozen people and the atmosphere was decidedly strained. Scarlett urged everyone else to speak in Italian and not mind her, which wasn't a problem for Elisabetta, who was studiously ignoring her even while Aristide drew Scarlett continually into the conversation.

Cosetta chatted to her, referring to exclusive places in London that Scarlett had never visited and sighing about the amount of travelling she did as a model while interposing the monologue with clever little questions about when Scarlett had first met Aristide, when they had reconciled and numerous other little asides. Scarlett ducked and swerved and held on to her privacy while Cosetta disclosed certain facts…

Aristide and Cosetta had always moved in the same exclusive social circle. Translation: you're out of your league.

Aristide didn't commit because his family had put too much pressure on him to marry. Translation: you have no hope.

Aristide was exceptionally selective with women. Translation: the competition out there will slaughter you.

A sunny smile pinned to her taut lips as they climbed

the magnificent staircase again, Scarlett was relieved that Aristide had excused them from the dinner table as soon as he saw the first yawn creep up on her.

'I have the impression that Cosetta was not quite to your taste.'

'She was trying in the politest way to learn my deepest secrets—of which she learned none—and frighten me off by intimidating me with your high standards. I think she believes that she would make you the perfect wife.'

'That's Cosetta. She has always been her own biggest fan,' Aristide said with amusement as they walked back into their bedroom.

Scarlett gathered up her silk pyjamas and went into the bathroom to change. When she reappeared, Aristide was stripping, not a shy bone in his magnificent body. She studied his lean strong back, the ripcord muscles rippling as he bent down in his boxer shorts, and forced herself not to stare like a sex-starved woman as she plumped up the sofa cushions and arranged her makeshift bedding before climbing in.

'I've been mulling over what you did to me all evening and I've reached certain conclusions. I ought to tell you what they are and clear the air,' Aristide startled her by confiding quietly.

'Okay,' Scarlett agreed nervously.

'I realised that if your husband hadn't died I would never ever have known that I have children.'

In consternation, Scarlett rolled over and almost dragged herself up into sitting position on the sofa. 'That's a dreadful thing to say!' she argued.

'But it's true. Luke *wanted* to be their father. A rich birth father in the wings who wanted to get to know his children would have been a threat because you didn't include me from the beginning. When were you planning to tell the children that he was *not* their father? The older they became, the harder that would have been and you would probably have avoided it,' Aristide contended, green eyes hard as iron on her troubled face.

Scarlett stared at him where he reclined, apparently fully relaxed against the headboard of the bed. He wore black PJ bottoms, nothing else. Bare-chested, he was a study of crow-black curls and polished bronze skin sheathing well-honed muscles in the softer light. 'I didn't avoid anything—'

'Well, you certainly were not active in informing me that I had become a parent. Did you consider contacting me in the months since Luke died? Did it occur to you that the twins no longer had a father of any kind and that there was space for me to be acknowledged? My best guess is,' Aristide intoned levelly, 'that you were *never* going to tell me because that was the easiest thing to do. And don't say again that that's nonsense. If I hadn't attended the memorial service and followed that up with a visit, you would have had *no* immediate plans to tell me. Did the sight of me jog your conscience? Is that why I'm finally being informed that I'm a father?'

Scarlett was pale as milk, her blue eyes dark with strain. 'Finally? They're *only* eighteen months old, Aristide—'

'Eighteen months I've missed and can never recapture. Their birth, their first steps, first words,' he enumerated in a roughened undertone. 'What did I do to you to deserve that loss?'

Scarlett felt her tummy roll sickly and lay back down again on the sofa, no longer able to look at him. Remorse was roaring through her.

'I wasn't a drinker or an abuser and I was never unfaithful despite what you believed,' Aristide stated levelly. 'I didn't lie to you either. And yet you have behaved as if I wronged you terribly in some way.'

'You've said enough. I understand your feelings,' Scarlett mumbled wretchedly, hoping to bring the character assassination to an end. She didn't want to throw up his habit of dangling the threat of other women over her head. She didn't want to provoke an argument when both of them were already overwrought and she herself was exhausted.

'I had to speak up to have any hope of containing this anger,' Aristide confessed in a raw undertone. 'I trusted you until the day you sent me a text informing me that you were going to marry Luke. You have now betrayed that trust twice. With that sudden marriage *and* with the concealment of the twins.'

Her lips trembled, her eyes prickled, but she couldn't possibly cry with Aristide in the same room. He doused the light and she lay in the moonlight darkness staring emptily into the shadows while silent tears ran down her cheeks. She should have told him that she was pregnant right from the moment she found out and steeled herself against whatever his reaction might have been back then. Sadly, she had not been able to bring herself to break her parents' hearts.

And right now, she was learning something that she hadn't known about Aristide. He could control his temper, speak with clarity and hit every lethal target with accuracy and all without raising his voice in the slightest. He was so disciplined he had contrived to make light conversation over the dinner table with the parents he thoroughly disliked and he had not displayed a shred of the angry frustration that his most recent words had communicated to her. *You have now betrayed that trust.* That made her feel as though she had stuck a knife in his back the minute he'd turned away from her.

And was it true? Could it be true that there had never been another woman while she was with him? Had their relationship been more stable than she appreciated? She could see now that she had subjected him to unfair treatment. She had panicked when she conceived. She had attempted to build herself up to the point where she told Aristide but she had failed time and time again and her insecurities had taken charge of her instead. As the weeks had passed, she had drowned in an ever-growing spiral of anxiety and then Luke had made his offer and it had seemed to her then that it was the perfect solution for a woman who wanted to keep her baby and a man who didn't want a baby. But, far too late to change anything, she was discovering that there was no such thing as perfect when it came to solving human dilemmas.

Aristide shifted position in the big bed. He knew she was crying. She hadn't made a sound, but he just knew it the same way he knew the sun would rise in the morning. He also knew that an intervention would be unwelcome. He wanted to grab her off the sofa and close his arms round her, but he knew she would lose her temper if he dared. But he had had to get it all off his chest before that anger flamed out of him in a much more damaging way.

Aristide was very practical. He didn't want to fight with Scarlett about decisions that could not be changed. He was well aware that if he wanted his children in his life, he had to accept the current situation with as much grace as possible. He had to move on, fix the damage and leave regrets and judgements in the rear mirror. What came next was more important than past mistakes.

Scarlett lay sleepless half the night, feverishly going over and over what Aristide had said. She began to see that she had made a crucial error right from the moment that she had realised she had conceived. It had not occurred to her that while Aristide might decide he no longer wanted *her* he might still want to be part of his child's life. She had tangled up their relationship with the baby she carried, not appreciating until now that they were two *separate* issues, two separate relationships, and that Aristide was quite entitled to break up with her and still be involved with his child. That was where she had gone wrong in her decisions, telling herself that she was choosing the best option for all of them, saving her pride sooner than face Aristide ditching her.

Her shoulder was lightly shaken. 'Breakfast is out on the balcony,' Aristide informed her.

Scarlett sat up with a start and discovered that she was now in the bed and alone, because Aristide was fully dressed and already disappearing outside again. She scrambled out of the bed in haste and pelted into the bathroom to splash her reddened eyes and clean her teeth before running a brush through her hair. Unless you were a vampire of myth, nobody looked good with red eyes, she decided ruefully. Back in the bedroom she put on the robe she had left on a chair and searched out the package she had dug out of her luggage and hidden on the floor of a dressing-room closet the night before.

She had to move on from the previous evening and all the horrible feelings that had surged up inside her after Aristide had admitted how he felt about what she had done. Somehow, she would make it up to him, she told herself ruefully, even if she didn't know how. She located her bag and took out the little photo album, swallowing hard as she gathered up her courage.

Aristide was talking in Italian on his phone when she joined him at the table. She set her birthday gift and the album down in front of him, watching an ebony brow arrow upward in surprise, and then she poured coffee for him and tea for herself. A selection of elaborate mouth-watering pastries and fruit was on offer and she helped herself because she was hungry, having been too stressed to eat much the night before.

Aristide put his phone down.

'How did I manage to end up in your bed?' she asked.

'You were tossing and turning at dawn and I lifted you in. You snuggled down and went straight into a sound sleep.'

Scarlett shrugged. 'Well, thanks. Happy birthday!' she added with determined brightness when clear green eyes collided with hers and she could feel her face burning up hot.

'Didn't you feel more like throwing it at me after last night?' he quipped lazily, relaxing back in his seat. 'Am I getting the album as well?'

'Yes. I should have told you that yesterday. I put it together for you,' she admitted stiffly, watching him flip through the photos again, pausing to treat some of them to a more thorough appraisal.

It was a beautiful day with a perfect blue sky and brilliant sunshine. She doffed the robe because she was too warm, all her attention locked helplessly to Aristide. Green eyes as translucent as sea glass, black lashes spiky and velvety dark, he was an incredibly beautiful guy and his hotness factor, she acknowledged, was off the scale. He smiled as he lifted her gift and began to unwrap it and she was grateful that she had thought to get him something because it was a much-needed ice breaker following that confrontation after dinner.

Aristide indicated the slim leather-bound copy of Andrew Marvell's poetry with a flashing smile of appreciation. 'This has to be the most thoughtful gift I will receive today and I'm grateful. I like to remember Daniele on our birthdays and reading some of these lines will bring him back just for a moment,' he confessed.

'How long has it been since…?'

'Six years. He took his own life, which was the hardest fact for me to deal with because I tried to stay close enough to him to give him my support,' he admitted. 'He was an artist, very talented, very sensitive and bipolar, but he wouldn't take the medication that kept him on an even keel because he believed it stifled his creativity. He was already cut off from the family because he had dared to walk his own path. The artist's model he was crazy about cheated on him and he fell apart. He was in New York when it happened. I don't know that I *could* have changed his mind but at least I could have made the attempt if I'd been there.'

'Nobody's fault,' she whispered. 'Sorry, I didn't mean to rouse unhappy memories on today of all days. I just remembered out of the blue that you once said Andrew Marvell was his favourite poet—'

'You haven't roused bad memories. I make a point of remembering the good times on this particular day,' Aristide murmured smoothly. 'Now, tell me about Rome and Alice, what they like, what they don't like. I want you to flesh them out for me before I meet them.'

Relief spread through Scarlett, diluting her weighty sense of guilt. She went through the album with him and shared little stories until it was time for her to go and get dressed for their lunch out.

As she walked towards the bathroom, Aristide caught her hand in his. 'Thank you for not being defensive or moody or angry. Thank you for sharing the twins with me. We have to consider them and overcome our differences.'

Scarlett hovered, troubled eyes brightening as she met his intense green gaze. For an instant there was nothing inside her head but him and her whole body was warming at his proximity. She stretched up to try and kiss his cheek in an unstudied moment of affection but she couldn't reach him because he was far too tall. He laughed with rich appreciation, disconcerted by her approach but seemingly pleased at the same time. His hands settled on her hips and he lifted her up against him.

'Let me help, shorty,' he teased softly.

Predictably, Aristide did not aim at her cheek, he let his mouth drift gently across hers in an opening caress before crushing her parted lips under his with all the raw passion he had restrained when she had been in his arms the day before. Her head swam, her tummy flipped and her toes curled as he kissed her breathless. Excitement hummed low in her stomach and pinched her nipples into tight little buds. She closed her arms round his neck and kissed him back, revelling in the erotic flicker of his tongue delving and sliding against hers, enthralled by the tightness of his hold on her and the sensations engulfing her.

Aristide settled her down again on the rug below her bare feet. He skimmed her swollen mouth with the tip of a forefinger. 'Later,' he muttered thickly, his stunning eyes heavily lidded on a gleam of smouldering hunger.

In a daze, Scarlett walked into her bathroom and shed her pyjamas. What was she doing? What was she inviting? Wasn't she muddying the waters of their platonic agreement? Why was she suddenly thinking that Luke had had his nights out during their marriage and had not been a faithful husband while she had stayed celibate? Luke had told her that she was free to do as she liked but Scarlett hadn't believed that she could cope with that sort of freedom within marriage. In any case, there had been no one else for her after Aristide, nobody she ever wanted or missed more than him.

She had been heartbroken when he went out of her life. Of course, she hadn't given him an option, had effectively staged her own exit by telling him that she was marrying Luke. She couldn't blame either Luke or Aristide for her poor choices. She had to stand up and be strong this time around with Aristide and, whatever happened, always tell him the truth. No more secrets or half-truths. And she wasn't about to make a fuss about a stupid kiss, was she? After Aristide had finally told her the story of his brother's death, they had both been in an emotional state of mind and they had got a little carried away, no big deal.

Elegant in a lavender shift dress of designer cut, Scarlett sat down at the beautifully furnished small table in the lush, leafy courtyard. Paper lanterns hung from the trees and glimmered in pretty colours in the sunshine. Soft guitar music was playing very quietly somewhere in the background. 'It's really beautiful here.'

'It's incredibly exclusive and the food's amazing,' Aristide said as their drinks and menus arrived.

Scarlett sipped her wine and chose her meal, taking note of his suggestions. For the first time since she had left home, she felt relaxed, even though the party still lay ahead of her. So far, Aristide had reacted incredibly well to the revelation that he was a father and she was already looking forward to him meeting the twins, but she was also apprehensive about what the future might now hold. What would Aristide want from her? Shared custody or something more? Or even a lesser arrangement with only occasional visits? she ruminated worriedly.

Aristide removed something from his pocket and settled it down on the pristine white tablecloth. It was a small leather box adorned with the logo of a famous jeweller's.

Scarlett leant forward, tensing, her eyes enquiring. 'What is it?'

'Open it and see.'

She clicked open the lid on a magnificent diamond and sapphire ring. 'What's this for?'

'I want you to wear it this evening because I'm planning to announce our engagement.'

'Our...*what*?' Scarlett questioned in astonishment.

Aristide spread lean brown hands as if to soothe her. 'News of the twins is sure to make it into the media and I don't want you to be embarrassed in public. I'm aware that you work in a faith-based school. If we appear to be engaged and on track to getting married, it will lend us a respectable patina. For the present, it's a harmless pretence which will offer you protection.'

Aristide marvelled that he was speaking with such assurance, offering an engagement ring on a foundation of complete practicality when in truth he didn't know what he wanted to happen in the future. In fact, he was in turmoil. He was still angry and bemused by Scarlett's revelations *and* her behaviour but he already knew that he didn't want revenge and he didn't want to hurt her. In short, he wanted his children. He also wanted his children living with him but he had yet to work out how he could best achieve that ultimate aim. The ring created a link between him and the mother of his children and right then, it felt sufficient…as if he were protecting her and the twins by officially binding her and them to him.

Scarlett was stunned by the suggestion, still staring down at the gorgeous ring as though it might yet leap out of the case and bite her. 'But…but—'

'You know it makes sense. Those children are mine and I will be making all the legal moves necessary to have their birth certificates updated to reflect their true paternity. DNA tests will be required. It must be done,' Aristide insisted. 'There are inheritance interests to be considered. If anything were to happen to me tomorrow, I want to be confident that both you and the children are left financially secure.'

'Don't talk like that,' she urged, having lost colour. 'Not after what happened to Luke.'

Perspiration dampened her brow and she breathed in slowly and deeply to complain, 'You're throwing a lot at me without warning.'

'We're flying back to London tomorrow. I haven't got much time to work with,' Aristide pointed out levelly. 'Think it over. No matter what happens between us, I don't want anyone to think that I am ashamed of my children or of you. I'm not trying to trap you, *bella mia*, I'm trying to show you respect.'

And while he was showing her that respect, he reasoned grimly, he would be working on how best he could safely claim his children.

Scarlett's gaze dropped to the plate set in front of her. An array of tiny tasting dishes arrived next. She scooped up the ring box and placed it on her lap. Fake girlfriend to fake fiancée, it was a meteoric, speedy rise. And in reality, she was as stunned and breathless as if it were real rather than yet another pretence. He had laid it all out for her, nothing hidden, nothing that was really unexpected. It couldn't hurt Luke now if the twins' true paternity were to be legally established, nor did she have the right to deny her children their right to both the Angelico name and inheritance. And if the whole blasted, mortifying mess of her private life did contrive to make it into the tabloids, it would surely be less embarrassing to have a ring on her finger, even if it were only a temporary detail. Below the level of the table, she extracted the ring and slowly eased it onto her engagement finger.

'Let's eat,' Aristide urged, smiling as the ring flashed in the sunshine while she served herself.

'You do realise that your mother will be absolutely raging about this,' she warned him in an undertone.

'It's my life, not hers.'

In something of a daze at the speed with which Aristide was changing the path of her life, Scarlett returned to the palazzo to get ready for the party. It was only a fake engagement, she recollected, but it was hard to look at that ring on her finger without remembering how it would have made her feel had he offered her such a commitment two years earlier. Only he *hadn't*, she reminded herself ruefully. It wasn't real, nothing about their current status was real and it was ridiculously sentimental for her to wish that Aristide had offered her a genuine commitment. The time for all that was long past.

The ground floor of the palazzo was busy, professional caterers interspersed with the household staff hurrying in and out of doorways, emptying vans and wheeling trolleys of equipment and china. Cosetta was putting the finishing touches to a wonderful flower arrangement, which Scarlett paused briefly to admire.

'That looks marvellous,' she said warmly.

Cosetta's eyes flickered. 'The florist created it. I'm only deciding where it will look best.'

Aristide's fingers flexed against her taut spine and Scarlett moved on towards the stairs. 'That was you being told that she considers flower arranging beneath her.'

An involuntary grin chased the tension from Scarlett's mouth. 'Oh, I know.'

'I'll see you later,' Aristide informed her, leaving her at the entrance to the bedroom they had shared the night before. 'I have business to discuss with my father. He runs our Italian office.'

Scarlett walked out to the balcony and scanned the fabulous view of the woods and the lawns and the glorious countryside in the distance. It was so beautiful that it felt almost unreal, rather like the fabulous diamond and sapphire ring adorning her finger. Settling down into a seat, she dug out her phone and rang her mother-in-law, Edith, to check on her children and share what had been happening since her arrival.

'Tom and I have been preparing for this to happen since Rome and Alice were born. Our only fear is that their father will want to exclude us from their lives,' the older woman confessed anxiously.

'I wouldn't allow that to happen. In any case, you're pretty much likely to be free of all competition in the grandparent field. I doubt if there will be much enthusiasm from Aristide's parents,' she admitted, having moved quietly back indoors lest she be overheard.

Aristide rapped on the bathroom door when she was putting the final touches to her make-up. 'Time to go down for dinner,' he warned her.

Straightening the straps on her beautiful gown, she walked out, registering that he must have got showered and dressed elsewhere, for there Aristide stood, poised, sleek and sophisticated in a tailored dinner jacket and narrow trousers, the lean dark beauty of his face spectacular.

'You look stunning,' Aristide commented with approval. 'I'll announce our engagement at dinner.'

'Isn't it a little too soon?' she pressed nervously.

'No, family members and close friends should be informed first.'

On this second evening the dining table was clearly going to be packed. Aristide threaded her through the chattering cliques, introducing her to aunts and uncles and cousins and one or two familiar faces she recalled from two years earlier. As she renewed her acquaintance with one of his friend's wives, she was asked where she had disappeared to back then and she laughed, reddened and bypassed the question, only then appreciating that Aristide had not shared the news of her marriage with anyone.

And then that same woman said, quite loudly, grasping Scarlett's hand and raising her fingers to the light, 'My word…is that an engagement ring? Does this mean what I think it means?'

As heads turned, Aristide smiled. 'Exactly what it looks like, although we haven't set a wedding date yet,' he admitted, moving through guests to reach Scarlett's side and curving a supportive arm round her.

Mere feet away, Scarlett saw Elisabetta Angelico freeze, outraged dark eyes welding to Scarlett like stabbing icicles.

'I was planning to announce our engagement over dinner, but Christine's eagle eye beat me to it,' Aristide quipped. 'This is Scarlett, my future bride and already the mother of my children.'

Scarlett paled and tensed, unprepared for the second half of that announcement and the outcry of confusion that those words invoked.

'Yes, twins,' Aristide was soon explaining cheerfully, as though such news were mere commonplace. 'A little boy and a little girl, eighteen months old.'

A welter of congratulations followed. Scarlett was surrounded by women admiring the ring on her finger. They moved into the dining room for the meal and even by then talk had moved on to the subject of weddings and heaps of advice came her way. She pinched her thigh at one point to persuade herself that she was even figuring in such conversations, reminding herself that it was all fake and that no wedding was on the horizon for her and Aristide. Over coffee, she excused herself to go to the cloakroom and when she emerged, Cosetta awaited her, looking very much like the evil fairy attending a christening party in her sleek black gown with its plunging neckline.

'Surprise, surprise,' she murmured smoothly. 'You've played a long game with immense patience and now you think you're about to reap the benefits.'

'Do I?' Scarlett fielded, exasperated that the other woman was efficiently blocking her exit. She supposed, however, that Cosetta's ambition to marry Aristide had received a shocking dent and maybe she couldn't blame the beautiful blonde for such an attack.

'Aristide has you right where he wants you. He'll marry you and then claim custody of the children. That would be a win-win on his side. He divorces you, regains his freedom and no longer needs to consider a wife once he has gained the heirs this family needs.'

Scarlett shrugged a slight shoulder, wishing she did not still have to look up at the beautiful model in spite of wearing the highest heels she had ever worn. 'Aristide is a law unto himself. But I doubt very much that he would do anything likely to hurt his children. Don't worry about it. It's not your problem.'

'I was warning you for your own benefit!' the blonde snapped as she finally stepped away from the door.

'Mind your own business and I'll mind mine,' Scarlett advised in a mild undertone as she made her escape. She would pay no heed to Cosetta's doom-laden warning because Aristide had no plans to marry her.

Aristide was measured and cautious in most actions he took. He had stage-managed their entire relationship two years earlier, never ever promising what he had no intention of delivering. He had controlled and lowered her expectations of him with little occasional remarks that had always made it clear that he saw her as only a temporary amusement in his life. It was little wonder, she conceded then, that she had been riddled with insecurity when she was faced with telling him that she had conceived.

So, no, while he might not have lied to her or cheated on her, he *had* manipulated her by ensuring that she had little faith or trust in their relationship or its staying power. Only, she was now acknowledging, that latter truth did not excuse her silence about the existence of the twins. Indeed, it merely accentuated the reality that she should have told him she was pregnant instead of going to great lengths to hide the fact.

Guests were already arriving for the party. Aristide stood with his parents, smiling and laughing as though he had not a care in the world. For a moment she envied him that cool, calm facade and then she recalled his unhappy home life with his brother and the moment of envy ebbed away. Scarlett had been very much loved by her adoptive parents and had grown up in a happy stable home. While it was true that she had devoted a lot of attention to gratefully fashioning herself into exactly the daughter they had seemed to want and expect, she had never faced the kind of critical censure that was so clearly Aristide's experience with his parents. The senior Angelicos had wanted to hand-pick their surviving son's bride and Scarlett's reappearance and fertility had wrecked their ambitious plans and hopes.

As she walked over to join the group, Aristide immediately guided her away, doubtless protecting her from his mother's venomous gaze and waspish asides. He walked her down a short corridor into a magnificent ballroom, stowed her in a comfortable seat and signalled for drinks to be brought. Champagne was poured by a uniformed waiter, bubbles tickling her nose as she sipped. 'Why does your mother hate me so much?'

'Social status means everything to her. My father comes from a family that stretches back hundreds of years and was once titled. You don't have anything to boast about in your family tree and you are not rich. That's all Elisabetta cares about,' Aristide advanced grimly. 'She married my father for his superior social status and he married her because she's loaded. It was a suitable match made more by their families than by them. They don't even like each other.'

'What a depressing way to live. Well, no doubt they'll be very relieved when we split up again.'

'That's not quite the comfort you might think,' Aristide imparted. 'Your son and daughter will soon be my official heirs. Whatever happens in the future there is no way of getting around that fact. If it's any consolation, it's only my mother who is furious about our engagement. I don't think my father *cares* who I marry. We've never been close.'

The room began to fill up and the party got going. Aristide was hailed with birthday greetings and many gifts. Introductions were made over and over again. Scarlett's social smile began to make her facial muscles ache. They were constantly interrupted and her ring was repeatedly shown off and treated as though it were the eighth wonder of the world. Getting an engagement ring from Aristide Angelico appeared to be a feat of no mean order in the eyes of his guests. She knew what people were thinking: that he was marrying her because she had his children and for no other reason. It embarrassed her to be aware that that assumption was being made, even though it was the truth, and she scolded herself, telling herself that their pretend engagement would make their relationship look a bit more official, a bit more serious even when they eventually broke up.

'Did you ever see more young, beautiful women assembled in one place?' It was Christine Moretti speaking, the wife of an Italian industrialist with whom they had once dined out regularly in London.

Scarlett turned to the other woman with amusement and chuckled. 'No.'

'His mother has invited old flames of his and innumerable potential new flames to this party,' the brunette pointed out with a grin. 'You must be the most hated and envied woman in this room and you took him off the market *before* the party even started.'

'Not quite,' Scarlett parried, watching a ring of gorgeous young women gathering round Aristide as he talked to a friend at the edge of the dance floor. 'It wasn't quite that simple.'

'Yes, but you were never one of the little yes-girls he used to date, and he was with you for a very long time in comparison to your predecessors. And then you simply vanished—'

'No. I married someone else,' Scarlett confided, knowing that Christine was trustworthy and her husband, Matteo, one of Aristide's closest friends and that that particular truth would be common knowledge sooner rather than later.

Christine's lips rounded into a circle of astonishment. 'Oh, so that's why—' And then she sealed her mouth closed again and grimaced. 'Sorry, I was about to be terribly indiscreet.'

Scarlett was mortified by her eagerness to know what her companion had almost revealed. But Christine switched the conversation to Rome and Alice and nothing more of a gossipy nature was voiced. *That's why what?* she wanted to gasp. *That's why what?*

The second surprise of the evening occurred a couple of hours later when she was crossing the room in search of Aristide, and his father, Riccardo, intercepted her and asked her to dance. Disconcerted by the invitation though she was, she accepted with a smile and contrived to move around the floor to an old-fashioned dance tune without stumbling over the older man's feet.

'My congratulations are a little overdue, for which I apologise,' he told her awkwardly. 'But I didn't want to risk causing a public scene with Elisabetta, who always expects me to take her side. Take it from one who knows, Aristide deserves a little happiness in this life and if you can make him happier, you have my vote and my support,' he told her with a warmth he had never shown in his wife's presence. 'I'm in London every month and I would love to meet your children.'

Taken aback by that speech, Scarlett sought out Aristide, extracting him with some difficulty from the group of glamorous women demanding his attention. 'You'll never guess,' she said then breathlessly. 'Your father asked me to dance and made a lovely speech. He's totally different away from your mother.'

Aristide frowned. 'I can't imagine that.'

'I think he's scared of her,' she whispered. 'But I'm sure you know more about that than I do.'

'I've had very little to do with him,' Aristide admitted. 'When I was growing up, he was always at the office or I was at school. If he was pleasant to you, I appreciate it, but it's still a case of too little, too late…'

'I suppose so,' Scarlett sighed, realising that she was scarcely entitled to an opinion on the strength of one friendly approach from the older man. Dropping the awkward subject, she moved closer and said, because a DJ had just taken over and the first energising beats of a tune were sounding out, 'We could dance…'

Aristide groaned. 'You know I don't dance.'

'Just stand there. I'll dance round you,' she teased. 'That's one of my favourite songs.'

Aristide stayed on the edge of the floor watching her lose herself in the music, fluid hands swirling, feet moving to the beat. The fabric of her dress drifted against her shapely body and then flipped back to outline the firm swell of her full breasts and the bodacious curves of her feminine hips. He was mesmerised by her. A surge of lust roared up inside him with hurricane-force efficiency and he went hard as a rock in response.

Stalking forward, he reached for her and tugged her into the circle of his arms. '*Be* with me tonight,' he urged in a raw, hungry undertone.

CHAPTER SIX

ARISTIDE SENT SCARLETT a winging glance from scorching green eyes and her tummy flipped and her mouth ran dry but she knew she wasn't going to say no the same way that she knew she needed to breathe. She felt alive again, she felt wanted, *needed.* Intelligence was telling her not to make too much of the attraction that had always flared between them, but her body and her heart were singing an entirely different tune because this was Aristide and he made her feel stuff no other man had ever matched. In an atmospheric silence, he walked her out of the ballroom, which was already thinning of company as midnight was long behind them, and directed her upstairs.

Scarlett walked over to the dressing table and began to reach up for the clasp of the diamond necklace.

'Allow me,' Aristide murmured, his silhouette tall and strong and dark in the mirror behind her.

The silence smouldered. She trembled as cool fingers brushed her nape and he leant forward to place the glittering necklace down. The scent of him, warm and male with only a hint of cologne, flared her nostrils, the aching familiarity sending her back in time.

His lean brown hands dropped down to lightly rest on her narrow shoulders.

'Is this a yes or a maybe…or a no?' he asked sibilantly.

'Yes,' she pronounced shakily, terrified in one way of what she was doing, wildly exhilarated in another.

He ran down the zip on the dress, tipped the shoestring straps down and let it fall to her feet. She was so on edge, so worked up before he could even touch her that she almost gasped. She stood there frozen in her very high heels and the flimsy lace strapless bra and beribboned panties she had selected to wear with the dress.

'*Madonna mia…*don't wake me up. I've died and gone to heaven,' Aristide groaned in a roughened undertone.

'I didn't have the right bra to go with this dress. It's not for you,' she gabbled, defending herself against the suspicion that she could have dressed up in the lingerie just to tempt him. 'I thought we were going to be in separate rooms—'

He entwined her fingers with his and guided her over to the carved ottoman at the foot of the big bed. He stationed her between his lean powerful thighs.

'What are you doing?' she gasped.

'I'm savouring you like a fine wine,' Aristide told her, pistachio-green eyes roaming over the proud swell of her breasts, which segued down to her shapely waist and full feminine hips. Breathing in deep, he shrugged off his jacket. 'You look extravagantly gorgeous. Like a mirage—'

'What's got into you?' Scarlett demanded, losing patience. 'I don't like standing here like an artist's model. My body's not the same any more. I've got stretch marks and a C-section scar. I'm nobody's gorgeous mirage—'

'Nobody's but mine,' Aristide growled, levering her down into his lap, pausing to slip off the ridiculously high heels as he kicked off his own shoes, peeled off his socks, gathered her close. 'C-section?'

'Last-minute emergency. The cord had caught around Alice's neck—'

Aristide paled. 'Was Walker with you?'

'Not until afterwards. Edith, his mum, was there. Luke was interning at an office miles away that day. The twins came early. Edith was better than he would have been anyway because the surgery would have freaked Luke out. He was very squeamish.'

'I would have coped,' Aristide proclaimed with pride. 'And I should've been there when my daughter's life was at risk—'

'We were lucky. It was a very good maternity unit.'

'I should've been there,' he said again with regret.

Scarlett framed his high cheekbones with her hands to distract him from that sensitive subject and teased her lips along the edge of his.

Aristide took the invitation with alacrity, driving her soft lips apart in a ravishing, possessive kiss and then standing up with her still held in his arms. He brought her down on the bed and stood over her, ripping off his shirt, unzipping his trousers. As he came to her, Scarlett ran her finger down the intriguing little line of dark hair bisecting his flat stomach and he shuddered with gratifying responsiveness.

'Not likely to last long this first time,' he said raggedly, coming down to her with one driving kiss.

Scarlett speared her fingers into his curls to break the kiss and collided with glittering emerald-green eyes, her own anxious. 'You need to protect me. I'm not on the pill any more.'

Aristide stalked into the dressing room. Doors slammed open and shut. He reappeared and slung a handful of foil packets on the bedside cabinet. She looked at him as he came back down to her again, scanning the lean powerful musculature of his torso, the tautness of the muscles rippling with every movement and the awesome outline of the erection the boxers couldn't hide. He gave her a sudden flashing grin. 'See anything you like?'

Her face was hot but Scarlett merely inched a slight shoulder up in a shrug. 'Maybe,' she said.

'You want me as much as I want you…don't you?' he prompted, all of a sudden less confident than he had seemed earlier.

'Yes.'

It was a whisper because once she had made serious decisions about intimacy with him, but they were not in that familiar place any more. What they had now had no safe boundaries. She was running a risk and she knew it, but she didn't want to think too deeply about it, lest her pride and her common sense force her to go into retreat. No, this way, this way, she thought ruefully, was easier. She wanted Aristide more than she had ever wanted him in her life and she had not the smallest wish to miss out on an opportunity that surely wouldn't come again.

He ran sure hands up over her hips and waist to release her bra. The cups fell away from the lush mounds, and he buried his face there for several seconds. 'I love the scent and taste of your skin.'

His lips engulfed a prominent pink nipple and her breath caught in her throat. Even as an arrow of heat darted down into her pelvis and made her squirm, memories were making it a challenge for her to stay solidly in the present. She remembered Aristide once returning to her after a few days' absence and ambushing her in the hall of his penthouse apartment, so impatient to be with her again that he took her against the wall, hard and fast. Now, as he teased at her sensitive buds and shaped the swell of her breasts, she was light-headed with the flood of sensation assailing her, awakening her body again after what felt like a long winter.

He traced the heat and dampness at the heart of her and excitement raced through her in an intoxicating surge. When he followed up by shimmying down her body to tease the most tender and responsive bud of all, her body went liquid and then shot up the scale to the sharp feverish edge of desire. She lifted her hips, twisted and arched her back while he toyed with her, knowing exactly what drove her crazy and providing it. The pulsing ache of desire controlling her rose to a high she could not contain, and she went soaring with a cry into a concentrated climax that made her flop back against the pillows like a boneless doll.

Aristide skimmed off his boxers and ripped open a condom packet with his teeth.

'Risky,' Scarlett told him, twitching it from his fingers and sitting up to smooth the contraceptive down his boldly virile shaft with a fierce determination, born out of a need not to run the smallest risk of another accidental pregnancy. After all, the likelihood was that the twins had been conceived because one of them had been careless without even realising it.

Aristide was taken aback by that gesture. It was the first time she had done that with him. Was he a fool to have simply assumed that she had been faithful to a husband who had had no sexual interest in her? How did he know that there had not been other men? Well, that move had filled him with suspicion. That instant of disquiet, however, didn't lessen his fierce arousal one jot.

Why was he even thinking of something so trivial? Emptying his mind of such disturbing, confusing thoughts, Aristide shifted over her, lithe as the superbly fit male he was. She closed her arms round his neck and knocked him back in time to the night he had called her a spider monkey for the way she wrapped herself round him in bed. He washed out that thought for being inappropriate. All of a sudden, he was on his guard again, awash with lust, but now wary and striving to be cautious. Pushing her thighs back, he sank into the hot, tight welcome of her with a sound of deep masculine pleasure. And then there were no more thoughts, not a single one.

* * *

Still floating on a sea of endorphins, Scarlett moaned as his fast penetration stretched her tight channel and he drove deep. An eddy of blissful sensation spread through her lower body and she gave herself up to the enjoyment, rising up against him as he plunged into her, the ferocious beat of hunger pounding through her as fast as her racing heartbeat and pulses. Excitement seethed like a cauldron inside her and the knot of tension building within again rose to an agonising peak. A split second later, she convulsed under him as he vented a groan of harsh masculine satisfaction and she writhed, caught up in the same frenzy of excitement until the throbbing waves of sweet pleasure washed through her sated body and left her limp.

'Even hotter than I remember,' Aristide said raggedly, springing off the bed to stride into the bathroom. 'Do you want a bath?'

'Yes.'

A little spooked by the speed with which he had vacated the bed, Scarlett was still searching for her wits. Recalling that she hadn't even taken her make-up off, she scrambled out of bed and snatched up her robe, tying the sash with shaking hands. Had she done the wrong thing? Had she made a fool of herself when she fell back into bed with him? How would that renewed intimacy affect their already complicated relationship? She suppressed a sigh, knowing it was too late for regrets.

While the bath filled, she took off her make-up and removed the rest of her jewellery. Aristide was in the shower and the sight of his tall, bronzed body through the misted glass took her back in time again. *Stop that*, she told herself. *Wise up, this is now and everything's changed...everything's different...although not the sex.*

She had missed Aristide. She had missed their physical connection as well. Was that all this had been? A sentimental walk down memory lane? She doffed the robe, studied the wildflowers floating on the surface of the water and the scent of aromatic steam rising. He had always prepared baths like that for her and once she had thought it was so romantic, when he automatically bought luxury bath treatments for her. Had he readied the bath for her this time without even thinking? Or was he making some sort of point?

She sank into the water with a sigh of appreciation. A hug would have meant more to her than the bath though, she reflected ruefully.

Aristide emerged from the shower and towelled himself dry, wrapping a dry towel round his narrow waist and lingering.

'You put the contraceptive on for me...you never did that before,' he remarked abruptly.

Already flushed from the heat of the bath, Scarlett was mortified. 'No, it was my first time, but you seemed...careless with it. Hasn't it occurred to you that I'm terrified of getting pregnant now?'

Aristide nodded slowly and the brooding expression on his lean, dark features cleared and the stiffness dropped from the set of his broad shoulders.

'I spent weeks and weeks trying to work up the courage to tell you I was pregnant,' she reminded him.

'And why didn't you?'

Scarlett hugged her knees and rolled her eyes simultaneously. 'It wasn't that simple. I thought you'd blame me. I thought you'd want me to have a termination and I didn't want one. It's all very well talking about an unplanned pregnancy civilly but you're talking now with hindsight and the one thing I did know at the time was that you definitely didn't *want* a baby!'

Aristide elevated an ebony brow. 'Did you?'

'Not at first but I warmed to the idea after the first ultrasound. They became real little people to me very early on and I just loved them instantly,' she confided softly.

Aristide stretched down a hand. 'Come on, it's very late...back to bed.'

Scarlett smiled up at him, sunny, natural. Aristide tensed and then she grasped his fingers, and he hauled her bodily from the water. He enveloped her in a towel as she complained about the water streaming everywhere, and patted her dry.

He lifted her naked and threw back the bedding to settle her down again.

Leaning over her, he stroked a strand of hair out of her eyes. It was messy and tousled because she had put it in a bun for her bath and let it down again. For the first time since he had seen her again, she seemed relaxed. His mouth drifted down on hers in search of her sweetness, her unique taste, the caress travelling down her slender neck to linger at her pulse points and suck on the sensitive skin.

'Don't you dare give me a love bite,' she said, breathless in the wake of that erotic onslaught. 'We're not teenagers.'

'I'm feeling as randy as one, *bella mia*,' Aristide confided with a slashing grin, shifting against her to acquaint her with his erection.

She rolled against him, fingers splaying across his chest, eyes closing, lips curving up as he carried her hand downward to encourage further exploration.

'My blood's running too hot for this,' he said raggedly only minutes later, reaching for contraception before lifting her bodily onto her knees and thrusting deep.

Scarlett gasped, her excitement on the rise again, and what followed kept that excitement at a sustained high for long, breathless, sweaty minutes. Surging over the peak of pleasure again, she collapsed, boneless.

'I'm never going to move again.'

'Is that a challenge?'

Her eyes were drifting closed as she closed an arm round him. Minutes later, she was fast asleep.

Aristide, in comparison, emerged from that surfeit of pleasure with a sense of shock. He knew that he hadn't enjoyed himself to that extent for years, but he also knew that he was fishing in dangerous waters. He didn't want to slide into a rerun of that past relationship with Scarlett, did he? No, of course he didn't, he assured himself squarely. He dared not trust her. They were already stuck in a fake engagement for the foreseeable future. It could get messy, *very* messy considering that she was the mother of his children. He had allowed his libido to overrule his good sense. He would have to make it quite clear where they both stood in the morning.

* * *

Scarlett woke to breakfast in bed.

She was embarrassed as the maid furnished her with a lap tray. She had slept in. Aristide had kept her awake half the night and as usual had risen with the dawn, unaffected by his own athletic performance between the sheets. As she pulled herself up against the pillows, carefully keeping the sheet raised to conceal the fact that she was naked, she noticed that their cases were lying open in the dressing room and being filled by another maid.

At the point where she was wondering where Aristide was, he strolled in from the balcony, a cup of coffee cradled in one lean hand. 'Sleep well?' he asked lazily.

Although he was smiling she could feel the tension in him and she wondered why he was trying to hide it. 'Like the dead. Could you throw me my robe?' she asked.

Setting the lap tray aside, she dug her arms into the sleeves of the robe and wrapped it around her before leaving the bed to head into the bathroom and freshen up. If there was one thing guaranteed to make a woman uncomfortable it was being forced to greet Aristide, fully clothed in an elegant suit, shaved and immaculate, when she hadn't even had the chance to brush her hair. She packed up her toiletries at speed and dropped them into the case being packed for her before extracting her outfit for flying home and setting it aside.

'How long do I have before we leave?'

'An hour,' he told her.

'You should have wakened me earlier.'

Scarlett was hungry. If she hadn't been she would have pushed the tray away and got dressed. She ate her pastry, cut an apple into segments and drained her milky coffee while Aristide moved restively around the big room. Setting the tray down, she went to get dressed, emerging fifteen minutes later in a sundress with her make-up done.

'You suit dresses—'

'Aristide, just tell me what you're here to tell me,' Scarlett sliced in. 'Or save it for the flight.'

'Am I being that obvious?'

Scarlett released her breath in a soft hiss. 'Pretty much. If it's about last night, keep it to yourself.'

His brows drew together, his lean, darkly handsome profile taut. 'I've got us both into this no-man's-land. I should be the one to steer us out of it again.'

'Well, start steering,' Scarlett advised curtly, walking into the bathroom to pack her cosmetics and grab her brush, dropping them into the case for the maid and gently closing the door on her presence.

'Put your engagement ring on,' Aristide reminded her.

Scarlett rammed the sapphire and diamond ring back onto her finger and added the rest of her jewellery more slowly. 'I know this is all fake,' she reminded him. 'I'm not expecting anything more from you.'

'Last night was ill-advised—'

'Wonderful how it took you all those hours before the dawn to reach that conclusion,' Scarlett sniped helplessly, so hurt and so angry she wanted to strangle him.

In the interim the dressing-room door opened and

their luggage was wheeled out, the bedroom door finally flipping shut while the silence between her and Aristide stretched longer and drier than the Gobi Desert.

'You're annoyed with me.'

Scarlett spun to look at him, her dark blue eyes very bright. 'Was it revenge?'

'What on earth are you talking about?'

'Sexual one-upmanship. Let's face it, you're much angrier with me for staying quiet about the twins than I am angry with you,' Scarlett stated.

'It's not like that. I'm not that petty,' Aristide proclaimed with distaste. 'But this has been a roller coaster of a weekend from the moment you informed me that I was a father. I haven't been myself. When I suppress things, the tension only rises. Sex is a terrific release for tension.'

Scarlett walked into the bathroom, filled a glass of tap water and walked back out again to fling the contents at him. She didn't even have to think about doing it. Hitting back was automatic.

'Porca miseria!' Water sprinkling his face and soaking his shirtfront, Aristide stared back at her in a shock that would have been comical in any other circumstances.

'And I'm not going to apologise,' Scarlett declared defensively. 'Because that's the least that you deserve. Don't tell me that you used my body to get rid of your tension unless you're prepared to take the consequences. When you get cold feet, just call it cold feet. An explanation is unnecessary. We got carried away.

It was a one-night walk down memory lane. It's never likely to happen again. Can we please forget about it now?'

Pale beneath his bronzed complexion, Aristide stalked into the dressing room to change his shirt. When he reappeared, he said, 'I want to go straight from the airport to meet the children. Please organise that.'

She remained rigid, her flushed face expressionless. 'I'll tell my in-laws.'

'What do they have to do with it?'

Scarlett flashed him a look of reproach. 'Who do you think has been caring for them while I'm away? Edith and Tom are very attached to the twins.'

Aristide's lips compressed and he said nothing more. Indeed, neither of them exchanged another word during the drive to the airport. Buckled into her seat on the jet, Scarlett lifted a fashion magazine and stared numbly down at it. She was devastated and she knew it, but she didn't need to advertise the fact. The huge pain, the emotional wound of his rejection, threatened to pull her into a black hole of despondency but she resisted it like a soldier on the front line. Aristide had hurt her before with stray phrases—Shakespeare he was not and would never be. He was more like a machine gun spitting out unstoppable fire. She would deal with the hurt *later* and in the meantime she would be the soldier doing her duty.

Everything between them had changed. The past was dead and gone. Aristide was currently back in her life in a totally different guise as the twins' father.

She would have to cope with that without getting emotional or reliving what he had once meant to her. She didn't have a relationship with him any more, but he *would* have an ongoing relationship with her children. Welcome to learning the art of being civil, she thought facetiously. How could she be polite and distant with him when she now hated him?

Scarlett assumed that she would learn, and probably the hard way since that seemed to be the way she learned most things with Aristide Angelico. She hated him but she hated herself more for being so foolish, for ditching her pride and sense of self-preservation in return for intimacy with the man whom she had once loved. What else had it been? Aristide would never allow it to be anything more than sex with her. She was the ex; she belonged in his past and not in his present.

So, why was she *so* hurt? Aristide was not a forgiving sort of person. He would never forget that she had once married another man and hidden his children from him. Whichever way she looked at the situation, she had wronged him. Why was that reality so clear to her now when she had not seen it two years ago? But she knew why. She had panicked. She had chosen ditching Aristide and running away into a safe marriage with Luke over simply telling the truth. And Aristide despised her for that choice. Could she really blame him?

Scarlett did, however, blame him for the night that had just passed, for the intimate ache of her body and the use he had coldly, cruelly made of it. He had ripped away the pretence that she could *ever* be indifferent to him. Now, here she was, shattered into so many broken pieces. She had acted like the most stupid fool, and she had stirred up feelings again, feelings that belonged only in the past. Her damage was self-inflicted, and she wasn't allowed to start feeling sorry for herself. Last night, Aristide had given her plenty of opportunities to back off and say no. He hadn't lied to her. He hadn't seduced her. He hadn't made any smooth promises. If it had been an act of revenge on his part, he certainly hadn't shown any form of satisfaction at the end result.

And the end result for her, anyway, was turmoil. Turmoil she did not need to be experiencing on the brink of letting Aristide meet his children for the first time. Nothing could change what had happened between them. She already regretted throwing that glass of water at him. She shouldn't have shown him how upset she was, shouldn't have put her *hurt* on display like that…

CHAPTER SEVEN

SCARLETT LEANT ACROSS the aisle to settle the engagement ring down on top of Aristide's laptop as the jet taxied back into the airport in London.

'You agreed and you need to keep up that pretence for your sake and for the children's sake,' Aristide intoned grimly, while he wondered how he had contrived to mess up their present relationship quite so spectacularly. 'We won't gain anything from you taking the ring off—'

'There is no "we",' Scarlett riposted.

Aristide gritted his even white teeth, despising the drama he had unleashed with every fibre of his usually disciplined being. He tossed the ring back to her with studied casualness. 'You wear the ring for the present. It makes sense. You know it does. The public at large prefer romance and reconciliation to a former couple who are bitter enemies engaging in a custody battle.'

As Scarlett lifted the ring again before it could roll onto the floor, she froze into icy dread. *Custody battle?* Was that first mention of legal action a throwaway threat offered in the heat of the moment? Or a taste of what lay in her future? Whatever, the mere suggestion that he could fight her for custody of her children chilled her to the marrow. Reluctantly compliant, she thrust the sapphire and diamond ring back onto her finger, willing to admit that she had tossed it back at him in a rather juvenile gesture.

He brought out a side of her she seriously disliked. She compressed her lips over that continuing self-denigration. Beating herself up for her mistakes would do her no favours. At the end of the day, she could not escape Aristide's determination to become a part of the twins' life. What she had yet to learn was how to handle that development with grace and style. It was all the personal ramifications of further exposure to Aristide that were causing her grief. She was too sensitive and emotional about Aristide and that did have to change because she was the only one of them likely to be hurt by any fallout.

Aristide reappeared from the rear cabin, more casually clad in jeans and a long-sleeved green tee. 'I assume that this is more suitable clothing for meeting young children,' he said, skimming an almost self-conscious hand off a lean, taut, denim-clad hip.

Aristide was nervous, she recognised in surprise. 'How much do you know about toddlers?'

'Next to nothing. There are young kids in the wider family circle but none that I've had anything to do with. Only a few of my friends have children and, again, I've had little personal contact with them.'

'Rome and Alice are very sociable. I shouldn't think you'll have much of a problem getting acquainted,' she told him soothingly, aware that it would be easier for all of them if the first meeting went well.

* * *

Aristide studied Scarlett covertly when the limo got stuck in traffic. He hated the silence, the absence of her sunny smile and her chatter. But he had done what had to be done, he told himself squarely. He had redrawn the boundaries between them. *Again?* He flinched from that sarcastic inner voice. So, he had a weak spot when it came to sticking to business with Scarlett. He would deal with it and move on, get back to his life, full closure achieved, wouldn't he? How soon, though, would he manage to stop craving her like some toxic, mind-bending drug?

She was dangerous. She knocked him off balance, came between him and his wits. But he had too much pride to be sucked in by her again. He couldn't trust her, he *knew* that he couldn't trust her. She was seriously bad news for him, so why was it such a challenge to keep his distance?

It was true that once she had made him incredibly happy, but the aftermath of that experience had proved to be a punishing, horrible challenge. He wasn't going to put himself through hell and rejection again. From now on, he would respect boundaries and it would benefit both of them. *Accidenti!* So, why was he still looking at her and thinking about her?

Sooner than Scarlett had deemed possible they arrived at the apartment she had once shared with Luke. In the midst of reacquainting Aristide properly with Edith and Tom, she was swarmed by Rome and Alice and almost unbalanced by their enthusiastic welcome home.

Laughing, eyes damp with guilty tears for having left them in the first place, she stumbled into the living room and got down on the floor with them, abandoning Aristide to his first meeting with her in-laws.

'Edith and I will bow out now and leave you in peace,' Tom said from the doorway, as always a sensitive, discreet man.

Scarlett rose to give him an impulsive hug of gratitude, knowing that the older couple were the parents she would have chosen for herself, had there been a choice, because they were so much more open, liberal and young in outlook than her adoptive parents had been.

Aristide sank down on the leather sectional and Alice surged over to him instantaneously to lean up against his knee.

'She likes men,' Scarlett muttered awkwardly, watching Rome hover warily beside his building blocks as if he were awaiting some kind of threatening move from Aristide.

'She must miss Luke.'

'They were only babies when the accident happened. I doubt if they remember him now.'

Alice clambered up on the seat with Aristide, stuck her thumb in her mouth and steadied herself on his shoulder.

Almost mesmerised by her proximity, Aristide studied her vivid little face and her huge smile when he smiled at her. 'She's ridiculously pretty.'

Not to be outdone by his twin, Rome climbed onto the seat too and then climbed over Aristide as if he were a mere obstacle in his path.

'Rome will be more of a challenge,' Aristide guessed, lifting Alice down onto the floor and advancing on the building blocks to pile them up into a tower.

Rome smashed them down and chuckled with delight.

'We could take them into the garden so that they can play…or to the playground at the park,' Scarlett suggested, trying to be helpful as Rome raced about the room with a toy aeroplane making loud noises. 'They're very active for a very short time and then they need a nap.'

'Playground,' Aristide selected. 'We'll be alone there.'

'We are alone here. Edith and Tom won't interfere,' Scarlett said mildly.

Scarlett tried to understand as she packed a bag for the playground to cover all toddler necessities. This was Luke's former home, photos of her late husband and of her with him and the twins everywhere, and if Aristide didn't feel comfortable here, she should make allowances, she reasoned ruefully. What she had not expected in the outing was Aristide's security team wanting to scout the location first and taking watching stances to observe from the tree line.

Luckily, it was late afternoon, and the park was mostly deserted. The twins swarmed over the infant slide with the interest of regular visitors, quite indifferent to the size of their audience. Scarlett saw Alice being tucked into a swing and giggling like a drain as Aristide pushed her and Rome clung to his legs, demanding his turn, and she smiled, aware that he was struggling to work out how to handle both children at once without disappointing either. She was seeing a side of Aristide she had never thought to see, a more laid-back, open side as he grinned at Rome screaming his way down the slide and then stamping with delight through a muddy puddle.

It really wasn't that long before the twins' boundless energy drained away and Rome cried when his increasing clumsiness led to him falling off the short slide steps. Alice sobbed when Scarlett lifted her out of the swing to give another child an opportunity.

'So, this is when they need a nap,' Aristide gathered, scooping up a complaining Rome in one powerful arm and heading back towards the car.

In truth, Aristide was shell-shocked by the experience of meeting his son and daughter properly for the first time. They were much livelier and more demanding than he had innocently expected, and he was unnerved whenever they fell over even when they were playing on a safe surface. His heart lurched inside him when Alice viewed him through tear-drenched green eyes full of distress. Rome simply sobbed and clutched at him, but two minutes later was willing to forget his annoyance at having fallen when something bright and shiny inside the car attracted his attention. It was Aristide's phone and he handed it over like a lamb to the slaughter until Scarlett filched it from him, substituted her own and located a toddler game for her son's use.

'Isn't he a little young for that yet?' Aristide remarked uncertainly.

'Yes, it's a fix for fraught moments only,' Scarlett told him.

Aristide was only now grasping just how much he had missed of their development. Rome and Alice were already little people with distinct personalities and as different from each other as he and Daniele had once been. He worked hard at suppressing his bitterness and his biting sense of injustice, knowing that such feelings would only cause damage in their current situation and that the clock could not be turned back. He accepted that he was still a stranger to his own children, that they hadn't even known what to call him and Scarlett had introduced him by his first name.

'I'm your *papà*,' he had told Rome in immediate contradiction at the playground, and he had seen the pink scoring Scarlett's cheeks at what she took as a rebuke even though it had not been intended as one.

'No more pretending,' he had said to Scarlett then, bright green eyes level and direct. 'There's been too much of that already and I don't want to confuse them.'

Scarlett knew he had had the right to say that to her, but a part of her tender heart burned with regret for the virtual burial of Luke's short-lived role as a father. Intellectually, she knew and accepted that Rome and Alice barely remembered Luke now and that she had to move on and adapt to a changed parental role as well.

Alice clutched Aristide's arm as though she were afraid he would disappear while Rome made another stab at getting Aristide's phone, only grudgingly accepting his father's occasional intervention. For the first time ever, she was not the centre of her children's attention and it stung a little.

While the twins were down for a nap in their cots, she made coffee for Aristide.

'So,' she said chattily and with more cheer than she actually felt as she sat down opposite him. 'How do you see you and the twins developing a relationship?'

'Something normal,' Aristide said rather drily. 'And the way everything's arranged now and the children are living, it's not normal.'

Her mouth ran dry. 'I don't see it that way—'

'Of course you don't because this is the system that *you* chose. Grandparents who aren't grandparents in reality and a father who wasn't their father.'

'Edith and Tom really *love* Rome and Alice—'

'I'm not denying that and they appear to be decent people but they will inevitably see less of the children now that I will be part of their lives.'

Scarlett breathed in slow and deep, conscious of Aristide's shrewd scrutiny, determined not to show her dismay at his attitude to her in-laws, whom she was very fond of. 'All I want is what is best for the twins,' she said simply. 'I don't want to be selfish or possessive or to impose my views on you.'

'I'm seeing my legal team tomorrow and we'll do this legally.'

'That's a rather daunting announcement.' Scarlett lifted her chin. 'For the moment, can't you just get to know the children without all the legal stuff complicating things?'

'I need Rome and Alice to have my name.'

'I understand that,' she conceded. 'But I'm completely willing to be flexible about access arrangements for you to get to know the children.'

Aristide released his breath in a sudden hiss of frustration and leant back, lean strong face taut, jawline stiff, green eyes sharp as blades. 'It will be rather difficult for me to accomplish that. You live on the wrong side of the city. I travel a lot and, while I will naturally try to spend more time in London, it is not my home even if my business headquarters is based here. How am I supposed to become a father on a daily basis, rather than a visitor who simply arrives with gifts and offers occasional adventures?'

'I'm not sure that there's any way that you *can* accomplish that now,' Scarlett admitted with a harried look of regret. 'But I don't see how bringing in the legal profession will change that at present because the twins are too young to do without me.'

'I'm not trying to separate you from them,' Aristide censured quietly. 'I'm not stupid. I can see how much you are their safe place and that my relationship with them will only be enhanced by your presence.'

Scarlett swallowed hard and nodded, not quite sure where the dialogue was heading but a little less unnerved after that concession on his part.

'That's why I want to ask you and the twins to move into the townhouse with me. The school term has ended and you're free for the summer. If you're all living with me, I can build a more normal family relationship with them before you return to work.'

The breath rattled in Scarlett's throat because, once

again, Aristide had blindsided her with a proposition she had been wholly unprepared to receive.

'When I'm working I rely a lot on Edith and Tom for childcare and that only works well because I live here. I'm afraid that living with you would be too difficult for me, especially after what happened between us in Italy,' she dared to remind him through lips that felt stiff.

'I'm not changing my mind about what I said earlier. We can't be together as a couple, but I believe we both have enough sense and concern about the children's welfare to act like adults for their benefit,' Aristide intoned.

Her mouth ran dry, a flare of pure panic rippling up through her tense body. 'No, I'm not doing it. I need my own space. I'm entitled to my own space. I'm not moving into your townhouse for you. That would be very uncomfortable for me. You're my ex!' she reminded him thinly, her voice rising in spite of her attempt to control her volume. 'The answer is *no*, Aristide. I'm not giving up anything more because you've given me a guilty conscience over the choices I made two years ago!'

Anger lent a reckless glitter to Aristide's lean, hard face. 'Then we go the legal route and we do everything by the book.'

'You make that sound like a threat,' she condemned unevenly. 'I've bent over backwards to try and make amends, but I can't let you take over my entire life!'

'Is there a boyfriend in the background?' Aristide enquired flatly.

Furious with him now, Scarlett sprang upright. 'No, of course there isn't and you should know better than to ask that question after I was with you in Italy! Whatever else I am, I'm not a cheat—'

'Yet you were quite happy to let *me* think you *were* for two years,' Aristide reminded her in a harsh undertone. 'You didn't care what I thought of you then, when you told me you were marrying Luke!'

Disconcerted by that unwelcome reminder, Scarlett made an awkward movement with one hand. 'That was different—'

'I don't see it as different. Why do you think I'm challenged to trust you in any field now?' he asked curtly, his attention locked to her full pink mouth as the tip of her tongue ran across her lower lip to moisten it. He shifted position, hunger stabbing through him like a secret silent menace.

'I agreed to be your partner at the party. I even agreed to the fake engagement but when is enough *enough* for you? It stops here and now,' Scarlett spelt out in furious warning, evidently impervious to the same susceptibility afflicting him, a reflection that could only incense Aristide more. 'I won't let you intimidate me into doing what I don't want to do!'

'I'm not trying to intimidate you. I'm trying to be reasonable,' Aristide flashed back at her. 'You created this horrible situation for us all and now I'm attempting to fix it the best way I can without injuring or intimidating *anybody*.'

Scarlett nodded slowly, sapphire-blue eyes suddenly wounded and accusing, dark colour warming her pallor. 'It takes two to create a situation, Aristide, and two years ago, you played a part in that situation that you are very reluctant to acknowledge. Whose fault was it that I was *terrified* of telling you I was pregnant even though it wasn't my fault? You see in black and white with no shades of grey. You spent our entire relationship warning me that I was only a temporary aberration in your life. I lived on my nerves with you and you *made* our relationship work that way.'

Aristide had paled and tensed in receipt of that candid comeback. 'I was determined to be honest with you at the time. When I said I didn't want to get married or have children until I was much older and more mature, it was the truth. It never crossed my mind that you could conceive because we were both responsible. Don't hold me to account for not foreseeing that development and the risk that you might choose to take *all* choice away from me.'

'It doesn't matter now.' Scarlett backtracked at speed, afraid that she had exposed herself too much and determined not to get any deeper into a pointless argument that would benefit neither of them.

As Scarlett sank back into her seat, she felt utterly defeated by the abyss of understanding that separated them until she collided without warning with a sizzling green glance from Aristide. A look so hot it should have burned her alive from the inside out. It shook her, that sneaky, momentary glimpse of what Aristide was trying so badly to hide from her. The same male who had rejected her that very morning still *burned* with hunger for her.

It was a revelation, a reassurance that Aristide was not anything like as cold and in control as he liked to pretend he was. He hadn't spent the night making mad, passionate love to her out of revenge or to release his stupid tension, he had spent the night making mad, passionate love to her because he *couldn't* keep his hands off her. Scarlett revelled in that little insight, that decided shift in the power base between them, angling back her shoulders a little, madly aware of the almost compulsive cling of his smouldering gaze to her every movement.

A smile slowly stole the stiffness from Scarlett's luscious mouth. Aristide stared with wary glittering green eyes, taken aback by that switch of mood but also utterly gripped by it.

'I'll *think* about moving into the townhouse,' she told him with quiet emphasis, startling herself almost as much as she startled him with that change of heart but in the space of a moment, in the space of seeing that look of need, of hunger in his gaze, everything had changed for Scarlett. 'But in return, you'll have to rethink your dismissive attitude to Edith and Tom. They're my family now. Our ties go deep. They became a second home for me from the moment Luke and I became friends in primary school.'

'I wasn't aware the ties went that far back.'

Scarlett wrinkled her little nose and smiled again. 'You were never much interested in the finer details of my life.'

Aristide almost winced at that revealing crack but her forgiving smile eased the sting. He recognised the truth of the criticism. To keep part of himself detached, he avoided the kind of emotional intimacy that others took for granted. He didn't let anyone close since Daniele's death, but he had let Scarlett come much closer than most. And look where *that* had taken him, he acknowledged with barely suppressed bitterness.

'I love Edith and Tom and the twins love them,' she continued quietly. 'They're the twins' grandparents and I want them to continue to be treated as such.'

'Done...' Aristide agreed straight away, struggling to understand what had changed inside her, what was making her smile back at him.

Sometimes Scarlett gave him whiplash, but he didn't much care at that moment because she had stopped fighting with him and resurrecting the past he couldn't stand to even think about, never mind relive. Furthermore, she had promised to 'think' about moving into the townhouse. And he wanted that, *her* and his children in *his* house, he wanted it so freaking badly that it was literally *all* that he could think about. He didn't understand it but he was past caring about understanding the urges and thoughts that attacked him in Scarlett's radius.

What was most important now, he told himself soothingly, was gaining the best chance possible to get to know Rome and Alice. Nothing else could or should matter at this stage, never mind whatever hoops Scarlett planned to put him through. There would definitely be hoops ahead, he reckoned, because he recognised that tricky glimmer of challenge in her lovely eyes and wondered where she was planning to take him with it.

* * *

'Move in with him?' Brie echoed in horror some hours later as the two young women shared a bottle of wine in Scarlett's living room. 'Which one of you is out of his or her mind?'

Scarlett laughed, convinced she had already experienced the worst that Aristide could do to her after that dismissal in Italy. She refused to believe that he had any plan to take their children away from her. He wanted to share Rome and Alice. He wanted to learn how to be a father. He wanted to forge his own relationship with them. She saw those objectives as perfectly normal and understandable.

'Moving in with separate bedrooms,' Scarlett extended in wry explanation. 'Not quite as groundbreaking a move as it may have sounded.'

'Well, I think it is,' her friend admitted, still shaking her head in astonishment. 'One minute you're doing the fake party girlfriend thing, the next he's stuck a ring on your finger and a split second after that, he's attempting to move you into his home—'

'I only said I'd *think* about it,' Scarlett reminded her friend. 'I haven't fully decided yet. Aristide likes and expects things to happen at the speed of light. I intend to make him wait.'

'You're getting your own back,' Brie assumed with a chuckle.

'Not in any way that could make anything more difficult between us,' Scarlett qualified, although she knew that she wasn't quite telling the truth because she had already made up her mind.

The school term was finished. They would move in. Aristide would get to play *papà*. Scarlett would get to work out what made Aristide tick, what was causing the stop-start sequence he had begun, because there was absolutely something wrong when a male famed for his cool decisiveness blurred the lines over and over again.

Maybe it was simply that he couldn't forgive her for marrying Luke and keeping his children a secret. Only she didn't think that there was anything exactly simple about the way Aristide thought and reacted. After all, there never had been. He had often said one thing to her and then done another, which hadn't given her very clear signals to follow in their previous relationship. He was a mystery and she was done with him being a mystery.

Mid-morning the following day she phoned him at the office. 'Er… Aristide?'

'Did it arrive yet?' he demanded with all the eagerness of a schoolboy.

Scarlett swallowed hard because she really didn't want to disappoint him. Edith was still in stitches in the kitchen over the size of the jungle gym/playhouse that Aristide had evidently purchased for the twins to play on.

'It's arrived,' Scarlett confirmed, grimacing as she glanced at the busy suburban street outside where the massive structure on a low loader and a crane were still snarling up the traffic. 'But I'm afraid there's a problem. It won't fit. It's far too big for the back garden. Put it in your garden at the townhouse.'

'I can't. I bought two of them,' Aristide responded in a clipped undertone.

'Then donate it somewhere where children don't have that kind of outside equipment,' she advised. 'It was a very generous gesture, Aristide, but you overestimated the size of the garden.'

'My apologies,' he breathed tautly. 'I'll be in touch.'

Scarlett winced as the phone call ended, having sensed his regret and feeling that rare failure for him. She was too soft, way too soft, she warned herself irritably. Before she could think better of the impulse she picked up her phone and texted him a concise list of the sort of toys and equipment that the children were currently able to use.

I can work with this. Thanks.

Relief spread through her and an hour later a beautiful bouquet of flowers arrived for her. Her eyes prickled at the familiar AA signature. She breathed in deep and slow. No, she wasn't about to get sentimental about this, wasn't going to risk catching feelings again. She had been so miserable for so long without Aristide...

But she had had to hide it and internalise her pain because Luke had believed that a wedding ring and a willing father to her twins were the perfect, complete cure for all that emotional stuff, only regrettably they hadn't been. Luke had never been in love, and he hadn't understood what losing the love of her life had felt like. And she wasn't returning to that better forgotten phase of her life when just getting up in the morning with a determined smile had proved a massive undertaking.

She had adapted to life *without* Aristide Angelico and this time around, once she got the new structure for their co-parenting efforts smoothly organised without some cut-throat legal eagle taking charge, she would return to normal. Well, a sort of *new* normal, she adjusted, now that Aristide would inevitably be part of the arrangement and on the outskirts of her life in the future.

More flowers arrived from Aristide the next morning and then an invitation to an exclusive restaurant for dinner the following evening. How could a guy be so sophisticated, successful and intelligent and yet remain so emotionally detached that he did not recognise that that kind of invite was inappropriate in their circumstances? They weren't dating any more. Neither flowers nor invites of that sort were suitable. It was like dealing with a split personality because Aristide *said* one thing and *did* another.

Swallowing hard, she turned down the dinner proposition even though with every fibre of her being she was longing to see Aristide again. Feed a cold, starve a fever, she recited the lesson to herself. Aristide came closest to being a fever in her bloodstream and she refused to put herself out there to be devastated again.

A week later, and only the day before she and the twins were organised to move into Aristide's home, Scarlett returned from some last-minute shopping to be greeted on her own doorstep by Edith.

'You have visitors,' she whispered in a hiss. 'Aristide's mother and some man.'

Scarlett went cold at the thought of Elisabetta Angelico in the sanctuary of her home and she knew that it could mean nothing good. Aristide had made no mention of the older woman having plans to visit and he had already visited three evenings to see Rome and Alice. Of course, Scarlett had endeavoured to stay out of his way during those visits, reluctant to let those boundaries get blurred again.

'Shall I take the twins upstairs?' Edith murmured. 'Or do you want to introduce them?'

Scarlett actually shuddered at that suggestion. 'Upstairs,' she said through numb lips, feeling that her children would be safer unseen by Aristide's unpleasant parent.

Foolishly conscious of her jeans and plain top, her unstyled hair and *au naturel* face, Scarlett squared her shoulders as Edith wheeled the twins in their buggy to the side of the house and her own entrance.

An untouched tea tray with biscuits sat on the coffee table. Edith had tried to be hospitable, and it had been rejected, Scarlett surmised. Elisabetta stood by the window, a rigid figure in a purple designer dress and jacket teamed with enough diamonds to sink the *Titanic*. Aristide's mother was very wealthy, and she liked people to know it. Beside her stood an older man with an air of solemnity much like an undertaker, dressed in an immaculate suit. A professional of some kind, she assumed. A bodyguard?

'Finally,' Elisabetta stressed with impatience as Scarlett appeared. 'I only waited because that woman said you were on your way home. *Home!*' Tiny beringed

and glittering hands lifted in a gesture of derisive dismissal. 'Where you are subjecting my grandchildren to poverty.'

Scarlett breathed in deep. 'Does Aristide know you're here?' she asked quietly.

'You only need to know that *I* will not allow you to *blackmail* my son with his children.' Elisabetta spoke English with a cut-glass accent worthy of a royal and she gave Scarlett a scathing up-and-down glance that made it very clear that she was unimpressed.

'I'm not blackmailing anyone. Aristide and I are engaged,' Scarlett reminded the older woman.

Elisabetta vented a derogatory laugh. 'Did you think I wouldn't guess that that was bogus?' she sniped with satisfaction. 'If you were genuinely reconciled with Aristide, you would be living in his house with his children. I know my son. Nothing less would satisfy him. I also notice that you haven't yet offered to let me even meet my grandchildren. Of course, there's no need: I've already seen them.'

As Scarlett's brow creased in bewilderment, Elisabetta extracted a handful of photos from her little clutch bag and tossed them down triumphantly on the coffee table. Scarlett was appalled to see images of her and the twins in the playground, taken recently and without her knowledge. Angry colour marked her cheekbones.

'What are you doing here?' Scarlett demanded tightly, resolved not to react to the photos when she could do nothing about pictures taken in a public place. Losing her temper with Elisabetta Angelico would be a serious misjudgement.

Elisabetta signalled the older man, who asked if they could all sit down and introduced himself as Mervin Hollanditz of Hollanditz and Associates. Scarlett sank down into a seat, deciding that he sounded like a lawyer and chilled by the suspicion. Unfurling a thick document from a briefcase, he outlined the very generous offer that Mrs Angelico was prepared to make in return for Scarlett signing over custody of her children.

'You can stop right there,' Scarlett advised as the older man momentarily paused for breath. 'Never, ever. That's my answer. No, I don't need to know how much money is on the table. There are some things that money can't buy.'

'You're so oblivious to the world I live in, it's ridiculous,' Elisabetta commented, undaunted. 'Give her proposal two, Mervin.'

Her sidekick threaded through his document and began to outline a shared custody arrangement.

'That's Aristide's business, not yours,' Scarlett objected icily.

'You are so naïve about my son that it's almost adorable,' Elisabetta murmured with caustic bite. 'Aristide is ruthless when he needs to be. Even in Europe there are countries that don't belong to the Hague convention and Aristide owns property everywhere, thanks to his grandfather. That means there is no reciprocal agreement with the UK when it comes to custody cases or...*stolen* children—'

'Mrs Angelico!' the lawyer tried to interrupt in dismay, clearly a law-abiding citizen.

But there was no stopping Elisabetta Angelico in

the full flood of her arrogance and her powerful sense of superiority. 'And you can't watch them all the time, can you?' she continued poisonously. 'Accept one of these proposals and you will have nothing to fear. Walk away from both and, trust me, you will learn to *live* in fear and regret.'

As her visitors departed, Scarlett's tummy had succumbed to a queasy roll and she was pale because she knew how very rich Elisabetta Angelico was and how formidable an adversary that made her. She knew that unscrupulous people could be paid to do immoral things like stealing innocent children. She knew that she didn't live in a perfect world. She knew that there was a genuine danger, just as she knew that while Aristide hadn't qualified for a cosy dinner, he was about to receive a visit at his office in the middle of his working day…

CHAPTER EIGHT

ARISTIDE STUDIED THE text and frowned.

Your mother visited me with a lawyer. I'm coming to your office to tell you what it was about.

Aristide was startled and he did something he rarely did. He called his father, Riccardo, to see if he could shed some clarity on the mystery because Aristide could not think of a single *good* reason why his mother might have visited Scarlett. It was not as though she particularly liked children of any age, having only agreed to entertain her own single pregnancy in the first instance because she recognised the need to have an heir to her family fortune.

'One son would have done...but *not* you, you are surplus,' she had once cruelly told Daniele.

At first, Riccardo Angelico had no inspiration to offer, admitting that he had recently seen little of his wife. Only when further pressed had he finally, grudgingly revealed that he was currently in the process of divorcing Elisabetta. 'I wanted to be discreet about it. You know how she is,' he mumbled while Aristide sat back in his chair in shock at that revelation that the worm had finally turned but was predictably staying well out of reach of the bomb he had thrown without warning into the family circle.

Aristide was well aware that a divorce would send his snobbish mother into a violent tailspin of outrage, disbelief and mortification. Nobody cared more about social appearances than Elisabetta Angelico. Nobody had ever been more scathing about other couples who divorced. At best she might have agreed to a separation, but never a divorce. Yet she deserved the divorce, he acknowledged grimly. His father wasn't a bad man, merely a weak man, but bad things had happened to his children on his watch and Aristide found it a challenge to forgive him for it.

Even so, Elisabetta had got thirty-odd years out of her compliant husband and even Aristide felt that Riccardo had paid his dues for marrying for wealth when his own father had demanded that he do so. After all, it was not as though the marriage had ever been a normal one. It was hard to respect a man, however, who bent over backwards to placate bullies and live an easier, more affluent life. Yet he had forgiven his twin for that same weakness, conscience reminded him. Aristide was never keen to concede that, while he might physically bear a close resemblance to his father, he had inherited his essential strength of character and hard, calculating streak from the mother he despised.

Scarlett had been tempted to rush straight out of the door and erupt into Aristide's office like a woman who had narrowly escaped a catastrophe, but she had more pride and control than that. She changed into the lavender shift dress she had worn the day he gave her the engagement ring and dabbed on a little make-up. She didn't need to embarrass him by appearing in public looking like a wreck, even if wrecked was how she felt in the wake of Elisabetta's insinuations and threats. But nothing could convince Scarlett that Aristide was equally involved in that display of menace. Did she still have too much faith in him?

The new Angelico office building in London was an impressive gleaming tower of glass and she was greeted in the marble foyer by a security man and escorted up to the top floor in what appeared to be a private lift. From the moment she stepped out of it again she was conscious of the attention she was receiving and belatedly she was even more relieved that she hadn't simply rushed out in her jeans. She was supposed to be Aristide's future wife. She only wished that his mother had believed in that fiction because, had she done so, it would surely have kept her at bay.

Aristide was pacing along the floor-deep windows filling his office with light. Tall, dark and stupidly, ridiculously handsome. She didn't think it was a character failing when, even in the midst of her heightened emotions, she felt a suppressed buzz and tightening low in her pelvis and her mouth ran dry. It was merely her unmistakeable constant reaction to him.

'Aristide,' she said a little breathlessly, struggling to regroup and digging into her bag to produce the handful of photos that his mother had left lying on her coffee table and set them down on his immaculately tidy desk.

Aristide frowned down at the photos she had fanned out for his examination and glanced back up at her in bemusement. 'Where did these come from?'

'Your mother had them,' she whispered shakily, quick to plunge right to the heart of the matter. 'She had a lawyer with her as well. She wanted me to sign over custody of the kids or agree to share custody with you—'

Dark fury lit up Aristide's narrowed green gaze like a threatening storm. 'But custody issues are nothing to do with her! She may be their grandmother but that doesn't empower her legally or in any other way.'

'Well, I didn't think so either,' Scarlett continued with greater confidence. 'But she doesn't believe in our engagement—'

'She doesn't need to,' Aristide asserted calmly. 'What she believes is unimportant—'

'I don't think it's quite that simple… I mean, I would like to believe that it is,' she responded in a troubled rush of words. 'But then she mentioned countries that aren't signed up to the Hague Convention, you owning property in such places and *stolen* children.'

Aristide swung away, rage thrumming through him in a lightning bolt of reaction, colour accentuating his slashing cheekbones. It seemed he could fully depend on Elisabetta to destroy any hope he had of gaining access to his children. How dared she imply that *he* would act in such a way?

'I mean, I trusted you. Was that foolish? Would you really consider something like that? Or is this her acting on her own agenda?' she prompted in an anxious surge.

Aristide strode round the desk and reached for both her hands in a sudden powerful movement. 'I swear on my life that I would never ever do something of that nature to you,' he promised in a savage undertone. 'Rome and Alice need your love and attention too much. It's something my brother and I never had and I would be the last man alive to deprive our children of a caring, loving mother.'

That touched her heart because she sensed that response came right from his deepest being, both that admission about Elisabetta and the sentiment he expressed. He was shocked and disgusted by what his mother had done and evidently Scarlett's instinctive trust in his moral values had not been misplaced. The strength of her relief on that score left her feeling almost dizzy. She hung onto his hands for an instant before letting them drop again, needing to recapture her dignity.

'Thank goodness we're moving into your house tomorrow,' she conceded unevenly. 'I wouldn't feel safe from her threats otherwise.'

'I'm relieved. She's lashing out at you and at me because *her* life is presently being derailed. She's a bully and that's how bullies behave under threat,' Aristide acknowledged in a savage undertone. 'And right now everything Elisabetta most values is being threatened. Her social standing, her role as an arbiter of good taste and refinement, her phoney support for the church. My father is divorcing her.'

Scarlett was thoroughly taken aback by that news but made no comment. She did wonder though if that had anything to do with Riccardo's friendly approach to her at Aristide's birthday party. Had Aristide's father already been embracing the new independence on his divorce horizon and making it clear that he did not share his wife's opinion of her?

Aristide ordered coffee and spoke in Italian on the phone for several minutes. The tension in her stiff shoulders easing a little, Scarlett sat down. 'Are the children safe from your mother?' she pressed worriedly.

'I'm putting security on them,' Aristide admitted as he tossed down his phone.

'But will that keep them safe?' Scarlett continued with a furrowed brow. 'What if one of your security men is bribed or something? Your mother made me very conscious that there are a lot of people out there who could be persuaded to do anything for the right price.'

A tray of coffee was set down on the small table in the corner. Scarlett leant forward from the sofa she was sitting on to pour. Aristide watched her slender dainty hands move back and forth, noting the tremors in them, inwardly cursing his mother for her innate cruelty. He decided to be honest.

'The only guaranteed safeguard I could possibly offer you is marriage. As your husband with shared custody of the children, I could fully protect them,' he confessed. 'Elisabetta is—'

'Crazy as a loon,' Scarlett interrupted apologetically, thinking of how the older woman had slung her warnings with such self-satisfied menace.

'Oh, she's not crazy,' Aristide assured her with a grim darkness shadowing his eyes. 'She's angry, bitter and vicious and, unfortunately, that's her natural state of mind.'

'But why is she like that?' Scarlett whispered with a frown. 'If she was halfway normal, I would have been happy to share the children with her even though she dislikes me—'

'I wouldn't let you. I wouldn't allow her to have access to the twins,' Aristide disconcerted her by admitting. 'She doesn't like kids, couldn't be trusted alone with them. She should never have been a mother. As to why she's like that…after what she did to you today, you deserve the truth.'

Her brow furrowed. 'The…*truth*?'

'When she was a young woman, Elisabetta was actually engaged to my uncle, Stefano, my father's older brother. On a tour of South America, they were attacked and robbed. Stefano was shot dead trying to protect her.'

Scarlett paled, her heart going out to any woman who had endured such a loss. 'She lost the man she loved, I assume—'

'Yes, and it… Riccardo was persuaded into marrying my mother in his brother's stead because both families still wanted the marriage. It was essentially an old-world-new-world connection with the Angelicos providing the class and social status and her family the cold, hard cash,' he told her drily.

'It sounds like their marriage was a disaster in the making right from the start.'

'It was. My parents didn't even like each other and it was never a normal marriage. Daniele and I were test-tube babies made in a lab. I often think that that is why my father could not relate to us. We didn't feel like *his* children. To him we always felt like *her* children and he hated her and didn't take the smallest interest in us.'

'That's very sad,' Scarlett whispered, shaken by the family history he had laid bare and finally understanding why he had never been able to understand the strength of her attachment to her parents or even Luke, who had been the brother she had never had.

'And then there was my twin's experience,' Aristide admitted thickly. 'Daniele fell madly in love with one of his models. It was a very passionate affair but she ran him into debt quite quickly and I urged him to be more careful because I suspected she was only after his money. She moved in with him and then one night at a party he found her having sex with another man. Daniele couldn't handle her infidelity. He had believed that she was perfect and he could neither forgive her nor move on from it. That's why he took his own life.'

'I'm so sorry,' Scarlett murmured softly, full of compassion and hope because it seemed to her that Aristide was finally beginning to trust her when he was willing to confide in her.

Love, family warmth and support hadn't featured anywhere in Aristide's childhood with the single exception of his twin and, tragically, he had lost him as a young adult. He had also grown up witnessing the chilling relationship of his estranged parents and it was hardly surprising that he had decided to stay single until middle age. For a moment she wished she had had access to that background of his years sooner. Only what difference would it have ultimately made? she chided herself ruefully. She hadn't been secure enough with him, hadn't been mature or strong enough back then to step up and tell him about her pregnancy.

'So, where do we go from here?' she asked chattily in the comfortable silence, dipping her chocolate digestive into her coffee and licking off the melted chocolate topping with unselfconscious enjoyment. 'Apart from into your house?'

Aristide shifted in his armchair, murderously aroused by that licking of the biscuit, which took him back years. She had always been the *only* woman to be absolutely herself around him. That quality had been so obvious in her from their first meeting and it had had amazing appeal for a male accustomed to glossy sophisticates.

He watched the tip of that little pink tongue like a hawk and even questioned how he could possibly make the offer he was about to make and stand by it. As his current track record showed, he was no good at resisting Scarlett, in fact he was abysmal at resisting Scarlett. But all the same, he *owed* her because it was his duty to protect her and his children from his lady mother, who was like a shark in the water around those more vulnerable and sensitive.

'I suggest that we go for the marriage option,' Aristide intoned flatly. 'It blocks my mother. She can't touch you as my wife and she won't dare to try and snatch the kids—'

'But why would Elisabetta act against *you*? I thought she adored you.'

'Only when I do what she wants, and I don't any more. I started this bout in the war between us, Scarlett. When I showed up at the party with you on my arm, it was the same as waving a red rag at a bull. I set her off and I did it deliberately,' he admitted in a tone of frustration and regret. 'Because I don't like her and I annoy her whenever I can. If I can strike back in even a small way, it helps me live with what she did to my brother.'

This was Aristide unveiled, admitting stuff he would once never have thought of sharing with her, and Scarlett was transfixed by every word he spoke. 'I can understand that.'

'Can you? Daniele loved her and never stopped looking for love from her even though she despised him. He didn't understand my attitude.'

'But I do. Maybe he saw an idealised version of her as she might have been if life hadn't tripped her up when she was younger,' Scarlett murmured. 'The marriage option? What did you mean by that?'

Aristide yanked back his wandering thoughts, currently anchored on the shift of her shapely legs as she changed position, roaming upward only to note the faint smudge of chocolate on her luscious lower lip. He tensed, wiping his busy brain clear of all such physical impressions. It didn't ease the pressure pushing against his zip but he needed his concentration back.

'We marry for the sake of the protection it grants you and my children. But that's all. We don't have sex…and then when all of this furore calms down and my *crazy* mother turns her malicious streak onto my father and the divorce she doesn't want, perhaps you and I can better decide where we stand then. But right now, you all need my protection. I must be honest with you. I will not want a divorce. I don't want my children growing up in a divided family.'

Scarlett nodded very slowly but she was drenched by the most ridiculous surge of disappointment, drowning in the sensation. That was the riveting moment when she realised that she was *still* in love with Aristide, even more in love than she had been with him two years earlier. She would've stampeded him to the altar if he had offered her the real thing on the matrimonial front. But he *wasn't* offering her that. He was offering her a lifelong commitment in marriage but still *not* a proper marriage.

'I should say what is it about me that I get two men in a row who want to marry me but don't want to sleep with me!' she riposted lightly, determined not to reveal the pain of yet another rejection from Aristide.

He couldn't forgive her for marrying Luke in the first place, never mind depriving him of the knowledge that she had conceived his children. He wouldn't give her a second chance. He didn't believe in second chances. He didn't do forgiveness either. And how could she blame him? He wasn't in love with *her*. He was only trying to keep them all safe from the kind of madness that Elisabetta Angelico was clearly capable of unleashing on all of them. He knew as well as Scarlett was now learning that, while they remained unmarried, his mother could well try to snatch the children for her own benefit to control her surviving son.

'One of those men was gay,' Aristide pointed out gently. 'I'm not gay but—'

Scarlett lifted a silencing hand in a sudden gesture. 'You don't need to say it a second time. I know it doesn't make sense for us to get involved again. We won't be a real couple.'

'No,' Aristide conceded, strangely unwilling to accept her making that point for him, wondering why that should be so when he should be relieved by her quick understanding.

He wasn't offering her a separation or a divorce in the future. Indeed the mere idea of Scarlett moving on with some other man, who would become a step-parent to his children, turned Aristide's stomach.

'I would suggest a register office civil ceremony for us as soon as it can be arranged.'

Scarlett nodded again, feeling ridiculously like a puppet having her strings pulled, but then there was no room for her to give him an honest response. Yes, she was willing to marry him to keep anyone from threatening her children's safety and security. But no, she didn't want to marry him on false pretences because that would be painful for her to endure. Greater exposure to Aristide was not a good idea for her when her feelings were not returned. Doubtless, however, she would learn to handle it and become accustomed to his proximity.

'There is one point I should make, although I would hope that the independent legal counsel you will have before we marry would also point it out. At present I have no real rights over the twins because I'm not married to you,' Aristide confided, compressing his shapely mouth as he made that frank statement. 'When I am married to you, and once all the DNA testing and putting my name on their birth certificates is done, I will have those rights automatically.'

A wry smile drove the tension from Scarlett's lips. 'You didn't have to tell me that. I already knew it. But I always expected to agree to sharing custody with you. It wouldn't be fair to do anything else now that you know you're their father.'

Aristide veiled the surprise in his eyes by bending to reclaim his coffee. He had believed that that fact could be a sticking point for her, which was why he had brought it up in advance. Her easy acceptance shook him because he inhabited a world where nobody ever gave up an advantage without demanding something in return. It also revealed that Scarlett had a greater generosity of spirit than he had shown her over past events.

Faint discomfited colour scored his hard cheekbones. He asked himself where that generosity had gone two years earlier when she had condemned him out of hand and walked away. And there was no satisfying answer to that conundrum. Maybe some time, he reflected hesitantly, he should talk to her about that. As quickly as he considered that idea, he discarded it again.

Some men might share their worst experiences. Aristide wasn't one of them and he remained proud of the fact. There was no point parading old wounds when it was too late to do anything about them. He was pragmatic about such matters. How could he be anything else with a mother like Elisabetta, who had ensured that his and his brother's childhoods had been a nightmare? Daniele had been a nervous wreck by the age of eleven but Elisabetta's spiteful tongue and behaviour had simply hardened Aristide, filling him with a fierce desire to find his freedom and keep it for as long as he possibly could.

Scarlett was studying her fake engagement ring, reckoning there would soon be a fake wedding ring beside it, giving her a perfect phoney pair. She should *not* be thinking overly romantic thoughts, such as what an amazing coincidence it was that Aristide should have given her an engagement ring she adored, if it wasn't real, well, real in the sense of being an expression of love and caring. It was the round setting that she preferred, not too large for her relatively short fingers and it was a sapphire surrounded by diamonds, which she loved as well. No doubt the wedding ring would be equally perfect, a simple display of Aristide's essential good taste, she thought limply.

'I'll have the wedding organised asap,' Aristide told her briskly, shooting her out of her far too sentimental reflections with a vengeance.

He sounded unemotional, practical, both traits that Aristide excelled at exhibiting.

Once he had ignored St Valentine's Day, seriously disappointing her at the time because it had been the first such holiday when she had had an actual boyfriend. He had also never given her flowers until recently. Instead, he had given her loads of sexy lingerie and jewellery that she suspected was so expensive it would give her a heart attack to know the cost of it. Those kinds of gifts had made her feel rather like the secret mistress of a rich married man, underlining her insecurity about a relationship that appeared to be travelling exactly nowhere.

'It's an unconventional choice but it suits you amazingly well,' Brie chorused admiringly as Scarlett twirled in her electric-blue wedding dress twelve days later. 'And this house is totally amazing. I'm envying the socks right off you right now!'

Scarlett aimed a still appreciative glance at her opulent, highly comfortable surroundings. Even a guest room was three times the size of her former bedroom. It was over ten days since she had moved into Aristide's townhouse with the twins to discover that Aristide had already hired Estelle, a nanny from a famous college, to help out.

She had had an argument with him on the phone about that piece of bossy interference. Aristide had got her to agree to his requests, had accompanied her to the legal meetings required for their matrimonial plans and had then taken off to New York on business for what remained of the week. By the time he had finished describing the nanny's excellent security training should any kind of threat arise, however, she had had to agree with the friendly young woman's employment. Mercifully, though, there had been neither sight nor sound of Aristide's mother since Scarlett and the children had moved out of the apartment.

'I still think that you could've gone for the white or the parchment shade,' Edith told her regretfully. 'I mean, when you and Luke got married in church, you wore a plain short dress—'

'Only because I looked so pregnant,' Scarlett reminded her. 'And my parents were so embarrassed about that, I didn't want to add to their stress by sporting a wedding gown because they wouldn't have approved of that either.'

'They were so out of touch with young people today,' the slender blonde sighed in recollection and then she glanced up and winced. 'My word, I'm sorry, Scarlett!'

'No need to apologise when it's the truth!' Scarlett laughed.

'I'm just disappointed on your behalf that you never got to do the whole bridezilla thing,' Edith lamented.

Scarlett laughed again, thinking that Aristide would be taken aback quite sufficiently by the sight of her in her long lace and beaded gown and all her diamond and sapphire jewellery. Brie excused herself to change her shoes in the room next door.

'And he may even be a little disappointed too,' Edith murmured. 'I mean, the man's besotted with you. I saw that at first glance.'

Scarlett raised her brows in silent disagreement as she bent her head to slide her feet into her high heels. She hadn't told her in-laws the truth about their marriage, deciding that they would be happier to remain in ignorance of Elisabetta's threats and to believe that she was moving in with Aristide and marrying him for all the normal reasons.

'It made me feel guilty,' Edith admitted. 'If he *always* felt that way about you, we were wrong encouraging Luke to marry you—'

'Oh, stop worrying,' Scarlett urged the older woman with warm affection in her eyes. 'Aristide was *not* in love with me two years ago. I may not know much but I do know that.'

'I hope you're right, because if it *was* the other way—'

'Of course, it wasn't. Marrying Luke was not a mistake,' Scarlett declared confidently to ease her companion's anxiety. 'Luke was there for me when nobody else was and I'll never forget that.'

Arriving at the register office for the ceremony, it was a challenge for Scarlett to look at anyone but Aristide. It might have been a civil ceremony but Aristide had invited his friends, Christine and Matteo Moretti, just as Scarlett had brought along Edith, Tom and Brie. Greetings exchanged, she went back to feasting her attention on the bridegroom, dangerously elegant and sexy in a sleek silver-grey suit of unmistakeable Italian cut. Encountering glittering green eyes, she smiled.

Aristide decided on the spot that Scarlett looked amazing in that colour and wearing all the jewellery he had once bought her. Copper hair tumbled round her shoulders framing her vivacious face, blue eyes as bright as the sapphires she wore with such panache. His broad chest tightened and he had to snatch in a deeper breath.

And then the atmosphere changed as the doors were swung wide to allow the entry of another small, rigid figure. Involuntarily, Aristide froze and then he strode forward to deal with the problem.

'I'll never forgive you if you marry her,' Elisabetta warned him tremulously. 'She's nobody, she's nothing—'

'You're only welcome here if you're prepared to congratulate us after the ceremony,' Aristide murmured quietly. 'I don't want any drama spoiling my wedding day and if you attempt to intervene you will be carried from the premises, which would be embarrassing with the paparazzi waiting outside.'

High colour bloomed over Elisabetta's thin cheeks. 'I will no longer recognise you as my son,' she threatened.

'I'll live,' Aristide riposted as he strode away again.

CHAPTER NINE

SCARLETT WAS THINKING drowsily of that scene before the ceremony as she curled into her comfy bed onboard Aristide's private jet.

Aristide had insisted that they had to enjoy, at the least, a long weekend away after the wedding to look 'realistic'. Edith and Tom were taking care of the twins with Estelle and staying at the townhouse. Scarlett had not understood why Rome and Alice couldn't come with them as well but, on a flight that was to take something in the region of fourteen hours, she could see little point in exhausting their children with such a journey. Where on earth were they heading? Apparently, Aristide was keen to surprise her and she wasn't good enough at geography or flight lengths to make a good guess. But she did naturally think that it was far too long a trip to make for the sake of only three days. She hadn't said so though, indeed had studied to be diplomatic for once in her life.

Why?

Aristide had given her a lovely wedding day, even if it was a fake one. He had got rid of his ghastly mother without an ounce of hesitation. He had given her a platinum plaited wedding ring that was beautiful, informed her that she looked 'utterly gorgeous' in her dress and then kissed her chastely on the cheek after they were pronounced man and wife… Well, nothing was perfect. Afterwards, they had all returned to the townhouse to eat a wonderful meal and Aristide had treated Edith and Tom Walker exactly as though they were her parents—with respect and warmth and acceptance. And for that alone, she was hugely grateful to him.

There was something vaguely familiar about the small airport they landed at and her forehead furrowed as she tried to make the connection. Still slightly somnolent, after the past tiring days, she smoothed down her sundress and climbed into the SUV beside Aristide.

'You're going to love this surprise,' he assured her confidently.

They were married now, she registered, with that faint sense of wonder that only a very new wife experienced. If only it had been a *real* marriage, her comforter of a brain added, and she hushed it immediately. Her children were safe now from Aristide's mother's machinations. Nobody was likely to steal them, least of all Aristide. That was sufficient good news, she assured herself, determined to embrace a bright outlook and enjoy a couple of days in the sun while maintaining good-natured relations with the husband who wasn't really a husband. She could do platonic, of course, she could.

She still hadn't worked out where they were, Aristide noted, feeling very satisfied by that because it would make the surprise even bigger. He was doing everything he could to express his gratitude at the trust she had shown him in agreeing to marry him. A new holiday wardrobe awaited her at the villa, a wedding gift of jewellery on her bed, flowers everywhere because she loved flowers, and his housekeeper would have breakfast waiting for them on the terrace.

Scarlett smiled to herself. He couldn't have brought her back to the island of Dominica where they had spent their very first night together. That had been an outrageously romantic experience from start to finish even if Aristide couldn't have intended it that way. No, even Aristide had to be too intelligent to walk her back through those particular recollections when everything between them was now so different, Scarlett reasoned frantically.

He angled the vehicle down a steep lane, clearly newly planted up with tropical vegetation, and then she saw the even more familiar green roof, although that looked very much more extensive than she recalled, but still her heart was beginning to beat very, very fast in consternation.

'We're on Dominica,' Aristide announced with all the pizzazz of a showman pulling an entire flock of white rabbits out of a magician's hat.

'At the same villa…is it?' she queried in shock.

'Yes, you loved it here…loved the island as well,' he reminded her with vast insensitivity.

'Oh, this is a wonderful surprise!' Scarlett gasped with fake enthusiasm when, truly, she just wanted to slap him and scream at him to get with the new platonic programme.

'I've made some improvements since my grandfather's passing and I extended the house,' Aristide informed her chattily as he escorted her into the cool tiled, air-conditioned hall. 'This is our housekeeper now—Marthe. Her mother, Sandrine, has retired.'

A beaming dark-skinned woman presented her with flowers. Scarlett thanked her in schoolgirlish French, a language that Aristide spoke like a native, having spent vacations on Dominica with his grandfather as a boy. Aristide asked her whether she wanted a tour first or breakfast.

'I'm starving,' she confided reluctantly, recognising that she would have to keep her dissatisfaction with him to herself for the sake of peace.

'Me too…'

A guiding hand at her spine, Aristide walked her out to the terrace with its incredible view of the turquoise Caribbean Sea through the gently waving fronds of the palm trees. As she sat down she noticed the twisting torturous track down to the silvery grey strand below had been replaced by steps that looked a good deal safer. But for a split second all she could remember was running down the original path, giggling as Aristide teased her about something, and she had almost fallen and he had caught her to him and kissed her, a deep, endless kiss that had left her tingling and desperate for that something *more* that she had not yet experienced.

'It takes you back, doesn't it?' Aristide guessed, shaking his handsome dark head as if he were remembering as well. 'I know it was only about three years ago but we've both grown up a lot since then.'

'Yes,' Scarlett conceded, because certainly that was

true. Aristide seemed a lot more accessible than he had once been and she had no idea how that had come about. And she had matured because she had become a mother and having two babies had irrevocably changed what was most important to her.

She sipped her mango smoothie and selected a stuffed plantain cup filled with tiny segments of fruit, vegetables and meat. Aristide chose a slice of watermelon pizza. She added a Dominican baked roll to her plate and tucked in. 'I put on half a stone the last time we were here.'

Aristide studied her with amused emerald-green eyes that glittered in the sunshine and he just took her breath away in that way he did and nobody else ever had. Lean bronze features, perfectly sculpted and darkly shadowed with stubble round his stubborn, wilful mouth. 'You still looked fabulous. In any case, I've signed us up for a hike this afternoon.'

Oh, joy, she thought ruefully, good, clean, fun for the honeymoon couple since nothing else was on the table. She could look forward to snorkelling and trekking, pastimes guaranteed to exhaust them both and satisfy Aristide's need to be constantly doing something. On her last visit they had spent most of the time on the beach or in bed, fuelling up on snacks to keep up the pace. Back then, though, they had been locked in a powerful bubble of intimacy that now had the power to make her eyes sting with regret: for what they had once had, for what they had lost.

'I'll unpack first, have a shower,' Scarlett told him as she finished eating. 'Would you mind if I didn't do the hike? I sort of just fancy sitting on the beach with a book and being lazy.'

'We can do it tomorrow instead—'

'No, seriously, *you* go. I'm quite happy to be on my own for a few hours,' Scarlett slotted in with resolve.

Frustration currented through Aristide, who did not want to go trekking without her. But hold on, he reminded himself very seriously, this was now, not before when she had once done things she didn't want to do for his benefit. He couldn't expect that any more. Scarlett had been so happy here in the villa almost three years earlier and he had somehow miraculously hoped to recapture that with her.

Was that why he had brought her to the island in the first place? His ebony brows drew together in a frown of perplexity. Now that everything was so different between them, naturally the ambience would also be different. All of a sudden Aristide wanted a very strong drink but even more he wanted to see Scarlett smile again.

'That's fine,' he agreed, and she smiled with the genuine warmth that lit up her whole face like sunshine, and he gazed back at her feeling immensely satisfied by that result even if it did mean doing without her company for several hours.

Which was how things were now, he recalled afresh. He would be damned before he would go back…no, no, he wasn't going there again, he promised himself as scorchingly bad memories threatened to engulf him. With decision, Aristide rose from the table to go and get changed for his three-hour trek to Boiling Lake *without* Scarlett.

Marthe showed Scarlett to her designated bedroom in the new extension. She swept open the door of a built-in dressing room to show off the many clothes already hanging there. For an instant, Scarlett felt a sharp, sick pang in her stomach at the suspicion that Aristide had brought some other woman to Dominica with him and then she noticed the labels still attached and the obviousness newness of the garments and her tummy settled again. Aristide had bought *her* a summer wardrobe.

And that wasn't all he had bought her, she registered in dismay as she was climbing into one of the beautiful bikini sets on offer and finally noticed the substantial gift box waiting for her on the bed, adorned with a card and Aristide's initials. She opened the large, shallow jewellery box and her eyes opened very wide in stunned disbelief. A sapphire and diamond tiara met her gaze. Where on earth did he think she was likely to wear *that* in their pretend marriage? With pursed lips, she anchored it into her hair in spite of the fact that she was wearing a bikini. The tiara looked as stupendous on her as a crown. Well, might as well feel like a queen for the day, she thought ruefully as she gathered up a towel and book to pad down to the beach.

How was she supposed to handle these utterly inappropriate gifts from him? The clothes, yes, she could certainly use them in the short term and could even appreciate that he didn't want his wife garbed in the inexpensive items that comprised her wardrobe. But a tiara? On what planet did Aristide live on that he somehow thought she would have a need for a tiara that had undoubtedly cost him a fortune?

How did she know that? She had once, while she was still with him, had the sapphire earrings he had first bought her valued for the purpose of insurance and she had been shocked and ultimately horrified by how very valuable they were. After that discovery, bearing in mind that she was too poor even to afford the insurance payment, she had been sure to keep all that jewellery at *his* apartment.

Why had he ever spent so much money on those lavish gifts of jewellery when he wasn't even planning on staying with her? She had never understood that extravagance of his. Yes, she knew he was very wealthy but, even so, there should still have been limits on how much he spent on a casual girlfriend.

Aristide went straight for a shower when he returned from his lone hike. He had wanted to share that experience with Scarlett but sharing anything with him, he was dimly beginning to grasp, was not presently in her repertoire. He recalled how he had behaved in Italy and winced at the inept harshness that only *she* brought out in him. He would have to do better, much better with her, he acknowledged, wishing that life had not suddenly become so very complicated. Why had he promised to behave in a manner which went against his every natural instinct? Could this inner turmoil that he despised while the sheer weight of it tore him apart possibly be *all* his own fault?

That suspicion was enough to push him into pulling on a pair of board shorts and pouring himself a tequila. He strode out onto the terrace to espy Scarlett lying in the shade below the trees edging the beach, her spectacular hour-glass figure displayed in three flimsy colourful triangles. And what was that on her head catching the dappled sunlight as she moved? He grabbed up binoculars and focused them and then he laughed with rich appreciation at the sheer irreverent nonsense of Scarlett sporting her tiara on the beach. Only Scarlett would do that, only Scarlett rejoiced in that kind of individuality. All of a sudden feeling like some kind of a pervert for spying on his bride, he tossed aside the binoculars and had a second drink, because he accepted that he had an awful lot to think about.

Early evening, Scarlett reached the top of the steps that led up from the beach breathless and looked in surprise at Aristide lounging back against the table. 'I thought you were still out,' she confided. 'How was the hike?'

'It was good,' he said non-committally as if it had been miserable, but he was too polite to say so.

'Well, I dozed and read and dozed and read and feel much fresher. We made a long trip for a short stay.'

'Possibly not my cleverest idea,' Aristide breathed, disconcerting her with that admission.

'I'll be out to join you as soon as I have a shower,' Scarlett declared. 'You know, I wasn't criticising. It's beautiful here but—'

'Everything's changed,' Aristide slotted in with measured emphasis, disconcerting her for a second time.

What an odd, introspective mood he was in, Scarlett thought as she peeled off the bikini and walked into the shower to get rid of the sand coating her sticky, sun-lotion-drenched skin. Freshened up, she wrapped a towel round herself and walked back into the bedroom only to find Aristide there examining the tiara she had laid back in its case on the dresser.

'It's exquisite and thank you,' she said awkwardly. 'But it was a weird gift. When would I ever wear it?'

Aristide flipped shut the box and slowly turned round. 'There will certainly be important social occasions for us to attend as a couple in the future,' he intoned. 'It looked amazing on you when you came up the steps, *cara*.'

There was something almost vulnerable darkening his stunning green gaze as he stared at her, his lean, strong face taut, his lean, muscular torso bare above the shorts, and her heart squeezed tight inside her chest. 'What's wrong?' she asked.

'I still want you,' he breathed tautly.

Scarlett almost winced but chose not to lie or pretend. 'I worked that out already.'

Aristide swore under his breath. 'This whole situation I set up is…*wrong*—'

'It's not that bad,' she said soothingly, helpless against her overwhelming desire to comfort him when he was down.

'Being with you, not being able to touch you…*kills* me,' he admitted in a raw undertone, those expressive eyes of his holding her fast as she nibbled uncertainly at her full lower lip.

Her hand rose involuntarily and stretched up towards a strong brown shoulder. 'Me too,' she muttered, wondering as soon as she said it if admitting that was the stupidest idea she had ever had.

His skin was warm and smooth as satin and the scent of him that close was an aphrodisiac. He smelled of sunshine and clean, hot masculinity. Heat curled between her thighs, a hollow ache tugging at the heart of her. Aristide gazed down at her with smouldering desire and a split second later she was tilting her head back, her lips parting in invitation, and thought had nothing to do with either of those actions.

His hard, demanding mouth crashed down on hers with all the passion she craved. Her hands travelled up, tracing his abs, smoothing down his torso to the V-shaped muscles that ran down into his waistband. A shudder ran through his lean, powerful frame and she felt the towel fall away as he backed her down onto the bed to kiss her with mounting, urgent hunger. It was as if she had been starved of him, her arms locking round his neck, her body rising up to his and embracing his weight with a breathless sound of pleasure.

Satisfaction and relief were trilling somewhere in the back of her mind because she knew now that she had read him right when he had asked her to move into the townhouse with him. Aristide wanted her, Aristide had wanted her again from the very beginning of their unconventional reconciliation.

'Staying away from you was crazy,' Aristide growled, shaping her breasts with reverent hands before turning his mouth to her sensitive nipples, making her buck and moan in response under him.

'C-crazy,' she stammered when she caught her breath again.

'And it makes *me* crazy,' he told her, ravishing her pink lips with driving desire, and as their tongues swirled she detected the faint tangy flavour of tequila, which surprised her because Aristide very rarely touched alcohol.

The reflection quickly evaporated from her brain as Aristide bent his head to the apex of her body, dallying there with the electrifying skill of an artist until her heart was pounding, her hips were writhing, and she was pushed into an all-encompassing climax. But that once wasn't enough for him and the dusk light darkened deep until he had wrung several more from her. She surfaced from that boneless surfeit of pleasure slowly, seeing Aristide reach into the nightstand.

'Is this your room?'

'If you weren't here. Your clothes require more space than mine,' he teased, green eyes alight with wicked amusement.

'Well, if you will keep buying me more…'

An ebony brow quirked. 'We'll share now.'

His tone warned her that that was actually a question that she wasn't yet ready to answer. Once again, Aristide had changed everything between them and broken his own rules. He could be the most infuriating male, she thought helplessly, threading fingers happily through his black curls.

'It needs to be cut,' he warned her with a heart-stopping smile. 'So, for that matter, does our son's. He's a little boy.'

'Men wear their hair in all sorts of different styles these days. Long, short, tied back, buns, braids,' Scarlett told him loftily. 'You're just old-fashioned.'

Without warning a frown, his lean, muscular body froze and his lean, darkly handsome features clenched hard. 'This feels like a time slip,' he said curtly. 'We're talking too much.'

And before she could say another word he was kissing her passionately again, rekindling the feverish need that she could not withstand until she was clinging to him, her body lifting inevitably to his. He entered her with the scorching urgency she had never forgotten, filling her in a single slamming thrust. Hunger without conscience rose in her like a leaping flame. Burning heat engulfed her, driving her hips up to receive him. Nothing had ever felt so good, nothing had ever felt so necessary. Tightening bands in her pelvis thrummed with wild excitement and, a little later, the world went white behind her eyelids as the resulting explosion of lusty pleasure took her by storm.

She flopped back on the bed damp with sweat and the lingering pulses of physical bliss. So, they were to share a room now. That was a new beginning, she acknowledged with relief as Aristide slid off the bed with predatory grace and stalked into the bathroom. Then he swung round in the doorway.

'Marthe said dinner would be ready in…' He checked his watch and winced. 'Fifteen minutes left. I'll use the shower next door.'

And with that he was gone and Scarlett flew out of bed and headed to the shower alone, thinking absently of other showers they had shared in the past. Aristide had seemed oddly detached, as if he was locked up inside himself, looking at her without really looking at her.

Or was she being paranoid and looking for problems that weren't there? Why the heck would Aristide be behaving like that when he had gone out of his way to bring intimacy back into their relationship and give them a more normal marriage? Even Aristide could not be on the brink of backing off from her again, could he?

Marthe delivered a banquet of dinner dishes to the big table on the terrace. A net of twinkling fairy lights hung above them.

Aristide strolled out to join Scarlett clad in tailored khaki chinos and a white linen shirt. 'I've made arrangements for you to spend tomorrow at a nature spa being pampered,' he revealed. 'You enjoy that sort of thing.'

Yes, but not in the middle of a very brief honeymoon when it would separate them for another precious day. Was he avoiding her? Or was that a bizarre suspicion?

'Do you know it's only now occurring to me that, although we were together almost a year, we really knew very little about each other,' Scarlett remarked.

Aristide studied his plate. 'We knew pretty much everything we needed to know.'

'I don't agree,' she said in a mild tone. 'It's made such a difference to my understanding of you to know about your background.'

'You sound like a counsellor,' he scoffed lightly, pouring more wine into her waiting glass. 'And I don't do that talking thing. Keeping it all to myself always worked best for me.'

'I think you might understand me better if I told you about my family,' she murmured.

'You said they loved you. What more is there to say?'

'That from when I was tiny I was told what a *lucky* little girl I had been because they had adopted me, and as I got older I was reminded of who knew what horrors I might have endured in an orphanage or with an unsuitable family had they not picked me.'

Aristide sat back and frowned, his lean, strong face taut. 'Nobody should have been saying such things to a child.'

'But people did, and I always felt I owed a duty to my parents to be the young woman they wanted me to be...not the more adventurous and outspoken me that I actually am,' she framed uncomfortably. 'I worked very hard at being the perfect daughter and it was hard because I didn't think like they did and we'd nothing in common. It wasn't until I met my birth mother—'

'You *met* her?' Aristide incised in surprise. 'When did that happen?'

'When I was eighteen. Crystal had left me a letter on file and I asked her to meet me. It was a bit of a disappointment.' Scarlett grimaced. 'I was kind of looking for an ongoing relationship, but she wasn't. She was perfectly happy with her career and her child-free life but I saw a lot of myself in her. She was stronger than I had ever dared to be, more willing to speak her mind freely. I honestly do think that if I'd been a couple of years older and my parents had been gone when we first met that what went wrong between us wouldn't have gone wrong—'

'I disagree,' Aristide pronounced flatly, his Italian accent very strong.

That was rather a conversational killer, Scarlett conceded, and she gave her full attention to the beautiful meal instead, helping herself to rice balls stuffed with saltfish, crispy chicken wings and mashed breadfruit.

Eventually, Aristide made light conversation and her frustration increased because it seemed that he wasn't willing to discuss anything that might clear the clouds of the past that still hung over them. And those clouds were definitely still hovering, etched in the grim aspect to his taut cheekbones, the troubled light in his eloquent green eyes and his obvious tension. He *couldn't* forgive her, she recognised unhappily. He couldn't forgive her for marrying Luke and staying silent about her pregnancy.

When Aristide finally fell silent, she left him drinking on the terrace, staring broodingly into the darkness.

'Are you coming to bed?' she hung back to ask awkwardly.

His coal-black curls fell back from his perfect profile as he turned to look at her. 'Not yet. I think I'll go for a walk on the beach.'

Scarlett went to bed alone with a troubled heart.

CHAPTER TEN

AT FOUR IN the morning, Scarlett wakened after a bad dream and realised that Aristide still hadn't joined her. Rising, she pulled a beach kaftan over her head and went to check the room next door, but that bed was equally empty, the sheets undisturbed. Having checked the rest of the house for him, she walked out onto the silent terrace still illuminated by the fairy lights and walked carefully down the steps to the beach.

Moonlight lit up Aristide's white linen shirt and the tequila bottle in his hand. Her brow indented. She trudged barefoot through the pale gritty sand towards him. 'What is wrong with you?' Scarlett demanded worriedly. 'It's not like you to drink like this.'

'You might be surprised. Two years ago, I actually followed in my lush of a grandfather's footsteps for an entire two months,' Aristide declared thickly.

'What on earth are you talking about?'

Aristide sprang upright, his sheer height and width almost intimidating as he cast a long dark shadow over her. 'Nothing,' he said flatly.

Scarlett breathed in deep. 'Look, I'm not stupid, Aristide. This is all about the past—what I *did*, what I *didn't* do—and I very much regret it now. I wish you could accept that. I feel guilty…very guilty,' she said shakily, tears clogging her vocal cords. 'But I can't go back and change anything I did. It's too late. All I can say is that I'm truly sorry—'

A humourless laugh escaped Aristide, his eyes glittering dark and colourless in the moonlight. 'You don't understand what you did, though, do you?' he grated soft and low. 'That engagement ring I gave you… I bought it two and a half years ago!'

'Two and a half years ago?' Scarlett repeated, stunned by the reference to that time frame.

'While we were still *together*,' he emphasised, walking along through the surf softly bubbling and swirling onto the sand. 'I know I didn't get around to actually proposing but I'm a very cautious guy with women. I simply waited too long…at least that's what I *used* to think. That you had settled for Walker because he was offering you what you wanted and I had failed to do so. The truth, however, when you gave it to me that day on our flight to Italy and told me about our children, was even *worse*.'

Scarlett fell back from him in shock. He had bought that ring to propose while they were still together? How was that even possible? If that were true, he was telling her something that would blow her whole world and her belief in her own judgement sky-high.

'What are you trying to say? That you had…feelings for me back then?' she pressed dubiously. 'Aristide… turn round and talk to me!'

'I'm drunk.'

'That doesn't matter right now,' she muttered, her

fingers closing into the sleeve of the unbuttoned shirt he wore to pull on it.

'It matters to me,' he said flatly. 'My grandfather was a drunk, which is why I rarely drink. My father won't touch a drop.'

'D-did you have feelings for me two years ago?'

'What do you think?' Aristide turned the question back on her. 'We were virtually living together. I didn't slide into that kind of compromising arrangement with a woman without having *feelings* as you call them. However, you're right on one score… I didn't *want* to feel for you what I did feel because, right from the teenage years, I had promised myself that I would never fall in love with anyone.'

'But why?' she whispered almost brokenly.

'My grandfather's two nasty divorces drained the Angelico family fortune.'

'But you said he was an alcoholic and that can't have been easy on his wives,' she pointed out gently. 'You can't only blame the wives for the marriages that failed.'

'Scarlett, always so rational and seemingly so clear-headed.' Aristide saluted her mockingly with his bottle. 'But you didn't even *notice* that I was madly in love with you…'

Scarlett had lost colour and fallen still. 'I still find that very hard to believe because, the whole time we were together, you kept saying stuff like, "*If* we're still together next month…", "I'm *not* going to be with you for ever…", "We're together until one of us gets bored…" and, of course, I always thought that the one who got bored would be you.'

Aristide shifted position. 'So, there were grandfather's divorces, my parents' car crash of a marriage, my own unsavoury experiences with women and finally the nasty piece of work who betrayed Daniele. All of that made me very reluctant to trust a woman and marry and then *you* came along and all my good sense went straight out the window!'

'And that must've been when you bought the engagement ring. But, surprise, surprise…you never *gave* it to me!'

Her heart was breaking inside her. She was convinced that she could hear the roar as every one of her defences crashed because she had loved him so much back then, indeed, had never stopped loving him.

Aristide loosed a bitter laugh. 'I kept putting it off… I was scared. I wasn't sure I was ready. To put it mildly, getting hitched in my twenties wasn't what *I* had ever seen in my future!'

'And then it no longer mattered because I let you down,' Scarlett assumed as the silence dragged while the surf continued to wash their feet. Her face was wet with tears she didn't recall falling from her eyes. 'I was scared too. I ran off and married Luke.'

'That almost destroyed me. I was devastated. Words cannot describe what I went through in the months after that because I trusted you. I thought you cared for me too. It was the worst ordeal of my life…even worse than losing Daniele,' he breathed raggedly.

'And then you drowned your sorrows in a bottle,' she

guessed wretchedly. 'That two months you mentioned when I first came down here tonight. Was that then?'

He gazed out over the dark ocean and nodded jerkily.

'I extended the house here for us as well,' he murmured curtly. 'For the future I thought we would have then.'

How do I make this right? she thought painfully. And the chilling answer came back that there was nothing she could do to change the mistakes of the past. But they had both made mistakes, only he didn't seem to see that. He was still too angry, too bitter about the pain she had inflicted when she married Luke. Her heart bled at the concept of Aristide missing her, needing her, wanting her. Oh, what an idiot she had been to run away!

'I ruined everything we had together,' Scarlett conceded heavily, her distress perceptible in the tears sliding down her distraught face. 'Only who knows if you would *ever* have had enough faith in me to actually *give* me that ring? You could have changed your mind. You still didn't trust me enough and even now… Luckily though, knowing what I do now, I understand better. I understand why you said that we could never be a couple and why you backed off from me in Italy again. Only that seems like a loser's game to me, Aristide… and you're not a loser.'

'What are you trying to say?' he demanded starkly, high cheekbones glimmering in the low light, sculpted mouth compressed.

'All that happened a long time ago and we've both changed,' she murmured hoarsely. 'Why can't we have a new start with our children? I still love you. I've always loved you. We could have the world but you're denying both of us that opportunity because you won't give me a second chance and you're bitter...'

The sob trapped in her throat wouldn't let her say any more. She had shot her last bolt, she conceded unhappily. She loved him and evidently he had once loved her, but love wasn't always enough. Their physical attraction remained but possibly that was all there was left on his side now and even she was willing to admit that they would need more to sustain a marriage.

She climbed the steps slowly, carefully, desperate for him to follow her and to take that challenge, that invitation of hers, but she reached the bedroom alone. She closed the door, shed the kaftan and, not even caring about the sand still clinging to her feet, she climbed into bed and cried her heart out for what might have been—if only she had been stronger, more confident, more intuitive and he had been less distrustful and wary.

Thirty minutes later, Aristide glanced quietly into the room where Scarlett slept and withdrew with a sigh after seeing the tear stains on her cheek. Dawn was now sending glowing light and colour into the night sky. He entered the office he had had built and began to make phone calls, work out arrangements and cancel appointments. While he did so, he wondered why it had never occurred to him before that Scarlett was much tougher than he was. Tiny but with a backbone strong as steel and the tenacity of a bulldog.

* * *

When Marthe wakened Scarlett for breakfast and explained that she was being picked up soon for her spa trip, she also mentioned that Aristide had only gone to bed an hour earlier and Scarlett forced a smile. Tomorrow they would be flying back home, where they would no doubt be terribly polite to each other for everyone's benefit. She would survive, she told herself fiercely, she had survived losing Aristide once, she would get through it again…eventually. But just then she felt as if Aristide had wrenched her heart out the night before by cruelly telling her of what might have been between them.

The spa day sentenced her to hours of relaxation she didn't want. If she wasn't being coated in mud or some aromatic concoction and being massaged, she was soaking in one of a variety of natural hot-spring pools. Once that was complete she had a manicure and a pedicure and a blow-dry. Only neither the luxury treatments and soaks nor the awareness that she was looking her best improved her mood as she was driven back to the villa while practising her game smile.

Nothing, she decided, could make her feel smaller than having told a man that she loved him and being ignored like a silly child who had said something embarrassing in public. She had buried her pride, launched her thousand ships of persuasion but, sadly, she was no Helen of Troy. Aristide wasn't about to fight for her affections. No, Aristide was far too busy being cool and sophisticated and proud and bitter to see what she saw and that was that they still belonged together.

As she vanished at speed into her bedroom, Marthe informed her that dinner was almost ready. She shed her clothes and walked into the dressing room to select a long fancy dress the colour of a tart green Granny Smith apple. There was no need to bow out of Aristide's arid and unforgiving emotional life like a damp squib. No, she would go with a great big noisy bang. Piece by piece, she donned all the sapphire and diamond jewellery like armour, a not-so-subtle reminder of how much Aristide had once valued her. Tears stung the backs of her eyes and she blinked them back furiously because she was done crying over the past. He wanted platonic? He wanted a detached marriage? Well, he was about to get platonic and polite with bells on!

Marthe had really pushed the boat out for dinner. The table was set with a cloth and loads of candles and even rejoiced in a picturesque trail of scattered flower petals. Aristide's green gaze locked to her the moment she appeared and he sprang up to pull out her chair.

'You look magnificent,' he told her. 'Let's eat.'

Scarlett rammed down her insecurities when she noticed that he had dressed up as well as though the meal were a special occasion. He wore a tailored dinner jacket and narrow black trousers that enhanced his tall, lean, muscular physique. Only the taut line of his cheekbones and the lines bracketing his passionate mouth warned her that he was very tense.

'Not before time,' Aristide quipped as he poured wine for her and passed her the first serving dish. 'Did you enjoy the spa?'

'Yes.' She began to make selections to fill her plate, her soft mouth down-curving. 'It was a real treat.'

'Since we talked in the middle of the night, I've learned a great deal about my true nature,' Aristide told her very seriously. 'I'm too emotional and very intense, rather like my late twin without, thankfully, his instability. But when I get down in mood, I do tend to wallow in my misery, only last night, you *fixed* me, cured me, whatever you want to call it.'

Her smooth brow indented as she toyed with her delicious food. 'What are you trying to say?'

'That I lost you once and lived to very much regret it…and now I will not allow *anything* to come between us, least of all my own faults.'

'But you're still angry and—'

'I'm not angry any more,' he hastened to declare. 'Last night was a wake-up call for me.'

'Bitter?' she queried with a perplexed frown.

'Not since a certain wonderful woman told me that she still loved me even though I *was* angry and bitter. That very brave woman still loved me even when I was destroying my second chance with her. Still loved me in spite of all the mistakes I made,' Aristide assured her, green eyes bright but anxious resting on her shaken face. 'And it may be hard for you to believe it but, no matter how angry and bitter I was, I still *loved* you as well.'

'Accepting that is a tall order,' Scarlett muttered unevenly.

'The minute I knew you were unattached again, I *had* to see you. Not at the funeral, though, where you would've been grieving for another man, so I made myself stay away until the memorial service. I told myself that I only wanted closure.'

Scarlett studied him with wondering eyes.

'I wouldn't let myself think about what else I wanted from you, but my real motives still bled through. I came up with my first excuse to get you back into my life when I asked you to come to my birthday party and it just went on from there. By that first morning in Italy, I was determined to get that ring on your finger,' he admitted. 'And finding out about the twins may have made me angry and bitter, but please note that it didn't stop me coming up with all the excuses of the day to persuade you into accepting that ring.'

'You were very smooth about it,' Scarlett commented as she tried to eat, only she was so hyped up, it was a challenge to swallow.

'And then we ended up in bed and I…panicked afterwards. I didn't want you to suspect that I was still in love with you, even though by that stage I was pretty sure that I was being rather obvious.'

'No, you hid it very well,' she conceded. 'And then you asked us to move into your home.'

'I wanted you close and even though I knew it was too soon to ask that of you, I had to try. When my mother came after you, however, it lit a fire under me. I would have done anything to keep you and our children safe from any kind of threat.'

'I realised that, which is why I trusted you enough to marry you.' Aristide reached across the table and laced his fingers with hers and she smiled again, a warm glow rising in her chest because she was beginning to believe, to accept that Aristide could finally be hers.

'But why on earth did you insist on a fake marriage?'

'I was still trying to protect myself from being hurt again. I told myself that I could resist you, but I can't.' Aristide sighed. 'I've never been able to resist you and, by the way, I no longer blame you for running off with Luke.'

'Seriously?' she gasped in astonishment.

'I did purposely keep you on edge throughout our previous relationship,' he acknowledged reluctantly. 'I was too insecure to tell you the truth about my feelings. I didn't want to raise false expectations, so instead I told myself that I was managing your expectations. Ironically it was only the day that you texted me that you were marrying Luke that I realised once and for all that I loved you one hundred per cent—'

Scarlett's eyes stung. 'I must've hurt you so much. I didn't realise that I *could* be that important to you then. I had accepted that I was just a casual girlfriend who would never be anything more. I didn't want to land you with the responsibility for a pregnancy I believed you wouldn't want...and Luke *did* want my babies.'

'I made the biggest mistake of my life when I didn't confront you about that text. I was too proud. Instead I chose to believe that you must've had something going on with Luke while you were still with me. It was pride and anger and jealousy and nothing more important that kept me away from you. When you finally told me about the twins, I was shocked out of my skull.'

'I know, but you did try *really* hard to deal with it,' she said softly.

'I did and I didn't. I got hung up on what I had lost out on rather than what I had *gained*,' Aristide reasoned with regret. 'In one sense it was a slap in the face finding out about our children because we could have had our happy ending without Luke, if even *one* of us had had the courage to tell the other the truth two years ago.'

'I never thought of that angle but it's true. If I'd admitted that I was pregnant then, you might have told me that you loved me after you got over the shock of learning that you were an expectant father,' Scarlett conceded ruefully.

'So, now I do what I should have had the guts to do two years ago,' Aristide pronounced, clasping her hand to raise her upright.

In bewilderment, Scarlett watched him get down on one knee in front of her. 'What are you doing?'

'Will you marry me...*again*? In a proper church, wearing a ravishing white dress, because I want you to have that experience. I've deprived you of enough. I want to start this reconciliation on a high, positive note.'

'But we can't get married twice over—'

'No, but we can have a blessing and all our friends present to see us get married the way I should have married you the first time.'

Scarlett tapped a toe with a huge smile, happiness dancing through her like shards of sunlight. 'Do I get a real honeymoon next time?'

Aristide groaned. 'Well, we're getting the honeymoon *ahead* of the church blessing,' he explained. 'I phoned Edith and Tom this morning first thing and asked them and the twins and the nanny to fly out here and join us tomorrow. Tom spoke to his partner and has freed himself up for two weeks, so all the arrangements have been made. I've rearranged my schedule and you're already free. We're very fortunate that I extended this house.'

Scarlett flung her arms round him in wonder and excitement. 'Edith, Tom and Rome and Alice will be with us tomorrow? Oh, that's wonderful news…it'll be like a family holiday!'

'Which means that if I want to chase you naked round the house, it *has* to be tonight while we're still alone,' he warned her teasingly.

'I'll meet you down on the beach,' she promised as she laced her hands round his neck to pull his head down to hers. 'And you're still going to keep on getting your curls shorn, aren't you?'

'Yes…won't lie about that,' he declared with amusement.

'Give me five minutes,' she urged, but he locked her to him and kissed her with hungry fervour.

'You'll need my help to get all that jewellery off.'

Scarlett just laughed. 'You'd grab any excuse to follow me into the bedroom right now.'

'A man should only marry a woman who knows his weaknesses.'

Scarlett grasped the hand that had reached out to enclose hers in a possessive hold. 'That is not a weakness.

It tempted you out of suppressing your feelings and made it possible for you to share how you truly felt tonight. I was brave last night. Tonight it was your turn.'

'I almost wakened you this morning to admit that you had brought me to my senses with a bold speech.'

'I wish you had. I spent a miserable day fretting and regretting stuff.'

'There wasn't really any way out of that. I wanted everyone here at breakfast tomorrow to surprise you,' he confided. 'I'm trying—not very well—to say I'm sorry for all the misunderstandings. I've never stopped loving you either. You took my sex drive with you when you married Luke.'

'I beg your pardon?' she whispered as he removed her necklace for her and she took off her earrings.

He unzipped her dress. 'I haven't been with anyone but you since I met you. Maybe that's why I was such a pushover in Italy,' he murmured with some defensiveness.

Scarlett whirled round, her eyes wide. 'Honestly…'

'I got burned with you and then I discovered that I've outgrown casual affairs. I needed more and nobody came along who fitted the bill until you walked back into my life.'

'You *lured* me back into your life with that party invitation and I felt guilty about the twins and decided it was time to come clean—'

'And instead, we got down and dirty and it was amazing,' Aristide teased with a wicked grin as she tossed her dress on the bed and kicked off her heels before speeding into the dressing room to retrieve the dress she had worn on the beach almost three years earlier. 'I can't wait that long,' Aristide confided, removing the dress from her hold and drawing her close. 'I want to make love to you over and over again tonight.'

'Ambitious.' Scarlett ran her hands up over his muscular torso below his jacket and he tipped it off.

'Always. Also very turned on,' he confided in a roughened undertone. 'I love you, Scarlett. I love you so much that I will never give you up.'

'I love you too and you're not getting away either,' she whispered as he eased her down on the bed and then he was kissing her and talking died a natural death.

While he kissed her she was thinking about how he had attempted to recapture their original happiness by bringing her back to the island. Even before he'd fully accepted that he still loved her, he had attempted to restore what they had once had. And now that love, fully acknowledged between them for the very first time, was flaring up like a wildfire, sealing them together with fresh confidence and happiness.

Much later they escaped down to the beach, giving Marthe and her daughters the time and freedom to prepare the rooms for the family members due to arrive the next morning. After snacking on a late supper, they skinny-dipped in the shallows and then, damp and laughing, they ran up the steps and returned to their room, having decided that comfort and luxury were even better than reliving a memory to the authentic last note.

'I'd love another baby…some time,' he admitted as Scarlett blinked in surprise at that frank admission.

'Maybe next year,' she suggested, gazing down into emerald-green eyes that reflected all the love and appreciation she could ever hope to receive.

'You're amazing,' he told her appreciatively.

EPILOGUE

THREE YEARS LATER, Scarlett smoothed her dress down over her barely perceptible bump. She was five months into her second pregnancy and had stayed wonderfully small this time around because, mercifully, she was having a single baby. Rome and Alice were getting a little brother they planned to call Luca after Aristide's grandfather.

It was their third wedding anniversary and they were staging a fancy dinner to celebrate in London ahead of a trip to Dominica, where they would relax and enjoy being a couple, although she had already warned Aristide that he could forget the hiking trips.

Aristide was very excited about the baby, had accompanied her to every medical appointment and diligently provided his support in every way possible. He was a terrific father, which she hugely appreciated when his own father had set him such a poor example of fatherhood.

Riccardo Angelico had gradually become a regular part of their lives. He got on very well with Edith and Tom and, since his divorce, he and Aristide had had the freedom to get to know each other properly. Aristide had had to be honest about what he and his late twin had endured at Elisabetta's hands and Riccardo's unvarnished shock and dismay had done much to give father and son a better understanding of each other.

Elisabetta had given Aristide and Scarlett a very wide berth, refusing their invitation to attend their Italian church blessing. Scarlett had insisted on sending that invite but had not been too disappointed when Aristide's mother had turned them down. They had had a wonderful day and a party without her. Scarlett had been less certain of the right response when Elisabetta fell ill shortly after her husband divorced her.

The stress of the divorce, which she had contested at every opportunity, had left her with health problems and when she suffered a heart attack, it had been Scarlett who persuaded Aristide to visit her, even though he had been convinced that it was a false alarm, designed to bring him to heel. Unfortunately, heart surgery had not saved Elisabetta because she had passed away a few weeks afterwards from an unexpected complication.

Aristide had thanked Scarlett for persuading him to go to the hospital and make his peace with his mother. He had done it in his brother's name, moving on from the past and overcoming his own reluctance to go anywhere near the older woman. She had left her entire fortune and her jewellery to Aristide, which had been a surprise when Aristide had expected to be fully disinherited by her.

Rome and Alice were now sturdy four-year-olds, who talked a mile a minute and attended nursery school. Alice had stayed tiny while Rome grew and grew like Jack's beanstalk. He was crazy about football but Alice, who was a true tomboy, was even better at the game.

Scarlett no longer worked. During her pregnancy she had resigned, too tired to cope at school and have sufficient energy for her own children and Aristide.

Aristide walked through their bedroom door and said, 'I thought you were wearing a short dress tonight—'

'Not since my ankles swelled, so I put on a long one to hide them.'

Frowning, Aristide wrapped both arms round her and hugged her. 'You're gorgeous whatever you wear. But perhaps you should be taking it easier—'

'It's just the hot weather,' she argued.

'It'll be hotter on Dominica,' he reminded her.

Scarlett ran appreciative hands up under his jacket over his muscular chest. 'Yes, I'm looking forward to the skinny dipping already—'

'Not when you're pregnant.' Aristide shaped her protruding midriff. 'The bump is for my eyes only.'

'So, this is what you do. You get me pregnant and then start restricting my activities—'

'Not *all* of them,' Aristide asserted with a wicked grin and a smoulderingly sexy appraisal that made heat curl in her pelvis. 'I'll skinny-dip…you get to watch—'

'Promises…promises,' she teased, gazing up at him with warm, adoring eyes, revelling in the way he hugged her with such ease, for the children had taught him the value of affection.

'I love you so much, *cara*.' Aristide extracted a long, lingering kiss that curled her toes and then raised his head again. 'Edith and Tom have arrived and they've taken the kids out to the garden.'

'Is this opportunity knocking?' she whispered.

'Afraid not…we've got to be horribly grown up and join them for drinks out there before dinner…but later, I will make you a very happy woman.'

'I'm already a very happy woman.'

'There's always room for more happiness. You taught me that.'

Scarlett smiled and clasped both his hands in hers. 'I love you, Mr Angelico.'

'Not half as much as I love you,' he told her with satisfaction.

* * * * *

A WEDDING NEGOTIATION WITH HER BOSS

CATHY WILLIAMS

MILLS & BOON

CHAPTER ONE

'TELL ME I haven't caught you sleeping...'

Helen Brooks sat up, blinked at the telly—which appeared to have changed programme from the detective series she'd been watching to something about over-sized mansions in LA—and cleared her throat.

'Of course you haven't!'

It was Saturday. It was a little past nine-thirty and, yes, she might not have been *sleeping* but she'd definitely been *dozing*. More to the point, why was her boss calling her at a little after nine-thirty on a Saturday night?

He read her mind. 'Because it's only nine-thirty UK time, if I'm right. Shouldn't you be out and about, now that I think about it?'

Helen heard the amusement in Gabriel's voice and she could picture him without any trouble at all—unfairly sexy, black eyes framed with lush lashes most women would have killed for and a body that was all muscle and sinful perfection. She had been working for him for a little over three years and she knew, just *knew*, that her uneventful life was a source of constant amusement for a guy who never stood still.

He played hard, worked harder and seemed to thrive on no sleep at all. When he wasn't working, he was having fun with sexy blondes who all seemed to run to type. And she should know, because she'd met a number of them over the course of time: pocket-sized, big-breasted, breathlessly seductive and, it always seemed, eager to please. It annoyed her just how much time she wasted thinking about her boss and his ever-changing parade of girlfriends. Frankly, it annoyed her just how much time she wasted thinking about the man in general.

'That's right,' she said. 'And how can I help you?'

'That's very formal, isn't it?'

'Gabriel, why are you calling me on a weekend when you're in California and should be… Wait, what time is it over there?'

'About one p.m.'

'Why are you calling me on a Saturday evening?'

'It's work-related, I'm afraid.'

Helen was instantly alert. When it came to work, he could count on her, although wasn't he supposed to be taking a vital one-week break before the work began?

'It's Saturday, Gabriel. Surely anything to do with work can wait until after the weekend?' She hesitated. 'And, um, I thought you were there with… I forget her name…'

'Fifi.'

'Oh, yes, of course—Fifi.' Fifi, whose real name was a more pedestrian Fiona, had been on the scene for a little over four months. Helen had sent flowers to her twice, arranged multiple dates for Gabriel and her at the theatre and various fancy restaurants, had supervised the purchase of an extremely expensive bracelet and had physically met her once a few weeks earlier when she had shown up, unannounced, at the eye-wateringly beautiful offices in the City that housed Gabriel's UK headquarters.

Fifi was small and busty with a tangle of bright-blonde curls that fell to her waist and which had been artfully scooped up in a ponytail on the day she had showed up in a very tight keep-fit outfit. This was, she had explained in a high, breathless voice, because she'd just come from the gym and thought it would be nice to go for lunch somewhere with Gabriel if he wasn't busy.

'Weren't you having some long-overdue time off relaxing with… Fifi…before you met Arturio? I'm sure that's what you told me.'

'That was the plan.'

'I don't suppose she'll be impressed that you're on the phone to your secretary on a Saturday to discuss work,' Helen pointed out.

She muted the volume on the telly and curled into the sofa. Somewhere deep inside, she was conscious of feeling a little guilty and a little exasperated with herself that the sound of his disembodied voice down the end of the line made her feel like this.

She was twenty-eight years old. Perhaps she should have been doing something more adventurous, something *more fun* than watching telly after a vegetarian pasta dinner for one, but she had never been into clubs and bars, and she had never seen the point of forcing herself to take an interest in them simply because she happened to be in London. She had a small circle of girlfriends and she occasionally went out for meals or to the theatre or cinema with one of them. If she chose to stay put on a Saturday evening, she wasn't going to beat herself up about it. A quiet life growing up in Cornwall had set a path for her that she wasn't ashamed to follow.

Until her boss's amused voice got under her skin and made her think again. Outside, the setting sun had left behind a pale-grey sky streaked with watercolour-orange. It was still summer-balmy and through the windows she could hear the laughter and voices of people passing by, people out there having the sort of fun she, annoyingly, now felt she should be having.

She absently played with her ring finger, brushing the

spot an engagement ring had once encircled, and pushed aside those intrusive thoughts.

'Hard to tell because she's not here.'

'But I booked her into the same hotel as you. Did I get the flights wrong? I'm sure I booked her on a first-class flight to get in the day after you arrived, which should have been two days ago!'

'Calm down, Helen. You did and she arrived.'

'Then I don't understand...'

'Long story. No, scratch that—really short story. Suffice to say that things didn't work out between us and she stormed out earlier this morning.'

'Ah.'

'Am I reading judgement behind that "ah"?'

'Not at all. I'm sorry things didn't go according to plan, Gabriel. But I still don't understand what that has to do with anything.'

Judgement?

Helen would never have gone beyond her brief to tell her boss exactly what she thought of his attention span when it came to women, because it was none of her business; but, yes, there had certainly been judgement behind her softly uttered, monosyllabic comment on what he had said.

She had no idea why women were so helpless when it came to him, because take away the crazy good looks and the over-the-top generosity and, at the end of the day, what they were left with was a rich guy who couldn't commit and didn't have to.

A little voice whispered that that one-dimensional picture certainly didn't do him justice, but Helen was adept when it came to swerving away from the disturbing notion that she knew all too well what women saw in her sinfully gorgeous and charismatic boss.

Easier to stick to the basics, and the basics remained that, in all the time she had worked for him, she couldn't remember any relationship lasting longer than a handful of months. Between these relationships, there would be pauses but never for that long.

He had form. Surely those women knew him for what he was? He was like a toddler with an attention span of five minutes when it came to relationships. It wasn't as if he didn't make frequent appearances in the glossies at some event or other with a woman on his arm, smiling up at him with adoring eyes. There was ample pictorial evidence on record of a guy who didn't have staying power, so why bother to go there?

He represented the very last sort of man on earth she would ever allow herself to get emotionally involved with, whatever his looks, charm and bank balance. Irritatingly, it just beggared belief that her body sometimes refused to play ball with what her head told her, so that the mere thought of him could set up a chain reaction inside her than had her nerves jangling.

Such as now. She surfaced to hear him saying something about an accident and she immediately asked him to repeat what he'd just said. Her pulses quickened and she straightened, all meandering thoughts put to one side.

'Thought I'd hit the gym when she flounced out and seems one of the weights I decided to tackle was a little too adventurous. Picked it up and managed to twist my hand in the process.'

'You *twisted your hand*?'

'It's shocking, I know, but I'm only human after all.'

'That's awful. Are you in pain?'

'Thank you for the concern. It was nicely bandaged by an attractive redhead and nothing stronger than Paracetamol called for, you'll be relieved to know.'

'You don't seem too distraught that Fifi has left, if you don't mind my saying.'

'I don't mind, and I'm not, as it happens.'

She heard his momentary hesitation down the end of the line and wondered whether he was tempted to tell her what had happened.

He never had in the past. Relationships came and went and she usually found out when the flowers were being sent to a different name at a different address.

Cut to the chase—what he got up to was his business. They couldn't have been more compatible when it came to work. It sometimes felt as though they could interact on the work front without saying anything at all. That said, forays into her private life were not encouraged, and that was something she had been firm in pointing out from the very moment she'd joined the company and started working for him.

Yes, he knew the basics. He knew where she'd been born, where she'd studied for her qualifications and knew the nuts and bolts of the academic journey that had led her to his towering offices in the City. Everything he knew about her he had gleaned from the impressive CV she had produced for her interview over three years ago.

But her private life? Of that, he knew nothing.

He knew absolutely nothing about the guy to whom she had once been engaged. He knew nothing about how perfect she had thought George Brooks was for her, the perfect guy for a girl who had been conditioned by her background to avoid the risky unpredictability of the fast lane, who had learned to prize safety and stability. She'd been to school with him and had dated him from the age of seventeen. All their friends, not to mention his parents and her dad, had seen their marriage as a foregone conclusion. In the little town in Cornwall, where everyone had known everyone else, theirs had been the fairy-tale romance—just without the fairy-tale ending.

It had been for the best—she'd told herself that a thousand times. If things hadn't been right for him, then the marriage would have come unstuck sooner or later. And he had been right: right to break up before vows had been exchanged; right to follow his heart, which had taken him straight into the arms of another woman within months of their break-up; and he had been so gentle when he had let her down, careful with his words and concerned for her well-being.

And yet, to be ditched was to question one's own worth, wasn't it?

She had moved past that miserable time, had weathered the well-intentioned, cloying sympathy of friends, had removed herself for life in London and had taken valuable lessons with her.

She'd toughened up. When it came to guys, she had built a wall around herself because she never wanted to be hurt again. Her past, her wounded heart and her insecurities when it came to men, would never be open to public scrutiny, least of all by her boss who would never understand where she was coming from.

She thought now about Gabriel breaching that unspoken divide between them and letting her into his personal life. She decided, with a suddenly fast-beating heart, that that was something she didn't want because there was no way she'd ever want to be tempted to return the favour.

They were worlds apart when it came to their views on relationships and she felt painfully vulnerable at the thought of her confident, sexy boss having any insight into what made her tick. There were boundaries in place between them and she liked it that way. She always had. Her right to privacy was non-negotiable, because if any cracks appeared there then who knew where that might lead? And, deep inside, she knew that there was a dark, unsettling awareness of him as a man that could prove way too threatening if it was ever allowed oxygen.

'So you've called me because...?' Back to work, back to familiar terrain.

Gabriel's voice softened. 'Arturio is in the vicinity, as it happens. Decided to come earlier with his wife for a little holiday and wanted to check out the vineyard himself to see whether the grapes would complement his own high-quality product. As you know, for him the sanctity of the Diaz label has to be preserved.'

Helen smiled. It was something she and Gabriel had discussed when the deal to take over Arturio's vineyards in Tuscany—a worthy addition to Gabriel's in California—had first been mooted well over a year ago.

Although Gabriel was based in London, and always had been, his roots were in California, and many years ago some of the vast fortune left to him when his parents had died had been invested in a vineyard that had drifted into neglect over the years.

Gabriel had hired the right people to do the right things, thrown money at the venture and then had decided to go further just as soon as his Californian grapes were doing their thing. He'd told her he'd decided that drinking good wine was not nearly as satisfying as watching how good wine got made, and he had promptly scouted around for an Italian vineyard, a reconnection with the country both his parents had left behind.

He had found more than he had expected. Casual at first, his hunt had led him to a family connection that had lain buried for years. Arturio, as it turned out, was connected to Gabriel's family on his grandfather's side, and establishing that connection had been the cement to Gabriel taking over which would otherwise probably never have got off the ground.

Arturio's high-quality vineyards were perfect, and over the months Gabriel had become more and more personally involved in their acquisition. Reading between the lines, Helen had worked out that he had immersed himself in something that represented a link to a past he had never explored, or even known about, and it had grown into such significance that even she was anxious that nothing jeopardise the final closing of the deal.

'Worked well, what with Fifi leaving,' Gabriel was saying down the end of the line. 'I'm not sure she would have appreciated having to be side-lined. Of course, Arturio was full of apologies about arriving ahead of schedule, but it worked well, getting my guys to give him a guided tour of the vineyard before he signs off on this deal. And I'll admit, I like having him here, like showing him that he has nothing to fear when it comes to selling to me. Means a lot that he enjoys the idea of everything being kept in the family.

'I'll get to the point. I've brought the whole thing forward by a week now that Fifi has returned to the UK and I need you here.'

'But you were going to manage the whole business yourself!'

'When it was just a case of preliminary steps, but it seems Arturio is keen for a conclusion. Wants to get on with the business of happy retirement. He's well over seventy, after all. Who can blame him? Personally, I can't think of anything worse than retiring, but he tells me that he has enough kids and grandkids to keep him busy for the next hundred years. At any rate, there's going to be a hell of a lot more detailed work to be done once the all-clear is given and I'll need you to be on hand with that. Aside from which, there's a limit to how much I can do with my right hand strapped up for the next couple of days. I'm capable of a lot but I still haven't got to grips with ambidexterity.'

'Me come to California?'

'You come to California. Is there a problem with that?'

'Well, not as such…'

'You *do* have a passport, don't you?'

'Of course. Yes.'

'And it *is* up to date, I take it?'

'I suppose so, yes. Of course.'

'Splendid. I'll want you over in time for us to go through the nuts and bolts of this deal. Tomorrow would work.'

'Tomorrow?'

'Helen, why am I detecting a certain amount of hesitancy? You'll be here for three or four days max. I've already assembled my legal people and, whilst it still has to be finalised, I don't anticipate any last-minute hitches. It should just be a case of sitting in on a few meetings and taking minutes.' He paused. 'Late notice, I know, but I'm really not seeing what the issue is. This is important. Dogs and men will have to be rearranged for a few days. Where's the problem in that?'

'Dogs and men?' Helen parroted faintly.

'Can't account for any other obstacles to your getting on a plane and coming over here which, I don't have to remind you, is all part and parcel of a job that pays very well indeed.'

'I realise that, Gabriel,' Helen said stiffly.

There was no question that she was paid well over the odds. In the space of three years, she had had several pay rises, not to mention two very generous bonuses. It was his way of making sure she didn't defect. She wasn't indispensable, because no one ever was, but she was pretty close to being that.

From everything she'd heard from friends and colleagues she worked alongside, his longest serving PA had been a middle-aged lady who had been with him for donkeys' years until she had decided to up sticks and move to Australia to be closer to her only daughter and her grandchildren. After her had come a series of ‘unfortunate events’, as Karis in Accounts had drily told her a few weeks after she’d joined. Girls who hadn’t been able to function at all in his presence, who became nervous and tongue-tied the minute he was around them, who developed girly crushes on him and then proceeded to show up for work in ever more inappropriate clothes.

For all his colourful and ever-changing love life, he was deadly serious when it came to work, and Helen knew that he would do whatever it took not to jeopardise the relationship with the one person with whom he worked so well.

Hence the fact that he was always happy to accommodate her wherever he could. But there were limits, and she realised that she was butting against those limits now. He wanted her there, and there had been steel in that mildly spoken remark about her duties and her healthy pay cheque.

‘No dogs,’ she said quickly.

‘And men?’

‘That’s none of your business,’ Helen returned coolly, because it *wasn’t*, and she heard him laugh softly under his breath. She couldn’t remember if he had ever asked her directly about her private life. Had he? Maybe he’d thrown out one or two general questions about what she’d done over the weekend, now and again, but never about men. He had a vibrant and energetic sex life. Had he ever stopped to wonder about hers? Or did he think that she had none, that she stayed in every evening while the world turned around her?

It gave her goose bumps to think of her sexy boss speculating on her private life; it made her wonder what it might feel like if their worlds collided and if those dark, lazy eyes turned in her direction and saw her as a woman instead of just his trusted employee. Would her need to be safe be blown to smithereens? If she were ever to trust a guy again, it certainly wouldn’t be a commitment-phobe like Gabriel.

And yet there were times when she looked at him from under her lashes and felt the force of his compelling, powerful sex appeal trying to suffocate her resolve.

'Of course it isn't.'

'You may not mind the world knowing what you get up to with women, but some of us are a little more circumspect when it comes to things like that.'

There was a telling pause down the end of the line and Helen could have kicked herself for falling into the trap of saying too much.

'I… I'll let you know what flight I've booked.' She rushed into speech to cover up her discomfort and to paper over the awkward silence that had greeted her impulsive little outburst. 'It may not be possible to find anything at such short notice.'

'It won't be a problem, Helen. There are always available seats in first. You know where I'm staying. Probably the most convenient thing would be to book yourself into the same hotel, and feel free to go for the most expensive suite on offer. I wouldn't want you to be uncomfortable while you're over here.'

Because she'd kicked up a fuss about going in the first place, much to his bewilderment? Because she was paid a small fortune and going abroad on business was all part of 'the generous package'?

Had there been sarcasm in that remark he'd made?

Helen was a creature of routine, someone who liked being in her comfort zone. He wasn't to know that, of course. He wasn't to know that the circumstances of her life had made her the person she was now, and that stepping out of that box always seemed to take so much courage, even when she knew that those steps were tiny and insignificant.

Things would have been different for her, but she had lost her mother and brother long ago in a car crash. She'd barely been eight when it had happened, and it had been a big deal. She had read about it long afterwards, scouring the newspaper clippings about the tragedy on the M4 when a lorry had jack-knifed, causing multiple crashes and twelve fatalities.

In the aftermath, her father had become a changed man. She could vaguely remember someone more relaxed, someone laid back and carefree, but those were distant memories, overtaken by the reality of a dad who, having lost his wife and son, had become so terrified of losing his daughter that he'd wrapped her up in cotton wool and taught her the value of never taking chances.

'Stay safe and take no risks': that applied to everything, from the emotional to the physical, and Helen, who absolutely adored her father, would never have dreamt of going against the grain.

She'd studied hard, skipped school trips abroad—because who knew what could happen on those ski slopes?—and had never been out too late when it came to teenage parties, because she couldn't be sure that drink and drugs might be going to feature.

When she and George had become an item, her father couldn't have been happier. George had been a known quantity, destined to become an accountant, to work in the nearest town and to look after Helen in the way her father had felt she should be looked after.

Looking back, she could see that she had been seduced by the notion of a safe future over and above everything else. She'd been too young to appreciate that there was a lot more to a for-ever relationship than feeling safe within it. She'd been in love with the idea of being in love, and only in hindsight did she see that there had been a lot missing from their relationship; that, although 'safe' was a good thing, there really was such a thing as 'too safe'.

Leaving to work in London—her one big adventure—

had been her only deviation from everything she had absorbed over the years and she still smiled when she thought back to her dad's reaction to her decision. Even now, he remained fond of warning her about anything and everything that could be found lurking down mysterious dark alleys and behind corners. But, disillusioned and desperate to see a different world out there, staying in Cornwall and finding work at the one of the local offices had been inconceivable. She had dug her heels in, and in fairness, although her dad had raised the usual worried concerns, he had caved in without too much of a fight. He'd understood that she had to do that for herself, for her recovery.

Her relationship with Gabriel obeyed all the laws she had laid down. She kept her distance. She worked hard, was extremely clever when it came to IT and could arrange his life with absolute ease, but never had the line between them been crossed.

She felt comfortable within that boundary. This was the first time a trip abroad for business had happened. Largely, when he went abroad, he handled things himself. The business with his hand, combined with the acceleration of this vineyard deal with Arturio, had skewered that, and she could hardly blame him for expecting her to go out to pick up the slack.

Yet the prospect of interacting with him beyond the office confines in London was oddly intimidating.

Nuts. Why should it be? They would still be working, even if the scenery would be different.

'Of course.'

'We have everything online but make sure you bring the physical files as well. Arturio has only recently stepped foot into the dawning of a new century. He delegates, but over here he'll be flying solo, and he might want to flick through the paperwork.'

'It's nice that he's old-fashioned like that.' Helen half-smiled and thought of her dad, who was the same, even though he was much younger. He used to work as a scaffolder but, now that he was retired, he had taken up his lifelong passion for fishing, and dabbled in some lucrative fishing for Cornish crab, which he sold to some of the restaurants in the area. What use had he ever had for IT skills? Perhaps his curiosity had died when his family had been lost to him and he had never bothered to breathe it back into life.

'Nice but time-consuming,' Gabriel remarked with wry, affectionate indulgence. 'Having to go through everything with pieces of paper and written reports. That said, I'm fond enough of him to indulge him in however many paper files he wants us to provide him with. I had no idea you were fond of the basics, considering you're the smartest person I know when it comes to everything to do with tech.'

Helen blushed and was relieved he couldn't see the hectic colour in her cheeks.

'His love for tradition goes beyond the superficial stuff of wanting everything in hard copy,' Gabriel continued into the silence.

'What do you mean?'

'He's a family man. You've met him a couple of times—you can see that straightaway. He carries an album of pictures of his kids and his grandchildren on him, in his briefcase—showed them to me the last time we met—and I must say there's something a little unfamiliar about seeing the faces of people whose blood I share. I know more names of sons and daughters and their many and varied offspring than I would ever have imagined possible when I first thought about scouting around for a vineyard I could buy close to the place my parents were born.

'It's a blessing that Fifi decided to cut short her stay here, to be perfectly honest. I have a feeling Arturio would have been a little disconcerted by her if they had happened to meet. He's laid it on thick about the importance of family and preserving the tradition within the company, and I suspect Fifi might not have played into that mindset.'

'But you're single,' Helen said, astonished. 'What does that have to do with the deal?'

'Nothing at all,' Gabriel drawled. 'He is the way he is, and this is a fledgling family bond I don't want to risk losing, never mind the tangible practicality of what I'm buying.' He laughed softly and mused under his breath, 'There's a part of me that thinks that the bond with Arturio and his family might actually trump the dry, financial business of buying his vineyard. If he chooses to think that I'm built along the lines of his own children—who all seem to have bought into the joy of weddings quickly followed by the pitter-patter of tiny feet—then I would hate to disappoint him.'

'Well, I'm sure he'll be pleased with its success when you take charge,' Helen said vaguely, nimbly steering the conversation away from anything personal, although she was aware of the faint buzz of curiosity inside her.

Why had his hot blonde decided to leave? Surely a different country, beautiful scenery, the end word in luxury and having one hundred per cent of Gabriel for the better part of a week would have been conducive to keeping her glued to the spot? Had they had some kind of argument because Arturio had shown up unexpectedly and Gabriel had tried to side-line the blonde? That would not have gone down well. From what Helen had seen, she didn't think that Fifi was the kind of woman who would take kindly to maintaining a low profile to accommodate Gabriel and a business deal.

'I'll email you the details of my flight, shall I? Although there's no need for you to change any plans you may have made for the day. I can easily find my own way to the hotel and contact you once I'm there.'

'I'll ensure a driver is waiting for you.' Helen heard his soft, amused laugh down the line once again and gritted her teeth.

'Perfect. I'll see you in due course. Goodbye.' And she disconnected the call before he could say anything further to unsettle her.

Helen had booked the hotel for Gabriel and Fifi without paying a scrap of attention to the details. She had been given the name of the place, had called it and had reserved the most expensive room. Fifi had done the sourcing of the place and Gabriel had acquiesced without demur. The eye-watering price of the room would not have raised an eyebrow.

She could have checked out the place herself now, and had vaguely planned to, but at the back of her mind she'd associated Fifi with somewhere incredibly expensive and incredibly busy, a place where she could bask in the admiring glances of people around her. She'd ended up way too busy to bother checking out where she would be heading to.

She had a smooth trip over—made all the more seamlessly comfortable because, as a first-class passenger, she had actually been able to sleep because the seat had reclined into a bed. Helen only felt a twinge of curiosity about where she was going when she was ensconced in the chauffeur-driven limo Gabriel had organised for her. All glass, perhaps? A skyscraper with uniformed guards outside and the frantic bustle of millionaires entering and leaving? All of the above?

She had never been to America in her life and, as she gazed through the tinted windows of the long, black limo, she felt transported into another world entirely, so different was it from London, from Cornwall—from every destination she had ever been to.

The skies were a milky cornflower-blue and the sun

streamed down like honey on a drive that skirted a stretch of coast with water as turquoise and as still as a giant lake. The Pacific coast, the driver explained, glancing at her in the mirror. He was obviously proud of his city. He pointed to the drama of the mountains that rose in majestic peaks behind the town, explained that Santa Barbara was referred to as 'the American Riviera' because of the gorgeous weather and boasted that the beaches were the best in the country, as were the restaurants and cafés that lined them.

There were no frantic, gridlocked roads, just beautiful winding little streets with picturesque boutiques and wine bars, and there was greenery everywhere, showing her that she'd never be far from nature in this part of America.

'I'll have to make sure to take a day off to explore,' Helen said politely, although she had no intention of doing any such thing, because this wasn't going to be a sightseeing, tourist's holiday.

She was busily scouring the skyline for the modern, glassy and expensive skyscraper she'd been expecting and was disconcerted when it failed to materialise.

Instead, the tour-guide conversation from her driver turned to the beauty of the foothills of Santa Barbara. 'Open space,' he boasted proudly, taking one hand off the wheel to make a sweeping gesture encompassing the scenery they were now passing, 'With brilliant views of the oceans and the mountains and a playground for all sorts of incredible wildlife. Hawks, coyotes, a thousand different species of birds, and of course the exclusive real-estate reflects the demand for a place like this.

'And where I'm taking you…' he threw in as an aside, 'Couldn't be more secluded…'

'I beg your pardon?'

'It's incredible. Could never afford to stay at a place like that myself, but my, I've driven a couple of people out there—and, well, if I win the lottery that'll be number one on my go-to list.'

'Secluded? *Secluded?* It's a *hotel.*' Secluded was not what she'd expected, because somehow secluded was something she associated with 'laid back' and laid back was the last thing Fifi was. Had she been remiss in not doing some due diligence before she'd headed over? Or had she been so wrapped up thinking about her boss in a different setting that practicality had taken a back seat?

'Sure, ma'm, but it's a hotel with a difference.'

'What do you mean?'

'You'll see! You'll find it's a bit different from your London, ma'm. Although, you have your royal family, and that's the next thing I'll do with my winnings! A trip to that palace of yours to see those guards with the big, furry hats! My wife would love nothing more…'

Helen was barely listening. She'd expected something big, modern, expensive and impersonal—part of a chain of five-star hotels, something stuck in the middle of the city, in the heart of the action, surrounded by night life, and noisy with the bustle of tourists.

With dismay, she discovered that she couldn't have been more off-target in her assumptions. There were no city lights where they were heading. Instead, the limo slowed in surroundings which, in the fading light, seemed to be a wondrous panorama of landscaped acres interrupted by towering sycamore trees, and fragrant with the smell of citrus and olive groves.

She rolled down her window and breathed in the aroma of blossoms, jasmine and magnolia. Everything told her that Fifi had done her homework.

She'd turned her back on what Helen would have expected and gone for out of the ordinary. No impersonal, height-of-luxury, five-star hotel but…*a ranch*? Or something that looked like a ranch. Definitely not a hotel along the lines that she'd been expecting.

Her heart flipped and dropped.

Her driver had mentioned the adjective 'secluded' and he hadn't been lying. This place was tucked away. It nestled into the greenery and was part of the magnificent landscape, and there was nothing built around it as far as the eye could see.

'Secluded' didn't come close. This was more than secluded. This was...*romantic.*

'Here we are.'

'This is the entrance?'

'I'll help you with your bag.'

'It's okay. It's not terribly heavy. I can manage.'

'No trouble.'

Her bag looked ridiculously out of place here, Helen thought as she stepped out into the balmy evening air.

There was just a hint of a cooling breeze, carrying with it the fragrant smells that had wafted into the car. But they were more intensified, sweet and aromatic, now that she was hovering outside the brightly lit reception area. To one side, a young couple walked past into the night, murmuring in low voices.

Blinking, she turned to retrieve her bag, which the driver had hoisted out of the car. He laughed and shook his head and then, when she spun back round, there he was—her charismatic boss. Framed in the doorway, hands shoved into the pockets of his trousers, looking every inch the drop-dead gorgeous billionaire that he was.

But this drop-dead gorgeous billionaire wasn't in his dark suit, white shirt and hand-made shoes. This drop-dead gorgeous billionaire wasn't attached to his laptop, firing out instructions and attired for work. He was attired for fun and frolics. He was wearing a white short-sleeved polo shirt, cream chinos and a pair of tan loafers.

Breathing in deeply, Helen walked towards him while behind the driver followed with her minuscule pull-along into which she had crammed sufficient work clothes for three days.

'You're here.'

'Where else would I be?' She stopped to look up at him, taking in the rakish stubble on his chin, and thinking that none of this was what she'd had in mind when she'd booked her plane ticket. Not the rakish stubble, not the casual gear and not the romantic setting.

The polo shirt stretched taut across broad shoulders. When she tore her eyes away from the breadth of his chest, they collided with the length of his muscular legs encased in those cream chinos, the easy grace of a hard, sinewy body that was shockingly attractive because it wasn't sheathed in work attire. She felt faint.

'Who knows?' Gabriel drawled with amusement. 'After all the umming and ahhing, it did cross my mind that you might just find an excuse to wriggle out of coming.'

'I wouldn't have dreamt of it.' Helen cleared her throat, eyes skittering away from his suffocating physicality. 'As you pointed out, I'm here to work. It's what I'm paid to do.'

Gabriel's lips twitched.

'Of course you are.' He stood back, allowing her to brush past him into the foyer of what was, in essence, a one-storey, uber-luxurious cottage surrounded by all manner of plants, flowers and foliage. The only indication that it wasn't someone's house was the marble reception area and the two cheerful young girls manning it. 'How could I forget that when you're here in your work clothes, ready and eager to send emails and read reports, even though you've just spent over ten hours on a plane?'

To which there was no answer, Helen thought.

This banter… She had strayed beyond her comfort zone,

and she grappled with sudden unease, but he was smiling and she returned the smile, because it was late, she was tired and tomorrow was another day. Things would be back into perspective tomorrow. Work would be on the agenda. This crazily sexy guy would conveniently be back in his box.

But somewhere deep inside her a little thread of nervous tension began to unfurl. She had to remind herself that the professional hat she wore, the one she had been at pains to keep firmly in place, was far too secure ever to be dislodged just because familiar signposts had temporarily been removed.

CHAPTER TWO

GABRIEL FOLLOWED HER through and took charge at the reception desk.

'Nice passport picture,' he murmured, holding it up for scrutiny before handing it over to the girl manning the sleek marble desk, and then grinned at her stony expression. 'How was the trip here?'

'Very comfortable, thank you.'

'Good.' He eyed her outfit, standing back while the young woman at the desk blushed and went through the usual check-in stuff, her eyes studiously averted from him. 'Why are you dressed for work? Surely you didn't expect me to greet you with a list of things to do? I believe in a hard day's work but I'm not that much of a task master.'

Yet had he expected anything different? Gabriel had never seen his dutiful, hard-working, talented and exceptionally self-contained secretary in anything other than formal clothes: suits, white blouses and neat jackets, all in a range of colours that reminded him in no uncertain terms that life was serious business and the work arena was no place for frivolity. Strangely, they had always made him wonder what she and frivolity might look like if they were ever to come up close and personal.

She was a little over five-six, with brown hair that dropped in a shiny, straight curtain to her shoulders, although in fairness most of the time that shiny curtain of hair was pinned back. She was slender, with wide-set brown eyes, a neat little nose that tilted just the tiniest bit and a little sprinkling of freckles across the bridge of her nose that made him think that she burned in the sun.

He dated sexy, voluptuous women, women who enjoyed displaying their assets, and yet he had always thought that there was something curiously compelling about his quiet, serious little sparrow with her clear, smooth skin, her considered conversation and her unexpectedly husky voice.

'I'm not dressed for work.'

Gabriel pushed away from the marble desk, told Pammy, the woman at Reception, that he would deliver his guest to her quarters and retrieved the pull-along from the ground, tut-tutting when Helen tried to take it off him and point out the fact that his hand was bandaged.

'My other hand is in fine working order,' he told her. 'So there's no need for you to worry on my behalf. If that's what you were doing.' He grinned and changed the subject. 'There's a nice pool here. You should try it. Relax a little, and don't tell me that you're not paid to relax.'

'Okay, then, I won't. This isn't quite what I was expecting.'

'No?'

Walking alongside her, Gabriel felt some of his edginess dissipate. The time-out holiday with his now departed ex couldn't have gone less according to plan. Instead of fun and frolics, he had found himself in the eye of a hurricane almost before the last item of clothing had been unpacked from her Louis Vuitton suitcase—one of three he had bought for her because she'd wanted to travel in style.

She had stepped out of the very same limo that had just delivered his secretary and looked around her with an expression of satisfaction. Something in her purposeful stride had warned him that all was not going to be smooth sailing.

That said, he had not been prepared for the sudden upping of the ante in their relationship, which she had brought to the table without any warning before romance had had much of a chance to blossom.

She had wound her arms around him, breathed huskily into his ear, drawn his attention to the extraordinary romance of their setting—which had made him think that she had chosen the venue for that very reason—and whispered that it was time to take their relationship to the next level. At which point, things had gone downhill at speed.

Gabriel shoved that to the back of his mind and slowed his pace as he ushered Helen out through the landscaped grounds to where she would be staying.

'I expected something more conventional,' she admitted.

'When you say "conventional"...?'

'A big hotel,' Helen confessed. 'Somewhere a little more in the thick of things. I didn't see the need to look up the place before I arrived.' And that was what came of jumping to all sorts of false conclusions...

'I was a little surprised myself by what I found when I got here.'

'Didn't you discuss the choice with...er... Fifi?'

'She said it was going to be a surprise and I was more than happy to leave it at that.' He shrugged and swung a sharp right under a little avenue of trees with branches charmingly entwined to form a canopy. They emerged into a delightful clearing in which a handful of beautiful little cottages was spread against a picture-perfect landscape of climbing plants, mature trees and scattered benches. Each cottage had a porch and was fronted by three broad steps.

'Here we are.' He nodded to another of the cottages. 'Mine's that one. Slightly bigger but no more luxurious.'

'I'm in a cottage...'

'And behind this little cluster of cottages is the swimming pool, although you'd never guess that it was man-made. They've done a great job of blending it into the backdrop.'

He swiped a card and nudged open the door with his shoulder, stepping back to let her pass.

The space was far from impersonal. Helen stepped through into a front room that was adorned with a range of artefacts and artwork that spanned the continents, from a bold abstract painting on the wall above the stone fireplace, to a series of exquisite African sculptures ranged along the window ledge.

She turned full circle and stared. The wooden floor was warmed with faded Persian rugs and through an open doorway she could make out a grand four-poster bed with requisite canopy and soft net drapes that fell to the floor in a swirl.

'Wow.'

'All the cottages have their own small private plunge-pool—added seclusion. Step outside and you can enjoy breakfast brought to you sitting on the veranda at the back which overlooks hillside gardens.' He laughed. 'I'm beginning to sound like a tour guide. Frankly, I thought about switching to something in the city centre, but in the end I didn't think it was worth the effort.'

He watched as she strolled off to inspect the rest of the cottage. She dumped her handbag on the sofa, along with the jacket she had been wearing, and tucked her hair neatly behind her ears.

Eyes on her as he leaned against the wall, Gabriel absently reflected that she was the only woman who was happy to ignore him, and in that extremely polite way of hers was never afraid to tell him exactly what she thought. It was curiously appealing. The less she said, the more he wanted to know.

She might not offer opinions on his love life, but did she really imagine that he didn't know exactly what she thought of it? She had just the right turn of phrase when it came to revealing her thoughts without actually having to be blunt. She kept herself to herself, and made sure never to encourage curiosity, yet he recognised that curiosity was never far away when he thought about her.

She was still young, yet he had never got even the passing impression that away from the office she was doing all the stuff most girls her age did. Had she had her heart broken? Was she still clinging to lost love, stuck in a moment in time and unable to move on? Never in the slightest curious about the women he dated, he could never resist letting his imagination wander when it came to his secretary.

'Is it going to be convenient doing business…er…here?'

'Come again?'

'You know what I mean.' Helen raised her eyebrows and stood in the middle of the room, hands on her waist. She nodded at her surroundings. 'Is there a conference room on the grounds, for instance? If lawyers and accountants have to gather, where are they going to do that?'

Sensible questions and yet, looking at her as she stood in front of him, the very essence of matter-of-fact practicality, he couldn't resist lowering his eyes to say with a contrived frown, 'I think it could work very well, having everyone here in these pleasant, informal settings. My cottage is bigger than this. There's a very useful table that seats six. As an alternative, we could always choose to discuss the details by the pool…have drinks and food brought to us. The restaurant here comes with an excellent reputation.'

His lips twitched as she stiffened and he burst out laughing. 'Relax, Helen. I have suitable arrangements in place at one of the hotels in the city which is close and convenient. I also have a timetable, you'll be pleased to know. Tomorrow, meetings are lined up with the lawyers. Day after, we consult with the finance guys. Day after that, we can run through the finer details, after which you are free to leave.

I will see Arturio on my own to explain what's in place and work through any further concerns he might have regarding the rights of all his employees—all the business stuff that's quite separate from everything else. Especially considering a fair few of them are related to him.

'Everything is in writing and pored over at length, but my gut feeling is it's something that will be raised again, and I want to make sure signatures are all in place before I return to London. So, formalities will be strictly observed, rest assured. Although…you'll have ample free time to practise your swimming in the pool. There's no need be shy about that.'

Looking at him, Helen suddenly felt the ground shift ever so slightly beneath her feet.

Of course he was gently teasing her about everything being in place work-wise, just as he had gently teased her about the formal clothes she had opted to wear for the trip over. Why on earth was she so uptight about a little bit of banter? It wasn't the first time he'd smiled and said something he knew was mischievous, knowing that it would get under her skin. So why was she unsettled now? Was it the change of scenery? She was going to be here for three days, after which she would head back to London and, as he'd made clear, their days would be accounted for.

So, relaxing around a swimming pool? Not going to happen. She hadn't brought a swimsuit with her, anyway.

She smiled and nodded.

'Sounds good.'

'I expect you're tired, and you'll probably find that jet lag might kick in tomorrow, so I've made sure that nothing kicks off until late morning. You can lie in.'

'I'll be fine.'

'Have you ever done a trip of this length before to a country with this time difference?'

Helen reddened. She thought of her dad, his fussing and his worrying when she'd been younger. And then in the blink of an eye she'd been making all her girlish plans for a wedding that had never happened. In between all of that, she and George hadn't given a moment's thought to travelling anywhere, because they had been too busy putting money aside to leave their rented accommodation and buy somewhere of their own once they were married.

So much planning, and yet he had walked away, and the woman with whom he had settled down in record time had been the very opposite of Helen.

'No,' she admitted shortly.

'Then don't underestimate the effects of jet lag,' Gabriel murmured softly. He looked at her for a few long, silent seconds. 'I don't want you to feel that you have to snap to attention if you're exhausted, Helen.'

'I wouldn't do that.'

'Sure? Because everybody needs to unwind now and again, especially when they work in a high-stress environment as you do, and you won't be judged if that happens.'

With Helen making no response to that, Gabriel straightened and continued briskly, 'Right. I'll leave you to it. You can order in whatever you want and I'll let you have breakfast whenever you please tomorrow morning. You can have it delivered to the cottage, or you can head to the restaurant, which is through the clearing and straight ahead in the building alongside where we checked you in.'

'Thank you. And where and when shall we meet to head into town?'

'Eleven. Reception. My driver will be on standby to take us for our first round of meetings.'

He half-saluted with his bandaged hand, and she breathed

a sigh of relief as he vanished into the night, leaving her to get on with the business of getting her thoughts in order.

Racing pulses and a foolishly hammering heart, because she happened to have been swept away from her usual safe environment for ten minutes, just weren't going to do.

She'd grown up since George and had had time to evaluate her choices and firmly establish herself as a woman with her head very firmly screwed on. Her sexy, charming boss wasn't going to mess with any of that.

Gabriel was waiting for her at eleven sharp the following morning. Helen spotted him chatting to Pammy, of the long, blonde hair, and from her heightened colour and bright eyes she could see that the twenty-something woman was thrilled to bits to have this striking Italian guy flirting with her.

Because flirting was surely what he was doing, half-leaning on the counter, with his bandaged hand making him even sexier than he already was for reasons she couldn't fathom.

Honestly. No sooner had one girlfriend disappeared through that revolving door than another potential was in the offing. Didn't the man need any breathing space at all? Ridiculous. Superficial. Typical!

She cleared her throat and looked at him coolly as he slowly turned to her, gave her the once over and then strolled unhurriedly in her direction.

Again, he was casually dressed. He wore a different pair of trousers, grey this time, and a grey-and-white-striped polo shirt with a distinctive logo on the pocket. Helen instantly felt uncomfortable and over-dressed in her dark-blue knee-length skirt and, to accommodate the heat, a short-sleeved shirt buttoned to the neck, the little pearl buttons somehow feeling like the height of frumpiness.

She had her laptop bag slung over her shoulder, along with her handbag.

'Ready?' Gabriel raised his eyebrows but said not a word about her choice of clothing, another nod to the fact that she was here to work.

'I've collated all the relevant information on the deal in one file,' she said, turning away from the flustered young girl at Reception and staring out to where the limo was waiting for them. 'I thought it would be easier than trying to retrieve strands from various places. All the documents to do with the legal side of things are in one place and I've emailed it all to you.'

'Excellent. Very efficient.'

'Have you checked?'

'Not yet, no. I'm assuming this will all go smoothly because so much fact-checking has already been done. These are mere formalities, even if there promises to be quite a bit of them. And naturally, unless they're all in order, there's still an outside chance that things might hit a roadblock. Unlikely with me at the helm,' he murmured in a low drawl. 'Bandaged hand or no bandaged hand. How did you sleep?'

'Very well. Thank you.' Helen slipped into the back seat through the door the driver had swept round to open for her. It was another glorious day and the rich, heady scent of flowers filled her nostrils. For a fleeting moment, she almost lost herself in the illusion that she wasn't here on business. The illusion didn't last long. In fact, it was comprehensively dispelled when Gabriel joined her in the back, angling his big body against the door so that he could look at her.

'This is a beautiful part of the world,' he said, snapping shut the partition and then devoting all his focused concentration on her.

Suddenly the intimate, confined space felt stifling and Helen breathed in deeply. Gabriel was very good when it came to making a person feel as though no one else in the world existed. She had seen him in action with a couple of women in the past: had seen the way he had perched on his desk when one of them had happened to drop by unannounced; had seen the way his dark eyes had lasered them to the spot until they were blushing and coyly responsive. When he'd politely but firmly ushered them out after five minutes, they hadn't seemed to feel rejected. Even in meetings, he would focus on someone and that someone would hesitate and then do exactly as he wanted.

But with her? They worked together in absolute harmony but that focused concentration was something he had only ever applied when discussing something of a work nature. Now, for some odd reason, Helen felt a tingle of sexual awareness stir inside her and she was confused and horrified in equal measure.

She drew in a hitched breath and reminded herself that the occasional surreptitious glance at a guy who was undeniably sexy was nothing to be particularly concerned about. Yet she found herself adjusting her position to quell the tingling between her thighs.

'Yes.' She rushed into speech, but her nerves were all over the place, and her usual calm had decided to desert her. 'Your...your driver told me a lot about the place, the cafés and the restaurants, and of course the scenery is beautiful. Breath-taking—the trees and the flowers. Yes, really beautiful...' Her voice fizzled out but his eyes remained on her, pensive and, she thought, a little amused.

This wasn't her at all. She didn't do girly—never had. She had always been serious and controlled, her life running on carefully regulated tracks, but right now she felt *girly*, and it was disconcerting.

'I imagine we'll work for a couple of hours, and probably break for lunch to be brought, but what remains of the afternoon will be free.'

'Yes, well, if I have to work on the minutes then I shall be more than happy to return to the hotel if you want to stay on and enjoy whatever there is to enjoy in the city.'

'That's extremely diligent, Helen.' His dark eyes were serious and his voice was mild and thoughtful. 'Of course, I would expect nothing less. However, this came as something of a surprise for you and, that being the case, I insist that you see something of the place while you're here. There's no need to bury yourself in front of your computer. Meetings will kick off tomorrow at the same time and you can do whatever needs to be done in the morning.'

'Of course, but…'

'No buts. I'll show you around.'

Gabriel looked at her with lazy concentration, his lush lashes masking what was going through his head.

He could feel her discomfort in waves. She was dressed for the office and any deviation from the script had not been predicted. Yet how hard would it be for her to take some time out with him? What was the big deal? He didn't intimidate her. He knew that for a fact, sensed it in the way she was never afraid of telling him what she thought, even if the criticisms were always wrapped up in polite packaging he could never fault. So why the hesitation?

She was a girl in her twenties, yet she behaved like someone twice that age, and here, under a syrupy sun and an alien landscape, Gabriel was suddenly intensely curious to find out what made her tick.

Broodingly, his dark eyes roved over her, appreciating her slender, pale-skinned delicacy, the Cupid's bow of her mouth, the intelligent slant of her calm brown eyes and, dropping down, the jut of small breasts pushing against her top.

Far less than a handful, he mused.

He frowned, shifted and dragged his wayward thoughts back to what they had been talking about.

'Let's go through what we need to cover,' he said more brusquely than he intended, because somewhere in his head his thoughts were still drifting in unfamiliar waters, playing around with images that were off-limits. 'We both know how much lawyers can waffle. The less of that, the better.'

He wrapped it up fast. He felt his eyes straying to her slight form positioned just to the right of him. Out of the corner of his eye, he could see her frown and the concentration on her face as she annotated details of what was happening, pulling up relevant pieces of information at the speed of light, and printing it all off on a printer which, at his request, had been installed within touching distance.

She moved quickly, confidently and gracefully. Once or twice he asked her something, and she knew exactly where he was going with his questions and responded accordingly.

Lunch was brought and eaten while work continued, and at a little after four everything was done and dusted and there was the usual round of barely concealed self-congratulatory noises on a job well done.

Gabriel switched off. He'd sat through many a conclusion to thorny, detailed work and all he wanted to do now was relax.

'Brilliant work, Helen.'

Those were his first words to her as they left the hotel, moving from air-conditioned comfort out into the sultry summer heat.

'Thank you. It all seemed very straightforward. I'm very happy to explore on my own if you have better things to do.'

'My calendar is oddly empty,' Gabriel murmured drily.

Helen wondered whether boredom was driving him into occupying himself with second best—Plain Jane secretary because sexpot girlfriend was no longer on the scene. She could do without him feeling sorry for her, or anyone else for that matter, seeing her as a second-best filler-in when there was no one else more exciting to play with. Being ditched all those years ago had made her proud, had made her learn the value of detaching and concealing what might be going on under the surface. Gabriel's staggering self-assurance, that came from money, power and good looks, made it seem even more important that she stuck to the script and maintained her cool.

'I expect you've been here before?' she asked politely, although her attention was going this way and that, taking in the perfectly arrayed line of shops, the quaint street, the patriotic flags over doorways and the bustle of very affluent tourists.

Tall palms and swaying trees lined the streets and avenues and there was a jostling, cosmopolitan feel that was vibrant and invigorating.

'I don't tend to do the sightseeing stuff,' Gabriel admitted with a shrug and Helen briefly turned to look at him.

'I'm sorry Fifi isn't here to share it with you. That must be disappointing.'

'I find that it's no big deal.' His expression was veiled as their eyes met. 'I know this part of the world because of the vineyards I inherited, but my parents never stayed too long in one place. And I grew up in England, even though I suppose you could say that my origins were split between Italy and America. I have no issue reacquainting myself with the place on my own.'

'That must have been odd for you, never being in one place.'

'Life happens.' He closed the conversation down and, in so doing, left her wanting more.

More ground shifted from under her feet, because here they were, straying beyond their boundary lines, leaving her confused and ill at ease. Her neat skirt and blouse, which had been fine when they'd been working in the boardroom, made her feel uncomfortable and out of place.

As though reading her mind, he said gently, 'Have you brought anything more casual to wear, Helen?'

'Yes. Of course.'

'Then why don't you think about wearing it tomorrow? This is a casual sort of place. Even the lawyers were in tee-shirts and cotton trousers.'

'I…'

'And what about a swimsuit? It's hot and there's that pool, and you can't leave without using it.'

'I didn't bring one of those.' She almost heaved a sigh of relief.

'Of course. Because you're here to work.'

He was laughing at her and she suddenly felt dull and unexciting—the dutiful secretary incapable of letting her hair down. The dutiful secretary, still in her twenties, incapable of letting her hair down, which made things worse.

'Because I'm not going to be here very long and I didn't see the point of banking on time off to swan around.'

'In that case, we should remedy the situation. An hour relaxing in a pool after a hard day's work is hardly what I would call *swanning around*. It's called *recharging your batteries after slaving over reports and facts and figures without a break.*'

Helen burst out laughing.

'What's so funny?'

'You make it sound as though I've been chained to a desk, starved of food and forced to work for days on end without sleep. We had a delicious lunch brought to us, and it was a shorter than usual day, in actual fact. My batteries don't need that much recharging, as it happens.'

So he thought that she was hard-working but dull,

wrapped up in doing the perfect job to the point where she had to be ordered to down tools and relax… What would he think were he ever to see a different side to her—a side that was wild and reckless? The thought took hold and it was a little scary, making her think that safety might not have been all it had always been cracked up to be.

When had she ever let herself go? she wondered. When had she ever dared to turn her back on all those life lessons that had been embedded in her from such a young age?

A thousand thoughts flitted through her head, darting like quicksilver.

George had been her rock, or so she had thought at the time, and he had also been her shield. The big, bad world was out there and he had been the protector she'd thought she needed. But as it turned out she hadn't, because she'd moved to London and managed the big, bad world just fine. Hadn't she?

Okay, so she didn't do clubs and bars. She didn't sleep around or try guys out for size. But that didn't mean that she was a bore, she thought now; didn't mean that there wasn't a sense of daring lurking beneath the surface.

For some reason, Gabriel's amused teasing, those sexy, dark eyes appraising her in these new surroundings, stirred something inside her that wanted to show him that there were sides to her that might be unexpected—wanted to show *herself* that there were sides to her that might be unexpected.

She drew in a sharp, unsteady breath.

'But you're right,' she murmured. 'I love swimming and I was always very good at it. It would be brilliant to have a dip in the pool. I haven't even seen what it's like.' She looked around her. 'There must be a shop here somewhere that sells swimsuits.'

She glanced at him and felt a stab of triumph at the momentary flash of surprise on his face. Had he thought her so predictable that she would retreat from the horror of relaxing when she was here to work? Would allow him to gently tease her, safe in the knowledge that she would always scuttle away from facing him down when it came to anything of a personal nature?

'Lots.'

'I'll have a wander around and find one.'

'I'll come with you. Like I said, I'm familiar with the area.'

'No need, Gabriel. I'm not completely at sea when it comes to exploring somewhere new.'

He stood back, fidgeted hesitantly for a few seconds and raked his fingers through his dark hair.

'I can find a shop, buy a swimsuit and make my way back all under my own steam.'

'Of course…'

'So I'll see you in the morning? I don't seem to have any jet lag at all.'

'You're very welcome to join me for dinner with Terry and his wife.'

'No thank you, Gabriel. You've said that they're long-standing friends of your parents whom you haven't seen for years and I'm sure they'll want to have you all to themselves.'

For a few seconds, their eyes tangled and she felt her breath hitch. He had amazing eyes—so dark, so piercing and so disturbing when they were pinned to her, as they were now. 'Your hand may not be in great working order but I don't think I need to come with you to cut up your food and feed you, do I?'

'Since when do you do sarcasm?'

'I'm sorry. Seldom.' Helen lowered her eyes. She wasn't sorry. She never, ever shared any personal opinions with him but something about being here, away from their usual surroundings, made her feel restless with the trajectory of her life, dissatisfied with her own predictability.

'No need to apologise,' Gabriel drawled softly, his voice sending shivers up and down her, reminding her that sometimes it felt safe to get close to the fire until you suddenly went up in flames. This? This felt a bit like getting close to a fire.

That said…she knew that she was far too controlled ever to get burnt. Buying a swimsuit, taking a dip in a pool, relaxing when she knew that her boss wasn't going to be around anyway—why should any of that constitute grounds for panic?

She'd spent over three years working with this guy, and sure she could stand back and appreciate his crazy sexiness and his charismatic allure, but she wasn't one of those blondes who swooned at his feet. She'd proven that. She was detached when it came to her boss. She would never in a million years go for someone like him which made her immune to everything about him that seemed to suck women in.

And, if he'd suddenly fired up something inside her that wanted *change*, then that wasn't a bad thing. Was it? Being careful was very different from never taking chances. What was life without taking the occasional risk? She gone down the uber-safe route with George but hadn't that been a mistake? Climbing out of her work gear and lightening up with the man now watching her through narrowed eyes was hardly going to break the bank when it came to risk taking!

'So, tomorrow…' she threw into the lengthening silence between them. 'Timings?'

'No need to rush out of bed. It will be the same routine as today.'

'Lovely.' She stepped back and made a point of looking around her. 'I'll head off now, if that's all right?'

'No reason it shouldn't be. But getting back to the hotel? Forget about taking a taxi. I'll get my driver to collect you.'

Helen smiled, shrugged, dutifully put all the details of his driver into her phone and listened politely while he gave her various helpful hints about where she could go if she fancied something to eat or drink. She frowned and stifled a sigh when, eventually, he asked her whether she was absolutely sure she was going to be okay, left to her own devices.

'I'll manage,' she said with a stiff smile, 'And, if I find I can't, I'll make sure I get on the phone and call you immediately so that you can come and rescue me.' She smiled sweetly and, wow, did it make her feel good when he shot her a disconcerted frown in response.

If there was one thing guaranteed to make her change gear, it was Gabriel de Luca treating her as someone who might be sharp as a tack in front of a computer but as clueless as the village idiot when it came to everything else…

CHAPTER THREE

IT WAS A long evening. Or rather, it felt like it. Gabriel had been distracted at the restaurant bar and then had caught himself glancing at his watch as he made small talk with Terry and Caro over lobster and champagne.

He would rearrange, make it up to them, wine and dine them another night. But he had to go…a thorny problem with a big deal…time was money…

And he *would* make it up to them—in style. After all, he hadn't seen them in a while, and he was extremely fond of them. In the preposterously lavish but uncertain world he had inhabited as a kid, they had been more of a constant than his own parents had been.

They had been neighbours, two vast estates sitting alongside one another. His parents had chosen to use their sprawling house as a base, leaving the upkeep of it to other people so that they could travel the world and do very little, aside from have fun. But Terry and Caro, considerably older, had seldom travelled, preferring to enjoy their surroundings and taking pride in everything they did to their house and its huge grounds.

The couples had met over drinks at the local members-only club and somehow it had been established, in not so many words, that Terry and his wife would somehow 'keep an eye' on Gabriel when he was on his own, with only two nannies and various employees there to supervise him.

In hindsight, Gabriel wondered what Terry and his wife had made of the situation. What had they thought of his parents who had had the freedom to indulge in one another and pursue their heady, selfish lives of uninterrupted enjoyment, in receipt of their huge passive income from family holdings which had been set up to virtually to run itself, thanks to people who had been put in place years before? They'd never said and he'd never asked. He'd formed his own conclusions about his parents all by himself.

From the age of six, he could remember the older couple swinging by for him, gathering him up to take him out for ice-cream, a meal somewhere, some fun fair or other that had been passing through or to hit some balls on the three-hole golf course they had had landscaped, because Terry had been fanatical about the game.

Through all this, his own parents had been globetrotting, descending now and again with armfuls of gifts from whatever exciting countries they'd visited. They would stay for a couple of weeks, just time to catch their breath, then once again would come the round of nannies and caretakers and, through it all, Terry and Caro picking up the slack.

At the age of eleven, he'd been shipped to boarding school in England, never to return to America to live, but always keeping up with the childless couple who had been there for him, especially following his parents' deaths. He had leant on them as a source of support in his own solitary, independent way.

So looking at his watch, being distracted enough to wind up the evening prematurely? Unacceptable. And yet he had been on edge, his thoughts returning to his secretary and that sudden unexpected glimpse of fire simmering beneath the cool, placid surface.

One flame—the glimmer of a burning spark… How much more to see? Where had she been hiding that fire?

Somewhere deep inside, he recognised that that flame had always been there, flickering steadily behind the contained demeanour. She would lower her eyes and half-smile at something he'd said and he'd feel that feathery frisson, as though something had passed very softly over his skin.

It was a reaction no other woman had ever been able to rouse in him, and he had always uncomfortably pushed it aside, but out here… Out here, the barriers had been broken through. Heck, that was why he'd spent the evening with her in his head.

He didn't want to be curious but he was. He didn't want to think about her as a woman he wanted to touch, but he did. Had he always wanted to touch her? It was an unsettling thought. He wondered whether the fiasco with Fifi had shifted something inside him, made him confront a life spent without any commitment whatsoever. A life spent indulging his own physical desires whilst shrugging off the responsibility of taking those desires and trying to turn them into something more significant.

That was an unsettling thought. Was he so different from his parents? Wasn't all self-indulgence the same, even if no kids were involved?

He would never make the mistake of handing over his heart to anyone, of losing control emotionally, but was there some other way that didn't involve a parade of beauties coming and going without ever leaving a dent in his life?

And, underneath all those discomforting questions, the image of his quiet but curiously compelling secretary shimmered and beckoned.

He'd made his excuses and left with the sun still shining and the evening barely beginning.

He reckoned the only way to take his mind away from

those forbidden places was to work. He would head back to his cottage and throw himself into work, and by morning whatever passing fever that seemed to afflict him would be gone.

Truth was, whatever passing fever this was, it *had* to go because he had no intention of doing anything that could possibly jeopardise the vital working relationship he had with his secretary. Temptation could be fought and conquered. There was no choice here.

She was the best he'd ever had. They were tuned into one another in ways that never failed to astonish him. She was so much cleverer than she probably gave herself credit for and he was amazed she hadn't taken her qualifications much further and gone to bigger, more rewarding places. Not that he was complaining. He wasn't. He made sure to pay her what she deserved and then double, ensuring loyalty.

She liked her privacy and he'd made sure never to overstep boundary lines, even though they puzzled him. Surely lightening up a little wasn't a crime? Even when she was with some of her colleagues, he could see that underneath the laughter and the gossip there was always something holding her back. Why?

That was a curiosity he had always made sure never to indulge. She was smart enough to get a damn good job anywhere and he was smart enough to make sure he kept her close. But what made her tick? Had there been a man in her life? Was there someone? No one? Surely there were guys out there who could see just what he saw—a woman with depth and substance who was as sexy as hell underneath whatever drab outfits she chose to wear?

Because they were out here didn't mean he was going to play fast and loose with three years' worth of sensible good intentions, however. And Gabriel knew himself well. *Sensible* good intentions and *women* didn't always go hand in hand. He enjoyed women. He liked the thrill of the chase and, if boredom inevitably followed, that didn't negate the thrill of the chase.

He enjoyed women but the chase always ended and that was how he liked it. Until now. Who wanted to play catch for ever? But that didn't mean the only alternative was love.

Love, to Gabriel, was a destructive force. That was what he had learnt from his own parents. It burnt like a raging fire, out of control and all-consuming. His parents had loved one another to the exclusion of everything and everyone, including him.

Why else would they have left him to his own devices from the time he'd been able to walk? They had been so involved with one another that there had been nothing left over to give him or anyone. They had both been only children, heirs to vast personal fortunes, and they had done nothing with their lives but take advantage of the privileges of their birth. Maybe, if they had needed to work, reality might have made an appearance at some point but they hadn't. They'd been the original trust-fund children with the world at their disposal.

And love? It had made them selfish and single-minded. It was a blessing they had both died together because he was sure that neither would have survived for long without the other. If the only people they'd needed were each other, then removing one would have killed the other. So, love? *Thanks, but no thanks.* The thought of ever putting himself in the position of being vulnerable in a life where his heart made the decisions and his head obeyed was repugnant.

Yes, there had been other examples of love. Terry and Caro were one of them, but they were few and far between, and for Gabriel the very prospect of handing himself over to someone else was to be avoided at all costs.

He could identify with Helen's need for control because it was a trait he shared with her.

Maybe, down the line, he would contemplate marriage, which admittedly had certain advantages—who could maintain a revolving carousel of women for ever? But, as and when that time came, it would be a well-considered situation with a woman with whom the primary aim would be compatibility—two adults who got along. No highs and lows, no agonising and no vulnerability. Affection made a lot more sense than love, and even he knew that the time came when passion ran its course.

So the women in his life came and went and he never bothered to fight temptation when it came to sex. Two consenting adults made for a very happy equation. He never made promises he couldn't keep and never spoke about a future he knew wouldn't happen. Only now had the ground begun to shift under his feet.

It was frustrating to realise that he was somehow starting to think of Helen as more than just the quiet, understated woman who worked so well alongside him; beginning to see what he had successfully managed to ignore for three years. But he couldn't afford to think of her in any other terms. He would have to make sure his head did the thinking and his body did the obeying.

The hotel was quiet when he arrived back, his chauffeur-driven car noiselessly circling the courtyard to deliver him in front of the flamboyant flowering trees that guarded the reception and the various pathways that led to the clusters of cottages on the grounds.

It was still warm, although the sun was beginning to dip. He headed straight for his quarters, brushing past the exuberantly romantic canopy of trees, thinking ahead to what he could accomplish in the hours ahead.

He was barely looking left or right.

The romance of the setting was beginning to get on his nerves. His erstwhile girlfriend might have thought long and hard about finding the right place to seduce him into the sort of commitment he had no intention of making, and he might have found it reasonably charming, had she still been on the scene minus unreasonable demands. But, given the circumstances, all this lush foliage, mouth-watering scenery and tantalising shaded pathways were a nuisance. When his thoughts were all over the place, the last thing he needed was damn romance.

In the midst of brushing some blossoms from his shirt, he stilled at the faint sound of water, of splashing. Someone was swimming in the pool behind the cottages.

Gabriel hesitated.

But then curiosity got the better of him, and he was irritated with himself even as he followed the path that wound alongside the cottages. It nestled amidst stunted trees and over-sized flowering shrubbery in a way that had been artfully created to give the illusion of it being hewn from the rocks, stones and earth through which it threaded, rather than purposefully engineered by men in hard hats sitting in digger trucks.

He knew what he was expecting. He half-hoped that he was wrong; that the splashing, which was barely a sound quivering in the still air, came from other occupants eager to take advantage of the late-summer warmth and sunshine.

He emerged by the pool and stood completely still.

She was as graceful in the water as a fish, her slender body encased in a black one-piece, slicing through the blue-green, barely needing to tilt her head to draw breath.

Gabriel felt he had never seen anything like it.

How could dreary office suits and buttoned-up blouses conceal a body that was so slender and so perfectly proportioned? Even as she moved, he could make out strong, well-shaped legs, arms that carried definition and the curve of her narrow waist.

He breathed in sharply, unable to move forward but incapable of beating a retreat. Images that had been playing in his head coalesced into a reality that was a thousand times more alluring. Standing in the shade of overhanging trees, he watched and then flushed when she came to a stop by the side of the pool, her hand on the *faux* mossy ledge, and turned towards the cottages.

He should have walked away when he'd had the chance.

Too late.

Their eyes tangled and eventually he propelled himself forward, because heading towards her in a natural and easy manner seemed the better of two options, the other being shiftily skulking off in plain sight.

'I see you decided to try the pool,' he drawled, when he was within earshot.

The pool, shaped to resemble a very large pond, was dappled from the setting sun slanting through the overhanging trees.

Her hair was wet and clung to her cheeks and her skin was smooth and flawless.

'What are you doing here? I thought you were having dinner with your friends.'

'Work.' He pulled across one of the wooden chairs, largely the only concession to the fact that this was actually a swimming pool and not a natural body of water in the middle of a glade. He sat and promptly leaned forward, his arms resting on his thighs. 'Thought I'd cut short the evening and see if I could work through some of the details that still need ironing out. How's the water?'

'Please don't let me keep you if you've returned to work.'

'Maybe I'll join you. I haven't been in since I got here, and it's a nice evening for it.'

Damn, he couldn't take his eyes off her. How had he not paid more attention to just how huge her eyes were? How long, lush and dark her eyelashes? Or how her mouth was so beautifully full and defined?

'I was just getting out, as it happens.'

Helen could have kicked herself. What had possessed her to say that?

One minute she'd been swimming, loving the glide of cool water over her and the peaceful, noiseless silence of the pool. But the next, there he was, lounging against one of the trees, his hand indolently shoved in the pocket of his loose cream trousers, looking every inch the sophisticated billionaire.

Shock at seeing him had ripped through her, bringing her out in goose bumps. He'd walked towards the side of the pool and, the closer he'd come, the more her nervous system had plunged into disarray.

She felt exposed. Here in the deep end, she was treading water, one hand on the ledge to support herself. The pool might have been fashioned to replicate a pond, but the water was chlorinated and clear as crystal, and she was horribly aware of the distorted image of her swimsuit-clad body under the surface.

'Were you?'

'I…'

'I'm very sorry if I interrupted your enjoyment. Feel free to ignore me. I'll sit here and take the weight off before I head in to work. What did you do about dinner?'

'Gabriel, I haven't eaten yet and—and I'm just about to head in.'

'You haven't *eaten* yet?'

'Gabriel…'

'I blame myself!'

'What are you talking about?' Treading water whilst trying to ignore the movement of her body under the surface was exhausting but the man showed no sign of going anywhere.

'You're far too polite, Helen. There's no need to feel awkward about ordering room service or going to the restaurant to eat!'

'Whoever said anything about feeling awkward?'

'Of course, I'm just glad that you decided to drop the work routine for five minutes so that you could enjoy this pool—and, I must say, you seem to be a very strong swimmer. But I hope you weren't thinking of grabbing something from the mini-bar in the cottage and working after hours!'

Helen was beginning to feel a little cold now that she was no longer burning energy swimming. The light was fading fast and shadows were beginning to replace the dappling of the setting sun.

She began levering herself out, self-conscious and clumsy, feeling his dark eyes boring into her, and she was rudely brought to her senses when he reached out with his unbandaged hand and effortlessly hoisted her to her feet. He simultaneously stood up and she stumbled into him as she lost her balance, trying to sweep her hair from her eyes and extract her captured hand at one and the same time.

She reached out, flattened her palm against his chest and almost passed out. His tough, masculine body was as hard as steel, his chest tightly packed with well-honed muscle and, in his nearness, came the fragrant aroma of whatever woody aftershave he used.

For a fleeting second, she breathed him in, nostrils flaring, swept up in a moment of searing heat and a hot, sexual awareness that shocked and terrified her.

She raised alarmed eyes to his and was ensnared by the glittering, dark depths of his, and the way they drifted from hers to her mouth and lingered there. He reached and traced the contour of her mouth in a shockingly intimate gesture.

It lasted a second then he dropped his hand as she sprang back, almost stumbling again. But, instead of releasing her, he held her arm, although at least their bodies were further apart and her addled brain had a chance to clear.

'You okay?'

'Of course I am!'

'Good, because we don't need another invalid.' He held up his bandaged hand and waved it but his eyes were focused on her, deep, dark and riveting. And not obeying any of the parameters they had in place, trampling all over the work boundaries that were never, ever crossed.

Or was she just imagining that? Because, right now, her fevered senses could be getting up to who only knew what tricks of the imagination. She hadn't imagined the touch of his finger on her mouth, though. That was seared into her mind with the red-hot burn of a branding iron.

She was breathing fast, as if she'd been running a marathon.

'Let me go!' She yanked her hand away and he stepped back.

Gabriel had never felt tension like this in his life. The charge flowing between them was electric. She'd been in his head, sending his thoughts in a tailspin, and now here she was and every pore in his body yearned to touch.

'My apologies,' he said huskily. His voice was cool and controlled but his thoughts were all over the place, and he could feel the steady pain of his erection shamelessly pushing against the zip of his trousers.

Helen spun round and ducked to fetch her towel. The swimsuit was clammy against her body and she was aware of the tautness of her nipples against the damp fabric, stiff, sensitive and achingly responsive.

She took a few steady breaths and reminded herself that this was her boss. *Her boss!*

She would do well to remember *that* little technicality!

'I'll head in now.'

'Of course.' Gabriel turned and began heading away from the pool. He could *feel* her tripping alongside him, but he didn't dare look at her, because one more glance and that erection, which was thankfully beginning to subside, would barrel into life again. Had she noticed the bulge under the trousers? If so, she gave no sign.

He clenched his jaw. In his mind he saw the fall of her small breasts as she had leant to retrieve her towel from where she had hung it on the low branch of a tree by the side of the pool. What the hell had possessed him to touch her like that? It had lasted a second, but still—there was no excuse. Since when had he ever allowed his body to control his head?

He delivered her to her door and watched as she fumbled to fetch the key from the cloth bag she had taken to the pool.

An urgency to straighten that kink in their otherwise smooth relationship was suddenly overpowering and, before she stepped through the door and shut it on him, he placed his flattened palm on it and followed her through.

'What are you doing?'

Helen swivelled to face him and took a couple of steps back. She'd wrapped the towel around her waist but was conscious of her upper half and the scant cover provided by the swimsuit. She didn't want to think about it, but she was well aware that her cleavage was on display, such as it was, the shadow dipping into the V of the swimsuit.

She folded her arms and stared at him, heart thumping and mouth going dry. He'd never looked at her like this. His dark eyes were narrowed with intent. She longed for the safety of her work clothes, her laptop in its neat little case, an office chair in front of a desk—a great, big desk which would provide much-needed distance between them, a much-needed physical barrier, reminding them of their roles.

Reminding *her* of *her* role—because right now she was suffocating from the weight of his presence. Even when she'd been engaged to George—had thought he was the one for her—he had never made her feel like this. He had never made her feel as though she was going to burst out of her own skin, as though every square inch of her body had suddenly been sensitised.

She hated Gabriel for making her feel things she didn't want to feel. Was it just this damned place with its heavy scents, leafy glades and fairy lights all over the place? Was this what had stirred a recklessness inside her, or had that recklessness been waiting in the shadows for just the right time to appear? And, if it had, why on earth did it have to manifest itself with this particular man?

But she knew why. There'd been those little sidelong glances over the years…the hum of electricity when he'd got too close… She'd hidden behind her prim work clothes, kept her guard up, but nothing had been able to stop her eyes from wandering and her mind from playing games.

'Please leave,' she said tightly.

Gabriel raked his fingers through his hair.

'Back there, at the pool…'

'I don't want to talk about this.'

'I—I touched you and that was inexcusable. I have no idea what came over me.'

'I don't know what you're talking about. I'm beginning to feel cold and I think it's time you went back to your—your room. Didn't you say you returned early so that you could do some work?'

'Helen…'

'No!'

They stared at one another and the silence was so thick, she could almost hear the wild beating of her heart.

'Nothing happened there. *Nothing.*'

'If that's how you want to play it,' Gabriel muttered, 'Then it's not a problem. Nothing did happen there but, just in case you were to revisit that conclusion, I want to assure you that…' he breathed in deeply '…that nothing will ever happen. That… I don't know what that was, but I value you too much to ever jeopardise your position as my employee.'

Helen knew that she should breath a sigh of relief that normal play had been resumed but she was still in another place and his reassurances, instead of relaxing her, made her feel angry and defiant.

He'd made an easy assumption that he could apologise his way out of that touch, the fleeting touch that had sent her into a panicked tailspin—that he could shrug and smile a crooked, bemused smile and muse that why he'd succumbed to that brief, out-of-character gesture was a mystery. *What the heck had that been about?* he would have asked himself with genuine puzzlement.

Of course he'd have no idea what that had all been about! He'd let his eyes wander over her swimsuit-clad body—and she didn't get why, because she certainly wasn't the sort of woman he would usually be attracted to. He'd had a momentary lapse in concentration because she'd taken him by surprise—because she wasn't in one of her usual working outfits, which always seemed to amuse him. And, naturally, he hadn't hesitated because he was a guy who was utterly assured in his ability to attract. It probably wouldn't have occurred to him that he might get knocked back.

Instinct trumped common sense. The urge to step out of the box, for once, was overwhelming.

'Thank you for that,' she said stiffly, biting down that temptation because, at the end of the day, she worked for him and discretion was certainly going to be the better part of valour.

But it was a struggle.

'I mean it, Helen. I respect you. I respect your boundaries. Like I said, I had no idea…' He shuffled and looked away, frowning, for a couple of seconds. 'I don't know what to say.'

'Nothing,' Helen muttered in a driven undertone, her small hands clenched into angry fists. 'Don't say anything.'

He ignored her. 'Let's just say we put this behind us and move on. I just wanted to set the record straight because I don't want you to feel uncomfortable, either here or when we return to London. You have my word.'

Helen gritted her teeth. She didn't know how they had managed to arrive at this quagmire but she felt as though, having got here, she either waded through it and emerged on the other side by standing up to him or she allowed herself to sink without defending herself. The latter option made sense but the former was irresistible.

'You have an ego the size of a planet, do you know that?'

'Come again?'

'You took me by surprise,' she conceded hotly, colour flaring into her cheeks. 'But you don't have to make a big deal of it. You don't have to bend over backwards to reassure me that it won't be repeated. I'm not going to shrivel up in trepidation whenever I'm with you. You're not my type, Gabriel. I work for you. You're my boss and the reason we work well together is that I'm not like—like—all those women who can't get enough of you.'

'I merely wanted to reassure you—'

'I'm not attracted to you!'

'No, I never said you were,' he muttered. 'Did I?'

For a couple of treacherous seconds, Helen was almost tempted to smile. Firstly, she'd never seen her boss so discomfited before, and secondly, the very thought of someone not finding him attractive was obviously a concept he hadn't quite taken on board. His mouth was saying one thing, his awkward scowl and dark flush were saying another.

'Want the truth?' she continued, side-stepping the diplomacy she had been determined to hang onto. 'I don't approve of your behaviour with women.'

'Sorry?'

'I know I probably shouldn't be saying this but, now that we're clearing the air, I feel I should make my position completely clear so that you don't have any misunderstandings.'

'I'm all ears.'

'I don't have a lot of time for guys who play the field.' She crossed her arms and watched as his mouth fell open and he stared at her with narrow-eyed incredulity. His quiet, obedient secretary had opinions! She felt a surge of satisfaction, which was far more powerful than any fear she felt at saying things she might live to regret. 'You think I'm helpless. Or maybe hopeless would be a better description.'

'That's ridiculous!'

'Is it? You think I'm so gullible that one passing touch from you and I risk falling apart at the seams from now on. You think I'm utterly wet behind the ears when it comes to the opposite sex!'

'Are you?'

'No, I'm not! I was once engaged, if you really want to know!'

Gabriel's mouth fell open and he stared. Helen bitterly regretted every word that had passed her lips. All her caution had gone down the drain in a single explosive confession.

'What happened? You never breathed a word…'

'Because it's none of your business, Gabriel! The fact is, I can handle what happened just then! You needn't fear that I'm going to go to pieces!'

'What happened? Didn't it work out?'

'Again, none of your business! I told you that because—because I wanted to reassure you that I just don't go for guys like you. So, there—we can now just consider this matter over and done with.'

'If you say so.' Gabriel shot her a slanting look.

'I do! So, if you'll excuse me…?'

'Of course.'

He began heading for the door. Every rebellious word she had uttered had whetted his appetite to hear more. An engagement? The depths he had glimpsed were now even more dangerously compelling.

He wasn't her type. Then who was? The guy she'd been engaged to? Was she still broken-hearted? Who the hell had the guy been? She'd probably been out of his league. It took a strong guy to deal with a strong woman and not be intimidated.

He'd done the decent thing and rushed in to reassure her that there was no need for her to be nervous around him. He'd laid it on thick about respecting her, and he'd been one hundred per cent honest. What had he expected her response to be? She might be reserved by nature, but she had opinions, and he knew that. When he replayed his little speech in his head, he could hear how patronising he might have sounded, even though that hadn't been his intention.

That said, he hadn't expected her to voice her opinions with such heat. He wanted to quiz her on what she'd said, prolong the conversation, find out more about her past.

Dangerous territory.

She'd laid it down—nothing had happened. He would go

along with that because allowing curiosity to get the better of him was not something he could afford to do. He shakily accepted that conclusion.

'Tomorrow…' He turned to her, one hand on the door, halfway out.

'I'll have everything ready and on hand to print for signatures. I'll make sure those niggling discrepancies are highlighted and ironed out. When Mr Diaz is ready to sign off, everything will be in place. Will we meet at the same time—eleven?'

She tilted her head to one side. Her eyes were cool and remote. The professional hat was back in place and Gabriel could scarcely reconcile his crisply spoken secretary with the woman who had stilled for a second as he'd touched her mouth; or with the woman who had let her fires rage at him for temporarily putting her nose out of joint. The woman who had been hiding a past from him he would never have expected.

Was he really not her type?

That physical response—surely it hadn't been one-sided? Yes, he'd touched her, but she'd responded—and it hadn't just been a case of being taken by surprise, as she'd claimed.

Did her aggressive denial of any attraction conceal a forbidden urge to touch him? Was that something she'd carefully hidden over the months and years, something she refused to acknowledge? Or was this his ego talking?

Did the lady protest too much?

It was one thing to have a clear idea of what the perfect guy might look like, and maybe she'd had that perfect guy before it had all fallen apart for whatever reason. But he was no more, and who knew? Maybe she was drawn against her will to the imperfect one…

Pointless speculation, of course.

'Eleven it is.' He mock-saluted her and looked at her from

under sooty lashes. 'It's all coming along very nicely. I don't foresee anything cropping up to throw this off course so, with a good following wind, you'll be back in Blighty the day after tomorrow and you can put all of this behind you...'

CHAPTER FOUR

'RIGHT.' GABRIEL SLAMMED shut his laptop and pushed himself back from the conference table at which were seated the five crucial players responsible for fine-tuning all the nuts and bolts on the deal he had just concluded. There were two highly qualified accountants, one specialising in tax, and two company lawyers to make sure every detail was in place.

And his secretary, sitting to the right of him, diligently taking minutes and printing out every piece of paper still awaiting Diaz's signature. Every so often, in her low, modulated voice, she pointed out things that might be questionable because, as she explained, Arturio wasn't au fait with modern-day tech-speak and altering the language slightly might work better for him.

This was how they worked—in tandem. Everything, was back in place, Gabriel thought, and all was right in the world.

Except…

He couldn't get rid of that memory of her from two days ago when he'd surprised her swimming in the pool…and then after, the blazing fire in her eyes when she'd told him what she thought of his lifestyle choices. And the proud tilt of her head when she'd informed him in a cool, husky voice that he wasn't her type, that she could look after herself, that she'd been engaged. She hadn't just broken through the neat little barriers she'd built up between them, the ones he'd taken care to keep in place for fear of losing her, she'd comprehensively obliterated them, wiped her hands in satisfaction and then promptly announced that the matter had been settled, to be put behind them and forgotten for ever.

He'd made sure not to utter a word about what had happened. He had seen her the day after and they had resumed their working relationship as though that blip had never taken place.

She was polite, friendly and, of course, as efficient as always… But, when he slid his eyes to the side, he could see her smooth fingers resting on the keyboard of her laptop, as though she might be on the verge of typing something, and he had to stop his imagination from going into overdrive. If he shifted just a few inches, he would be able to brush against her arm. He was desperate to know more about her and equally desperate to steer clear of asking.

'I'm seeing Arturio tomorrow,' he began, standing up and, on cue, everyone followed suit, packing away stuff and hurriedly shuffling to their feet. 'And everything is now ready for his paw print on the dotted line. I don't foresee any hitches, and that's down to a joint effort here. I want to thank you all for your hard work…'

He looked around him. They were a couple of guys in their fifties, serious and highly experienced in complex buyouts, and the other two in their early thirties, fresh-faced and keen. He'd noticed the way those two had both slyly glanced at Helen every so often. One of them was married, with a ring on his finger. Hadn't stopped his eyes from wandering Gabriel had gritted his teeth and said nothing. Of course.

'It's…' he glanced at his watch '…not yet five. I suggest we celebrate with some champagne and an early dinner.'

There were murmurs of consent as Gabriel knew there would be. When he issued invitations, whatever the nature of the invitation, acceptance was generally a given.

'If you don't mind…'

Helen's polite voice right next to him brought him to an abrupt standstill.

'I'll give it a miss. I fly out tomorrow and I still have packing to get through. I'm sorry I'll miss seeing Arturio.'

He turned and frowned, and she smiled serenely back at him as she continued busying herself, stuffing her laptop into the bag and faffing with the lightweight coat she'd neatly draped over the back of her chair. Her working wardrobe was firmly in place. Forget about the casual look he'd recommended—she wore a knee-length blue skirt, blue-and-white-striped shirt tucked into the waistband of the skirt and flat canvas shoes.

What had her fiancé been like—safe, steady? Wouldn't she see a guy like that as the opposite of him? Safe, steady... dared he say, a little on the dull side?

'You're part of this team,' he said grittily, in a low undertone.

'I'll make sure everything's ready by tomorrow, so all Arturio has to do is sign on the dotted line.'

'Helen...'

'My flight's in the evening, so there'll be time if I have to implement any changes.'

'If you're sure,' Gabriel said gruffly, knowing very well that she'd cleverly put him on the spot. He shuffled, raked his fingers through his hair and decided that it made no difference whether his secretary came or not.

Better if she didn't!

She was suddenly a distraction on a blockbuster scale and, the faster he got over that, the better. He might just tack on an extra week out here, catch up with Terry and his wife and check out the vineyards again. He could spend more time with Arturio when he saw him—quality time, nothing about vineyards or work.

He had asked about his family, which had been like asking about strangers, in a way, yet oddly satisfying. He'd had some pieces of a past he'd never known slotted into place. He'd rather like more of those pieces slotted in. He was beginning to find out what it meant to have a family, even if it was late in the day. It meant more to him than he could have imagined. So, yes, he and Arturio—it would be good.

It would also give his body time to recover from its unexpected response to a woman who was off-limits. He would make it back to London with his head screwed back on.

'I'm sure.'

'Come on, Helen…' A coaxing plea came from one of the young lawyers and Gabriel's teeth snapped together at the smile she flashed the guy—half-distracted, half-amused, full-wattage.

'Looks like you have an admirer,' he said tightly, dropping his voice.

'Nice, isn't it?' She was already making her way to the door, saying the usual goodbyes, shaking hands and laughing at something or other one of the older guys said, something about 'should she ever need a job this side of the pond'.

How had he not noticed just how dynamic she was in her own, very special, low-key way?

'He's a lawyer,' Gabriel returned, standing back with her while the rest filed out of the conference room, talking amongst themselves. 'I'd take what the guy says with a pinch of salt.'

'Thank you for your concern.' Her face fell into a wry smile. 'You're actually not telling me anything I didn't already know.'

Gabriel smiled back at her and there was a moment of perfectly shared compatibility.

Helen's breath caught in her throat. If she took away the surge of sexual attraction that had sprung up between them, and took away all these weird, disturbing interactions that had muddied the calm water between them, and what she got was this—the sort of easy familiarity where words were unnecessary and where entire conversations could be had in just one exchanged glance.

'You must be looking forward to having some time with Arturio, Gabriel.'

He'd told her of the family connection and now he flushed, before admitting seriously, 'I am, as it happens. Might make some time after everything's done and dusted to spend a little time with him.'

'You should.'

'Thank you for sharing your opinion with me.' But he was half-smiling. 'And, now we're in sharing mode, tell me what happened between you and your fiancé.'

'Gabriel…'

'What was his name?'

'People are waiting for you.'

'Not that I can see. Well?'

'George. His name was George.'

'What happened? And I can see that you want to tell me that it's none of my business.'

'Well, it isn't, as it happens.' But she was tempted. Barriers eroded, doors opened—what harm could it do? It was hardly a state secret. 'It didn't work out. We were very young and, before we could tie the knot, he came to his senses and broke it off.' She gazed away with a little frown. 'And, if he hadn't, I would have.'

Gabriel didn't say anything. Her reticence made sense. He wanted to pursue the conversation and ask her for details, but she was right when she'd said that the rest of the crew would be waiting for him.

The rest of the crew, including the guy with his eyes on

stalks. Had her thoughts begun to drift to resuming her single life, with her ex firmly behind her? Had the weird romance of the place turned her thoughts away from work and onto play? The place had certainly got to him. Had it got to her as well?

'Lost for words, Gabriel?' She had an insane desire to pull the tiger's tail. 'Maybe I needed a little break like this. It's certainly been very relaxing, having a handsome young guy flirt with me. Course, I told him I wasn't going to be here long enough to go out with him.'

She felt her skin prickle as again she ventured into foreign territory. She told herself that there was nothing outrageous about this conversation. It only felt outrageous because of the working relationship they had cultivated over the years, one in which personal things had seldom been mentioned.

'Who knows? Maybe if I'd been out here a little longer, I might have been inclined to go on that date he asked me on.'

'Go on a *date*? The guy asked you on a date?'

'It's what single people do. You should know that better than anyone else. Don't look so horrified, Gabriel.'

Gabriel relaxed and shot her a slow smile. 'It certainly is what single people do, Helen; and if I look a little startled maybe it's because I'm suddenly seeing a side to you you've been so busy keeping under wraps before. Maybe I'm liking this new side to you.'

Helen blushed and tried to recover lost ground because his soft, lazy drawl made her skin tingle and reminded her of how his finger had felt on her mouth.

'I should go.' She backed away. 'I have a lot to do.'

Gabriel raised his eyebrows. He was still grinning, a wicked grin that got to all parts of her. 'If you're quite sure you won't join us…'

'I'll see you tomorrow, Gabriel. Let me know if there are any amendments you need me to do before I submit everything.'

He watched her vanish through the revolving door into the summer sunshine, as slender and graceful as a ballerina.

Drinks and an early dinner didn't hold a huge amount of appeal, but he had to show his thanks to the hard work the guys had put in. He would go beyond and arrange a weekend for they and their families—somewhere suitably luxurious. He would doubtless use their skills again at some point and loyalty was a great thing.

He thought of one of those guys sneakily making a pass at his secretary and it made his teeth snap together. Yet she was perfectly correct—he *had* urged her to relax, to let her hair down, and if her back story had come as a shock it was only because he hadn't credited her with such a riveting one.

Broken engagements, shattered hearts… What next?

She'd never given him the slightest inclination that she was somehow trapped in a physical deep-freeze. He'd just read the outward signs and come up with his own, as it turned out incorrect, interpretation of the woman who worked so diligently and uncomplainingly for him.

And he was honest enough to admit to himself there might be just the tiniest bit of egotism behind those assumptions. He knew the power of his own personal magnetism. He'd cultivated it from a young age, flung into a boarding school on the opposite side of the world when he'd just been a kid. He'd learned that, to avoid being bullied, side-lined or mocked as an outsider with a foreign accent, it was imperative that he was accepted and, beyond acceptance, that he was admired and, ultimately, feared and respected.

He'd been clever, athletic and had learned to charm. It had been a very successful front for those feelings of hurt buried deep inside him. The hurt at how his wealthy parents had treated him had felt a lot like abandonment.

It was something he'd taken for granted over the years and he wondered, now, whether that was why he'd rushed to foregone conclusions.

Had he thought that his perfect secretary wouldn't be able to resist the occasional remark? Wouldn't be able to resist the force of his personality when he'd initially tried to tease casual chit-chat out of her? He hated to think that his ego was as big as she'd informed him she found it, in no uncertain terms, but he had to concede that there had surely been a reason he hadn't just accepted the obvious. She was a sexy woman with a very healthy personal life who just didn't want him involved in it on any level.

Especially seeing that she'd written him off as a womaniser who played the field—probably from the very beginning, he figured.

He was half-occupied with those thoughts during the course of drinks and dinner, which was much earlier than he would usually eat, because the older guys needed to get back to their homes.

All were instantly grateful at the suggestion about a long weekend with partners and, when he magnanimously told them to agree on where they wanted to go and his secretary would sort it out, they beamed from ear to ear. 'Something beachy in Mexico' was suggested as they gathered their belonging to leave.

He called Helen the second he was on his way back.

'A couple of things to discuss…'

'Sure.'

Helen listened while he discussed two points belatedly raised over drinks, neither of which were in any way crucial to the deal, but both of which could be sorted in five minutes with an alteration to some of the wording.

She'd returned to the cottage with the sun still shining and so little packing to do that she'd finished it in under five minutes.

She should have stayed. She'd shared a bit of herself with him but then, all of a fluster, she'd made a point of leaving and afterwards had felt a bit of a fool. Now here he was, coolly talking about work, because the fluster had been all on her part…

'There's also a little trip I want you to arrange for me,' she surfaced to hear him saying. 'A weekend somewhere. I'll fill you in on the details at a later date, but a beach somewhere expensive in Mexico looks like a likely candidate.

'This can all wait, to be honest, until tomorrow morning,' he added.

Helen had frozen at the mention of Mexico and a weekend away. That had all the hallmarks of one of his romantic rendezvous and she wondered who the latest blonde might be. Surely not…?

There was a sour taste in her mouth when she thought about it and it horrified her to think that that sour taste was plain, old-fashioned jealousy. She'd opened the door a crack and now look at the result!

'No,' she said sharply, 'It's no bother for me to sort everything out this evening. It's not even eight yet.'

'Don't you want to relax on your last night here?'

'I can come to the meeting room; just let me know what time you'd like me there.'

'Helen, there's no need for such formality. You don't have to take notes. I can just verbally brief you. I really shouldn't have interrupted your evening but I'm on my way back now. Probably have a drink on the veranda at the cottage. It was a ludicrously early dinner, but the older guys wanted to head off.'

'I'll come to your cottage. You can fill me in. It's no bother at all.'

How had it been professional to scuttle off like a scalded cat earlier? Did she want him to get the impression that he got under her skin? That he made her feel hot and bothered? She'd told him about her broken engagement because she'd wanted to point out that she wasn't an ingénue, utterly clueless about the ways of the world. So why was she behaving like one? Why was she letting him get to her like this?

She had to play it cool. She had worked late into the night in his office many times, with a takeout between them as they had pored over whatever thorny issues required completion to a deadline. Twice, she had been summoned to his magnificent house in Holland Park, and had worked in his home office there for a couple of hours, because he'd had everything set up for complex co-ordination of external meetings on different time zones.

She'd never run scared on any of those occasions! Why should it bother her now to sit outside with him and go through stuff for half an hour? To be her usual unflappable, reliable self?

'Fine. Meet me there in half an hour. That suit?'

'Yes,' she said firmly. 'That suits me fine.'

Gabriel was having a whisky when he heard Helen knock and sauntered out to open the door to her.

He wasn't sure why he'd called her. Nothing needed to be done as a matter of urgency. That said, as he pulled open the door he was glad he'd made the call, because the evening suddenly seemed a little less insipid.

She'd changed into a pair of faded, light jeans and wore a

tee shirt that hung loosely to the waist so that, if she raised her arms, he would be able to see a sliver of skin.

And, of course, she'd come armed with her trusty laptop. Gabriel didn't mind. He stepped aside and she swept past him straight into the small living area before spinning round to face him.

'So…'

At her brisk, no-nonsense voice, he smiled and was suddenly at ease in himself.

'Drink? I'm on the veranda at the back. Splendid view, even with the sun fading. They've done clever things with the lighting so that it's somehow possible to see for quite some distance before everything disappears into fields and open land.'

He spun round on his heels and she followed but, instead of following him out, she plonked her bag and belongings on the table in the living area and took up residence on one of the chairs, ready and poised to take notes.

A drink? A romantic view from his veranda? A twilight vista studded with fairy lights in the trees and twinkling stars in a velvet-dark sky? *No, thanks.* Table in the living area bathed in bright overhead lighting? *Yes, please.*

He got the message and sat opposite her, but the way he sprawled in the chair somehow detracted from the businesslike atmosphere she was aiming for.

He talked to her about the tweaks she would have to make to the wording of the agreement, which would then be perfect and waiting only for final approval from Arturio.

It was straightforward.

Helen relaxed.

'And,' she said, tweaks done, 'You mentioned something about Mexico?' Her voice was clipped as she reached into her laptop bag for the slim notebook she always kept there.

'Ah, yes.'

Gabriel sipped his drink and eyed her over the rim of the glass, noting the faint tinge of colour pinking her cheeks.

'If you tell me the sort of thing you have in mind, I can make the necessary arrangements.'

'I've never actually been to Mexico,' he said, dumping his squat glass on the table and then relaxing back with his hands folded behind his head. 'Don't suppose *you* have?'

'I haven't, as it happens,' Helen returned politely. 'Although I'm struggling to see what that has to do with anything.'

Gabriel decided that he very much liked this new version of his secretary—polite but a different sort of polite from what had been on offer before. A more nuanced and *impolite* polite, if there was such a thing. The politeness of someone who'd opened up and probably regretted it. The politeness of someone who had tossed him titbits of her past which had really inflamed his senses. It challenged something in him and was as invigorating as the fizz of expensive champagne after a diet of soda water.

'If you had to go there—for a long weekend—what sort of thing would you say would appeal to you?'

It was a provocative statement...and yet Gabriel didn't regret asking the question because he enjoyed the way her colour deepened, and the way she suddenly fiddled with the ring on her finger and then lowered her eyes to stare at the blank page of the notebook on her lap.

What was going through her head?

He knew what was going through her head. *He knew women. And he knew her.*

He was treading on thin ice, and he had no intention of continuing the trek to see what was on the other side.

'Beaches?' he prompted, voice oozing suggestiveness, dark eyes lazy, slumberous and amused. 'Sun setting when the violet hour comes on waves crashing on sand on an empty coastline? The distant sound of coconut trees swaying on a night breeze?'

'I had no idea you were so poetic,' Helen said shortly.

'I sometimes surprise myself,' Gabriel murmured in response.

'Well, I'm sorry, but I can't help you on this. If you want to take your new girlfriend somewhere romantic, then you'll have to come up with the destination by yourself, and of course I'll make all the necessary arrangements.'

'Oh?' Gabriel's eyebrows shot up. 'Is that what you think I'm doing—new girlfriend? How fast do you think I work? That's very cynical of you, Helen, I must say.'

'Why else would you want a romantic getaway in Mexico? Look, I don't care what you do, but please don't expect me to have input into the itinerary.'

'Would it bother you?'

'Yes, of course I would rather not do that!'

'Why?' he queried softly.

'Because...'

Helen looked at him, their eyes collided and she suddenly felt the ground collapse from under her feet. Those eyes, the amused tilt of his head, the sexuality emanating from him in waves that made her feel giddy... She found it hard to think in a straight line.

'Because?'

'Because that's not in my brief, Gabriel, and you know it isn't. So don't...don't...'

'I absolutely agree one hundred per cent, even though you've never complained before about it not being in your brief!' he retorted, standing to fetch himself another drink and then returning to the table. But he perched against it, drink in his hand, sipping and looking at her with the sort of focused intensity that would make any woman's head turn to mush.

'You do?'

'I wasn't talking about you arranging a weekend for me and a woman!' He dismissed the notion with a wave of his hand.

'Then, I don't understand.'

'The guys who were working on the deal—I told them, as a reward for some admirable focused, precision work, I would treat them to a long weekend, partners included, at a place of their choice. They came up with Mexico.'

Helen stared at him for a few seconds in open-mouthed silence.

He'd been toying with her. He'd introduced that conversation about a weekend in Mexico to…what?…gauge her reaction? He was clever when it came to the opposite sex. She'd told him that that silly business of a couple of evenings ago was nothing, nothing at all, but had he believed her? She'd let him into a sliver of her past so that he could see that she was a woman well able to deal with emotions, but had he believed her?

She snapped shut the notebook, seething with anger, and flew to her feet. She was stuffing everything into her laptop when she felt his hand on her wrist, a gentle pressure that made her skin burn.

He knew that he had an effect on her, whatever the heck she'd said, she thought in panic. It defied all common sense but she found the man attractive and now, over here, the door between them had opened a crack and he had been given an opportunity to peer through, to see that weakness inside her.

She snatched her bag from the table and stormed towards the door of the cottage.

'Helen…'

'This isn't funny.' She whipped round to look at him and

wished she hadn't because, even fuming as she was, she was still overwhelmed by his beauty, by the force of his personality, by the dark, mesmeric depths of his eyes. By a pull that was rooted in much more than superficial physical attraction, whether she faced up to that or not.

'No, it's not.'

She had moved towards the door but he was blocking her way out and, knowing that, he shifted because he didn't want her to feel cornered.

He really didn't know what the hell he'd been playing at. He just knew that he found her physically compelling and that attraction had wreaked havoc with his usual ferocious self-control.

'I could apologise till the end of time but you should know that I find you physically attractive.'

'No! I don't want to hear this!'

'Because it's out of order? Or because you're terrified that it's returned?'

'Gabriel, I don't know what's happened over here…'

'Life got in the way of common sense. Neither of us can take back what has been shared. I want you.'

'You can't say stuff like that.'

'What would you do if I kissed you?'

'I would… I would…'

'Kiss me right back?'

He leant into her and Helen knew what was going to happen next. He was going to kiss her and she wanted him to: wanted that with every ounce of her being; wanted to feel the coolness of his mouth heating her up; wanted to feel his touch rouse her even further. She was so wet for him right now that her mind was alive with images of his hand down there, cupping her wetness, exploring her with his fingers.

She stood on tiptoe, her eyelids fluttering, and put her

hand behind his neck to draw him down to her, losing herself in the sweet taste of his mouth as it met hers with a hunger that matched her own.

She stifled a cry of pure, forbidden pleasure.

Their tongues meshed and he propelled her back against the door, breathing hard, his hand contouring her waist and pushing up under her top, finding her breast sheathed in its cotton bra and caressing it until she wanted to wrap her legs around him and have him take her right here, back to the door.

He pushed the bra down, his mouth never leaving hers, found her nipple and she whimpered with uncontrollable pleasure. She wanted nothing more than for his mouth to leave hers, to move to her breasts, to suckle on her nipple.

The knock on the door was so shocking that it took a few seconds to penetrate the haze of lust, but it did, and Helen scrambled back and looked at him with wide, horrified eyes.

Neither said a word and there was another knock, this time a little harder. Gabriel raked his fingers through his hair and stared at her, but then he opened the door a fraction—enough for him to see who was out there and for Helen to hear them. The soft, confused Italian accent apologised for dropping by.

She straightened herself, breathed in deep and stepped around Gabriel, because she couldn't hide in the bathroom, duck under the bed or try an escape route out back.

It was perfectly acceptable for them to be doing some work together. She tried a smile as she met Arturio's gaze, but she could feel red-faced guilt stamped all over her face. She had met him a couple of times. He was as old-fashioned as they came and the look he was giving them both now bore that out.

'Have I interrupted something? Please accept my apologies.'

'Work!' Helen's eyes glassed over. 'It's—great to see you.' She tugged at the tee shirt as she felt the blazing heat in her cheeks.

'You two… My dear, I didn't know.' He turned to Gabriel. 'You should have mentioned that you were going out, Gabriel!'

'We're…we're…' Her voice petered out…

Arturio's surprise had turned to delight: he and Helen had hit it off the first time they'd had met months ago.

She glanced across at Gabriel and he returned her gaze but only briefly, for a few seconds. He knew what she was going to say. The truth—that they weren't going out.

But then, what were they doing? She was in his room and any idiot could see from the flare of hectic colour in her face that, whatever they'd been doing, going over the books hadn't been top of the list.

A little bit of 'hanky-panky'… Arturio would get it. He might be a traditional Italian family man but he was also a man of honour and, if he disapproved of a little bit of 'hanky-panky', then it wouldn't stand in the way of their deal.

Or would it? There was nothing wrong with fooling around between two consenting adults although, frankly, that brief moment hadn't felt like it at all. Not as far as his definition of it went. In fact, several months with his ex had felt more like fooling around than ten seconds with his secretary… What was that all about?

For the first time in his adult life, Gabriel was lost for words. Realisation surged through him with force, a realisation of how much he wanted this old man's approval, of how much he wanted this deal…and of just how much this deal was more than simply the purchase of some vineyards that belonged to a distant relative.

Gabriel had had no contact with any other distant relatives on either of his parents' sides. Only children, both of them and he an only child—their lineage fading away because it hadn't been looked after with love and respect. His self-centred, self-obsessed parents had flown the nest and never looked back. And he had flown even further, leaving America at eleven, by which point he'd had nothing to do with any Italian relatives. He had never given much thought to his relatives in Italy, or anywhere, for that matter.

But then he had decided to expand his vineyards and thoughts of his native land had seeped through his general indifference. He had targeted the region where he had been born. Had that been a subconscious urge to form links with a past he had never known? Maybe. Maybe it had been a whimsical link, but then fate had stepped in, and the link had developed a solidity he could never have predicted.

He liked, respected and admired Arturio. He looked forward to getting to know him better over time. He wanted to meet all those family members, many of whom worked in the vineyards in some capacity or other.

His parents had ditched their past because the present had been way more interesting to them. He wanted to be a different man to them.

Deep inside, he knew that Arturio would be disappointed in a guy who fooled around with his secretary. Disappointed with a guy who made fooling around with women his stock in trade because he wasn't interested in committing. He shifted uncomfortably as parallels formed in his head, parallels with his parents, who had shunned committing to parenthood just as he shunned committing to anything beyond work and making money.

His priorities were ones that would be alien to the old man looking at him with a question in his eyes.

Helen stared at this big, powerful, self-assured man as he raked his fingers through his hair and struggled to find the right words to say that would somehow rescue the situation from sounding tawdry and distasteful.

She had never seen Gabriel vulnerable before, but he was vulnerable now. Had he ever in his life been at the mercy of his emotions? Standing there, did he even recognise that that was what was happening?

She felt sure Arturio wasn't going to pull out of the deal because he disliked the conduct of the guy buying his vineyards, but something would be lost to Gabriel in the process—perhaps a relationship he had never foreseen but had grown to want, whether he could admit that or not.

Arturio was a passport, of sorts, to the sort of family life he hadn't had, from the little she had read between the lines.

She took a deep breath and smiled at Arturio.

'Yes, Arturio, we're going out.' She smiled. 'We work together, so we haven't been shouting from the rooftops, and it's early days yet.'

She wondered what Gabriel was thinking. Was he shocked? More unexpected behaviour from his predictable secretary! It was oddly gratifying to think that. Besides, the gesture had made her feel pretty good. She would be gone the following day and this inconsequential little white lie would, at least, allow him to follow the path that had unexpectedly opened up to him.

She cherished the bond with her father. She had no idea what life would be like without him and without the various members of her extended family they saw on a regular basis. It touched something in her that Gabriel could be moved by the unexpected family connection he had discovered. It showed a side of him that was poignantly human, a side he guarded so well, despite his apparent openness when it came to his varied and chequered sex life.

She slid a sideways glance at him and then shivered as he

reached to rest his hand on her shoulder, a touch that made her body hum in pleasured response.

For just a split second, she wondered whether the recklessness that had been washing over her ever since she had arrived in this magical place was quite as harmless as she'd imagined.

But then she reassured herself that this was just a simple favour she had done. She had grasped the situation and acted accordingly because…because…

Her mind skittered away from the thought that what she felt for her boss might be more than just physical attraction.

It settled on the more harmless conclusion that she had acted like a friend because, after all, weren't they friends at the end of the day? She'd helped him out as a friend.

CHAPTER FIVE

'YOU DIDN'T HAVE to do that...'

They were still standing outside. Arturio had made exclamations of delight, profuse congratulations and a thousand apologies for showing up unannounced but, 'Isabella insisted on spending one night at one of the cottages because they looked so romantic!'. He had now vanished back to whichever cottage they had managed to secure for the night.

Gabriel might have mentioned where he was staying over the phone, when Fifi had made the arrangements, never thinking that a few words thrown into a conversation would have the repercussions that they had.

Now, he stared down at Helen's upturned face, her fine bone structure highlighted by the twinkling fairy lights strung everywhere, which had switched on as the sun had disappeared.

He was disconcerted to think how easily she had read him and how smoothly she had rescued him from a situation he hadn't anticipated. Had she somehow known just how much this whole deal meant to him? How much he had ended up investing in a family he'd previously never given a passing thought to?

Did the woman know him that well?

It was an unsettling thought and he abruptly decided to focus on the basics and not allow his mind to start wandering too far off the lead.

'No, I didn't.'

Then why did you? was the question he fought against asking, because the answer might not be one he wanted to hear. It was one thing to have affairs with women who didn't come close to getting into his head. It was another to look at this woman and realise that she might be the one person who did.

'But thank you for the spontaneous gesture,' he drawled, drawing back slightly. 'The deal isn't signed off yet and we both know how much I'd like to get my hands on that vineyard.' He paused, clenched his jaw and averted his eyes from hers. 'A bonus is definitely on the cards for you, Helen, and it'll be a generous one.'

'That's not why I did it,' Helen said quietly. 'I don't care about getting a bonus.'

'Maybe you were just on a high after what happened between us,' he suggested in a roughened, wicked undertone.

'It's not always about—the physical, Gabriel.'

'I know.' He raked his fingers through his hair and shook his head. 'At any rate,' he said gruffly, 'thank you.' He meant it—and yet he would have rescued the situation somehow. She had cleverly stepped in but he hadn't needed her. 'Need' was not something in his psyche.

He rushed into speech. 'It's getting cold out here. You—you should head in. Last day tomorrow. No need to do anything at all. Enjoy the place. Go into town. Clear your head.'

Helen realised that actually he was the one who needed to clear his head. Hers felt fine. She'd succumbed to the moment and she didn't regret it. A little less comfortable was what she and Gabriel had been doing when they'd been interrupted.

Did she regret that? Since the business with her broken engagement, she'd stuffed her sexuality in a box and pretended that it didn't exist. Working for Gabriel, it had been all the more imperative she never acknowledge what her own body might feel like were it to be aroused because, somewhere at the back of her mind, she accepted that her boss could very well be the guy to show her.

She was so used to caution ruling her life that the very thought of letting herself go to something that was bigger than her was inconceivable. But out here the ground had shifted and she'd opened the door to temptation. She'd let him touch her because she'd wanted it—and she'd rescued him from an awkward situation just then with Arturio because he got to her in all sorts of ways that weren't altogether physical.

He was a physical guy whose brain travelled on a one-way track but that wasn't her.

Confusion and trepidation tore into her. What would he do if he started thinking that she had feelings for him? Did she have feelings for him? She couldn't have. He wasn't her type.

George hadn't worked out but that didn't mean that her choice of guy had been completely off-target. It just meant that youth had stopped her from exploring what else was out there first. She had been conditioned by her over-protective father to gravitate towards safety and she'd jumped in at the deep end without giving it as much thought as she might have. She still wanted someone who believed in love, believed in marriage and wanted security and stability, just as she did.

Gabriel wasn't that man. He was sexy, so she'd been attracted to him. She was only human, after all. She was still young, she was a woman and she decided that, however imprudent her behaviour had been, there was nothing really to be ashamed of. She'd let nature get the better of her for once. And, if she'd been savvy enough to gauge the situation with Arturio and act on it, then it was because it had really been no skin off her nose. Besides, whilst Gabriel might not be her type, she still liked him and could still appreciate those qualities in him that made him a man worthy of respect.

Gabriel, though… Was he torn with guilt? Would he think that she had over-stepped the brief by what she had said to Arturio? Worse, would he get it into his head that she had been expressing some kind of secret desire for them to be an item?

It made her break out in a cold sweat.

She could downplay that bit of it, bury it under the tug of war that had been going on between them on the physical front, he'd get that. For both their sakes, it would work.

'We need to talk this through,' she said firmly. 'Maybe the bar? I could have something to eat. I haven't eaten yet.'

'You want to talk about it?' He sounded startled. 'I didn't think that you were open to discussions about things that happen that shouldn't have happened.' He shot her a wicked, sideways glance. '"Sand" and "ostriches" spring to mind.'

'I know I said before that—yes, okay—what happened a few days ago was a blip that should never be mentioned again. But what happened…' She drew in a deep breath. 'What happened back there was more than a blip…' She shot him a quick glance and gathered her scattered self-control. 'I also don't want you to start taking the blame for anything.'

'Helen, I'm not a fool. I'm a man with a great deal of experience, and of course I hold myself responsible for my shocking lapse in good judgement.'

'Let's just say that it takes two to tango.' She began walking towards the reception area, behind which was the gorgeous bar that gave out to the fields and open land behind, and which was bedecked with lanterns and clusters of sofas, chairs and thoughtfully positioned outdoor heating for when it was a little chilly.

She was so aware of him striding alongside her that it

made her body go hot. She thought of them together, and she wanted more, and then she went even hotter when she wondered how long that want had been brewing away under the surface. He would shoulder the blame for what had happened and that said so much about the man that he was. He might pick women up and drop them just as fast but he played fair because, as he had once murmured in passing, he never promised anything. And that was an intensely attractive trait.

'And did you enjoy the tango, Helen?'

'I…' She blushed. 'It happened and…and…'

She shot him a sideways glance as they were ushered to their tables in the bar that, thankfully, was free of Arturio and his wife.

Barely glancing at the menus that were brought for them, she ordered some tapas and a glass of wine, and then sat forward to meet his dark gaze head-on.

From being the dutiful secretary, she felt oddly empowered as their eyes met. Their unusual interlude had altered the balance of their relationship and there was no point trying to unpick the situation. Maybe it was a good thing that he had seen beyond the professionalism to the woman underneath.

He was a guy in the enviable position of being able to have whatever woman he chose, and the women he chose all seemed to be women who would do anything for him. She would just have to make sure he knew that she didn't include herself in that category, whatever had happened between them. She might fancy him, but she hadn't joined his fan club. Things would revert to what they had been once they returned to reality, but he would no longer smile those annoying, amused smiles because she would no longer be the person he'd assumed she was.

'And?' Gabriel prompted, settling into the chair and giving her his undivided attention.

She raised her eyebrows, going for light-hearted and steering clear from serious. Light-hearted was the response of a woman in cool control of a situation, whatever had happened. Shame she didn't quite recognise that version of herself.

'And I don't regret it,' she told him simply. 'Like I told you, I was engaged once, and maybe over here it felt right, even though it was probably a little crazy.' She smiled and kept her cool—just.

'I like a woman who doesn't have regrets.'

'Have you had a lot of experience with ones that do?'

'Enough.' He ran his fingers through his hair and looked at her steadily, seriously. 'But only with women who ended up wanting more than was on the table, than was ever going to be on the table.'

'Like Fifi?'

Gabriel grimaced. 'Correct.'

'What happened there?' She never asked him anything truly personal, but this was personal, and it felt exciting and alarming to have this conversation.

'Like I said…' his dark eyes were lazy, yet focused '… didn't work out.' He sighed. 'She decided that it might be a good time to explore other options between us—options that might involve rings and jewellery shopping in the not-too-distant future. I was astonished and then I made the mistake of bursting out laughing.'

'Poor woman.'

'Why?'

'She just wanted a serious situation.'

'And she deserves one. Just not with me.' Gabriel paused. 'Although…'

'Although?' Helen broke eye contact, sipped some of the

wine and dipped into the tapas which had been brought to them. Her voice was light but she was tense with the realisation of just how far out of both their comfort zones this conversation was taking them.

'Although,' he said smoothly, 'those tapas won't stay hot for ever.'

Helen blinked. He'd closed the conversation and that was a relief, she told herself. Trample over the boundary lines too much, and how on earth would they be able to put them back up? It was a sobering thought. He had come close to saying…what?

She'd told Arturio that she and Gabriel were an item. Had he been about to stress his lack of availability just in case she'd got it into her head that the fiction she'd concocted might turn into reality?

She took a deep breath and decided that she might as well address the elephant in the room and get things back on as even a keel as she could. If he got it into his head that she might become another Fifi—unlikely, but who knew?—then her continued presence around him at work would end up wrecking their working relationship and her job, which she loved and which was so well paid.

'About what I told Arturio…'

'That we were involved in a hot, clandestine affair?'

'That's not what I said.'

'He's traditional and he's a romantic. The family fortune was split several ways when various members died. It wasn't a sprawling family. Arturio got the vineyards, and of course all the land and estates that went with it. My father got the shipping business, which ran itself, and of course coincidentally married a girl whose family fortune made his own pale in comparison. Where Arturio worked from dawn to dusk to make the most of his unpredictable inheritance, my parents washed their hands of Italy and were happy to tour the world and live off an income that dropped into their bank accounts without having to do the graft to put it there.'

'You admire him a lot, don't you?'

'He's more of an example than my own father ever was,' Gabriel admitted. He grinned and looked at her with his head tilted to one side. 'His wife's father worked for him, but he said that it was love at first sight, despite the fact that they came from wildly different backgrounds. Passion, love… heady mix. I fancy that's what's going through his head at the thought of the boss and his secretary—a couple of lovebirds who just couldn't resist the heady mix.'

'That's ridiculous…'

'Who knows what scenarios he's concocting in his head?' Gabriel was still grinning with wicked amusement. 'I don't have a romantic bone in my body, but it doesn't take too much imagination to work out what he must be thinking.'

'Well, he's way off-target with that one,' Helen said briskly.

'Yet you can't blame him. He caught us red-handed, after all. He was probably tickled pink.'

Patches of bright colour stained her cheeks.

'Well, isn't it just as well that I'm leaving to head back to London tomorrow?' she said. She focused on London, the office, his desk, her work outfits—she focused on remembering that those were the things that mattered. His words were so evocative, made her feel so hot and bothered. She thought that, however much she made a deal of being in charge of her emotions and in control of what was happening between them, she really lacked the experience to deal with a man like Gabriel. It was important he didn't realise that but it was hard to meet those lazy, penetrating dark eyes without breaking out in nervous perspiration and giving in to the temptation to dab her forehead with the linen napkin by her plate.

'Isn't it?'

The wretched man was still smiling. She cleared her throat and angled her head haughtily. 'I shall head into town first thing. When you see him, you can say that that was always the plan—which it was—and that I wanted to get some last-minute shopping in before I left for the airport. Because he thinks we're some kind of old-fashioned, romantic couple doesn't mean that he'll expect us to be glued to one another's sides.'

'That might very well be the case.'

'And I just want to say that—being out here—we were in a bubble. When we're back in London, there's no bubble and…' she breathed in long and deeply '… I want this to be put behind us.' Her head said this was imperative; everything else said that it was easier said than done.

'Think it's going to be as easy as that?' he said, reading her mind.

'It has to be because, if it isn't, then I'm going to have to hand in my notice and I really love what I do.'

Their eyes met. She sipped her wine and looked at him, her face revealing nothing in the subdued lighting while her heart was beating like a sledgehammer inside her.

Gazing right back at her, Gabriel could only admire her cool.

She'd been swept up by something bigger than both of them, just as he had been, and in that crazy place there had been no room for rational thought.

But that didn't matter.

She'd thrown down the gauntlet—forget this ever happened or she'd quit—and he knew that she meant every word she'd said. When he considered her doing that, he drew a blank.

'Arturio will never be the wiser that we're not a couple,' she said, breaking the silence as he sampled the tapas between them. 'Your deal will go through and at some point when you see him again…'

'Relationships end, and even the die-hard romantic can appreciate that.' Gabriel filled in the blanks and she nodded.

It all made sense and, truth was, he couldn't envisage walking into his office without the expectation of her being there. But forgetting that it had all happened—how easy was it going to be to shut that open door? He still wanted her and she still wanted him. They'd both let the genie out of the bottle.

Yet his hands were tied and that, in itself, was new for him.

'Agreed.' He reached out to shake her hand. 'Back to the status quo in London and picking up where we left off…'

Helen thought she'd handled the situation really well.

The following morning, as she flung the rest of the stuff into her case she had brought with her, she reflected that she had successfully managed to get on the front foot.

Inside? She was all over the place, emotions running high, head filled with questions, doubts and a reckless sense of daring that made her light-headed, frightened but excited, as though one foot was poised, outstretched, taking a different path in her life.

Outside? She was cool, calm, mature and laying down all the rules and boundaries she knew had to be laid down if they were to continue to have any kind of working relationship. Gabriel had crept through a side door and entered her personal life, and she knew that she couldn't allow him to remain there.

When she thought of him, she shivered. He was so wildly different from any image she'd ever had in her had of the perfect guy, and yet so powerful in the position he now occupied. Maybe those snatched moments with him had been important when it came to showing her that the time had come for her to move on with life and start dating again.

Naturally, not with someone like Gabriel, but perhaps someone in between…

Once upon a time, growing up in the shadow of her father's loving anxiety and desperate need to protect her from anything and everything, safety had been paramount. Whilst it was still important, London and working for her charismatic boss had opened her eyes to what adventure might taste like. And, being out here, she had seized the opportunity to go where she had never dared go before.

It had been wise to lay down that ultimatum. It had been clever of her to put up the sort of defence that would protect her from—weakening.

She zipped up her case and for a few moments looked at herself in the full-length mirror, making sure the image would be just right when she next saw her boss. She saw average height, slim build…a coltish figure, which some might like but many might not…with chestnut-brown hair and eyes with just a hint of green.

She'd never given much thought to her looks, and had certainly never considered herself to be anything but averagely attractive, but when Gabriel had touched her she had felt *oh, so sexy.* Even thinking about it now made her shiver.

They had agreed that they would have breakfast together, a perfunctory meeting to go over any final bits of work, and then the rest of the morning would belong to her, with a taxi coming to collect her just after four.

Accordingly, she had dressed for shopping, relaxing and seeing Gabriel in a multi-purpose outfit: light cream trousers, a sensible cotton shirt with a round neck and buttons up the front and her trusty flat shoes. No laptop bag to hide behind, but her backpack and a little nylon bag strapped round her waist for easy access to her phone.

She had no idea how she would feel, seeing him after the night before, but she told herself that it would be a good opportunity to reinforce the message she had sent. He'd always been the one to do the walking away. She knew that. How would he feel now that the shoe was on the other foot? When she thought that he might just see that as a challenge, she shivered with a dangerous mix of dark excitement and thinly suppressed panic. No—it was a definite plus that she had slammed down her boundaries.

She swung into the restaurant, where the buffet was laid out to the left in groaning splendour, cast her eyes around the room, which was filling up, and then abruptly screeched to a halt and stared.

From the opposite side of the room, Gabriel spotted her roughly at the same time as she spotted him, and he read the expression on her face with ease.

Oh no, help...!

He couldn't blame her. Her bright plan to disappear back to London without seeing Arturio was now in tatters because Arturio and Isabella were both right here at the table with him. A pleasant surprise for him, a nasty shock for her.

He waved, rose to his feet and then walked to meet her. It was a nice opportunity to lean into her, a gesture of love and affection, he hoped, because they were in full view of Arturio and Isabella. He whispered into her ear, 'You need to brace yourself.'

'I didn't expect Arturio and his wife to be joining us!'

'Smile and look loving.' He swung round with her, holding her close, but there was no chance to say anything else. 'Remember that we're an item…'

Arturio was already standing. He and Isabella were smiling, and Helen wondered why she suddenly felt a frisson of apprehension trickle through her. The warning 'brace yourself' seemed ominous.

Arturio was a short, plump man with thinning grey hair and a face that was weathered from the sun and a life lived outdoors. In contrast, his wife was tall, willowy and, for a woman in her seventies, remarkably youthful-looking and rather beautiful, with striking dark eyes and grey hair pulled back in a bun. It was easy to picture the beautiful young girl from the opposite side of the tracks who'd captured his heart.

She had no idea what to expect and was determined to wriggle out of a lengthy breakfast which would be spent pretending to be someone she wasn't, in a relationship that was fictional, even if she had been the one to kick-start the fiction.

She went beetroot-red as Gabriel pulled out a chair for her and simultaneously dropped a kiss on the side of her neck, just a brief, passing caress that feathered on her skin. Just what she didn't need when she had done her utmost to recalibrate their relationship.

Helen hoped for some polite chit-chat and, as soon as she was sitting, said that she couldn't stay.

'I'm leaving later today.' She smiled and eyed Gabriel's hand on the table before reluctantly linking her fingers through his to maintain their charade. 'So, a bit of retail therapy is called for.'

Gabriel squeezed her hand.

'So,' she continued, 'just time for a quick cup of coffee and then I'll be off.' She looked at Gabriel and kept the smile on her face. 'As we, er, discussed last night...darling.'

'We certainly did,' Gabriel agreed warmly.

'How are you both? It's so exciting about this marvellous deal and the fantastic family connection. I know Gabriel will be brilliant when it comes to carrying on the tradition at your lovely vineyards and, of course, expanding and updating a lot of processes, which is what we discussed.'

She was smiling a full-wattage smile, conscious of background noises, the sound of people moving around, eating breakfast, chatting and waiters weaving between tables with trays and pots of coffee. Mostly, though, she was conscious of the Italian couple beaming at the both of them in a way that was vaguely disconcerting.

Her voice petered out but the smile remained in place.

'So…' she said vaguely.

'I don't suppose Gabriel has had a chance to tell you…' Arturio's dark eyes twinkled and his wife leaned forward with a smile.

'Er…?'

'Arturio and I have had wonderful thought,' Isabella said. 'This deal with our vineyards—this wonderful family connection that is already bringing us so much joy… Over the past few months, we've come to see Gabriel as a son as well as a businessman, and to hear that you and Gabriel are going out… We thought it would be lovely if you both came to Italy from here to meet the other members of the family.'

'Sorry?' Helen sat forward, detaching from Gabriel's linked clasp at the same time and shoving her hands on her lap. Her eyes had glazed over.

'We can tell from what Gabriel has told us before you came that what you have is serious—we know that he isn't the sort to get involved with someone working for him unless it is, which we appreciate. We understand more than most how sometimes relationships can overtake common sense and, when that happens, it does no good to wage war on it.'

Helen was straining towards the elderly couple. She wasn't sure which strand of information was most appalling: an invitation to Italy as the couple they weren't, where they would have to cement their lie yet further; the generosity of Arturio and his wife, who now saw them as part of their own family; or the weight of trust placed in every single word spoken now.

She'd never felt more of a fraud. She'd landed them in this situation. It had never dawned on her that, during the many conversations Gabriel had had with Arturio, he had promoted himself as the sort of guy he knew Arturio would thoroughly approve of. The sort of guy who would never get caught red-handed in a clinch with his secretary just for the fun of it.

She shot them a ghastly smile, stumped for anything to say.

'I have told Arturio,' Gabriel murmured from next to her, 'that you have responsibilities in England which might make it difficult for you to contemplate their kind offer.'

'Yes...'

'Family responsibilities, my dear?' Arturio ordered them all coffee and Helen settled into her chair, deprived of all hope of heading off to town without having to spend time in their company promoting a falsehood she was coming to regret. 'Gabriel mentioned something of that nature.'

Helen looked sideways at the brooding guy sitting next to her and, in silent response, he reached out to squeeze her hand.

'My dad,' she said jerkily, determined at least to be truthful from this point on rather than get mired in yet more falsehoods. Gabriel knew next to nothing about her personal life but, where only a few days ago sharing on this level would have appalled her, it seemed insignificant given the current situation. The rule book had been tossed through the window.

'He lives on his own,' she said. 'Quite far from London. Cornwall, as a matter of fact. I—I try to visit him at least once a month. He worries, you see.'

'I understand.' Isabella patted her hand. 'We parents make a habit of worrying about our children. It is only natural.'

Helen thought of her father—the cards he sent her on a regular basis, the long, casually worded emails that couldn't quite hide his daily anxiety that she was okay, the absolute relief and love on his face whenever she went to visit him. He never *said* anything, but she knew that it had taken a lot of courage for him to let her fly the nest without protest, to understand.

And now here she was, gazing into this lovely woman's concerned face, wondering how she could wriggle out of the situation she and Gabriel had jointly brought on themselves. Well, largely her, if she were completely honest.

'My mum…' her voice was low and quiet '…and my brother died in a car accident when I was very young. My dad never really recovered. He became very protective of me and even now—and I'm twenty-eight years old—he's still very protective, always scared that something's going to happen to me. So I try and get back to see him as often as I can, just to reassure him that everything's all right. It means the world to him.'

'Oh, my dear.' Isabella reached out in a spontaneous gesture of sympathy. 'That poor man, and you, poor child. Of course we must not interrupt that routine! We would so have loved you to have met all our family who work in the vineyards but naturally another time—yes, it was just a spur-of-the-moment invitation. Another time, perhaps, and you must bring your dear father!'

'Yes.' She thought of Gabriel and wondered what this strong, invincible and yet vulnerable guy had said to Arturio in passing when they had met in the past. She thought of the reason why he would have been driven to want the good opinion of someone when, she suspected, he had never cared what anyone thought of him. That one little white lie had now come back to haunt her.

She felt faint. She *did* have feelings for this man. Just acknowledging that fact made her giddy, as though she was at the bottom of the ocean speeding to the surface without sufficient oxygen to take her back to safety.

She'd started this. Might it be up to her to finish it? Would those boundary lines, and her ultimatum about packing in the job if they couldn't put this behind them, still hold up should she spend yet more time in his company? They were finding out about one another and it felt dangerous.

It also made her feel *alive*.

'I'll come. *We'll* come.' She looked at Gabriel and their eyes met, although she couldn't begin to work out what was going through his head. His expression was tender—loving, as a besotted boyfriend's should be—and completely unrevealing.

'I'm not due to visit my dad for another week or so.' She managed a smile as she was swept away on a decision that made her pulses leap. 'And I think he'll like the thought of me seeing a bit of Italy. I haven't travelled much.'

'Are you quite sure, my darling?'

'Yes.' No going back now.

The conversation flowed around her in waves. She was saying stuff but she wasn't sure what. Whenever she glanced down, she saw Gabriel's brown hand on hers, an intimate gesture that reminded her of this unexpected turn they had taken—thanks to her, because he had given her an out clause.

She could have been vague. She could have stuck to what she had said about unavoidable commitments—no one would have questioned that, least of all uber-polite and emotionally generous Arturio and his wife. Maybe she needed this. Maybe she had to address whatever wayward feelings for Gabriel had taken root inside her. Things had become muddled and perhaps she had to wade through the muddle to emerge on the other side and not walk away from it in the hope it would disappear in time.

At any rate, she'd made her bed. She was going to have to lie in it.

'Well, that came as a surprise.'

Helen blinked and realised that Arturio and Isabella had left. She must have said her goodbyes, barely aware of what was going on, her mind way too cluttered with the business of repercussions.

He had dropped her hand and was sitting back in his chair, staring at her.

Gabriel had spotted Arturio and his wife just as soon as he'd entered the restaurant. They'd waved, hurried over to him and, before he'd finished his first cup of coffee, had sprung their idea about a few days in Italy to meet the family.

Gabriel had done well to disguise his shock. He'd thought of how that suggestion might go down with Helen and come up short, but he'd smiled and murmured something about perhaps her not being able to make it over at such short notice.

They'd wanted them both to fly directly to Italy from America and swing by for a few days—rather as if it was as convenient as stopping on the way from work to buy a pint of milk.

He knew why and had himself to blame. Having spent a lifetime cultivating an armour around his emotions, he had found himself courting the old man's good opinion. Why? Because a door had been opened to what family life looked like? And not just any family life, but his flesh-and-blood family life. Arturio had been cut from such different cloth from that of Gabriel's own irresponsible parents, that he had sought to impress. Having a fling with his secretary didn't come under the heading of making a good impression.

He had been incredibly pleased when Helen had come up with her little fabrication. He hadn't thought that anything further would come of it.

He'd been wrong.

He'd waited for an explosion when the idea had been excitedly mooted, but she'd handled the situation with admirable calm. Definitely not a woman prone to hysteria—admirable, really.

Of course, he could feel her shock and tension in the cool clasp of her fingers dutifully entwined with his, but he'd given her a way out of accepting their offer. He'd opened the door to an excuse involving *family* which was broad enough to include anything: babysitting duties; a favourite cousin's upcoming wedding; a mother in hospital…

The possibilities had been endless.

And at no point had he guessed which road she would travel down. At no point had he contemplated a response that had shocked him, and he certainly hadn't imagined for a passing second that she would actually go and *accept* their offer.

And the crazy thing was that he didn't know which had shocked him more—that sliver of revelation about her personal life or the fact that she'd agreed to go to Italy at the behest of the Italian couple.

'I'm sorry.'

'They can be charming and persuasive.'

'It's only for three days, so I suppose…'

'Helen, this isn't part of the plan for things to revert to normal between us.'

'I know. I couldn't help myself. I like them and I could see how enthusiastic they were to have us over.' There was a lot more she could have said but that would dig deep into personal areas yet again. She decided to stick to vague basics. 'I hated the thought of their disappointment and I hated just—lying more to them.'

'And will you be issuing more threats in due course about moving on, about my mentioning nothing or else you walk? No? Because I made sure to give you a handy excuse for making your apologies.'

He watched as she squirmed, and then he sat forward, leaning into her. His voice seductive, sending little shivers racing through her, he murmured, 'But, seeing that you failed to take up my helpful get-out clause, I think it's time we started finding out a bit more about one another, wouldn't you agree? We wouldn't want Arturio and Isabella to start harbouring shady suspicions about our relationship, would we?'

CHAPTER SIX

HELEN CALLED LUCY. Who else but her best friend would do? The following morning, she and Gabriel would be flying to Italy. She still couldn't believe that she had gone and thrown herself in the deep end when, as Gabriel had calmly pointed out, she had been given a very nice road-map out of the dilemma.

'It's mad,' she said in a hushed, furtive voice as she eyed the bags of purchases Gabriel had informed her she would have to get for their extended trip, and which she had duly bought earlier on company expenses.

Helen had done her training with Lucy and they had remained firm friends ever since. They had both veered off into careers with powerful, wealthy men and mutual venting had been invaluable over the years. Over time two, more PAs had been added to their social media group—Top Secret Secretaries to Billionaire Bosses, as they wryly called themselves—but she and Lucy had their own friendship quite apart from anyone else.

'It's mad,' Lucy agreed.

'I have no idea what happened.'

Helen was not the sort who shared confidences, but with Lucy confidences had been shared over the years, each safe in the knowledge that neither knew each other's boss and so secrets were safe. They trusted one another implicitly. On so many levels, Lucy was the best friend Helen had ever had, so open, straightforward and bubbly.

'It never pays to kiss the boss.'

'Big mistake.'

'But I'm not surprised. You've had a crush on him for a long time.'

'I...' Helen quailed inside. Having a crush on her boss was the last thing she wanted to have confirmed by someone else, and yet of course it made sense, now that her friend had addressed the elephant in the room without bothering to beat about the bush.

Why else did she feel that tingle of forbidden excitement whenever she was in his company? Why else had she postponed getting back into the dating game, even when her head had been telling her that it was time to move on from George? Why else did she never have a problem working stupid hours when he asked her to because some piece of work or other needed to be done faster than yesterday?

A crush that would never come to anything had been safe but taking it to the next level of a kiss no longer felt safe. And she now recognised what she felt for Gabriel was more than a crush but less than...anything dangerous. Surely less than love...? She licked her lips and pushed that thought aside.

'Enjoy the break.'

'Enjoy the break?'

'Well, Italy *is* very beautiful, and I know you've been hankering go there for ages.'

'With Gabriel? In a phoney relationship? Pretending to be someone I'm not in front of people I respect and like, from the little I've seen of them?'

'What other choice do you have at this point?'

'Zero. Why are you always so upbeat?'

'Comes from being one of six kids.' Lucy laughed with just a hint of wistfulness. 'No room to think too much. You just have to always go with the flow or end up being left behind, and sometimes you have to talk louder and faster just to get yourself heard over the din. Remind me to give you the lowdown sometime.

'My advice? My billionaire boss is in a league of his own as well, and has no problem playing by his own rules and to heck with the rest of the world… Take it as it comes and remember that a crush is different from the head-over-heels "in love" thing. Now, the head-over-heels "in love" thing? *That's* dangerous.'

Helen wasn't exactly sure whether she felt better or not after that phone call. There was too much going on to feel anything but low-level panic, which made her think that the best thing she could do was to try really hard not to over-analyse the situation.

When she looked at the brand-new suitcase containing the brand-new outfits for three days of a brand-new *her*, however, her stomach did a few nervous flips and she broke out in a cold sweat.

Because, as well as telling her that she would have to buy some more stuff to tide her through the next three days, Gabriel had also informed her that it might be an idea to think about him when she was choosing what to buy.

'Why would I do that?' Helen had asked, instantly walking into the trap he'd set for her.

'Because,' he had murmured with silky smoothness, 'Bearing in mind you shot down my opporunity to avoid this situation, we're going to have to present a convincing façade to Arturio and his wife and whatever assorted crowd we're going to meet.'

He'd looked at her carefully then, and said in a low, deadly, serious voice, 'This means a lot to me. Not just the deal—buying a vineyard, however much money I make from it, is just something to add to my portfolio. But you can't buy family connections. We are where we are and it's important that we are convincing.'

'I get it, Gabriel,' Helen had said with gruff honesty. She wondered whether he realised just how many inroads had been made into the barriers between them. She thought of his husky, passing confidences, uttered with such sincerity, and her heart clenched.

'He has no idea what sort of clothes your girlfriends like to wear.' She had moved the conversation on, half-smiling, when she remembered the last outfit she had seen Fifi wear to the office—cling-film-fitting hot-pink gym gear, only to be worn by the bold and adventurous, neither of which was Helen.

'Ah.' He had shrugged. 'But *you* know, and it's going to be more convincing if he sees my eyes light up the minute my soul mate and partner walks into the room.'

Their eyes had tangled and for a few seconds Helen had felt the ground unsteady under her feet, but then the moment had passed and normality had been re-established.

They would be flying out together the following morning, arriving only slightly later than Arturio and Isabella, who had already left. They had no idea where exactly they would end up because the vineyards had already been visited and looked at from every angle by Gabriel and his highly experienced team of professionals.

They could have waited but, Gabriel has explained with a shrug, it would be less of an interruption to follow in their wake than if they were to return to London, wait a while and then make the trip over. Helen had seen exactly where he was coming from. If appearances had to be maintained, then there was no point prolonging the situation.

But did he honestly expect her to dress the part of one of his flamboyant girlfriends, when he knew that she was someone who seldom strayed far from sobriety when it came to choosing outfits? He'd really only seen her in work stuff, and here in sensible informal clothes.

So much straying from the norm had happened, though, in the past few days… How did he see her now?

It was an alluring thought—exciting.

He wanted her to "dress the part"—well, why not? That was what had gone through her head when she had sprinted from boutique to boutique, caught up between a sense of cavalier recklessness and the forbidden thrill of wondering whether she was doing the sensible thing. To heck with common sense, for once!

She was less convinced of that particular response now that she was facing the reality of she and Gabriel, and this crazy farce, even though it would only be for a very short while.

There was a knock on the door, and she sprang into action. Gabriel was swinging by for her and they would head to the airport together.

Before pulling open the door, she paused to eye her reflection and was pleased with what gazed back at her. She saw comfortable clothes, but classy with no expense spared, as befitting her new elevation to the role of 'girlfriend of billionaire Gabriel de Luca'—a woman who worked hard but knew how to play as well, and was comfortable in the shiny world of the mega-rich.

A complete transformation. She'd felt guilty at the amount of money she had spent on a few outfits but, then again, playing the part with conviction wasn't going to be a cheap exercise, and she knew him well enough to know that he would be quietly disapproving if she decided to skimp on cost.

He wanted flamboyance? Then he was going to get it. She'd shopped with his reaction in mind. But for the flight over she had gone for cool and elegant in loose linen culottes with a drawstring so that they slipped just a little down her narrow hips, and a sleeveless silk vest, both in shades of cream, and some tan loafers.

Gabriel had stood back and was glancing at his watch when the door was pulled open and, for a few seconds, surprise knocked him for six.

Because this was the first time he had seen his secretary in anything other than what he knew to be off-the-shelf, cheap, cheerful, comfortable clothes for blending into the background. He'd privately always suspected that she scoffed at the sort of expensive designer stuff his girlfriends paraded in. She oozed sophistication, from the willowy lines of her graceful body, to her proud carriage and the way she held herself.

This was a charade, but for a moment it flashed through his head that this was a woman he wanted the world to think was his.

'All packed?' His eyes wanted to linger, to take their time absorbing what they saw.

'And ready to go,' Helen said briskly. She nodded to the two cases on the ground. 'I'm afraid I had to buy a case for the extra wardrobe.'

'You could have bought an army of them if you wanted.' He swung round and stood aside so that she could brush past him in a waft of highly feminine, floral scent.

Her hair was loose, and the sun and heat seemed to have lightened it. It fell in a shiny, streaky curtain to her shoulders.

'I also have my laptop at the ready,' she said, walking quickly past him and towards the reception area, where she knew their driver would be waiting. 'I thought we might do some work on the trip over. Never mind this deal; I've had a few emails from that construction company poised to start work on the eco-village near Dundee…'

Before the rule book was completely tossed through the window, Helen did her best to remind them both that they worked together—first and foremost, whatever had happened.

Gabriel fell in step alongside her. Dundee… Eco-village… *Right.* That floral scent was penetrating his nostrils, blending with all the other floral scents outside. She was so unbearably fresh, and *pretty*, that it took his breath away.

He dragged his brain back to the present and, for the next couple of hours, managed to immerse himself in the barrage of work-related issues she insisted on dealing with, both on the way to the airport and then, after a brief respite, once they were settled in the first-class compartment of the plane.

'Enough of work,' he ordered when they were cruising and champagne had been brought for them.

He rested one finger on the lid of her laptop and eased it shut. 'I get it that you want to remind me that our peculiar situation doesn't negate the fact that you're still my secretary—and not, as appearances would have it, my girlfriend—but we still have to fill in some blanks before we get to Italy. You never mentioned anything to me about your mother and brother being involved in a fatal car accident—and, first off, I want to say how sorry I am for your father and for everyone else who must have been affected by it.'

Helen's heart sped up.

He hadn't said a word about her outfit, but she'd seen the quick flick of his eyes over her, the way he had quickly lowered them to guard his reaction, and sexual tension had sizzled through her like a live electric charge.

She wanted it and she didn't want it. The conflict inside was sweet torture.

This was all new to her. Life had always been so well organised. This…? She could write off a silly crush, and she could almost shut the lid on those stolen moments between them, when things had got out of hand, because thankfully they had come to their senses. She could very nearly blame it all on being in a bubble, back there in that ridiculously romantic hotel where barriers had been blurred just for a moment.

But now Helen was agonisingly aware that the sand was shifting ever more beneath her feet. She'd felt it before, and the feeling had lodged deep inside, impervious to being dislodged just because she would rather not address it the way it needed to be addressed.

She didn't want some kind of voyage of discovery.

No... She was terrified that part of her wanted it way too much for her own good.

She knew the kind of guy her boss was and she knew that it would be fatal to let herself get sucked into his magnetic orbit. But here they were, and he had a point—they could hardly present themselves as a loved-up couple if a simple question thrown at them at some point in the next couple of days resulted in the whole farce being exposed for what it was.

Her fiancé would know at least one or two basic details about her past! And it wasn't as though she would be divulging some deep, dark, state secrets, even if it might feel a little like that—a little like another chip was being made in the wall she had constructed around herself, the wall that had defined the relationship she had had with him.

'Thank you.' She blinked her way back to the present and to her sexy boss, who was looking at her from under his lush, dark lashes.

'It must have been very hard for you. How old were you at the time?'

'Gabriel...' She turned to look at him, her hazel eyes colliding with his curious, dark gaze. 'I know we have to know a few basic facts and figures about ourselves if we're to be convincing, but honestly, there's no need for detail, is there?' She smiled to temper the cool curtness of her response and hoped he couldn't sense the fear underlying it, fear that her self-control was fraying at the edges.

His eyebrows shot up and he tilted his head to one side. 'I thought what I asked was a basic *facts and figures* question,' he replied. 'So why the secrecy?'

'Because...' She looked at him and sighed. 'I'm your secretary.' She lowered her voice and took a deep breath. 'And not actually your girlfriend, so we don't need to get too much into the details of one another.'

'You know pretty much everything about me. Besides, now that you've invested in this pretend situation, I think it'll work for you to take a little time off from being my employee. Is it really so hard for you to open up a little? You already have. The threshold has been crossed.' His voice was husky. 'I can be a very understanding boss, if you give me the chance.'

The threshold had certainly been crossed, that was for sure.

'Eight.' She looked away and sipped the champagne. 'I was eight at the time. I was at home with my dad, and my mum was with Tommy, who was my kid brother by three years. She was taking him to a birthday party. It was all just—a terrible, tragic freak accident. A pile-up on the motorway. I...' Her eyes glazed over and she drew in a sharp, painful breath.

'You?' Gabriel encouraged gently.

'It was a very bad time,' she confessed, 'if you really want to know.'

'I can only imagine.'

'My dad went to pieces. It took him a while to get out of that black hole but, when he finally did, he'd changed. He wasn't carefree any longer. He became very protective, and I only really noticed it when I got older—when I saw how much freedom other girls had.'

'How did you deal with that?'

'I never minded. I adored my dad and I still do. He was doing his best for me and I always knew that.' She glanced across to him and then laughed self-consciously. 'So, that's my story.'

'Things are falling into place,' Gabriel murmured.

'What is that supposed to mean?'

'Your cautiousness: was George your cautious option?'

'We weren't talking about George.'

'Mistakes get made when you're young,' Gabriel murmured.

'I never said he was a mistake.'

'Despite the painful break-up?'

'Okay, so maybe I played it a little too safe with my ex-fiancé. Maybe we do all make a few youthful mistakes! You must have made some of your own, now that we're sharing our life histories.'

'There are a couple of times I was a bit too impatient in selling shares…'

'I mean it, Gabriel,' she persisted. 'I've opened up, now that we're supposed to be involved and need to know a bit about one another to be convincing. So why should it be a one-way street?'

'If you want to know,' he replied with a thoughtful shrug, 'My parents set a good example when it came to teaching me what sort of mistakes never to make. They were so involved with one another that it was almost like a sickness. The sickness of losing oneself in someone else. So I never made any youthful mistakes. No broken engagements.'

'No broken heart.'

'That won't be my fate.' He frowned and fidgeted.

'You can't be sure about that. No one knows what fate has in store for any of us. Look at the way you and Arturio ended up meeting.'

Gabriel had to concede that she had a point.

'I mean,' she pressed, 'do you really never plan on settling down?'

'No plans at the moment.'

She really wanted to worry this, like a dog with a bone, but did she want to find out more about what made her boss tick? Wasn't that just a road that was going to lead to a life all the more complicated when they were back in London? When they both had to forget this interlude and pick up their normal working life where they had left off? They could step out of their boxes for a while but they would have to keep it light.

'Very wise.' She laughed. 'I don't think all those eligible women out there would ever be able to cope if you weren't on the scene as a prospective boyfriend. What on earth would they aim for?'

Gabriel didn't say anything for a few seconds and, when he did, it was non-committal, amused.

He knew what she was doing, just as he knew that she had felt vulnerable and uncomfortable sharing that snippet of her past with him. But then, despite his invitation to her to ask him whatever she wanted, wouldn't he have walked away from any real personal disclosures? 'Facts and figures', as she'd called it, were very different from the painful business of full disclosure.

He'd told her the truth when it came to his parents. He would never hand his heart over to any woman because he would never risk ending up in a place where uncontrolled passion became the sort of all-consuming fire that ended up burning everything to the ground, from common sense to responsibility.

He was more than happy for sporadic work to be done for the remainder of the flight. When that fizzled out, she read and he snoozed, chair angled back, because it was the only way he could be remotely comfortable, given his size.

They arrived at their destination as evening was falling, bathing the landscape in mellow light.

A chauffeur was waiting for them with a placard with their names on it.

'I don't even know where we're going,' Helen said, turning to Gabriel as a source of strength as she was bombarded by fast Italian accents and people everywhere.

'"Wait and see", was what Arturio said. Expect many relatives. It's a sprawling family.'

'Maybe that's better than just something small.'

'Less chance for anyone to eke out skeletons in the cupboards, you mean?'

Helen slid a look across at him and felt the tug of familiarity mingled with the excitement of the unknown.

'Something like that. Should we get our stories synchronised?'

Gabriel looked straight at her and grinned.

'It's not going to be an interrogation under a bright light with security at the doors in case we try to flee,' he said drily. 'Vague murmurings should be okay. We just needed to know one or two details about one another, and I think we've covered that.'

'I know Arturio and Isabella like me well enough, but I hope the younger family members—you know—don't find it a little odd that someone like you decides to go for someone like me.' Helen heard her own insecurities bounce around in the silence that followed and Gabriel stopped dead in his tracks and spun to face her.

He curled his fingers round her arms and looked at her with deadly seriousness.

'Where does that come from?'

'Nowhere. It was just a passing remark.'

'"Someone like me"? Someone like you?'

'Gabriel, please,' Helen said with an attempt at laughter. 'You're *you*. You're an eligible bachelor with a roving eye who could have his pick of women. Someone here would surely have spotted you in some tabloid or other with a *Fifi* wrapped round your arm—I'm just saying it might not be quite the easy sell you seem to think it's going to be. No matter; we're where we are and, before you say it, I know that I'm the one who managed to prolong this mess.'

'Run with me on this,' Gabriel murmured, hands still holding her still while people bustled around them on the way to collect bags from carousels. 'Yes, I'm a billionaire, and yes, I suppose there are women who find me attractive...'

'That's something of an understatement. Don't forget, I've worked with you for over three years.'

'My point exactly.'

'Sorry?'

'After a long line of Fifis, after a thousand nights out eating in expensive restaurants and sitting in over-priced front-row seats at theatres—after too many nights to count when boredom started setting in before the bedroom lights were dimmed—I finally discovered that what I wanted was right in front of me.'

'And what was that?' Helen whispered.

'The woman who has been at my side for years, who knows me better than anyone, who's smart and funny and unimpressed by all the things the Fifis of this world are impressed by.'

Silence settled between them.

Helen blinked, caught up in the narrative. For just a second, he was so persuasive that even *she* could believe every word he'd uttered. Of course, it was all a convincing falsehood, and the only reason he had just said what he had was to provide her with a plausible back story for an implausible situation.

She pulled away a bit and he abruptly dropped his hands, although his dark eyes were still riveted to her face.

'Nice one,' she said shakily. 'You're good.'

For a few seconds, Gabriel continued to stare at her in complete silence, then he raked his fingers through his hair and turned away.

'Right—bags, and then onward bound on our little unforeseen adventure.'

Helen wasn't sure whether the smooth ride in the limo was quick or whether she was so submerged in her thoughts that the time flew by.

There was no more conversation with Gabriel, because he spent the time on his phone, having extended conference calls because of his unexpected absence from his office for a couple of days. She zoned out because she was fed up gabbling about work-related issues as a cover to hide her growing apprehension.

Her thoughts made her feel queasy but the scenery rolling past them lulled her.

A thousand shades of green unravelled beneath gentle hills, and there were distant views of white villages clinging to the sides of the hills. The sky was milky-blue. It was like being immersed in a beautiful painting and even the passing of cars on the road couldn't quite detract from that sensation.

She blinked as the limo swerved off the main drag to make its way through lush terrain, and then the rise of white stone carved like a monument against a backdrop of clambering houses, variously painted in pastel shades but all red-roofed and symmetrical, like perfectly shaped boxes.

'My Italian roots stem from these parts.'

It was the first thing Gabriel had said for a while and now Helen looked at him with interest. He was leaning against the door, sprawled in his seat as he gazed at her.

'Does it feel peculiar?' she asked softly. 'Have you never been tempted to visit?'

'No point,' he replied. 'As you know, my parents emigrated to California to make their base there. They were sent abroad to study when they were young and that seemed to have killed any desire to return to Italy. I imagine they weren't close to Arturio and his clan. Polite contact might have been there at the start, when they first left Italy, but it was frittered away. There was certainly no mention ever made of anyone back here.'

'And you've never been curious?'

'Never. Life's too short to become immersed in a past you never knew. Besides, by the time my parents died,' he went on, 'they had exhausted a substantial amount of their joint inheritance. Because my father took little interest in the day-to-day workings of the various companies, he'd failed to see that many of the old stalwarts had retired and their younger replacement weren't quite as dedicated.'

'What do you mean?'

'I mean, I had to do a hatchet job on the failing arms of the business—get rid of the dross and build it back up before I could even think of doing my own thing. There was no need to go to Italy to oversee any of that because the head offices had long been relocated to New York.'

He looked at her. 'How do you manage to do that?' he murmured.

'Do what?'

'Get me to say things I wouldn't normally say.' His voice was a low, vaguely surprised murmur and his dark gaze was speculative as it rested on her.

Helen shivered and made sure to remind herself that the last thing she needed was a couple of throwaway confidences, dragged out of him because of circumstance, to get her imagining that she meant more to him on any level than what she was—his secretary.

She was also aware that there was a danger of him resenting her over time for knowing more about him than he had ever bargained for.

He pointed ahead of them and she glanced to see that their limo was beginning an ascent through the picturesque town towards a distant and sprawling villa, built along the lines of a castle, all white and grey stone that seemed to spring from the very rock on which it squatted.

'I was under the impression that Arturio and his family couldn't quite afford to modernise the vineyards, hence the sale...' she murmured, awestruck by the villa they were fast approaching.

'A castle takes some upkeep,' Gabriel returned wryly. 'Just between the two of us, there was an informal agreement I made with Arturio, that I would look around the place and see what I could do to save it from falling into more disrepair. It would barely make a dent in my finances. His kids have been after him to sell it for a long time, but the truth is the old man is attached to it—probably more than he should be—and I would want to preserve it.'

'A knight in shining armour—whatever the family connection.'

'Well, as knights in shining armour go, it's nice for me to find a role that I enjoy occupying, considering none of my exes would ever agree with the description.'

He looked at her, brooding and thoughtful. 'And with good reason.'

Gabriel looked broodingly at Helen's calm, intelligent, fine-boned features. He'd never contemplated anything serious with any woman, and it had been easy, because the women he had dated had been unsuitable for any role other than just to pass through. Had he subconsciously ambushed any possibility of commitment on any level by choosing the wrong types of women? It was an interesting thought.

He looked away. 'We're here; let the fun begin.'

And so they were. Arturio and Isabella were already outside. Just the two of them, although Helen could spot uniformed help behind.

Their chauffeur swooped round to open the door and the action began. The smile was already on Helen's face as Gabriel looped his arm casually around her shoulders, and it stayed there as they were welcomed with fanfare into the mansion. Then, with arrangements and timings made for drinks and dinner, they were shown to their bedroom.

CHAPTER SEVEN

GABRIEL LOOSENED HIS TIE. He couldn't remember the last time he'd worn a tie, but drinks and dinner with Arturio, Isabella and various relatives invited to a meet-and-greet seemed to holler for one. He'd suspected formality was something Arturio might appreciate and had packed accordingly: he'd been right.

Now, the evening was behind them.

The matter of a shared bedroom had been briskly dealt with by Helen the minute the bedroom door had been quietly closed behind them.

With a king-sized bed staring at them, she had spun round on her heels, hands on her hips, and informed him that he could take the *chaise longue* by the window, no ifs or buts.

There would also be a bathroom rota.

Gabriel had promptly agreed to both, but he had felt a suspicious quickening of his libido as he had coolly locked eyes with the pink-cheeked, fiery woman who seemed to divulge more and more compelling sides to her with every passing minute.

And, wow, had those sides to her he'd never glimpsed before come into their own earlier. He felt himself breaking out in a light sweat thinking about it. Banished to one of the bathrooms on the floor they had been designated—safe in the knowledge that the chance of anyone passing him was remote because the place was vast and their wing seemed empty—he thought back to the moment she had walked into the drawing room.

He'd gone down ahead of her to test the ground and fend off the brunt of the questions about them. It had been easy enough because everyone there was either far too polite and well behaved to display avid curiosity, or else too insecure in their English, preferring to dip in and out of Italian. Besides, they had all clustered around him, eager to fill in the gaps about a relative they had never met. That he had brought a woman with him was less significant.

He was fluent in Italian and was in the middle of an anecdote about his Californian vineyard when he stopped mid-sentence and stared.

He'd told her that, for their charade to pull out all the stops, his eyes would have to to light up when he saw her. He'd made some fatuous remark about her wardrobe, safe in the knowledge that there was no way she could ever break habits of a lifetime and really get into character for the part she was playing. The ground had shifted between them but *that much*? No—no chance.

But that outfit for travel had shown a departure from the expected, and when she'd paused in the doorway of the drawing room…

He groaned now, tugged the tie down and then began getting undressed, switching on the stuttering shower and keeping it cold.

Red…where had *that* come from? She'd been wearing red—a deep, sexy red, modestly covering most of her but cut in ways that showed off her elegant sexiness and revealed just enough of her cleavage to have him desperate to see more.

The colour had complemented her complexion and matched the shade of lip gloss she had chosen to wear. If she'd aimed to garner all his attention, then it had worked perfectly. And he knew that Arturio and Isabella had been looking at him with affectionate approval, because the dark flush slanting his cheekbones and his loss of speech had certainly pointed in the direction of a guy in love. Not true, but what else would they have thought?

And the remainder of the evening had passed in a daze. He'd talked and chatted as normal, autopilot taking over, but his eyes had kept straying to her, taking her in, appreciating every gesture and admiring the way she engaged with people she didn't know from Adam.

She had some Italian, and used the little she knew to draw in the younger contingent, of which there were eight, and laughing with delight, begging them to correct her.

The cold water barely contained a raging libido, and he was glad he'd invested in some very staid pyjamas, because had he done his usual and slept in only his boxers then his erection would have been way too easy to spot for his liking.

'Taking no chances, I see,' he drawled, just as soon as he was in the bedroom and had closed the door behind him.

She'd set up camp on the enormous bed and drawn the curtains around it, with only one side open, so that he could see her safely tucked away with her book in her hand and a tense expression on her face.

'I've put some linen on the *chaise longue*.'

'So I see. I'm not anticipating getting much sleep, if I'm honest. A hard five-five *chaise longue* isn't going to work wonders for a guy who's six-three.'

'I'm sorry about that,' she said politely, and Gabriel grinned and sauntered towards her. He thought back to the way she'd blushed and sighed when he'd touched her and he thought of how far they had strayed from their normal working relationship. This arrangement made sense but it certainly didn't take into account the vagaries of his imagination. Was her imagination doing loops as well? Or had common sense won out at the end of the day?

'Are you?'

'No.'

'Theoretically, I should get the four-poster with the curtains, considering this little adventure is all of your doing.' Then he laughed at her obvious discomfort and added, placatingly, 'Fortunately you're dealing with a gentleman, and I wouldn't dream of depriving you of your beauty sleep. By the way, you were brilliant tonight. I do believe you charmed your audience.'

Helen was busy wondering how a pair of very sensible navy-blue pyjamas could look so unfairly sexy on a man. She wanted to tear her eyes away but she couldn't. They surreptitiously roved over the way the sleeves were shoved up to reveal the dark hair on his sinewy forearms, and her mind was all of a tizzy, imagining what would be revealed if the drawstring of the bottoms was loosened.

'All in a day's work,' she said, clearing her throat, which was dry. 'If you want to lie in, let me know and I'll make sure I'm out of the room before you.'

'There's no need to be quite so formal, Helen, but, if it helps, I'll be up by five and I'll hit the ground running. If I'm to work on the place, fix it where it's in the process of falling down, then I'll need to get an idea of what work might need doing and start mentally doing some costings. So you can lock the bedroom door behind me and take your time getting ready.'

'Good. Yes.'

'There's a strict itinerary for tomorrow and then we can make noises about going. I haven't quite confirmed how long we can stay here, but Arturio knows it won't be longer than three days.'

'Great.'

'Additionally—and you'll be pleased to hear—there'll be some work to do tomorrow, despite the relaxation criteria laid down. I'll want you to schedule all the details of what might need to be done to this place so that I can put things in place as soon as possible.'

He raked his fingers through his hair and shot her a crooked smile. 'Don't fret, Helen, this will all be over in the blink of an eye, and we'll put the whole episode firmly behind us. Indeed, I'm thinking of flying straight to Hong Kong from here to start talks on a little company I'm thinking of merging with one of my own. By the time I'm back in London, you'll be surprised how all of this, everything, will just become a vague and distant memory…'

Time couldn't pass fast enough, as far as Helen was concerned.

She had no idea what she'd been thinking when she'd recklessly abandoned common sense and chosen a wardrobe to impress. Had she wanted to impress Gabriel—show off her assets?

Of course, she'd seen his eyes widen the evening before when she'd daringly worn red. But if anything he was less touchy-feely than before, now that they were here, and he was true to his word when it came to keeping to his side of the bedroom, as per her instructions.

She'd heard him breathing but the old-fashioned curtains around the four-poster bed had cocooned her from the nerve-racking sight of him on that *chaise longue*. Eventually she'd nodded off and he'd been nowhere in sight when she'd awakened the following morning at a little past eight-thirty.

And then there was work—exploring the vast, old mansion, which showed visible signs of decay; jotting down everything he said in a way that made sense only to her. Arturio was with them the whole time. Then they had lunch with Arturio and Isabella, when they discussed myriad possibilities for the place, including restoring one of the wings as a landmark treasure where visitors could pay to visit and sample authentic Italian cuisine in exclusive, traditional surroundings.

And now…another dinner, yet more people to meet, and another dress she wished she hadn't bought…

Because these outfits made her lose control of her thoughts: made her think of herself as a siren out to seduce her man; made her forget that she was just the secretary obeying an instruction from her boss that appropriate clothing would suit their temporary charade.

She eyed the blue number on the bed with a jaundiced, resigned look. It was a wraparound dress in silk that would fall softly to mid-calf, and in the process expose most of her back. She had felt like a million dollars when she'd tried it on in the boutique and she'd imagined the look on Gabriel's face when he saw her in it.

Now? Not so much. She hadn't bargained on wanting too much when she was in these clothes that made her feel sexy and expensive—too much of those dark eyes on her, too much of his hands on her, too much of everything. The confidences they'd shared had bridged a gap between them and it was hard to look at him and remain detached.

She strolled over and held the dress on its hanger up in front of the floor-to-ceiling mirror by the window, trying to work out whether her breasts would be visible under the thin silk. She was wearing only her cotton underwear and was barefoot—no bra, no shoes, no anything but her panties, and oblivious to everything but what was going on in her head.

She certainly didn't hear the door open, nor was she aware of the man framed in the doorway. She only came to when she heard a voice approaching, saying something from a distance, and when she focused in the mirror there was Gabriel, standing there, and then quickly turning to say something to someone before slipping into the room and firmly closing the door behind him.

She turned around, stared at him and the dress fell to the floor in a swirling pool of blue silk…

Gabriel couldn't breathe.

He leaned against the closed door and couldn't *not* stare because he had never seen anything so damned wonderful in his life.

Her small, high breasts were perfect, tipped with deep-rose nipples, her shoulders were slender and defined and her waist was the span of his hands.

The sun had turned her skin pale gold, but her breasts and belly were paler.

'Helen,' he croaked, wanting to tell her that he had knocked, that the door had been half-open when he'd spotted Arturio. He'd known that it would be bizarre for him to shut it, because it was supposed to be the love nest the engaged couple were sharing. It would be expected that he would be eager to step inside after an hour catching up on work in one of the rooms downstairs, rather than keen to beat a hasty retreat because a conversation with his host was more interesting than the woman waiting inside for him.

Her lips were parted and he propelled himself forward, at once trying to look away whilst simultaneously meet her startled gaze to reassure her that…that…

That what? That he was somehow immune to the vision of beauty standing immobile in front of him?

'My God, you're beautiful,' was what he heard himself saying.

Their eyes tangled as he moved closer to her until he was inches away, until the warmth of her body enveloped him.

He reached to cup her cheek with his hand and then trailed

his thumb across it, feeling the smoothness of her skin and the softness of her lower lip.

'I want you,' he said hoarsely. His finger was on the mouth he wanted to cover with his own and his erection was a painful rod of steel pushing against his trousers.

'This is crazy,' Helen whispered.

'I know.'

'But...'

'But...it's a craziness both of us need to get out of our system.' He wasn't going to touch her until she told him he could, but he was going to explode if she didn't. Worse, he would ejaculate in his trousers, and he wouldn't be able to stop himself.

She didn't speak. Instead, she took his hand from her mouth, put it on her breast and sighed as he began to stroke the rubbery stiffness of her nipple.

They were expected for drinks imminently. He'd already been running late when he'd headed up the stairs to quickly get ready and head back down.

To hell with imminent drinks.

He kissed her, plundering her eager mouth with his tongue, caressing her breast even as he eased her back towards the four-poster bed until she buckled against the mattress and tumbled back, landing softly with both her hands spread wide.

Gabriel stared, breathing heavily, looking at her spread in front of him. It was a struggle to undress, but undress he did, unbuttoning his shirt, stripping it off and then following that up with his trousers until, like her, he remained in underwear only.

The boxers bulged with the heavy weight of his erection. He was so turned on...

Was she as turned on as he was?

He stepped between her legs, which were dangling off

the side of the bed, reached down to cup his hand between her thighs and felt the tell-tale wetness of a craving that was equal to his.

His dark eyes never left her face.

He balanced on the palm of one hand, resting it flat on the mattress, while he gently eased the other under her panties until he was feeling the slickness of the groove there. He stroked and she squirmed and parted her legs wider, eyelids fluttering shut and colour rushing to her cheeks.

Gabriel was on fire.

He knelt between her legs, tugged the panties off and then rested his hands against the soft skin of her inner thighs so that he could spread them and open her up for his enjoyment, for his feasting.

He buried his head between her legs and breathed her in for a few seconds, and then he nuzzled the soft down before sliding his tongue into her, questing to find the stiffened bud of her clitoris so that he could tease it until she was gasping and desperate for more.

She smelled warm and musky, the smell of lust, passion and need, and it thrilled him more than he was prepared to analyse. He just kept licking, lapping her moistness and turning her on until she could no longer stop the unstoppable.

With a groan, she bucked and spasmed against his mouth, and only when she was utterly spent did he blindly fumble in the wallet that had hit the floor along with the rest of his stuff, extracting the foil packet he always kept there.

Heat was pouring through her body.

She half-opened her eyes and looked at him with glazed fascination.

Had this really happened? She'd been taken out of deep freeze and the burn of desire was tearing into her with devastating force. My goodness, never had she been pleasured in such a way before, feeling the earth swirl around her as she rose higher and higher to come straight into his exploring mouth.

Helen knew that she should have felt some sense of horror at barriers not just crossed, but thoroughly stampeded over, but she didn't. She felt powerful, energised and wildly replete.

She curved against him and her fingers trembled as they skimmed over his hard, muscled body.

'I'm sorry,' she murmured without too much regret in her voice. 'I should have waited, but I just couldn't.'

'Nothing has ever felt sexier,' Gabriel growled. 'Unfortunately, I'm so damned turned on that I don't think it's going to be a slow and lingering journey right now. I just want to feel you around me.'

Helen could think of nothing better. She was dimly aware of him donning protection, giving her body time to calm down a little, because after all this time being touched made her feel as if it was the first time.

He mounted her and entered in one deep thrust, and all those tingling nerve endings that had begun to flatten vibrated back into life and, as he pushed deeper and deeper into her, she could feel herself soaring once again, her whole body climbing up and up to an orgasm that was shattering when it came.

Reality only returned when her sharp, mind-blowing arousal and shattering orgasm ebbed away.

He'd rolled off her and was lying flat on the bed, staring up at the silk canopy above them.

What was he thinking?

Helen wondered whether she should be feeling regretful because she wasn't. She'd invited him to touch her and there wasn't a single part of her that wasn't content with the decision she'd made, even though it went against all common sense. In terms of her position as his secretary, frankly it couldn't have been worse.

She reached to cover herself and he stayed her hand, turning on his side to face her.

'Don't. I like looking at you.'

Helen adjusted her position so that she could likewise look at him.

'I don't think either of us can pretend that this never happened,' she said quietly.

'I feel that would be a tall order.'

'And I accept the consequences because I wanted this as much as you did.'

'The consequences…'

Helen breathed in deeply and her steady gaze didn't waver. It was distracting because he was playing with her hair, stroking it away from her face, and his slumberous eyes were doing all sorts of stupid things to her body and making a mess of her head.

'Where do we go from here? How are we supposed to just pick things up and carry on?' she said. 'I accept that you'll have no choice but to let me go.'

'I'm surprised that you feel you know what's going on in my head.'

'Isn't that what's going on in your head, Gabriel? You play the field with women and, when it's over, it's easy for you to move on because you don't have to carry on seeing them. Well, it's a little different in this case, isn't it? You'll have your error of judgement staring you in the face every day, and it would be unacceptable.'

'Who ever said anything about it being an error of judgement? You act as though this has sprung from thin air, but has it? We've been circling one another for days, chipping away beneath the surface. We've crossed more barriers than I even recognised were in place! And we both know there's been more than than—more than just finding out things about one another we never knew before.'

'I'm your secretary.' Her skin was hot and prickly, her body still tingling from being touched.

'You're a sexy, beautiful, smart woman I wanted to sleep with—who wanted to sleep with me.'

Helen blushed at his description. Smart—yes, she would concede that. But sexy? Beautiful? She'd never thought of herself as either of those things. With every word she could feel herself hurtling deeper and faster into the unknown.

'Just for the record, I still want to sleep with you.'

'Don't say stuff like that,' Helen whispered.

'Why not?' He trailed his fingers beneath her belly button and over the soft, downy hair between her legs, and her breath hitched.

'Because…'

'Do you still want this? Us making love?'

'Don't! I'm trying to be sensible.'

'Have you ever been anything but sensible, Helen? Have you ever dared to take a risk?'

'I…'

'Take this risk. We're here for another day or so. Let's enjoy one another—maybe hang around for a bit longer. I've earned the right to do what I want when it comes to showing up in an office and sitting behind a desk.'

'And when it's time for reality to kick in, Gabriel? To face me across the width of that desk and for things to return to what they used to be? How's that going to be possible?' Her words were a desperate plea.

'Have you thought that getting this thing out of our systems, whatever it is, is the very thing that will make it possible to face one another once, as you say, I'm facing you across the width of my desk?'

'I don't understand.'

'When this fire has burnt out,' Gabriel murmured, his hand drifting to her breast so that he could play with her nipple, which stiffened at his touch, 'What will remain will be fond memories of something that came and went. Who knows? Maybe this has been building between us from day one without either of us paying attention to it. It *is* possible, Helen, for two people to make love, to enjoy one another, to have something of a relationship and still be able to face one another afterwards...'

'You make it sound easy.'

'It's as easy or as difficult as you choose to make it.'

There was a flaw in that logic but Helen was struggling to see it, because his words were as soft and tempting as the darkest, most luscious of chocolate. She *wanted* to believe him because she wasn't ready to say goodbye to this wondrous thing he had stirred in her.

When she thought about the business of walking away—of giving up her job, of never seeing him again, hearing his voice or drinking in the way he smiled, the way he laughed, the way he frowned—she felt physically nauseous.

Was he right? Was this something that had been simmering beneath the surface for a long time, finally released into the open?

If people became lovers, wasn't it still possible to be friends afterwards? If people could get married and have kids and then divorce and end up friends, then of course it was possible!

She needed this. It was safe because she wouldn't be foolish enough to try and build anything from it. Surely she could dump common sense and chasing safety just for a while? She would never be able to give up those fundamental principles that guided her, but she could dare just this once, couldn't she?

And the bottom line was that if working with him proved

uncomfortable, because of this, then she could just get another job. Yes, she loved the one she had, but if because of this she no longer did then London was a thriving city and she would soon find something else.

'We should head down,' she said softly, but she was running her hand along his sinewy thigh and curling her own thigh over his, which made him smile slowly and with intent.

'We have a little time to ourselves…'

Helen smiled because, if she was going to succumb to this, then she was going to do it without reservation.

'Think you can be quick?' she asked daringly.

Gabriel drawled, 'Now, that's a challenge I can work at trying to overcome…'

Gabriel watched as their cases were being taken to the chauffeur-driven car waiting for them. For a few seconds, he appreciated the sun on his face, then the sound of voices reminded him that they were on their way.

They had stayed on for an extra day at Arturio's magnificent villa, and he and Helen had actually managed to get work done, as they had catalogued what would need to be done insofar as renovations went.

The more he saw of Arturio and his family, the more important it seemed that he discover more about his own lineage. His parents had dumped their country and severed the bonds that had held them there. It felt important that he not follow in their footsteps now that this door had been opened that led to a family he hadn't known.

All told, everything had worked out perfectly, and that included what had started life as a charade and had morphed into something altogether different.

He spun round, back to the present, and watched with satisfaction as Helen smiled and hugged the elderly couple, her warmth as natural as her gestures of genuine affection.

An extra week in Italy, playing truant for the first time in his life. In truth, Gabriel hadn't expected his desire to last as long as it had. Or perhaps, he hadn't expected his desire to last this long without showing visible signs of waning.

There was a big difference here. Even when it came to the hottest woman, he knew that his attention span was sorely challenged.

But with Helen? To see was to want and to want was to want more.

Rome, he'd told her…

'We can spend a few days there before we return to the grind in London.'

'I've never been to Rome,' had been her response, to which he had immediately wanted to say that there were a million other cities he could introduce her to, all different but equally captivating.

He'd kept quiet about that, however, because work would beckon in a few days and he wasn't into making promises he couldn't keep. A few days' worth of time out was one thing—but making a list of when those time outs would happen? No way.

He shook hands with Arturio, kissed Isabella on both cheeks and then, when he and Helen were finally in the car slowly driving away from the villa, he turned to her.

'Change of plan.'

'Okay.'

Helen sat back against the door, willed herself to relax and looked at him.

The past few days had been just incredible. She had seen her boss for the man he was underneath—the easy charm beneath the driving ambition and the core of steel.

She had seen him overtaken by desire, had seen him relaxed and sated and had watched him sleep, his breathing low and even, the years dropping from him in slumber. She had heard him laugh with genuine amusement, and seen how thoughtful he could be as they had gone from room to room in the sprawling villa and he had listened to Arturio and Isabella's concerns as the family finances were laid bare. They had welcomed him into their hearts and trusted him the way they would have trusted their own son.

There were sides to him she had only ever guessed at. The only one thing that remained a steady, beating constant was the acknowledgement that he would very soon call it a day and that she would fall in line and accept the inevitable.

What they had, however wonderful it was for her, was living on borrowed time.

He was looking at her now with something approaching gravity and she was already bracing herself.

'I said that we would go to Rome—'

'Which isn't necessary,' she interjected quickly. 'I do get it that time flies, and there's only so long the office can be left.'

'I happen to have some extremely capable people there who can pick up the slack at a moment's notice.'

Looking at her, Gabriel wondered if this was the reason he felt so comfortable with this woman, why his attention wasn't beginning to wander. Was it because she didn't cling? There was no fear that she would start getting the wrong ideas—ideas about settling down, going to bed with him at her side and waking up with him bringing her a cup of tea. She didn't want to domesticate him.

For a few seconds, he thought of settling down with her and going to sleep with her just there, within reach. For a few seconds, he accepted that playing the field was no longer how he wanted to spend his time, and Helen…

He felt comfortable with her—frighteningly so.

He frowned.

'At any rate, I've realised that Rome—enjoyable as it is—is painfully crowded during the summer months. Tourists everywhere, swarming like ants over everything.'

'Yes, I suppose so,' Helen agreed with a certain amount of wistfulness in her voice.

'So, instead of Rome, I am proposing somewhere closer to Genoa.'

'Sorry?'

Gabriel patted the space next to him and waited until she had shuffled from where she was sitting and strapped herself into the middle seat next to him, then he reached into his trouser pocket and pulled out a crumpled piece of paper which, as he smoothed it on his thigh, revealed itself to be a map.

'Old-fashioned, I know. Most people open a map on their phone, but for some reason I've always carried this around in my wallet.'

'You have?'

Gabriel shrugged. 'Did you know that once upon a time Genoa was one of the richest cities on the planet? It was because of its port. So many of the wealthy lived there that there was more money than good causes to spend it on. They built houses and mansions, and more houses and more mansions.'

'That'll be interesting.' Helen peered at the map, then she looked at him. 'But I don't understand, Gabriel. Why there?'

'Arturio and Isabella. They've opened my eyes to the value of the family I never knew through no choice of my own. My parents had no use for blood ties. It's time I corrected that oversight…and it will start with the place they once called home.'

CHAPTER EIGHT

GABRIEL DIDN'T QUITE know when he'd decided to abandon Rome in favour of Genoa, a place that had only existed in his head as where his parents had come from—the birthplace they had jointly vacated in their early teens, first to board at school in America, one in California and the other in New York and then later, when they were married, because they had found it boring and stultifying.

He would never know what might have happened had they come from larger, more united families. Would they have been duty-bound to stay? To supervise fortunes that would have been spread around family members?

'We're not a million miles away from the city,' he said now, 'so it's not as though it's going to be much of a detour—an hour or so. I've booked a hotel in the middle of the city for four nights.'

'Are you sure?'

'What's there to be sure about?'

'Well—retracing your past. Wouldn't you rather do that on your own?'

Gabriel flushed. 'That's over-romanticising the situation, Helen. I'm not embarking on a touching voyage of discovery, and I won't be investing time working out the family tree. That said, since when is it ever too late to be curious? We're reasonably close, location wise, and so why not? I've been to Rome a hundred times. If you'd rather I take you to

Rome, or anywhere else for that matter, then of course…' His eyes darkened as he brought this back to a level he found comfortable. 'Your body would turn me on wherever we choose to go.'

'Don't be silly.' Helen smiled but her eyes remained serious.

'Like I said, I'm curious,' Gabriel conceded with a shrug. 'Neither of my parents spoke much about the city that had raised them and, when they did, they were hardly flattering.'

'What do you mean?'

'Dull, antiquated, no fun at all… My parents placed a lot of value on having fun which is probably why they relinquished responsibility for me to people they could pay. I don't believe they thought a kid was much fun, far less a baby.'

When she looked at him, he threw her a crooked smile but his eyes were thoughtful. 'You make a ridiculously good listener,' he said gruffly.

'Surprisingly, so do you.' Helen blushed.

'I'll take that as a compliment.'

'You're very spoiled when it comes to women complimenting you, aren't you?'

'Is that because I'm amazing?' He grinned but his eyes remained thoughtful.

'In a way, I guess I could have done with a less devoted father,' Helen said slowly. 'The older I got, the more I understood why he was as protective as he was, but looking back?' She sighed. 'I drifted into that engagement with George because I suppose I was conditioned to be safe, and that was a safe relationship, a known quantity. It just wasn't the right relationship for me. I guess George drifted into it as well, if not for the same reasons. I guess he found it comfortable, and sometimes men can end up going down the road of least resistance.'

'And here you are now,' Gabriel drawled. 'Burning up the rulebook when it comes to safety.'

'Yes.' But then, she thought in confusion, why did he make her feel so safe if he was so emotionally dangerous for her?

'I can't believe you weren't just a little bit tempted to visit your roots before.' Curiosity brought her back to the topic they had started off discussing.

She thought about what he had said about her being a good listener and it warmed her inside, yet wasn't this a very special trait born from the fact that they had known one another for some time before becoming lovers? Wasn't there a familiarity there that had expanded now that the boundaries between them had become blurred? It was something neither of them had factored in, but it was why things felt so right between them for her, even though what they were doing was so foolhardy.

'It would have been out of my way,' Gabriel said prosaically. 'Now, though? I had no idea Arturio's place was within spitting distance, so to speak.'

'How do you think you're going to feel?'

'Not following you.'

'I mean…' Their eyes tangled and Helen reddened. At what point did she start overstepping the mark? At what point would his shutters come down because, no matter how cosy they got with one another, he would always have a wall up when it came to getting *too* cosy?

'Don't worry,' he said drily. 'You don't have to stock up on the tissues because there's a chance I'm going to break down and start crying.'

'No, I can't imagine you doing that…'

'And for the record? I've never appreciated girlfriends who go down the psychoanalysing route.'

'But I'm not a *girlfriend*, am I?'

'Touché.'

Helen reddened and wondered, if she wasn't a girlfriend,

then what was she exactly? A temporary plaything? That didn't feel good, but wasn't it a role she had volunteered for? She'd known from the start that he didn't do love, just as she'd known that that was what she wanted from any relationship. But things were changing for her and she was slowly starting to realise how much he could hurt her, how much *this* could hurt her.

'Does X mark the spot on the map?' She abruptly changed the subject.

Gabriel was silent for a few seconds. He thought of that map. It had been given to him by his father years ago. It had been a rare occasion when his parents had been around for a sustained period, something like three months, and he had seen more of them than he ever had before.

He must have been not quite a teenager, before he had begun closing down, forming hard and fast judgements on the nature of relationships that were so all-consuming they left no room for anything else. Before he had begun building his life along the lines of one where control would always trump spontaneity.

He could remember his father trailing his finger over the little icons, chatting about things in the city, the sights and landmarks there. They had both come from sufficient wealth that they'd individually been raised in small palaces although, he had confided to Gabriel, ruffling his hair, his mother had come with the bigger bag of gold.

'There are no spots marked,' he said, withdrawing, because it suddenly felt safer. 'But, I assure you, there will be many things of interest to see.'

'Including where your parents lived?'

'Let's ditch the questions,' Gabriel said softly. 'They bore me. Look at the scenery instead. It's incomparable.'

* * *

Helen recognised this for what it was—she was being reminded of her place.

As she gazed out, however, she saw the scenery was as incomparable as he'd said and he relaxed and became an informative guide, pointing out all sorts of things and filling her head with so many pieces of information about the country that she wondered whether he'd made it his mission to read up all about the place his parents had decided to leave behind.

Sepia fortresses rubbed shoulders with clusters of brightly coloured houses, and everything seemed to be embedded into the terrain, a wonderful mix of earthy tones mixed with the greens, greys and blues of undulating hills.

The car weaved through villages and towns at a leisurely pace. Inside it was cool from the air-conditioning but it was easy to feel the heat blasting down from cloudless blue skies. The sea was a constant presence, although it was hard to get a feel for how close or far away they were from it at any given time.

There was a sense of cliffs plunging into ocean, glimpsed here and there as they took a corner, and of entire villages clinging precariously to them, although they were surely in no imminent danger of erosion, because they all looked as though they'd been perched on the same spot for centuries.

She wanted to ask him how he felt, being here, even if he wasn't familiar with the place, but she'd been warned off and she knew how to recognise those boundary lines.

Watching her as she gazed in rapt appreciation out of the window, Gabriel was filled with a sense of well-being.

He actually hadn't got such a kick from sealing any deal in a long time. He was glad that he had branched out to make his own fortune, independent of the wealth he had inherited from his parents, which had still been considerable, even though much diminished from years of profligate spending. But nothing had felt as risky as opening up to Arturio and recognising family members he hadn't even known existed.

And his secretary had been with him for the ride from the very beginning. He'd told her that she was a good listener, and he'd meant it, and when he looked back to before they had become lovers he could see that he'd always found her relaxing to talk to. She didn't demand. She didn't nag. In return, he confided. It was a trade-off that had happened without him even really noticing.

He was looking forward to watching her various expressions of delight at the hotel he had chosen, for once doing his own legwork and sourcing somewhere suitably lavish, not to mention the various places they would visit during their brief stay.

He'd mentally made a list. He wondered what, if anything, she had seen of the world. Her father had been protective, but surely she would have done some travelling, if only to safe, touristy destinations?

'I know your engagement was broken off but where had you planned on going on honeymoon?' he asked curiously, and Helen dragged her attention away from the passing panorama to look at him.

'Nowhere.'

Gabriel's eyebrows shot up in surprise. 'Is that normal? I thought every young married couple was eager to make elaborate plans about where they would go on their honeymoon. The one time to throw financial caution to the winds!'

Helen reddened and she sighed.

'We thought it was more sensible to put the money aside to buy somewhere.' Of course, warning bells should have rung for her at the time for that very reason, she thought. She looked at Gabriel from under her lashes and thought that, for someone who wasn't interested in meaningful relationships, he was pretty emotionally shrewd.

'Don't forget that I was conditioned to be sensible, and maybe George simply fell into line because he was so mild mannered and really quite sensible as well. We both thought buying a house made more sense than frittering away what savings we had on going abroad for a fortnight in the sun. My dad couldn't afford to give that to us as a wedding present, not when he'd paid for the wedding, and George's parents were no better off financially.'

'You must have been very hurt when it all came crashing down.'

'I dealt with it.'

'With your usual cool? Sensible to the end?'

'If I were as sensible as you think, I wouldn't be here.'

'Very, very glad you realise that sensible only works if you dump it now and again.' Gabriel smiled, eyes darkening. 'Light and shade and so forth.'

He looked at her pensively, watching her blushing smile.

'And speaking of honeymoons…' she raised her eyebrows '…can I ask how it is that *you* never had one?'

'Interesting question.'

'Is that your way of saying that you're not going to give me an answer?'

'Does anyone know me better than you?'

'You're impossible.'

'Is that why you find me so sexy?' He enjoyed the way she went bright red at that—very satisfactory indeed.

'Impossible, and with an ego the size of a cruise liner.' She suddenly wanted him to touch her so badly that it was an effort not to fling herself on his lap and beg him to do with her as he wanted. Thank goodness the privacy partition was shut so that their driver couldn't hear the conversation although, if he glanced in the rear-view mirror, he would easily be able to see the deepening flush of a woman in the grip of lust.

Gabriel was looking at her lazily, reading the mood, which only added to the electrifying charge in the air.

He reached to slide across the screen so that the driver now could neither hear nor see them.

'What would you like to know?'

Somehow, the distance between them had closed. Had he shifted over to her? Had she moved towards him? Or maybe whatever charge had been released had just drawn them together.

'How is it that a guy like you isn't married?'

'Because a guy like me never had any interest in settling down.'

He slipped his hand underneath the knee-length skirt she was wearing, ran it up her thigh and then, eyes still pinned to her face, casually pushed his fingers under the crotch of her knickers, which were damp.

'You think too much about sex...' Helen breathed, her eyelids fluttering, and Gabriel laughed under his breath.

'Are you telling me you'd rather I wasn't doing what I'm doing?'

'This isn't—appropriate. Oh...'

'Shh...too much talking. We can return to the tedious honeymoon conversation just as soon as I've done this...'

He had managed to shove the crotch of the panties to one side so that he could explore her wetness, and this he did, fingers inserting deep inside her as she wriggled a little lower to accommodate them.

Outside, the scenery continued to flash past, a whirl of various shades of green, hills and mountains rising and falling, winding roads and clambering villages. All a background blur to the far more captivating sight of a woman in the throes of passion.

Her eyes were shut, her lips parted and her shiny, well-behaved hair was ruffled. Hectic colour was spread across her cheekbones and her breathing was soft and jerky, the breathing of someone who wanted to groan aloud but couldn't.

He could have watched her for ever.

He found the bud of her clitoris and stroked it, and nearly groaned out loud himself as she slid just a tiny bit further down.

He watched as she spasmed into orgasm, watched her colour deepen and her nostrils flare and the bumpy arch of her body, which she couldn't control.

There was privacy glass on the windows but even so the brightness of the sunlight pouring into the back seat of the car left nothing to the imagination.

This was passion at its most powerful and he wished, for a split second, that he could capture it for ever in his head, never to let it go, never to allow it to be become diluted over time.

'There now,' he murmured in a shaky, husky voice. 'Don't you feel a lot better after that?' He removed his hand, which smelled of her musky fragrance, and neatened her skirt.

Helen shuffled back into something resembling an upright position.

She'd never done anything like this in her life before, but then there was so much she'd done with this man that she'd never done before.

And every experience was backlit with something wild, soft, powerful and tender.

She looked at him, eyes widening, and then just as quickly she looked away, but her heart was beating madly inside her.

How had things crept up on her like this? How had she

found herself accepting the cards that had been dealt whilst desperately longing for them to be shuffled and re-dealt? He had got under her skin in ways that had been small and subtle but devastatingly significant.

And of course, she had noticed it. She wasn't a fool. She'd known that she was developing feelings for him, but it had been convenient to pretend that she could control those feelings and make sure they stuck to the plan. If she didn't actually give those feelings a *name*, if she didn't call it *love*, then she could tell herself that she was still in control, even when she felt out of her depth.

She'd done a good job at trying to kid herself.

He touched her and she went up in flames but, oh, it was so much worse than that. He smiled and her heart skipped a beat. He looked and she wanted to faint. He talked and she yearned for him to talk some more, to tell her what she wanted to hear—that he had feelings for her too. That this was more than just a dalliance that had happened out of the blue and taken wings because of circumstances neither of them could have predicted.

She'd been brought up never to take risks and, whilst she had felt protected by that mantra, she had failed to recognise how vulnerable it had left her—vulnerable to a guy like Gabriel, who was so far removed from anyone she could ever have imagined getting to her.

She was in love with the guy and as she sat, mouth dry, thoughts in a panic, she didn't know what to do with that.

She surfaced to find that they were nearing the small town where they would spend the next few days. Not actually in the city, as it happened, but in one of the picturesque little towns close to it, a base from which they could discover the city and its surrounds.

'You okay?'

Helen met Gabriel's confident, amused grin with a watery smile of her own.

'Perfect.' She aimed for crisp and light. She ended up with something of a sickly croak.

'Is it the drive?'

'Huh?' He had the deepest, darkest eyes, Helen though as she stared back at him. A person could drown in them. As she had—she and a million others.

'Some people can get travel sick.'

'Yes.' Helen clung to that excuse with the tenacity of a drowning person hanging onto an unexpected piece of passing driftwood. 'It's—it's my inner ear. It's always given me problems ever since I was a kid. Long drives, planes, boats and stuff.'

'I didn't think you'd done a lot of travelling,' Gabriel said with a frown.

'By car,' Helen answered quickly. 'Cornwall is far from everywhere.' She laughed weakly. 'Even going for a weekly shop could involve miles and miles of, um, travel sickness in my dad's car.'

'Must have been uncomfortable. And I suppose our little bout of activity didn't help matters…' He sent her a wolfish smile that made her toes curl and she heard herself mutter something and nothing before launching into a series of frantic questions about the area. At least when his attention was somewhere other than lasered to her face she could begin to get her thoughts in order.

What was she going to do? How could she have been so smug as to think that she could do as she wished without being affected? How could she have simultaneously spotted warning signs of emotional attachment while failing to take any safety measures to protect herself, to safeguard her heart?

She thought back to the way she had opened up to him,

gone from zero to full-blown rocket speed, in no time at all. A little sharing because they had got themselves in a charade; a few confidences so that they could pull off a relationship that wasn't there; then a few more...and now? Now every bit of her had blossomed and opened up, and she was as raw and helpless as a snail without its shell.

And Gabriel? Yes, he had shared stuff with her too, but he hadn't given any more than he could get back; hadn't gone and given her his heart while she had thrown hers at him, knowing he wasn't going to catch it and take care of it.

She was here for a just a couple more days and then they would return to England.

What next after that?

It was a blessing that he had no idea how she felt. She'd always been his calm, unflappable secretary and this arrangement, in his eyes, didn't change who she was. She was still calm. Not someone who was going to make waves that would require her dismissal, as had happened with Fifi.

She wasn't going to make waves now, she decided. She wasn't going to ask questions that couldn't be answered, and she wasn't going to give him any indication that she might want more than what they were enjoying.

For Gabriel, it was all about the sex, whatever personal snippets he had shared with her. He had confided, and she had absorbed those little confidences, and they had buried deep inside her and fed her feelings for him. She had confided and he had responded because he was interested and because they were lovers, but they hadn't fed anything in him, because there was nothing to feed.

And, if this was all the time left to her, then why shouldn't she enjoy it as well? Why shouldn't she feel like a woman. It had been so long since she had, and a few more days of stolen pleasure wasn't going to add to the pain. She was going to hurt, whatever happened.

When they returned to London, she would put a smile on her face and she would begin hunting around for something else. Maybe she would return to Cornwall. She could easily use that as an excuse if she wanted to avoid curious questions and raised eyebrows.

He was good at those two things.

'But it was very nice all the same,' she said weakly and he grinned.

'That's sounds a lot like me being damned with faint praise.'

'There goes your ego again,' Helen murmured, more in truth than jest, and he caught her eye and laughed.

'No one talks to me like that.'

'Maybe that's your problem,' she said drily.

'Who knows? You could have a point.'

She said what she thought. She always had. If she disagreed with him over something, or had a viewpoint that didn't coincide with his, she was never shy about telling him and she never feared the consequences.

He'd vaguely thought that that was because she was secure in her job, and knew he wasn't a guy who sacked anyone for a viewpoint, even though not many of his employees ever disagreed with his decisions. He'd also vaguely assumed that, because they weren't lovers, she wasn't in the same bracket as other women who tiptoed around him and were always eager to please.

But now they were lovers and she still didn't tiptoe around him. She *still* spoke her mind. She was still the same cool, composed woman.

Except, underneath there was a depth he hadn't seen before. She'd been hurt by what she'd experienced, and she'd grown from it. She had learned, as he had, that self-control was a good thing. They had both been formed from their backgrounds in different ways. Like him, she knew that life wasn't always straightforward.

His thoughts were running away at a tangent and as the grand, sepia-coloured hotel loomed ahead of them, uniformed attendants waiting to gather their luggage and usher them in, he decided that this had certainly turned out to be one of the best unexpected situations that had happened to him in a very long time.

He was going to enjoy playing tour guide for the next four days.

And he was going to enjoy so much more than that.

Helen looked at Gabriel, seeing him sprawled on the king-sized bed in the reflection of the mirror where she was sitting, brushing her hair.

The sheet was draped over him, just about covering the part of him he had only just very effectively used to bring her to a shuddering orgasm.

He'd offered to run a bath for her, when eventually she had found the energy to move, but she'd laughed and told him that a girl needed a bit of time to herself now and again.

So she'd had her bath, taking her time, and thought about how one pretence had led to another. Pretending to be an item had morphed seamlessly into pretending not to have feelings for him.

This was going to be their last night here. The past few days had been momentous. Today, in particular, her heart had clenched with love and empathy, for he had taken her to see the palace where his mother had grown up.

It had been sold many years previously and had been turned into exquisite apartments. The façade had remained the same, though, and, although he'd told her that it was a modest enough palace, it had still seemed vast to Helen, who couldn't conceive ever living in a place like that.

Sitting with strong coffee in one of the squares, people-watching, she had asked him questions and he had answered without his customary wariness, staring off into the distance, his voice low and thoughtful.

He spoke about his past the way someone might talk about a country they had once visited. Only once had she heard a curious hitch in his voice, a sign that underneath the cool exterior was an undercurrent of emotion of which, she suspected, even he was unaware. She had seen how momentous it had been for him to meet Arturio—life-changing, even if he might not have admitted it.

Helen had wondered whether this was what had sucked her in—a glimpse of someone powerful and impregnable who, without realising it, was also vulnerable and touchingly *human*.

'Penny for them.'

'Huh?'

'Your thoughts. Or I'm prepared to go higher if you'd like more. A pound, maybe?'

Helen laughed and swivelled round on the chair so that she was facing him.

'Much as I enjoy watching you brush your hair, I'd quite like it if you did it in the buff.'

'You can't always get what you want.'

'I've always been interested in challenging that particular theory. Tell me what was going through your head. You looked very thoughtful.'

'I was thinking that we leave tomorrow.'

'Has this part of the world lived up to expectations?'

His voice was still light but Helen felt that she could hear a very slight shift in it, so slight that it was barely noticeable, but she knew him well—well enough to know that he was waiting for her response, waiting to see what came after that remark.

He would always be the guy on guard for the clingy woman, the woman trying to pin him down and to make more of something than he was prepared to tolerate.

Even with her, even with someone he read as being as detached as he was from any emotional involvement, he *still* didn't quite trust her to obey the rules he laid down.

For a second she wondered what he would do if she confessed everything to him. How would he react? He would be appalled, and would see it as a betrayal of their understanding. When she thought of how his face would change, how he would begin to back-pedal, how that lasting memory of her would be one of shock and dismay, she felt sick.

She would never allow that to happen. She would always make sure that she exited without falling flat on her face in front of him.

'It has.' Helen's voice was normal when she answered and she gracefully rose from the chair to make her way to the wardrobe, from which she extracted what she would be wearing for their final meal in Italy. It was a soft, silk dress with a scooped neck in shades of rich blues and greys. It was very elegant and had cost the earth.

She could feel his dark eyes on her as she eased it over her head, over the bra and panties she had been wearing as she'd brushed her hair.

'It's a beautiful part of the world, Gabriel. There must be a part of you that wishes you could have spent more time here, growing up.'

'If wishes were horses…' But he grinned. 'And you still haven't told me what you were thinking when you said that this was our last evening here.'

'I was thinking that we've somehow managed to get very little work done, so there's going to be a lot of catching up when we get back to London.'

'And are you looking forward to that?'

'Catching up on tons of work?' Helen grimaced, scooped her sandals up with one hand and returned to the chair to slip them on; the straps were thin and fiddly. 'Does anyone look forward to catching up on tons of work?'

'You've never had a problem with tons of work.'

'That's true.' What a fool she'd been, slowly falling for this guy, never questioning the tons of work she'd always enjoyed doing, even when it had meant sacrificing a week-end. 'Actually,' she said slowly, 'I'm thinking that when I get back I might just take a week out to go visit my dad. Of course, I'll make sure whatever urgent work matters need doing get done before I go…'

She glanced up from fiddling with the straps to find him looking at her with a shuttered, thoughtful expression.

He'd asked her what she'd been thinking. What was going through his head now? Was he going to make a speech about the routine they would get back to once normal life recom-menced? Was he going to tactfully remind her that this was temporary, so she shouldn't expect it to carry on once they were back in London?

'This has been pretty intense,' she said seriously. 'There's no question it has to end once we're back in London but, realistically, we might both need a little time out before we face one another in your office. Don't you agree?'

Gabriel didn't say anything for a while.

His dark eyes drifted over her. She was saying all the right things, and he couldn't help but think about where all that common sense went the minute they were in the sack. When he thought of the way he could consign that practical side of her to a bonfire just by touching her, he felt himself getting turned on.

She did the same to him.

He was as cool and detached as she was—more so, if anything, because there was a sentimental side to her that he lacked—and yet she could rouse him with a look.

'What I'm going to say, Helen, is going to come as something of a shock…'

In a way, a shock to him as well. But things had changed. Fifi had showed up, and everything that went with her, from the demands for more than he could give to the tantrum and the flouncing out. It had made him think long and hard about the future of his choices. Then along had come Helen, as soothing as Fifi had been hysterical, competent and controlled…and, as the days unravelled, unbearably sexy.

Throw Arturio into the mix, along with a vision of family life he had never given passing thought to—and, to that mix, add this visit to Genoa, where he had felt the punch of what he had missed out on from the day he'd been born; the wrenching regret of a palace he had never occupied and the sound of family voices he had never had…

A revolution had been quietly happening inside him, and now…

Gabriel slung his legs over the side of the bed and stood up, unashamed of his nakedness although, as an afterthought, he looked around him, found his boxers and stuck them on before sauntering towards her, only pausing to drag up one of the chairs by the window to join her where she was sitting.

'What is it?'

'I'm asking you to marry me.'

CHAPTER NINE

HELEN STARED AT him in utter silence. Had she misheard? Had he just asked her to *marry him*?

She felt a slow, steady soaring inside her. She'd fallen for this guy hook, line and sinker. What had started life as an impossible, barely recognisable crush had grown at supersonic speed into something deep, powerful and overwhelming.

Looking back, she could see that love had been stirring inside her for a long time until, with circumstances changing the dynamic, things that she had bottled up had been given room to breathe.

Had it been the same for him?

He'd always had such a colourful love life but, underneath it all, had he too been drawn to her? Had love been building up for him as well until, as with her, it had surfaced and knocked him for six?

She blinked.

'Sorry?' she finally said faintly.

She teetered towards the nearest chair and fell into it, but she couldn't peel her eyes from him as her mind played with a series of lightning-fast thoughts, thoughts that were linking up and leading down all sorts of wonderful roads.

'I've never thought about proposing to anyone,' Gabriel said slowly. He stared off into the distance for a couple of seconds but then he was looking at her again. 'My parents…' He shook his head and shot her a rueful, crooked smile. 'Well, you know from what I've said to you that they weren't exactly the finest example of a responsible married couple with a child to consider.'

'I know they sent you off to board at a very young age,' Helen said softly. 'Maybe they lacked any examples of what responsible parenting looked like, if they were both the products of only children themselves and, like you, were dispatched to school when they were too young to really deal with it.'

Gabriel shrugged. 'I don't deal in the whys and wherefores. I prefer to look at the end result and the end result was an important learning curve for me.'

Helen nodded. She wasn't going to rush this. If dreams came true, then she wanted to savour the journey getting there, getting to the place where the first brick in the wall of happy-ever-after would be put in place. It had been a long time coming and she couldn't think of anyone she would rather spend the rest of her life with than this man sitting so close to her, his dark eyes so serious and focused.

It was a crazy thought, and yet it just felt right.

'Love? Wild, edge-of-seat, reckless love? Not for me. I lived through what the outcome of love like that could be and I wouldn't wish it on anyone.'

'Well…'

'So, proposing to any woman, signing up to having kids? Not a route I'd ever considered. But when I'm with you, Helen, I see a union that could work.'

'A union that could work?'

Something in this speech was beginning to make her feel a little uneasy. She had predicted where it would go. Her mind had gone hell for leather towards a future sun-filled and alive with possibility. If there was a similar heady excitement racing through him, then he was doing an excellent job of hiding it. He looked…serious and pragmatic.

'We've always got along. That I've known, but until our relationship developed into something else, well, I've come to realise that we're compatible in many more ways. Wouldn't you agree?'

'The sex is certainly nice,' Helen averred, clearing her throat.

Gabriel grinned. 'I feel I may be growing accustomed to your mastery of understatement. Fact is, being with you has shown me that there's an alternative to a tiresome parade of women, all eager to please and in the end—and I hate to say this—all disposable. I'll be honest, Fifi kick-started that particular line of dissatisfaction. That she wanted the whole package deal was ridiculous, but really, why? Why should the whole package deal be ridiculous? Yes, with Fifi it was, but with you? You came here and showed me that you fill gaps I never understood needed filling: compatibility; genuine friendship; no demands for emotional highs.'

'Disposable?'

'I don't miss any of them when my relationship with them comes to an end, nor have I ever questioned the business of simply moving on with someone else. It always seemed the only alternative to sticking with one woman and going down the marriage route which, like I've said, was off-limits for me.'

'Because you never found the right woman to love…?'

'Love isn't something I'm drawn to try out for size,' Gabriel said honestly. 'But until this—this thing that's evolved between us—I've never understood that there's a road between the two.'

'A road between the two?' Her head was swimming. It felt as though she'd started out on a straightforward merry-go-round ride, holding hands with the guy she'd fallen for, only to discover very quickly that after the merry-go-round came the ghost train and the guy she'd been holding hands with had disappeared just when she'd banked on him being there next to her.

It was disorienting, yet she kept a smile on her face while her mind continued to whirl.

She would have liked to place her hand firmly over that beautiful mouth but she also knew that she had to hear what he was going to say until there was nothing left to hear.

'There's no chaos with you,' he said simply. 'By which I mean, we're both on the same page. You don't do hysterics. You take me for the man I am, and you don't want to turn me into a man I will never be.' His voice was low, persuasive and thoughtful. 'I can see life with you because we complement one another, no questions asked.'

'So what you're saying is that we could get married and it would be a bit like a—business arrangement? One where all the right boxes get ticked and so it makes sense?'

'That makes it sound a whole lot less—hot than it is.' Gabriel's voice roughened and the vision of the sexuality between them charged the air with sudden electricity.

In a heartbeat, Helen knew where he was coming from. He had been hurt by his parents and had come to see them as an example of what love could do to a person, how it could consume and take over until two people got lost in one another to the exclusion of everyone else.

He'd been young when those impressions had been formed and, over the years, they had been cemented inside him as indisputable fact. In a way, not so different from her. She had embedded herself in the notion that safety was the top priority, because that was the lesson she had been taught growing up by her very protective father, and it was only when she had come to London to work and live that another reality had presented itself.

With Gabriel, he'd lived his life buried in the unemotional world of a high-octane work life with women as an enjoyment on the side-lines. He picked them up, he dropped them and they all seemed to blend into one another. Having worked alongside him for such a long time, she had long ago recognised the pattern.

Had the situation with Fifi changed something inside him? He'd pretty much said so himself. She had presented him with romance and an ultimatum, and he had ditched both at speed, but perhaps that had made him realise that he wasn't getting any younger and that settling down was really something he felt would work on some level.

And of course, having found family to embrace him, he had seen the other side of the coin when it came to marriage and family links.

He had glimpsed a middle road, a safe road where love wasn't a threat but companionship was a possibility—and here she was, fitting the bill. She was a known quantity. She was his efficient secretary who didn't make demands and always kept a cool head. She was also his lover now, and the sex was amazing.

So what if she'd told him that he wasn't her type? As it turned out, that was a lie, because he was very much her type and no doubt he'd sensed that. They were lovers and he knew just how much she wanted him. They wanted one another and they got along and, without love to complicate things, he had gravitated towards a proposal that made sense for him.

But for her?

It had been hard enough doing what she was doing now, having a sexual relationship with him while they were here because she was in love and she was greedy to make the most of him while she could. She knew that once they were back in London she would have to start looking for another job, because just facing him in the office would be tough.

So, a life with him from which there was no exit plan; being with him all the time, wanting more than he could give and taking the crumbs that were offered; a life of hiding how she really felt, knowing that to speak her feelings would be to risk it all: she couldn't begin to contemplate that.

'Gabriel, there must be a lot of other women out there you could find to fill the role.'

'Stop being so unemotional about it,' he said, only part in jest, just the slightest of frowns beginning.

'But isn't that what this is about?' she countered quietly. 'It would be a marriage, maybe not of convenience, but a marriage without emotion.'

'There would be a lot of emotion…' He smiled slowly and reached out to stroke her cheek, which made the breath hitch in her throat. 'I can guarantee that.'

'Sex isn't an emotion, Gabriel.'

'I feel I can convince you that it is. Anyway, it's not just the sex. It's the mutual respect we have for one another and the fact that we get along.'

'Thank you for the offer, but I'm afraid I'm going to have to say no.'

'What?'

'I don't want to marry you.'

'Why? You don't mean that.' He raked his fingers through his hair. His frown had deepened; he was perplexed.

'I wouldn't say it if I didn't mean it.'

'Then explain.'

'Because,' she said flatly, 'I suppose I know what love feels like, and if I enter into another long-term relationship then I don't want to think that I'm sacrificing my chance to find it again in favour of practicality.'

She looked away from him because it was easier to be composed when she could ignore his dark eyes resting on her. 'I want the crazy declarations of love, Gabriel. Yes, sure, the sex is good between us—okay, the sex is great between us—and you like and respect me, which is nice, but in between those two things? That's what I want. I want the thing that's in between. I want to be the person the man I marry just can't live without. I want all the highs and the lows and the stormy arguments that bring us closer together. I want the excitement of planning babies together. I want all the passion that has nothing to do with sex, and that relationship—'

'Can't be with me.'

'It wouldn't work out, because it's not a case of box ticking.'

Gabriel sat back and gestured expressively and, when he next looked at her, his eyes were shuttered but he smiled.

'Fair enough.'

Fair enough? He'd just proposed, she'd turned him down and his response was *fair enough*?

Yet, why would it be anything else?

Gabriel knew what he was bringing to the table. He was stupidly rich, sinfully good-looking and, all in all, a catch. Yes, she might have made noises about just enjoying what they had while they were here—but on some instinctive level he would have sensed her weakness. And that would have wiped out any misgivings he might have had about what she wanted or how serious she was about wanting to end things once they returned to London.

The equation, for him, would have been easy. They liked one another, they respected one another, they were compatible and they were hot for one another. And, if he had decided that settling down with a woman might have some advantages, then he had simply gone and drawn conclusions that had suited him.

He was, after all, a guy who was very, very accustomed to getting what he wanted when it came to the opposite sex.

But it still hurt that he could abandon his pursuit with so

little fight. For a couple of seconds, she wondered if, proposal rejected by Helen, he would make his next girlfriend a candidate for the role he now saw as vacant and desirable. Now that he had started thinking along the lines of marriage being advantageous, something achievable without real emotional investment, would his pattern of dating change? Would he stop the casual business of choosing women who were easy to walk away from? Would he now start interviewing for the one who would attach without making demands he would never be able to fulfil?

Marriage brought kids as well. From his interaction with Arturio and his various kids and grandchildren, he'd seen that there were up sides to family life, that making a fortune was meaningless if you had no one to spend any of it on.

Helen thought about working for him, and eventually having to see him get involved with someone on a serious level, and she quailed inside.

'So, let's put that aside.' She forced a smile while inside her heart twisted. 'And enjoy what's left of our holiday here. It's been such a great place—I've seen so many wonderful things.'

'Good.' His voice was clipped. 'Dinner awaits and then—I think I'll do some work. There's only so long a guy can play truant.'

Gabriel knew that it was stupid to be as unsettled as he was at her rejection.

He had never been rejected by a woman, but then he had never asked this question before. Was that it?

Replaying things in his head, he knew that he had somehow ended up making assumptions about her investment in what they'd shared.

What had made sense to him had stampeded through the reality that it wasn't a shared conclusion.

Marriage. Suddenly it had felt right for him to ask her. He'd seen family life at its best, thanks to Arturio and Isabella, and a series of events that he could never have predicted in a million years. And, even if he couldn't wholly embrace the business of love, even if his life lessons were just too deeply embedded, then he had realised how pointless it would be to die a billionaire with nothing left behind him in his wake.

He'd approached it from a practical point of view and because, like him, she was cool-headed and practical, he had assumed that his proposal would fall on fertile ground.

He was ashamed to think that any other woman would have bitten off his hand for a ring on her finger and all the vast benefits that came with that.

But she wasn't any other woman.

That said, he wasn't in the business of begging, but once he'd sat back and shrugged off her rejection he hadn't been able to face a night in bed with her.

It had grated on his nerves that she had been perfectly normal over an exquisite dinner he'd barely tasted. She'd smiled and chatted about the things she had enjoyed and, when that had petered out, she'd fallen back on the tried and tested work-related conversation.

He had no idea what she was thinking.

Now, back in London after a largely silent flight back from Italy, and after several days making do with a replacement because she had taken a few days to go visit her father, Gabriel sat at his desk, unable to focus on much, waiting for the door to his office to be pushed open…and only now realising how accustomed he had got to her presence.

It would be odd having her back, with all the water under the bridge, but it would be good, and things would settle right back into place: of that he had no doubt.

They always did for him. If he felt unsettled now, it was

just because he was dealing with a situation that many had faced, just not him.

He relaxed back into his chair, his back to the floor-to-ceiling panes of glass that separated him from the busy streets several stories below. He didn't stand when he heard the knock on the door, but he did push back his chair, folded his arms and tilted his head to the side.

Familiarity warmed him. She was back in the office gear, the clothes that had been abandoned during their brief time out in Italy: navy skirt, white blouse, flat shoes and, he expected, a neat jacket tucked away on one of the hooks in her outer office.

Her hair was tied back and the golden glow of sun-kissed skin was fading. For a few seconds, he found that he couldn't quite say anything but, when he did, he dived right in with what was expected of him.

'Thanks for that report on the Turner deal,' he drawled, tilting back the chair and folding his hands behind his head. 'Really no need to have interrupted your holiday with work issues.'

He glanced at his computer, which was whirring, and then rested his dark eyes on her. Irritatingly, memory mingled with common sense, and he had to fight from his thoughts unravelling.

He tore his eyes away, frustrated with his own weakness, and gazed at the columns and numbers on his screen, aware of her slipping into the chair facing his desk, as she always did.

Helen had steeled herself for this.

What could she expect? At any rate, it was something she had to get over and done with, and she'd been was glad of the break to see her dad, which had gone a little way to easing the ball of nerves in the pit of her stomach.

She noted that he could barely meet her eyes. There had been no flash of—*anything*. He was already over it, and she knew that she shouldn't be surprised, because that was how it worked with him. She might occupy a different rank to the Fifis of this world but that didn't mean that she wasn't disposable, just like the rest of his girlfriends—marriage proposal or no marriage proposal.

But her heart was beating so fast, and she just wanted to drink him in, to succumb to the onslaught of sweet memories.

She slipped the letter out of her bag and shoved it across the desk to him.

'What's this?'

'You should read it.'

Once upon a long time ago, she had told him that she would hand in her notice if he couldn't obey her 'Keep Out' signs; if he couldn't accept that one kiss would never lead to anything more. So much water had flowed under that particular bridge and now it was truly impossible to pick up the working relationship they had left behind them. That was the conclusion she had reached during her stay in Cornwall, when she had done nothing but think and think and think.

She could stay on working for him, but there was no point kidding herself that seeing him every day, remembering what had happened between them and being exposed to his wit, charm and wonderful, mesmerising charisma wouldn't leave her a broken person.

She would have to leave; she would have to move on, take charge of her life and not let memories of him dictate a future of non-engagement. She didn't want to get buried under sadness and disillusionment. There were positives in life to be found even in the darkest of situations, and she would have to think that he had shown her what it felt like to be really and truly alive. And even if things had crashed and burned, that in itself was a blessing.

She had hung onto that silver lining during her week away and made the most of it. She had phoned the one friend she knew who could yank her out of the doldrums and arranged to meet as soon as she was back in London. If she had to get back on the bike, the sooner she got on, the better and Lucy, who knew her better than anyone, would help with that.

She had been *proactive.*

Their eyes met and he slowly took the piece of paper, read what was written on it and pushed it to one side.

'No.'

'No what?'

'No, I don't accept your resignation.'

'You can't *not* accept my resignation, Gabriel.'

'This wasn't part of the plan!'

'Plans change.' She jutted her chin at a defiant angle and stared at him for a few seconds. 'I did some thinking when I went to see my dad and I realised that, after everything that's happened between us, working closely with you would be impossible for me.'

'Why?'

He pushed himself aggressively away from his desk and walked jerkily towards the bank of windows, leaning against one of the glass panes to glare at her.

With the sun streaming behind him, he was a towering, imposing silhouette—a dominant alpha male reacting to something he didn't like.

'Why do you think?'

'We agreed that we would only embark on—what we embarked on—on the understanding that it wouldn't affect our working relationship.' He knew—of course he did. Having always been the guy who did nothing without first working out possible consequences—the guy who knew how to control life, because it was better he control life than life control him—he had thrown it all through the window and galloped down a road that had led him right to this point.

'Maybe I can't be as unemotional about it as you, Gabriel.'

'What are you trying to say?'

His dark eyes skewered her with focused concentration.

Helen breathed in deeply and met that unwavering stare with equal coolness.

She remembered his mouth on hers, his hands touching her, his head buried between her legs, and a shiver of powerful awareness raced through her.

'Are you trying to tell me that…'

'I'm trying to tell you that life would be easier for me if I didn't have to work with you on a daily basis. I thought I could. I can't. Too much water under the bridge. It would be uncomfortable and awkward, and I wouldn't be able to get around that, and there's no reason why I should try. There's a thriving job market out there and I think I would be able to find a job without too much difficulty. Provided, that is, I get a good reference from you.'

'*Provided you get a good reference from me?* Who do you think I am, Helen? I really thought we knew each other better than that—better than for you to think that I could ever be the sort of person vengeful and spiteful enough to somehow make you pay for walking out on me.'

Helen flushed. 'I'm not *walking out on you*, Gabriel.'

'That's *exactly* what you're doing!' He shrugged elaborately. 'But, if that's the road you want to go down, then so be it. You will leave my employ with an impeccable reference, which is no less than you deserve.'

'Thank you.' She hesitated. 'You don't understand…'

'Really?'

'It's more than just the fact that things would be awkward between us.' She was thinking on her feet. 'For me, at any rate.' To leave with her dignity intact felt very important. 'Maybe that proposal of yours made me think—just as it probably made *you* think.'

'I'm not following you.' But a dark flush highlighted his cheekbones as he met her gaze with narrow-eyed, scowling intensity.

'Maybe,' Helen said slowly, 'it made me think that it really is time for me to get back into the dating scene.'

'The *dating scene*?'

'Yes, Gabriel.'

'The Internet is full of losers and men on the lookout for vulnerable women.'

'I think I'm grown up enough to handle myself. Besides…'

'Besides what?'

'Besides…' She was protecting herself, forcing him to see her not just as another of his women who would leave with a broken heart, despite her protestations to the contrary, but as her own woman capable of looking out for herself. 'There are other places to meet people. My friend Lucy is great fun and we're already planning evenings out. It's been a while coming.' It was not a lie; vague plans had been made. Saying it out loud though, felt committal. Like it or not, a future of moving on was taking shape at the speed of light.

'Evenings out? Where?'

Helen wondered what was so shocking about what she'd just said—nothing. Yet, judging from his tone of voice, anyone would think that she'd just told him that she'd signed up for a career in pole dancing.

Did he think that she was incapable of braving the big, bad world out there? Perhaps he figured that he knew her well enough to suspect that *evenings out* in search of a suitable partner would be way beyond her remit?

If she was honest, he had a point, but she had embarked

on this line of self-defence, so she would just have to see it through.

'Bars. Pubs. Clubs.' It was nerve-racking just thinking about it.

'Bars? Pubs? Clubs?'

'It's not beyond the pale, Gabriel. I'm young. It's what girls of my age do.'

'You're not a bar, pub or club person, damn it!'

'You don't know what sort of person I am!'

'We both know that's a lie.'

'Why would it matter to you one way or another if Lucy and I decide to go bar-hopping?' From vague plans to imminent bar-hopping. She had never bar-hopped in her life before. She had never pub-crawled. Her one time at a club had involved a broken heel of her brand-new high-heeled shoes.

'It doesn't,' Gabriel ground out forcefully.

The thought of her going from bar to bar, getting more and more intoxicated, made him feel sick. She barely drank. In his head, he had images of her being pursued by drunken strangers, misreading signals she wasn't sending out because she just wasn't a 'bar' person. He had no idea who this Lucy character was, but he assumed someone happy to lead someone else off the straight and narrow, even if that someone else was supposedly a friend.

Of course, what she did henceforth was none of his business, but was it any surprise that he was inclined to feel a certain amount of protectiveness towards her?

This wasn't just one of those women he dated who was experienced in the ways of the world.

'Good,' Helen murmured, looking down at her entwined fingers. 'And, just for the record, I have quite some holiday stored up, so I'm entitled to take it in lieu of working my notice.'

'This is crazy! You're acting as though…'

'As though…?'

'As though we're not friends,' Gabriel muttered with biting incredulity.

Helen whitened. In a nutshell he had found the core of her unhappiness and dragged it out into the open.

This man was more than just a guy she had fallen into bed with against all better judgement. This man was her friend, and the thought of walking out of these offices never to see him again was unbearable.

For a second, she wondered what would happen if she'd accepted his crazy proposal, but she reminded herself that storing up heartbreak was no way to spend her life. And, besides, it was a moot point because no sooner had that proposal been made than she had swiftly rejected it.

'I don't want you to think that,' she said gruffly. 'Of course we're friends. If you—really want me to stay and work out my notice, then I will.'

Gabriel waved his hand dismissively. 'Not important. You want to go? I wouldn't dream of standing in your way.' He moved abruptly towards her, towering over her, before reaching down, hands planted on either side of her chair, caging her in so that she could scarcely breathe for want of his proximity. 'But as your friend and, believe it or not, someone who cares about you, I would like to offer a word of warning.'

Helen didn't really want to hear about him caring about her because it was so far removed from the crazy passion she felt for him. They'd been lovers, but now that was off the cards and what remained for him was friendship.

Who wanted to be buddies with a guy they were in love with? That line of thinking gave her some much-needed backbone, powering her to withstand his chummy, patronising advice.

'What's that?'

'Pace yourself with the drinking and don't hand out your phone number to anyone, however convincing he might seem.'

Helen's eyebrows shot up and she offered him a wry smile. 'Repeat—I think I'll be okay out there in the big, bad world and, besides, I'll be with Lucy, my closest friend.'

Gabriel frowned.

'Mind me asking when this drinking session in bars and clubs is going to get under way?'

'Gabriel, I don't need your guiding hand when it comes to my social life,' Helen told him, but there was a slow heat burning a path through her and she wished he would just stand up so that she could get her breathing back under control. 'And, as for when we're going to have a night out, who knows? Maybe Friday. Everyone goes out on a Friday.'

There was no room for daydreaming. She knew that if she did that she would stagnate and the years would creep up on her while she busied herself thinking about the past. She might as well get her head around one or two concrete plans.

It was agreed that she would work to the end of the week. Julie, who filled in occasionally in Helen's absence, would temporarily hold the fort but would have to be shown the ropes.

'I'll leave it to you,' Gabriel said, stalking back to his desk and killing the personal and awkward conversation they had been having. 'I have several meetings that will take me out of London, so don't expect me to be around much.'

Helen smiled, annoyed with herself for not wanting that personal conversation to end; annoyed with herself for thinking that it showed protectiveness towards her, perhaps even *possessiveness*, and baulking at the commitment she had made to herself that Friday would be the start of a new chapter in her life. She didn't quite feel ready for new chapters just yet.

'Great.' She shot him a brittle, mega-watt smile and told herself that not having him around was going to do wonders for her nervous system.

Gabriel made it to the office a little after six on the Friday evening.

It was still way too hot and way too sunny. He'd just sat through a five-hour meeting and, even with the top two buttons of his shirt undone, he still felt uncomfortable. The crush of people on the streets threading their way through the city had got on his nerves.

Why was London always so busy? It had made him think of Genoa, the vineyards and a way of life that was calm, laid back and unstressed. At least, comparatively. The days there had melded into one another and the nights had been filled with making love.

Why couldn't she see what he did in the idea of a union that could work?

He clenched his jaw in raw frustration. His week had been hellish. True to his word, he had disappeared from his office, leaving Helen to work out the last remaining days of her notice, showing Julie the ropes.

Had he actually been able to concentrate, however? No. He'd found himself sitting in on high-level meetings, his mind a thousand miles away, contributing to proceedings without his usual incisive rigour.

Another woman, maybe? A return to his usual pattern of behaviour?

The thought of seeing someone else, of even getting in touch with another woman, had been enough to make him feel reasonably sick.

Truth was, *he missed her.*

He missed everything about her. He couldn't bear the thought of spending any amount of time in his office because he couldn't face her. And, somewhere along the line, he remembered what he had said when they had first embarked on their charade. She had asked him how Arturio would believe that a guy like him had fallen for his secretary, and he had mused that it was very credible that he had found that what he wanted had been right there all along—the woman who knew him better than anyone ever had.

How stupid and blind he'd been not to see the truth behind that throwaway remark.

He'd had the most precious thing in the world for a moment in time and he had thrown away the chance to show her that he… *That he loved her.* He'd been so securely locked up in his ivory tower, and so convinced that nothing and no one could make a dent in it, that he hadn't realised that this wonderful woman had entered through the front door and set up camp in his heart.

How could he not have guessed? Looking back, he'd treated her completely differently from every other woman he'd ever dated. He'd talked to her, opened up, revealed weaknesses without even realising; and, if he'd realised, he airbrushed over any discomfort at it.

He'd trusted her with his heart, whether he'd known it at the time or not. She hadn't seen it and he'd been too obtuse to point it out.

And now it was too late.

He thought about her hitting the singles scene and wanted to see the bottom of a whisky bottle to deal with the pain.

And, just like that, thoughts all over the place and barely aware of his surroundings as he pushed open the glass doors to the building in which his offices were housed, he saw her…

CHAPTER TEN

HIS BREATHING QUICKENED. She was in a pale-blue dress that was a couple of inches above her knees, had flung a silky cardigan over her shoulders and was wearing white trainers. The whole ensemble was quirky, cute and ridiculously sexy and he stopped dead in his tracks and just stared.

In the periphery of his vision, he made out her companion, a small, curvy blonde with curly hair who was wearing something or other. He barely noticed because his eyes were all for Helen who, after a moment's surprised hesitation, was now looking back at him with an expression he couldn't read.

She walked towards him and made polite introductions.

Lucy—the blonde companion intent on leading her astray although, in fairness, the blonde companion didn't look like someone inclined to lead anyone astray. Who knew, though?

'Apologies I haven't seen much of you this week,' he opened gruffly. 'But thank for keeping me updated on the transfer over of duties.'

Helen produced a tight smile. 'No problem. I think Julie is going to work out very well in the short term, although she's made it clear that she doesn't want a permanent transfer, as she's very loyal to Simon.' She turned to Lucy, whose blue eyes were darting between them with interest. 'Remember I told you that I'm leaving the company?'

'So you did. Bye-bye to the old and hello to the new.'

'So it would seem,' Gabriel remarked tersely, settling his gaze on the blonde as he detected something that sounded a little like wicked amusement in her remark. Or maybe she was just stirring the pot. 'Which clubs are you two going to target?' he asked with a lot of fake bonhomie.

His eyes were back on Helen. His mind was still playing with the realisation that he had fallen in love with her. Thinking about her deprived him of the ability to speak, it would seem, because she answered and he barely took in what she had said.

He was remembering how she'd looked after they'd made love, the flush on her cheeks, the drowsy darkness of her eyes, the soft curve of her body against his.

Conversations had been had, low and murmured, and he could kick himself now for never having worked out the significance of them—never having realised that, bit by bit, those conversations had changed the man he had been into a man he had never thought himself capable of being. Having spent his life vacating the bed as soon as the hot business of making love was done, he had found himself lingering between the sheets, warm, lazy and happy to talk with her curled into him, his hand stroking her hair.

The significance of that had foolishly passed him by.

'I… There are always any of the clubs I belong to.' He raked his fingers through his hair and forced a smile. 'You know which they are, Helen.'

'Indeed I do. I've made arrangements for several dinners there for you and one of your many Fifis.'

'Use my name. Don't pay for anything. You can put whatever you want on my tab. You've worked for me for years and—I would like to spare no expense on your evening out. I… Yes, well, whatever you want—lobster and caviar, champagne. Money's no object.'

'Thank you very much. It's a kind offer but I'm sure we'll

find somewhere nice enough and not too expensive. Won't we, Luce?'

'Sure will.'

Gabriel dragged his eyes away from Helen to focus on the small blonde next to her. He could see curiosity and amusement there, and he frowned.

'I know a couple of good places,' she said, glancing down but still smiling. 'Great places for two girls out to have some fun. I've been after Helen to get out there with me and for us to enjoy ourselves.' She dimpled and Gabriel's frown deepened.

'Is that what you want, Helen?' he asked brusquely.

'Course it is,' Lucy said airily. 'Isn't it, Helen? Loud music, guys buying us drinks, dancing round our handbags…'

'Yep.' Helen stared straight into Gabriel's cool, dark, disapproving eyes with defiance.

Was he going to give her another lecture on how to look after herself? Where would *he* be going later, anyway? He wasn't a 'Friday night is stay-at-home-night' kind of guy. He was more a 'where's my little black book and which gorgeous blonde shall I call? Because it's Friday, after all…' kind of guy.

Although, he looked tired. Haggard, even.

'Helen…' His voice was a little jagged. Why was he bothering to play the part of the guy who didn't care? He cared. He more than cared. If he hadn't bumped into her here, then he knew that he would have done what he intended to do now—he would have found her and begged for her time, flung himself at her mercy.

She'd said that she wanted the stuff that came along with the passion and the friendship, the stuff that made a relationship worth its salt—the stuff called *love*.

The very thing he'd removed from the table when he had asked her to marry him.

It was time to vacate his ivory tower.

'Gabriel, we should be heading off now.'

'Can we…talk?'

'Haven't we already?'

'Please.' He heard some soft laughter from the blonde with the smart mouth, but he couldn't get annoyed, because every scrap of his attention was focused on the woman she was with.

Helen hesitated. Gabriel was a guy who never begged. She'd never thought he had the vocabulary for it, and certainly not the disposition. But there was a pleading in his voice that made her breathing hitch and, looking at him more closely, she could see that he really did look haggard.

There was wickedness in Lucy's voice, next to her, as she murmured something about leaving them to it, that the pub wasn't going to go anywhere any time soon.

'Don't be silly,' Helen said a little weakly.

Were those new lines by his mouth? she wondered. Why did he look haggard? Was she being over-imaginative? Reading things into something that was straightforward? She thought of those times when she had seen him shorn of his usual self-assurance. He looked like that now: human; vulnerable; uncertain. And absolutely adorable.

When she next glanced away, it was to see her friend backing away and waving goodbye. And was that a wink…?

'Who *is* that woman?' He said this to buy a little time now that he was alone with Helen. He raked his fingers through his hair and was aware of a level of nervous tension he just wasn't used to.

'My closest friend. I should join her.' Considering Lucy

had disappeared, and Helen's feet were glued to the ground, this felt like an empty statement.

'Please don't. Please stay, hear me out. Please,' Gabriel said gruffly.

He was going to do it. He was going to do the one thing he never dreamed possible. He was going to spill his soul.

The love he felt for this woman was too heavy to carry around for ever without letting her know.

'I'm crazy about you.'

There. Why beat about the bush? He flushed darkly but he didn't look away.

Helen opened her mouth and stared at Gabriel. She wanted to shake those words out of her head because she didn't want them to carry her away on some stupid, hopeful, falsely optimistic journey.

'I know a wine bar just round the corner,' he continued urgently into the silence.

'Gabriel, we've done all the talking we need to do. I've told you how I feel.' Her protest sounded weak even to her own ears.

'But I am yet to tell you how *I* feel.'

He circled her arm and gently began ushering her out of the towering glass skyscraper.

It was busy, with people everywhere, inside the building and outside.

'Please, Helen,' he said quietly, although she hadn't protested. He dropped her arm and stood back, giving her the chance to blow him off and she wondered what he would do, how he would persuade her to hear him out, if she did.

Surely he couldn't blame her for her reluctance. How could he? He'd made sure to bang on about being unavailable, handing her so many warning notices that she could have papered a room with them. On top of that, she knew his form. Knew him inside out.

'Okay, but then I'm going to meet Lucy.'

'Thank you.'

He was crazy about her? She wanted to ask him to clarify but she wasn't going to.

They walked briskly round the corner to a wine bar that was brimming with people, full inside and with clusters of after-work groups hanging around outside, drinks in hand, relaxing after a week at it. The thought of joining them as she resumed life as a single ready to mingle was daunting.

They found a seat, which came as no surprise, because he was the sort of guy who *found seats.*

'Well?' They were both sitting with two glasses of wine in front of them. Helen looked at him and her heart skipped a beat. It hadn't been the same, being at the office without him there, knowing that she was saying goodbye to what had been a huge part of her life for years. She'd been giddy with misery and exhausted from having to put a smile on her face so that Julie didn't expect anything.

She'd managed to vaguely say something about having to quit because of personal problems, and it had been left there. To look as miserable as she'd felt would have courted the sort of quiet curiosity she hadn't thought she could bear.

'Well, I've done a lot of thinking, Helen. The past week has been…' He shook his head and raked his fingers through his hair in a gesture of wearied frustration. 'A mess for me.'

Helen lowered her eyes, blocked her mind from playing fanciful games and made an effort to stick to the programme.

'I'm sorry about the lack of notice. I wouldn't have done it if I hadn't thought that it would be for the best.'

'Naturally.'

'I may have dealt with a broken engagement but I'd had

the chance to leave, to make sure I put some distance between me and George. But to continue working for you after everything that happened? It wouldn't have been the sort of comfortable working environment I could have dealt with. And then, you would have picked up where you left off with other women… No, that's not something I felt I had to put up with.'

'I admit I've—not been exemplary when it comes to longevity and women,' Gabriel admitted heavily.

'That's the understatement of the year.' She gulped down some wine and tried not to wince at the size of the mouthful. 'It's not just that…' She sighed, fiddled with the stem of the glass and realised that, although there was noise all around them, the buzz of people laughing and talking, they seemed to be caught in a little silent bubble of their own.

'That…what?'

'It's not just that you haven't had longevity with any of the women you've dated. It's the fact that you're just not interested in having a serious, committed relationship with anyone. It's not a case that no woman has come along who captured your imagination. You haven't been looking for love and failing to find it. You're just not interested in looking at all.'

'You know my back story.'

'I know your childhood was an unhappy one, Gabriel.' She looked at him with empathetic, serious eyes which were nevertheless unflinching. 'If you've chosen to let that determine all the choices you make when it comes to involvement with someone else, then that's your business. I've had my fair share of learning curves as well, but in the end life goes on.'

'Yes, it does, and I've finally seen that.'

'What do you mean?'

When she looked at her glass, she was surprised to see that it was empty. She couldn't remember gulping down more wine but she must have done. He topped up her glass and she didn't stop him. There was nothing wrong with a little Dutch courage.

'You're right,' Gabriel said simply. 'I've always let my past determine my present and my future. My parents were absent, so wrapped up in themselves and in the business of having fun that there was never any real point of reference for me growing up. They seldom made it to parents' meetings when I was at boarding school. They never bothered with sports days. They couldn't. They were usually not in the country and it never occurred to them to make an effort to try to be. At the end of each term, I was collected by one of the staff, ferried to a private jet and taken wherever it was arranged I should go and, during the holidays, they might or might not have popped in.'

'I know. I feel so sorry for you. Money really doesn't buy everything, does it?'

Gabriel smiled with bitter irony. 'No, my darling, it doesn't. And yet for a long time I deluded myself into thinking that the only things I wanted were the things it could buy. It was my default position. There was safety in things that were tangible—in houses and cars and boats. Emotions? Love? Those were the things that caused pain and damage, and so those were the things to be avoided at all costs.'

'You're not telling me anything I didn't already know, Gabriel.'

Had he actually called her 'darling'? Or had her fevered mind played tricks on her?

'Here's what you don't know. You don't know how things changed for me. You don't know that I ripped up the road map I'd spent my life following without even realising it.

You don't know how it was that you came into my life and nothing was the same for me again.'

Helen's eyes widened and she tilted her head to one side, her expression silently questioning what he had just said.

Gabriel shrugged. 'I know. You don't believe me, and I don't blame you. I've been a fool, Helen. I don't know how else to put it. I never realised that over the years I became more and more embedded in you.

'You were the constant in my life. I thought I was standing still but, in fact, you were changing my direction and it all came to a head when we—when we went to America and the protective walls of the office were removed. I don't know if things would have changed for me, had we remained in London, had life carried on its same trajectory with you coming in, doing a great job at work and leaving the office—never letting me in. I think that eventually we would have ended up in the same place.'

'That's assuming I felt the same way, which is a pretty sweeping assumption.' Her words were firm, her voice was not.

'Did you?'

'I…'

'This is a time for us to be completely honest with one another, Helen. I—I'm not the sort of guy who does this emotional stuff, but I couldn't function this past week. Nothing made sense and nothing mattered. You were going, and I was broken up, because somehow I've managed to fall madly in love with you. The thought of never seeing you again is a thought that…'

He shook his head and briefly looked away, but his jaw clenched and his fingers tightened around the stem of his wine glass. He looked back at her. 'So…did you? Feel the same? Feel that we were both attracted to one another over the time we've worked together? That what happened between us in America was somehow inevitable?

'Actually, *attraction* doesn't begin to cover it. Not for me, even though that was the deal I wanted to kid myself was going on with you. No, for me, it would be more truthful to say that you became embedded in my soul, and the physical attraction that finally exploded between us was just a symptom of something a lot bigger that was going on underneath.'

'You—*you're in love with me*?'

Her heart skipped several beats. Was he telling the truth? His voice was raw with sincere emotion and yet it seemed unbelievable. But surely he wouldn't make something like that up because she'd rejected him and he wanted to have her back in his bed, whatever it took? Because he couldn't take no for an answer?

He'd said that this was a time for them to be honest with one another.

'If you were that crazy about me, then why didn't you say anything sooner?' she asked bluntly.

'Because, like I said, I didn't know how. I didn't have the words. I made assumptions about myself and believed them to be true, even when all my actions and all my thoughts were telling me that I'd changed.'

'I want to believe you, I really do,' she whispered, tentatively letting go of some of her suspicions as her heart opened up to what he was saying.

'Because?'

'Because…' she breathed in deeply '…because I feel the same way about you.'

There was a thickening silence. Gabriel reached out to link her fingers in his and his spirits soared when she didn't yank her hand away.

'But you turned down my marriage proposal!'

'Because I needed more than just a ring on my finger and good sex and compatibility. I needed more than just a business arrangement.'

'And you're ready to move on with me?' Gabriel asked quietly. 'No regrets down the road about taking the plunge and handing your heart over to the guy who always swore he'd never release his into anyone's safekeeping until now?'

'None,' Helen said with complete honesty. 'You know, I always believed in love. Dad went to pieces after Mum and my brother died, and he never met anyone again, but I was never scared of giving my heart away just because I knew that loving someone could lead to hurt. I thought I was safe with you because you weren't the sort of guy who would ever be on my radar, but I fell in love, and when I did I knew it had to be all or nothing with you, not a road in between. I love you, Gabriel, and I always will.'

'Then,' he said roughly, 'At the risk of being repetitive, will you marry me?'

Helen smiled and touched his cheek with her finger.

'Just try and stop me.'

The wedding was a small affair. Neither wanted to hang around, planning anything over the top, although the option was offered.

'Not me,' Helen had said. 'Not my style.'

She wore a cream silk dress that cinched in at the waist and fell in soft layers to mid-calf, and her hair was piled up and threaded with tiny flowers that matched the bouquet she carried.

Gabriel turned around, saw her as she walked up the aisle in the tiny local church where she had grown up in Cornwall and his heart had clenched with love.

He'd finally given himself permission to love and not a

minute went past when he didn't thank everything there was to thank that she was a part of his life.

He smiled, and when he cast his eyes over the congregation he felt a sense of satisfaction at the warmth and the love radiating from it.

He saw her father and her friends—including Lucy, who had told him what a lucky guy he was to have nabbed her best friend, a sentiment with which he couldn't disagree. And his friends, some from his days at university, and a couple from boarding school, all forming a tightly knit group in his life.

And of course Arturio and Isabella, who could not have been more delighted with the outcome.

And now…

Gabriel glanced over to where his wife was sitting, feet resting on an upholstered pouffe, television on in the little snug of the cottage they had bought on the outskirts of London—close enough for him to get the train into the City as and when, but far enough out that there was land and fields around them.

There was also ample room for visitors and her father had already visited several times since they had moved in.

'Anything?' he asked, nudging her feet a couple of inches with his and looking at her with love.

'Trust me, you'll be the first to know the very second I feel any twinges.' She glanced at her very pregnant belly and smiled at him. 'I'm only four days overdue. I could be another week. Who knows? Although…' she rolled her eyes '… I can't wait. I feel like a beached whale most of the time.'

'I can't wait either,' Gabriel confided in a husky undertone.

'You might not be saying that when your nights start getting interrupted with a mini-me yelling for milk.'

'Bring it on.' He grinned and rubbed his knuckle across her cheek. 'I can't wait to meet this baby we've made, my darling, and to carry on with this fantastic new chapter in my life.'

Helen smiled back and rested her hand on her belly. 'Nor,' she sighed happily, 'can I.'

* * * * *

TWINS TO TAME HIM
Tara Pammi

Sebastian rubbed a hand over his face. Any momentary hesitation he'd felt about having two little boys to care for, to nurture and protect, dissipated, leaving behind a crystal-clear clarity he had never known in his life.

Whatever instinct had propelled him to demand Laila marry him…it carried the weight of his deepest, most secret desire within it.

For his sons to be happy and well-adjusted and thriving, they needed their mother and he needed them. Ergo, his primary goal now was to do anything to keep Laila in his life.

And while he'd never have admitted it openly to his brute of a father, Sebastian had always known he could be just as ruthless as his twin.

He was keeping his sons and he was keeping their mother in his life, even if it meant he had to seduce every inch of logic and rationale out of Dr. Jaafri. And he would make sure she not only enjoyed the seduction but that she had everything she'd ever wanted. He would make all her wishes and dreams come true. It was only a matter of getting her to admit them.